COWBOYS

TO

CAMELOT

COWBOYS TO CAMELOT

A Novel

Mary Kay Leatherman

The Cowboy In Me
Words and Music by Craig Wiseman, Alan Anderson and Jeffrey Steele
Copyright (c) 2001 by Universal Music - MGB Songs, Mrs. Lumpkin's Poodle, Song Of Windswept Pacific, Stairway To Bittner's Music and Gottahaveable Music
All Rights for Mrs. Lumpkin's Poodle Administered by Big Loud Bucks
All Rights for Stairway To Bittner's Music and Songs Of Windswept Pacific Administered by BMG Rights Management (US) LLC
All Rights for Gottahaveable Music Administered by BPJ Administration, P.O. Box 218061, Nashville, TN 37221-8061
International Copyright Secured All Rights Reserved
Reprinted by Permission of Hal Leonard LLC

My Heroes Have Always Been Cowboys
Words and Music by Sharon Vaughn
Copyright (c) 1976, 1980 UNIVERSAL - POLYGRAM INTERNATIONAL PUBLISHING, INC.
Copyright Renewed
All Rights Reserved Used by Permission
Reprinted by Permission of Hal Leonard LLC

Ghosts That Haunt Me
Words and Music by Brad Roberts
Copyright (c) 1991 UNIVERSAL - SONGS OF POLYGRAM INTERNATIONAL, INC., DOOR NUMBER TWO MUSIC and DUMMIES PRODUCTIONS, INC.
All Rights Controlled and Administered by UNIVERSAL - SONGS OF POLYGRAM INTERNATIONAL, INC.
All Rights Reserved Used by Permission
Reprinted by Permission of Hal Leonard LLC

Copyright © 2016 **Blue Wave Press**
All rights reserved.

ISBN-13: 9781537659015
ISBN-10: 1537659014
Library of Congress Control Number: 2016915414
CreateSpace Independent Publishing Platform
North Charleston, South Carolina

Also by Mary Kay Leatherman

Vanity Insanity

Surviving Your Friend's Divorce: 10 Rules to Help You Both

Sharing the Faith with Your Child: From Birth to Age Four

Blue Wave Press

Dedicated,
with the greatest respect,
to my father,
to all of the cowboys who inspired this book,
and to the spirit of the cowboy in
so many people I've known

Table of Contents

First Quarter
Bone Collector

My heroes have always been cowboys.
And they still are, it seems.
Sadly, in search of, but one step in back of,
Themselves and their slow-movin' dreams.

—WILLIE NELSON

1

August 15, 2008

Annie

True love is like ghosts, which everyone talks about and few have seen.

—*Francois de La Rochefoucauld*

My cowboy ghost kissed me on the lips in the middle of the night in a rustic cabin just outside of Bailey, Colorado.

The sad, kind kiss was filled with understanding.

I call him my ghost because I really do think the ghost was trying to connect with me; he needed me as much as I needed him. And I know he was connecting with my four-year-old son, Oliver. He was protecting Oliver—from what, I'll never know.

I call him a cowboy because the sound of his boots woke me those nights in Colorado after I'd let go of the day, falling into a mountain-air-induced sleep in the uncomfortable, old bed next to Oliver's cot. As the hummingbird wind chimes outside my open window sang to the dreamers in the cabin, I heard a restless man walking in what sounded like cowboy boots, moving from room to room as if checking to make sure everyone was safe. *I'm here to protect you.* The first night he tucked Oliver in, the second night he plodded with palpable purpose throughout the cabin and then outside—his boots on the needles of the pine trees—and the third night he kissed me.

You're gonna be fine. Just get back to sleep, little one.

The barely audible whisper of a man woke me up on the first night of the Sawyer family reunion in August of 2008. I heard the voice, assumed it was one of my sisters' husbands walking Oliver back to his cot after a trip to the bathroom, and fell back to sleep.

"Thanks so much for getting Oliver back to bed last night," I said to Allen, my oldest sister's husband, at breakfast the next morning. The whisper had sounded most like him. My family hustled around the small kitchen, making a big pancake breakfast.

Allen looked up from his stack of cakes and shrugged. "Must have been your dad or Rick. Sorry, Annie. I would have done it if I had heard him." Allen looked at my dad. "Rollie, you up last night?"

I looked at Rick. I looked at Roland McGuire, my dad. They both looked at each other and shook their heads no in unison. "Slept like a baby last night," my dad said, sounding like a cowhand.

"I know I heard the voice of a man in my room. I swear." I drank the last swallow of my bitter cup of coffee.

"You were probably dreaming." Rick laughed and winked as my dad shook his head and furrowed his brow in the same look I'd seen for the past year whenever he dropped by my house to do his "fix-it" magic. *My poor little Annie*, Dad would say as he put up a fence or helped me clean out the garage. He never said the words, but his eyes carried on about his poor, newly single, pathetic daughter.

I hadn't really wanted to go to the Colorado family reunion to connect and revel in the updates of over seventy-five members of my mom's family at a campground with ten old cabins and a big dinner hall in the mountains. With only a week before starting a new semester of teaching high school English, I was not in the mood for small talk. I told my parents that Oliver and I wouldn't be able to make it on account of all the work I needed to do to get ready for the upcoming school year. Lesson plans for my American literature classes were weighing me down.

Maybe next time.

"We won't hear of it, Annie. We'll pay for your travel and lodging," my mother said in the same that-will-never-do tone I'd heard since my childhood. She knew I could teach my classes in my sleep in year seven of my job at Belmont High School in Omaha, Nebraska. Mom and Dad assumed money was at the core of my refusal. Actually, I just didn't want to talk to the Sawyer relatives about my own latest update and my newly acquired status following my ex-husband's affair with my ex-friend and new lawyer at his law firm: divorced, pathetic; see photo.

The last time I had seen most of the Sawyer relatives had been at my wedding ten years earlier. *Too fun to catch up. Should've returned that Crock-Pot you gave us for our wedding. What's new in your life?*

Caught up?

"We'll pick you up Friday morning."

My mom always wins.

The last night of the reunion, the sound of my cowboy ghost's boots woke me. I heard walking, walking around the cabin until the boots came into my room. The sound had never been so loud and close. The boot sound came into the room and stopped.

Don't open your eyes, I told myself. Don't let him know you're awake.

I wasn't afraid. Just anxious. My first ghost and all. I knew my cowboy ghost wasn't a stranger breaking into the cabin. I just knew that. I knew he wasn't a bad ghost, an evil force. I sensed a different presence as I lay in the little bed with my eyes shut tight. I felt a heavy sorrow mixed in with my cowboy ghost's busy energy, as if he had forgotten to do something when he was alive and was in an urgent state to get it done. As if someone had forgotten to tell him he was dead. I felt sad for him.

The presence in the room, no longer walking, seemed to be aware of my awareness of him. Strange how I sensed this.

Why me? Why had no one else in the big mountain cabin been awakened by the boots and the urgency? Even Oliver, to whom this spirit had spoken, said not one word about the exchange, not even a mention of a dream. I think my cowboy ghost sensed my great vulnerability that summer, almost as though he felt sad for me. In 2008, I was a raw nerve from rejection, a victim of alienation, shrapnel of a shattered American Dream. I was sad. My cowboy ghost knew this.

My shattered American Dream.

Six months prior to his exit, Jake Day, the once love of my life, and I had driven late one night by the lot we'd bought to build our dream house, Oliver asleep in his car seat, gripping his Woody doll, covered by his favorite ragged blanket. We were so excited about the builders coming the next day that we put a sleeping child in a car and drove across town to the development where our new life was about to begin. "In our new house, we'll have six more Olivers!" Jake whispered those words to me as we parked in front of our empty lot, which was strewn with heavy equipment and scattered supplies. Everything we had worked for. Jake and I got out of the car, ran onto the dirt someday-lawn, and looked at the spot where our perfect-future house would be. I looked up at my wonderful husband. Jake leaned down and kissed me. *Here's to our future. I love you, my sweet, sweet, little Annie!*

Sweet, little Annie. That was what Jake had called me, when he loved me. But then he changed his mind—about loving me, about his sweet Annie, about my American Dream.

So I lay in the bed in Colorado—a million miles from a night on a lot in Omaha—holding my breath, squeezing my eyes tight, trying not to move. My cowboy ghost was quiet. *Please go check on the others.* And then, even though the boots hadn't moved, I felt a kiss—the only way I can explain it. I didn't feel lips, but a pressure that was gentle and warm, slow and sad, on my lips. A warm spark. A connection. And then it was gone. And then he was gone.

When we checked out of the cabin on the last day of the reunion, I got out of my dad's car to return the coffee pot and iron with the four sets of keys to the main desk of the campground office. Two women dressed in white uniforms adorned with name tags began marking the items checked in on an inventory sheet. Dot, a bigger woman with hair the color and shape of the top of a vanilla cone and a uniform too tight for her large curves, smiled and spoke as if from a script. "Thank you for staying with us here at the Bailey Ranch Cabins. We sure hope your stay was relaxing and memorable."

The other woman, shorter and much younger, looked at the number on our keys. "Cabin number three. That's our biggest cabin. That big old wraparound porch with all those extra cots for kids. Did you turn off all the electrical fixtures and the water pump?" The name tag on her uniform read Vanessa. She didn't look like a Vanessa.

"We did. We just need to return the iron and the coffee pot here. We had a really nice time."

Vanessa moved a clipboard toward me. "Just sign on the line that says cabin number three, and we'll be good to go."

I signed the line, turned to go, and then stopped. Both women looked at me. Vanessa licked her lips. "Forget something?"

"No." I paused. "I just have a really weird question."

Dot looked at Vanessa. Vanessa smiled at me. "About your cabin?"

"Yes, about the cabin. Is there a…I mean, is it…"

Dot and Vanessa smiled as Dot reached across the desk and grabbed my hand. "He's not a bad one, hon. Not like ones in those scary movies. No Freddy Krueger or nothing. Harmless, really."

"And charming," Vanessa added. "He likes to play tricks, too."

"Are we talking about a…"

"Ghost," Vanessa said. Her mouth formed a perfect circle as she said the word. "We call him George. The stories that float around say he's buried in the hill that climbs up behind the cabin."

Dot walked out to the lobby from behind her desk. "The old guy who owns the gas station next to the Rustic Station Restaurant says our George was a gold miner when everyone came out here to strike it rich in the 1800s. Says he left a daughter and wife back east but never made it home. In the county records or something. Not sure how he died. Lot of those guys didn't survive the winters back then. I just know he's a busy one."

"We hear him all the time," Vanessa added. "When we clean the cabin, he's always in and out, in and out. One time, I was making beds by myself, and suddenly I felt someone right behind me. Turned around, and no one was there. Never alone in cabin number three. Dot, tell her about when you stayed there."

Dot shook her head as she adjusted her tight shirt. "I know George well. I had to live with him for three months when my house got cleaned up after a fire. My boss was nice enough to let me stay in cabin number three if I painted all of the rooms. At night, usually after midnight, I'd be trying to sleep, and he'd be busy, busy. I'd just yell, 'Knock it off, George. Trying to sleep here.' And then he'd stop. See? A nice one, like I said."

"Wow." I took a deep breath. "I'm not crazy."

Dot laughed and patted my hand. "Not crazy at all, hon. Just open to it; that's all."

A horn honked from outside.

"Thanks for making me feel better," I said. I felt better that I wasn't crazy but was still a little uneasy that I was so open to it all.

"Drive safe now," Dot yelled as I left the office.

My feet crunched against the gravel and pine needles as I ran to the car. "I'm not crazy!" I yelled to my parents and Oliver. My dad shook his head as he drove out of the campgrounds. *My poor, little Annie.*

I'm an open book, a person with no hidden agenda. I told my family all about my cowboy ghost and about the cowboy boots, which no one else heard. I told them about the blanket, moved from a chair to cover Ollie on his cot—a blanket I never touched. They all laughed and gave me a hard time when I told them all what my new friends Dot and Vanessa had said about our cabin. I told them almost everything.

I just never told anyone about the kiss.

2

August 20, 2008

Annie

The varsity football team found a human skull at the northwest corner of the practice field the day before school started.

Not the whole team. Just starting lineman Arty Elston.

"Did you hear that they found a skull on the Belmont High School football field yesterday? Crazy."

The two-pack-a-day voice on the morning radio show interrupted my daydream. I was still thinking about my cowboy ghost as I sat in traffic on the way to the first day of school, attempting to hold on to the enchanted residue of my memory of those nights in Colorado. Maybe my cowboy ghost really was a dream.

"So what do you think about the football field skull?" The gravelly voice asked his cohort again.

A second nasally voice on the morning banter responded to the first voice. "I'm sure the kid who found it is out of his head." Obnoxious laughter erupted as the music to an insurance commercial overtook the conversation.

I yelled back to the radio, "On the practice field, not the football field."

Already, the talk about the discovery was incorrect—and insensitive. I turned off the radio.

A slow news day for Omaha, the skull was the top story on the radio, the nightly news, and the morning and evening editions of the *Omaha World-Herald*. Reporters kept repeating the same words over and over. Human skull. Belmont High School. Football field. Center of the city. They might as well have said, "We really don't have a lot of information. Just juicy, sensational tidbits to tease you with, over and over again."

That a skull had even been found was the thing that set me most on edge, more than the exaggerated rumors that slithered through the building the days following the discovery like garden snakes through tall end-of-summer grass. Junior Arty Elston, a popular football player and a name on one of my class rosters for the upcoming year, had tripped and fallen on the skull when he was retrieving a football that had been overthrown in the rough terrain on the outer edge of the practice field.

"He screamed like a little girl," Coach Edwards told a few of us who were walking into the big "kick-off" teacher meeting in the cafeteria the afternoon of the discovery. "Then he ran around doing this little freaked-out dance. Big two-hundred-pound kid looked hysterical. I guess I would have been pretty upset seeing what he saw…I mean, you don't plan on finding a skull during football practice."

Theories throughout the staff were quiet but numerous as we prepared our classrooms for the two thousand teenagers who would be taking over the building in less than twenty-four hours. We heard the skull was that of a child or a woman. Someone else heard that it might be the skull of a Belmont High runaway who had disappeared almost a decade ago. The school nurse said authorities were looking at the dental records of a twelve-year-old boy from Iowa who went missing a few months earlier.

"We've practiced on that field for the past two weeks," Coach Edwards told us. "My new assistant coach had the boys running the rim of the field doing sprints after every practice, during both two-a-day practices. We held soccer camps on that upper field all summer. How we never came across that skull before is beyond me."

A human skull found on a high school campus is noteworthy, but its sudden appearance had authorities baffled. Had it always been there and then recently unearthed? The head of the Science Department, Hal Teller, thought that an animal may have transported the skull from another area. Construction on Dodge Street, the main road down the center of Omaha, had disturbed areas that had been covered down the road for a mile either way. It would have had to be a pretty big animal to carry a human skull in its mouth. Even I knew that.

So the first day of school held an uncharacteristic air of investigation drifting through the halls as a backdrop to what should have been the main events: that new school-shoe smell and the potential of a start-over year, getting better grades than last year, making the team, and meeting that special someone who might just be a homecoming date. Several times that first day of classes, police officers with dogs walked past my classroom as I introduced myself and the expectations for the year to the freshly new juniors. Did they think they'd find more bones in some lockers? All eyes of my new students looked to the dogs and then back to me each time they passed.

"In addition to the American literature we'll cover this year, all juniors will complete an eight-to-ten-page research paper second semester." (Pay no attention to the officer and dog ambling by classroom 213.)

In second hour, junior Mike Sheridan raised his hand. The tall, dark-haired, tan athlete with blue eyes was well known. Teachers, students—mostly girls—and all coaches knew the charismatic seventeen-year-old. Since I had never had him in a class or study hall, I wasn't sure if he used his powers for good or evil. He smiled at me and waited.

I looked at my seating chart even though I knew Mike's name. "Uh, Mike, you have a question?"

"Yes, Ms. Day." I still went by my married name for Oliver's sake. I wasn't sure how many students at Belmont knew of the marital unraveling

I'd been experiencing the past several years. "For that research paper you mentioned, are we able to pick our own topic? Just wondering." Again, the charming smile.

"Good question."

I'm pretty sure Mike Sheridan didn't really care if he could pick his own topic for a paper that wasn't due for another semester. So I wondered: What did we have here? A brownnoser, a heckler, a kid who wanted to connect with his new teacher? Maybe young Mr. Sheridan was just trying to calm the class on a day in which I probably wasn't the only one feeling uneasy about what was happening on our campus.

"You'll all be able to pick from a list of social issues. You will need parental permission on your topic. I'll have details for you next semester."

"Sounds like a plan," Mike said, and he looked to his right at Arty Elston, two rows over and right near the door. Finally, a face to go with the name of the skull finder. Arty looked at Sheridan and shook his head with a grin. Mike Sheridan looked to his left at James Wu, a tall, thin kid who also grinned.

That day, not quite twenty-four hours after the discovery of a human skull in our backyard, I gave my first-day-of-American-lit talk five more times. I talked to my new classes about the weekly vocabulary quizzes and my cheating policy. I handed out big American literature books, many of which were falling apart.

Students wrote their names and the year inside the front cover below the names of kids who had carried these books around dating back to 1998. They would check those same books back in nine months, two semesters, four quarters—whichever way you want to slice up the cycle of a junior year hanging out with Emily Dickinson and Boo Radley.

After most students had left the building smelling like hormones and promise, I pulled out a folder and a container of tacks and moved toward the back of the classroom to put up a bulletin board. Technically, all bulletin boards were to have been up the previous week, but since no bulletin board monitor had noticed my room void of any interesting pictures or sayings, I had gotten away with my delay. The goal, I guess, is to entice a young learner to want to learn about the magic of the classics or writing with style. For me, putting up bulletin boards was about as exciting as monitoring an ACT test: not at all.

I set the letters and pictures on the last desk of the row closest to the window. I pulled up a chair and grabbed the first set of letters. I never put up any gimmicky boards such as Take a Read on the Wild Side. I take the straight and narrow route and put up bulletin boards about the unit we're in. Henry David Thoreau. No messing around here.

Just Thoreau.

I stood up on the chair with a tack in my mouth and several letters in my hand, and a scratchy voice interrupted my project.

"So, how'd it go?" Nadine Pickering, Belmont's vibrant journalism teacher, leaned against the edge of the door to my classroom. With her short, black, spiked hair; funky earrings; and edgy clothes, Nadine might come across as an intimidating type, but she was one of the nicest people I knew on staff and a saint for putting up with me for the mercurial past few years.

"Tell me all about the wicked kids that you'll pass on to me next year. I always like the wicked ones. Spare none of the gruesome details."

"Too soon to tell." I smiled as I got down from the chair. "I do have the skull finder in my second hour."

"The skull? Oh, I almost forgot to tell you." Nadine darted down the long center aisle and then stood right before me. "I had the weirdest dream last night." Dream swapping was something Nadine and I did on a regular basis—sharing and analyzing. English teachers have to analyze everything, even when they're sleeping. "OK, so I was late to class… only I wasn't a teacher; I was a student in college, and I was at KU, but it didn't look at all like the KU that I went to. It felt more like Hogwarts or Russia. Oh, and I'm carrying this box of black puppies. Lots of really itty-bitty puppies. I keep running to get to class, and the puppies keep falling out. I pick them up and put them in and keep running. And then I see her in the doorway to my classroom." Nadine took the glasses that were attached to her neck with a long, colorful chain and put them on, then took them off.

"See who?"

"Uh, Becky. Becky Kershner. A girl I taught back before you got here. She was my editor of the yearbook, my right-hand man, quite a few years ago. I spend a lot of time with my editors. I've gotten pretty close to most of them, but Becky was pretty special. She was this pretty, independent girl who was just filled with crazy ideas. I just loved her. She and her two little girlfriends, not in journalism, would hang out in my classroom after school, like they felt at home. I thought we'd stay in touch. She graduated, and that was it. I never heard from her again. Had Zane try to find her on Spacebook—"

"Facebook."

"Whatever. She never stayed in touch. Anyway, in my dream, I just don't know why Becky's in the doorway of the class that I'm late to. She's standing there, wearing this fuchsia dress she used to wear that kind of made her look a little trampy. Never understood how her mother let her out of the house wearing it. Anyway, she's standing there with her arms crossed, like she wasn't going to let me into the room. She looked mad or scared. I couldn't tell. Or maybe she was the teacher? She was probably the teacher."

I raised my hand and cleared my throat.

"Yes," Nadine said, acknowledging my interruption.

"My turn now?" I asked as I put all of the letters and pictures for the bulletin board back in the envelope.

"Go!" Nadine pulled herself up on a desk to sit.

"OK, so the puppies in the box that you're trying to take care of are your sons. With Zane at college and Kenny almost ready for high school, you can't keep them in your box or home forever." I make air quotation signs as I say "box." And that probably explains going back to KU, since you just moved Zane into his dorm at Creighton. The puppies are falling out because you feel like you don't have control. Not sure why they're black."

"Yah, yah, definitely a control dream." Nadine took one of her large hoop earrings and started playing with it.

"And the whole 'being late' thing is universal OCD teacher. We hate not being prepared. Hello, it's the first day of school. And…" I paused for effect.

"And what?" Nadine actually looked panicked, as if I really had the answer for her. I loved this. I was at least twenty years younger than she was, yet she respected my thoughts and opinions.

"You think that Becky is the owner of the skull, a.k.a. our new neighbor." I motioned toward the window. A hundred yards from my window, investigators had roped off the area where the skull had been found and worked all day long doing what, I'm not sure.

Nadine stopped playing with her earring.

"Just my unprofessional analysis. I could be wrong…"

"What if it is Becky?"

"It's not Becky. It's a dream, Nadine. You're always telling me how our brain just dumps all our 'underthoughts' of the day or subconscious and then throws them up like a baby projectile vomiting on our dreams. I thought the *puppies as your sons* was a more relevant analysis. I mean, you're the perfect mom sending these perfect boys out into the world. And those puppies might not need you that much anymore. Puppies falling out of a box that protected them. I only hope I can be half the mom to Oliver that you are to your boys. It just makes sense that your brain, which has always wondered and worried about Becky, would dream about her the night after they find a skull on the grounds of Belmont High School. Right? And…you also talked about your dream right after I mentioned the skull."

"So serious on the first day of school already?" a man's voice said, interrupting our dream analysis. "You can't be serious until at least end of first quarter." Doc Winder, the oldest janitor on staff, pushed his cart of cleaning supplies into the room and took out a handkerchief to wipe sweat from his red face.

Nadine jumped off the desk and laughed. "Doc? You're kidding me. Annie gets Doc again this year? Why do I never get to have you clean my classroom?"

"Look a little overheated, Doc," I said as I put the envelope in my top drawer. One more day before the bulletin board would get done.

"Dangerously hot out there today, ladies. We spent a good part of the afternoon hauling dirt from the upper field to the investigation van down on the west parking lot. Not sure what the guys are doing with the dirt, but they seem to know what they're doing." Doc had always been my janitor. I think he purposely scheduled himself on my block or whatever janitors do when they split up areas of the building. He looked out for me.

Doc's blue eyes looked washed out against his red face. "I just felt real bad for those men who have been at it all day long. The Nebraska humidity is worse than it's been all summer. One guy said that it may have been 98 degrees, but it felt like 120 all day long. The assistant on the team passed out right before lunch."

"Hate to sound nosy…" Nadine sat back on the desk again. "Did they find anything? Or do they know anything?"

"Just that something's not right. Everyone looks pretty concerned." Doc stood up and put his handkerchief in his back pocket. "See there!" Nadine and I looked where Doc was pointing, out the far window near the undone bulletin board. "They're still at it."

We all moved to the windows to look out at the upper practice field edged up against the north side of the stadium. The seeping hot air created imaginary waves around the countless people combing the area, making the scene look like a dream sequence in a creepy movie. Yellow crime-scene tape connected by poles covered an area about half the size of a football field, and at least ten people and a few dogs were crawling around the area like ants on an anthill. The crime scene. What crime, I wondered? The practice field was more than likely not the scene where the owner of this skull had met his or her demise.

"They're calling him or her Mystery Doe," Doc said. "Poor thing. I just can't let my mind go there."

"Wow." Nadine pulled at her glasses again.

"Bad timing is all." Doc picked up my trash can and dumped the few wadded-up papers into a bag on the side of his cart. "Here we are, trying to get ready for the big evaluation team coming in, and then they find…" Doc shook his head as if to force the word skull away from the conversation. I had almost forgotten about the evaluation. The family reunion with my cowboy ghost and then the skull had kept me distracted from the evaluation. I can't remember how often the educational accreditation team came around to check out our high school for what seemed like a full year, making sure we met the standards for approval. I just know that whenever our year came up, we all went into performance mode.

"Got to get the school squeaky clean," Doc announced. "It's show time."

"I remember the last evaluation." Nadine jumped down from the desk. "There were all these gorgeous men in suits on that team. Have you seen any of the hotties in the hall yet, Doc?"

"Hotties? No, haven't seen anything like that." Doc had a smirk on his face as he took the wide dust mop from this cart and moved around the area behind my desk.

"Well, if you do, tell them about Annie."

"Nadine, stop," I scolded.

"I'm just saying, if these same guys come again—"

"Nadine Marie. I'm not interested in dating right now. Please, stop feeling like I need to have a man in my life. Been there, done that. And we all know how that turned out. Besides I'm way too busy for anything else in my life."

Nadine lowered her voice and looked at Doc as she started toward the door. "Just tell the hotties that Annie looks like a shorter version of Amy Adams."

"Who's Amy Adams?" Doc asked.

"OK, a younger version of Sandy Duncan with longer auburn hair."

"Who's Sandy Duncan?" I asked.

"Never mind." Nadine moved toward the door. "Meet me for coffee in the teachers' lunchroom before school tomorrow, Annie. Oh, and my middle name is not Marie."

"That one's a sparkler," Doc said as he pushed his mop to the back of the room.

"Agree," I said as I packed up my purse and the lesson plans I wanted to take home to review after Oliver went to bed. "Thanks for being my janitor again this year. You know I do appreciate it, Doc."

"You bet. Now go home, Annie Day. You've got to spend time with your little guy. Got to finish this wing and head home to Alice." Alice was Doc's ancient beagle who couldn't see too well. Doc's wife had died years before I met him.

"Have a nice night with Alice!"

I pulled my car keys out of my purse and locked my door. The long hallway to the central hall was quiet. The air conditioning had kept everyone who'd spent the day in the big high school building in denial of the intense heat awaiting them on their drives home. I turned left and passed the counselors' offices and the administrative office in the front lobby. Scattered down the hallway, a few kids sat on the floor with backs against the walls, lining the passage like the homeless people on streets of downtown Omaha. Instead of signs that said "Will work for food or money," their imaginary signs read "No one worries about me," "I've got way too much free time," or "A little angry at the world at the moment." Some looked down at cell phones. Some looked off into space. The lost angels. Every year, a cluster of kids, the same ones every afternoon, just hung around. At first I thought they were waiting for rides, but Fred Walters, one of the counselors, said most don't want to go home. They didn't make a team; probably never tried out. Didn't join clubs. Different faces and names each year. Same kids, though. Lost.

Once I opened the door to the air outside, the oppression of the humidity overwhelmed me. I walked down the twenty-five stairs that led to what, in 1962, had been a stately building. I looked out at the west parking lot; my car sat alone in the first row. Beyond the football stadium, dark, pregnant clouds hung on to the horizon, hovering and waiting to take over the city, the air thick and noxious as teen angst. I walked to my car. I was looking at a group of men walking from the practice field behind the stadium when a big green truck slowed down and the window rolled down.

"Did you hear?" Avery Kensing, the head of the grounds crew, looked as if he'd had a long day. He opened his mouth to display a crooked fence of teeth. "They found another bone."

3

August 20, 2008

Annie

The rain began and did not stop for six straight hours.

The deluge of showers that hit Omaha in full force at about five o'clock that evening poured relief from the heat and the tension of the first day of school, relief that felt like a great big breath in and then out. I kept the windows open on the main floor until bedtime, and the whole house smelled like the perfume of a windfall waterfall.

"Look at the rain!" Oliver pointed with his fork.

Oliver and I watched the rain from our table as we enjoyed two plates of leftover spaghetti for the second night in a row. Oliver, perched on his booster chair at the dining-room table, babbled about his day as calendar monitor at daycare while Atticus, our elderly golden retriever, watched for fallen food from his moving fork. After dinner, I gave Oliver a bath, both of us singing "The Wheels on the Bus" over and over again as I washed his hair and scrubbed his little body. We read *Goodnight Moon* and *Horton Hears a Who* twice. We said our prayers and blessed everyone we knew. I kissed Oliver goodnight, and Oliver kissed Atticus.

I shut the door to Oliver's room, leaving it about three inches open. As I moved quietly down the stairs, the third step creaked, as I knew it would. I knew this old house very well. I tiptoed down the remaining steps to the main floor and grabbed my softest throw and pulled it over me on the couch, with just enough light from a small lamp for planning my day. Jake and I had bought this house in the year 2000, following his first year of law school. Though only 1,600 square feet—including a musty attic and an unfinished basement that smelled as if a garage sale had exploded—the hundred-year-old white house still looked dignified and solid, like a little, old matriarch sitting upon a small hill.

Atticus sprawled on the floor beside me.

Rain poured on my roof like a comforting bear hug. I picked up my pen and looked at the lesson plans for the next week.

Another bone.

I put down my pen. Where were these bones coming from?

A very tall, thin man with bad teeth and fierce pride of his position as head of grounds had told me about the second bone. Avery, who actually looked like a young version of Ichabod Crane, had been mowing the area around the baseball field after school when he had seen some "annoying little junior high kids on the baseball bleachers." A boy and a girl, he said, must have walked from the junior high school about five blocks from Belmont. He wasn't sure if they were there to smoke pot or make out, but the girl looked down under the bleachers and saw the bone. Because both preteens had probably listened to the same radio station I had—or any station, for that matter—they knew about the skull. The girl screamed, and Avery, worried that the boy might be hurting the girl, stopped his mower and ran to bleachers.

By the time Avery got to the two, the girl was still screaming and pointing to the bone. Avery phoned one of his crew members who had been helping the investigation team on the practice field. Eric Foster had been keeping students from getting anywhere near the scene where Mystery Doe had been found as they went to their cars in the west parking lot.

"You might want to send some guys over here," Avery told Eric. "We found something on the baseball field." A group from the investigation team came and gathered at the site to collect the bone and soil samples.

After answering questions from the team, the junior high girl made her closing, junior high, dramatic comment, "It was just sitting there… almost like it wanted to be found."

Shortly after the second bone—a human femur—was found, the rain came. Oliver and I had just walked in the back door of our house when torrential rains took over the city.

I put my lesson-plan book on the couch and listened to the thrashing rain. A strong wind blew the branches of the big oak tree in my yard against the windows, scraping and clawing and begging to come in. Atticus whimpered in his sleep and settled himself closer to the couch.

If only bones could speak. I thought about the owners of the bones found this week. I thought about my cowboy ghost, whose bones lay in a grave on the hill near the cabin in Bailey. What would his bones say about the man who had connected with me in the middle of the night? Had he been a good man when he was alive? How had he died, and why was he still hanging out in a cabin in Bailey, Colorado?

I sat up. Atticus, not moving his body, looked up at me with one eye. My laptop sat on the coffee table in front of me, beckoning me to search. Did I really think I could find my cowboy ghost on the Internet?

I put my cursor in the search bar and wrote, "Colorado ghosts." Search.

Results: the haunting in the Stanley Hotel in Estes Park that had inspired the book and movie *The Shining*, the haunting by a child of the Henry Treat Rogers Mansion that had inspired the movie *The Changeling*, and hauntings in and about Breckenridge, which apparently hadn't inspired anything.

"Ghosts in Bailey, Colorado." Search.

Results: a brief Wikipedia blurb about William Bailey, the man who settled a ranch and built a stage station known as Bailey's Ranch in 1864, links to the history behind the gold-mine rush in 1859 in the South Park area where Bailey fell on the map, links about men heading to the lower Rockies in the mid-eighteen hundreds to strike it rich, a link to stories of ghost towns, and many other links to stories of ghost towns.

"Colorado cowboy ghosts." Search.

Results: A band called the Colorado Cowboy Hosts and Ghosts on tour in Denver, links to a few ghost stories in abandoned gold mines, more links to stories about ghost towns, and links inviting me to go tour the ghost towns for a small price.

Maybe my cowboy ghost wasn't a cowboy at all. Maybe he was a gold miner, as Dot and Valerie had said, a man heading after the big dream of making it big, finding the big gold nugget, and heading home to his family. Still, I could see or feel a tall man with a hat and cowboy boots. A very handsome (pretty sure) man who worked hard and cared. I'm sure he cared. I felt his concern in my bones.

"Cowboys." Search.

Results:

Synonyms: cowpoke, cattleman, cowhand, cowman, cowherd, herder, herdsman, drover, stockman, rancher, and broncobuster.

Definition: adventurer, venture—a person who enjoys taking risks; a person who is reckless or careless, esp. when driving an automobile.

Atticus sat up, his old body moving like a stubborn, old man with arthritis. He stared out the window and whimpered. Jake and I had gotten Atticus the day we found out Jake had been accepted to law school. Atticus was the last pup left in our landlord's litter. She had told us as we wrote the check for our new dog that golden retrievers were so sweet that they would hold the flashlight for the burglar, and we laughed the whole way home with joy about the future of Jake's career, of our new puppy, of our life together. We named the pup Atticus, after the father and lawyer in my favorite book, *To Kill a Mockingbird*. Life was perfect.

"What do you see, Atticus?"

A huge clap of thunder sounded as if it hit a house nearby, or maybe a tree. I heard little footsteps running above me; Oliver stood at the top of the stairs. With his cowboy Woody in one hand, he put his glasses on with his other hand and looked down at me. Several people told me that Oliver looked like a little Tweety Bird, with his big blue eyes, thick lashes, and big head of blond hair that always looked as if it had just rubbed against a balloon. He was beautiful.

"Can I come sit with you?" Oliver said in an urgent whisper.

I patted the couch. "Come on down, buddy. It's just rain. Everything's fine."

Oliver ran down the stairs with his hand holding the banister, gave Atticus a hug, and crawled up on the couch with me. "But it sounds bad. Really, really bad."

"Pappa Rollie used to tell me when I was your age that the angels were bowling when you heard the thunder. Thunder won't hurt you." I didn't want to tell him lightning could hurt you. Plenty of time in life to find out about the really, really bad things. "Your buddy Atticus seems to know when it's about to thunder."

"That's because Atticus is smart." Oliver pronounced each world clearly. Sometimes I forgot he was only four.

"He is," I said as Atticus sighed. "We don't usually stay up this late, but maybe just this once we can go on the porch and smell the rain and then come back here to rest a bit." I tried hard to keep structure in the unstructure of our new life, but I knew that sometimes I could let up a little.

"Smell the rain?" Oliver tilted his head.

"Yah, why don't we open up the front door and take a great big smell of the rain. Breathe in and breath out." Oliver was up and running to the door before I said "door."

After I unlocked and opened the door, Oliver, Atticus, and I went out on the covered front porch. Water from the rain rushed everywhere: from my drainpipes, down the street, off of trees. Rain was pouring in forked sheets, at an angle when the wind shoved it around. The air, pure as the dreams of young children, smelled like a really, really good day. A good rain could wash away all of the bad things in a day. I breathed in the cleansing air. Oliver giggled and put his hand out to catch the rain. Atticus sat close to the door and watched us.

"Can you smell the rain, Atticus?" Oliver asked. "Choochoo, come out here and smell the rain."

Choochoo was Oliver's imaginary friend. Nadine had told me that bright children usually created imaginary playmates; both of her boys had. Oliver, a great lover of cars and trains, told me more than once, "Choochoo is a train man." He would then pull an imaginary lever as his high-pitched voice shouted, "Choochoo!" All I knew was that Choochoo was a pretty bossy playmate.

"Choochoo is shaking his head no. I guess he doesn't like to get wet either." Oliver shrugged. He moved his hand out to the rain pouring down and laughed a belly laugh.

Suddenly, Atticus barked. This wasn't like his whimper before the thunder. He barked loudly and consistently, without stopping, for about fifteen seconds. At first he seemed to be barking at the flickering street lamp. A tall figure appeared under the light with a dog on a leash.

"Hey, Annie and Mr. Oliver." Fred Wagner, my neighbor, was walking Elsie, his spoiled little pug, in the rain. "If Miss Elsie doesn't go out now, she'll wake Nora and me up in the middle of the night. That bark of Atticus sounds pretty mean coming from such a teddy bear."

"Hi, Mr. Wagner," Oliver yelled. "We're smelling the rain."

"Smelling the rain? Sounds like a good idea to me. Have a good one." Fred picked up Elsie and headed toward his house.

"You too, Fred. OK, guys, time to head back in."

Oliver reached up and grabbed my hand, and Atticus waited until we both were in the door and then followed us. I locked the door, and the three of us went back to the couch. I covered Oliver up with my blanket and began rubbing his back, the best way for him to fall asleep. Atticus settled down again, crumbling to the floor, only this time with his chin on Oliver's legs over the blanket.

"The angels are bowling," Oliver said and then yawned. "Pappa Rollie is funny."

"Yes, he is," I whispered, rubbing Oliver's back.

"Choochoo says you're right. The rain won't hurt me." Oliver moved his head on my shoulder and then yawned.

Thank God for rainstorms. Because of the unfortunate first day at work with mystery bones, my obsession with a little paranormal activity in Colorado, and a great big rainstorm, I had gone a full day without thinking about *The Jake and Jaymie Show*. The little Catty Monster would usually rear itself in my brain almost every hour on the hour as I obsessed over the affair that had broken up my marriage. No one around me knew what I was thinking as I smiled and quietly steamed.

The way the planets lined up to create *The Jake and Jaymie Show* was really almost comical. Jaymie, with a *y*, had lived on my sophomore floor in college. I knew her before I met Jake. We didn't know each other that well; in fact, the only thing I could remember about her was that Jaymie had a full head of long, black hair and shocking brown eyes. I have one other fleeting memory of her: Jaymie had stood up in front of everyone at a floor meeting in our dorm to introduce herself and told all of the third-floor girls that her name was Jaymie with a *y*. "Why?" she had said. "Because I always add a little something extra to whatever I do." Why, yes, she does.

When I played back the phone message I got from her during the first year after Jake made partner in his firm, I struggled to remember Jaymie—*with a y*—Shimmer. "Hey Annie! This is Jaymie Shimmer, from Creighton. Wow, it's been like forever. Anyway, I found out through my cousin that you're married to someone at Delmar, Delmar and Smith. And I was like, awesome. I just happen to be interviewing there next week. I wondered if we could do lunch. Connections are important in the business world. Am I right? Call me."

What's really strange is that I worked hard, with great resistance from my husband, to have the two meet so that Jake might help Jaymie in the process. So, I guess it's really my fault that the two found true love in each other. Just a little matchmaker, that's me. I should get some kind of karma credit for setting them up. I wondered what *The Jake and*

Jaymie Show was doing on this rainy night. Probably cuddled up on a couch, drinking wine, and thinking only of themselves and their narcissistic world.

And the Catty Monster was back.

I shook the thought from my head and looked down at Oliver and Atticus. Life was still pretty good on my couch. I could tell from his breathing that Oliver had fallen asleep. I took off his glasses, picked him up, kissed him on the head, and carried him up to bed, the third step creaking as I hit it. I tucked Oliver in for the night, Atticus right behind me.

I crawled into my bed that night. The rain lulled me to sleep, my last thoughts of the day about bones that could not speak.

4

September 30, 2008

Annie

Mystery Doe Number One and Mystery Doe Number Two remained on everyone's minds, in the headlines, and as the top story for the days following the rainstorm.

Two weeks following the discovery of the two separate bones that had found their way onto two different athletic fields at the same school, authorities made a shocking announcement: both bones belonged to the same Doe. At least that was what the DNA told them. We were back to one Mystery Doe. Although reporters were confident—*investigators have very strong leads*—the city of Omaha was doubtful we would discover the cause or the place of death of its Mystery Doe, let alone the identity.

"Poor thing. Wonder what happened to that little angel." Twyla Cartwright, a little firecracker from Texas with ruby-red lips and robust perfume, was the queen bee of the Belmont High School cheerleaders. Mother of three now-grown Texas star cheerleader daughters, Twyla had appointed me her assistant at the end of my first year of teaching. All teachers usually have extra duties, and I guess my duty wasn't so bad since I was in charge of the logistics of our functions—tryouts, car washes, fundraising—and left the "smarkling" of the girls up to Twyla. "If y'all just keep me organized, I'll make sure the girls smile and sparkle—smarkle!"

"Makes you wonder," I said as I looked at the clock on the wall behind her head. We both had first hour as a planning period and got together weekly to go over cheerleader events.

"I mean, there's a story out there that we'll probably never know. He or she didn't die under a bleacher; that's for damn sure."

"I'm going to need to head to my second-hour class."

"Right. I'll get an announcement to the front office that the cheerleaders will meet Wednesday. If you could contact the fundraiser guy before then, that would be awesome!" Twyla said in a Texas accent thicker than true Tex-Mex chili, her words dripping with spicy seasoned expressions even though she had been living in Nebraska for fifteen years.

"The man from Cheerworld FUN Raising is stopping by this afternoon to go over the fundraising kickoff info. Different guy than last year. I'll get the information to you tomorrow, if that works." I hurried out the door and looked at the long hallway that would take me from one end of the building to the exact opposite side. I was a third of the way down the hall when the bell rang. Doors exploded on each side of me, and warm bodies poured out in a frenzied, overpowering urgency.

Must get to room. Need more energy to barge through the masses.

Lockers slammed.

"Don't you touch my stuff! Hey, check out this picture."

Warm bodies gave off heat.

"No, meet me in the east parking lot after eighth hour, not the west one."

Almost to room 213.

"Mrs. Day!"

I made it. Students were still leaving as I was moved into the room.

"Mrs. Day! Can I get that American Dream thingy to you by the end of the day and still get credit? Please, please, please." Kyle Goodman, twice as tall as I was and full of energy, walked with me.

"The American Dream essay, not thingy. You mean to tell me that you haven't written the essay that was assigned last Tuesday, Kyle?" I moved as I talked and finally got to my desk. "Can't you just get it to me fifth hour when you're in my class?"

"Well, you see, I'm a big inspirational kind of guy." Kyle leaned on my desk. "And I haven't gotten inspired by the whole American Dream thing…until today. But I'm superinspired now, so I'm going to write it in my eighth-hour study hall. I just want to make sure I don't get down-graded or anything since *technically* it's still the day it's due."

"But it would be *after* the school day is over. Technically, it would be late."

Kyle put his hands together in a prayer.

"But," I said as I pulled out the handouts for the next class, "I'll take it. Now go get inspired." Students poured into the room to their seats.

"Yes!"

"I'll be here for a little bit after school. But if you miss me…"

"Thank you, thank you. I'll be here right after eighth hour. Promise!"

"OK, second hour, give me what you've got!" I called out to the students. A handful of late students rushed in to get settled. "Please get out your essays and pass them forward. If you haven't already stapled the sheet that I gave you with the essay prompt on it, I have a stapler here to pass around."

"I need the stapler!" Cami Hollaway yelled out from the back of the room. She got up, pushed her blond hair back, batted her big brown eyes, and walked down the row to get it. Cami would take any stapler opportunity as a chance to parade up and down the aisles.

"As you're handing these essays in, let's review. The idea of the American Dream is going to be a thread that will pull all of the literature of this year together. Who can tell me a little bit about the American Dream?"

Several hands shot up. Second hour was really starting to grow on me.

"OK, Arty. Tell me all about it." The skull finder was focused.

"Well, the idea kind of started back when all the people were moving to America a long time ago. Like America was this magical place for people from other countries to come and strike it rich." Arty sat in the first row next to the door. His freckles, reddish blond hair, and big blue eyes made him look as if he had just stepped out of a sitcom in the seventies. "Everybody wanted a piece of the action." He smiled and shook his head.

"Yes, there was an appeal factor," I said. "Anyone want to add to that?"

Another hand shot up in the back of the middle row.

"Kinkaid?" A larger, really smart kid with bright-red cheeks and the tendency to hum when stressed had something to add. Kinkaid O'Neill was a bright and neurotic boy who had opted out of Honors English for an easy grade—or so he informed me on the first day of school—which proved that he wasn't that bright.

"But it wasn't like America was just granting those wishes." Kinkaid spoke as if reading from cue cards. "The dreamer's attitude needed to be right. You couldn't just come and expect to be rich. The dreamer needed to be honest in attaining the dream, and the dream needed to be worthy."

"Exactly." (Exactly from his notes.) "Optimism about the future in America was what moved some people to finally make those dreams a reality. So for the most part, we'll focus on the purity of the dream, but we'll start to become aware of the corruption of the American Dream in some literature as well."

Mike Sheridan raised his hand.

"Yes, Mr. Sheridan?"

"Speaking of dreams, I had a dream about you the other night, Mrs. Day."

Laughter and groans.

I was a little rattled; I won't lie.

I don't lie.

"Creeper." James Wu's response was disguised in a loud cough.

"Not like that, people. I just think this American Dream stuff is sneaking into my psyche. I dreamed that I was chasing an ice cream truck, and then it stopped, and there you were, Ms. Day, driving the ice cream truck. And you said to me, 'You better keep up, or you'll miss the American Dream.'"

"That's the dumbest dream ever," Arty said without raising his hand. "Hey, when I was little, my mom used to tell me that when the ice cream truck rang its bell, that meant he was out of ice cream." Arty laughed louder than anyone at what he had just said. "No joke. I'm totally serious."

"And I've officially lost control. All papers handed up the row. Now get out your notebooks. You're all going to need to be in note-taking mode. I have so much to pass on to you little groundlings. Why am I always giving, giving…" A hint of a smile appeared and quickly disappeared from a girl named Peaches Trumble, sitting directly behind Mike Sheridan. Peaches, a senior repeating junior English, was easily six foot three and 250 pounds. Her serious expression was both intriguing and intimidating to me. Two large earrings that looked like silver pinwheels floated on either side of her ebony skin, moved as if suspended without connection to her.

"OK, your pens better be hot. Here goes." I drew a big yellow star at the top of the dry-erase board. I turned around. Students looked, confused, at one another and then at me.

"Aren't you going to write that down?" Several students smiled at me as they all began drawing stars at the top of their notebook pages. I then took a green marker and made several little marks at the bottom of the board, creating a grasslike image. "Are you keeping up?" Students marked the bottoms of their notebook pages. I then took a black marker and drew a jagged line from left to right halfway between the star and the grass.

"What is this? Art class or something?" LaTrey Williams mumbled. LaTrey was short and feisty.

"Nope. You're about to learn about transcendentalism, the philosophy that Henry David Thoreau not only valued but lived to the extreme. He's one of the first American writers we'll be studying."

"*Trans* what?" LaTrey looked annoyed.

"Transcendentalism." I spelled the word out to the left of my artwork. "First you need to learn how to say it, right? See the word *dental* in there? Everyone say *dental-ism.*"

Students looked up at me and then at the door. A tall student stood in the door with a piece of paper, his head almost touching the top of the doorframe. Either tired or stoned, the young man held out a slip, his eyes hidden by long, brown hair. Kurt Cobain's face graced the black T-shirt.

"Can I help you?"

"Mr. Holmes gave me this paper to give to you." The voice was low and quiet. "Just moved to Omaha this week."

"Come on in. You have a name?"

"Donovan Hedder." He moved his head, and his dark hair swished to the side and then moved back to cover his eyes again.

"It's your lucky day, Donovan. You get to sit right next to me." I pointed to the first seat in the second row from the window, the only seat left in the room. I needed to let Mr. Holmes know second hour was packed. "If you could see me before you head to your next class, I can update you on what you've missed. OK, now you get to join our discussion on...Trans..." I looked to the students.

"*Trans*-vestites," LaTrey mumbled.

Katrina St. Martin raised her hand.

"Katrina."

"Transcendentalism," she said perfectly. "You were talking about Thoreau's philosophy that he liked." Katrina St. Martin, dubbed K-Mart during her run for class officer, was a quiet leader. Her long, dark, wavy hair struggled around a face where puberty was pretty busy at the moment, but I knew that time would chisel away the awkward factor and reveal a beautiful woman someday. K-Mart had made her mark at an all-school assembly the previous year when she stuttered to get out her speech and announced, "If elected, I will give my breast as a class officer of the class of 2010." Hands down. No contest. We had a winner. Especially after Mike Sheridan gave her his personal endorsement, announcing to all of his classes that he would vote for any girl who would give him her breasts. By default, Katrina won. By luck, the sophomores elected the most qualified representative. She was presently the junior class president.

"Thanks, Katrina. Donovan, we're taking notes." I looked at Donovan, who slowly pulled out a folded piece of paper from his pocket and pulled a pencil from behind his ear. "Back to the board. OK, first, the star. What is it? It's your ultimate goal in this life. It's happiness, it's peace, it's freedom from pain. Jump in. What's your star?"

"Summer," Cami yelled from the back of the room.

"Perfection," Kinkaid added.

"The American Dream with ice cream," Mike said with a huge grin.

"Nirvana," Arty said as he looked at Donovan.

"God," Katrina said.

"So what about the grass down here?" I pointed to the board. "Those little lines down there are actually all of you little groundlings looking up at the star. What about the black, mucky line? That muck there is everything that gets in the way of you reaching that star, your happiness. Drugs and crime. Bad days and rude people. Deadlines and rules." *People who add the letter y to their names to add a little extra something.* "What else?"

"Parents." A few people laughed as a boy named Phil Timmerman decided to join in.

"Homecoming," a voice grumbled from the back of the room.

"Skulls," Arty threw out.

Mike Sheridan shouted the rival team. "Millard North!"

"Thoreau!" LaTrey shouted. "He makes me want to *Thoreau* up."

"If I had a dollar," I said to LaTrey, "for every time I've heard that one. OK, so you get the picture I'm painting for you. There's this awesome state of mind where we want to go, and there's an awful lot of muck in our way. Transcendentalism comes in to save the day."

I went to the board and wrote several large letters on the board, each letter under the one before. S-S-S-M-I-N-E.

"Write this down. OK, in order to break through the muck—the problems, the rules, the bullies—Thoreau believed that you needed to live your life a certain way. In order to transcend the muck, you must first simplify. Write 'simplify' down after the first S."

Sitting in front of Arty, Maggie Whitehead raised her hand. An unfortunate name for any teenager. Why don't you just call her Zit.

"Maggie?"

"Are we going to be tested on all this stuff?" Maggie asked as she bit her lip, her face a pouty lemon.

"Yes, but I'm giving you this picture and this mnemonic device, or trick, to help you learn this pretty overwhelming idea. This will help as we study several of Thoreau's written works. You'll be fine!"

"OK." Maggie's brow furrowed as she pulled at her hair.

"So by 'simplify,' Thoreau meant 'get rid of the clutter,' and you'll feel better. Clean out the closet and give some stuff to Goodwill. Stay away from the drama that crawls through the halls out there. Don't be so busy. Simplify."

Good old Period Two. They were all taking notes. Donovan had even drawn little people and things that represented the muck in his life. Wish I could have looked closer.

"The next S: solitude. Sometimes you need to pull away from the hustle and bustle. In an experiment on the true transcendental life, Thoreau moved out to live by himself in a tiny little shack for a while. His budget for the year before he came back to society: twelve dollars and twenty-eight cents. The final S is self-reliance. The more you depend on others or technology, the worse off you are when they're gone. We depend on technology and become paralyzed when it crashes. Anyone ever lose a cell phone? A nightmare."

James Wu raised his hand.

"James."

"Once I wrote a ten-page paper and went to print it, and the electricity went out, and I lost the whole thing."

"Serves you right for writing a ten-page paper," Arty said to his friend.

"Exactly what Thoreau meant. OK, so then we hit the letter *M*, which stands for morality. Bottom line: be good. Say a prayer. Go to church. Life gets complicated when we do drugs or lie. We create our own muck. The letter *I* is something you all already get: individuality. Cast conformity behind you! Thoreau says, 'Do *not* follow the crowd!' The letter *N* is nature. He lived off the land that year of his experiment. If he had lived in 2008, Thoreau would recycle and probably crusade environmental issues. And then, finally, the letter *E*. Why are we all here?"

"Haven't figured that one out yet," LaTrey grumbled.

"Education, LaTrey. You meant to say education. When you learn, you grow. Education. Write it down. So three *S* words, *S* cubed, and the word MINE, like owning my journey. MINE. Maggie, just remember *S* cubed and MINE, the trick to remember the seven things to break through that muck. And after we read excerpts from Thoreau's *Walden* and *On Civil Disobedience*, you'll be able to recognize how Thoreau applied these tools to his life."

"Kind of unrealistic," Kinkaid said, mostly to himself.

"Well, for a lot of people, Kinkaid. Not everyone can do it. In fact, I'm sure few do every moment of the day. It's a challenge, for sure. You've probably heard expressions that are really saying 'Transcend.' Like 'Get over it' or 'Rise above it.'"

Peaches raised her hand, her first time to participate. Intrigued and intimidated, I called out her name. "Peaches, want to add something?"

"Just a question." Her voice was quiet and surprisingly calm. "If this Thoreau guy was so stoked to be a transcendental guy, then why did he leave the woods? You said he left the woods after a year."

"Peaches, you are a thinker! Thoreau did his little experiment, and while I buy into the fact that these seven 'transcendental suggestions' will make your life better, life is also about balance. Extremes of anything don't usually work—which is what Thoreau found out. I think the man got lonely, personally. The answer, Peaches, which I think you already knew, is balance."

Peaches smiled.

I gave my transcendentalism speech five more times that day to classes that weren't nearly as receptive to the idea as my second-hour class. After eighth hour, I sat down at my desk and pulled my stack of essays in front of me, grabbed my red pen, and sighed. Six times 30. I had about 180 essays to look forward to, along with 180 quizzes from the day before; I had gotten through about half. I grabbed the first essay from the top and began to read.

> The American dream is something most Americans understand, but it is something that everyone views in different ways. Basically, it means being successful in an area that you have interest and living a good life. I see my "American dream" as being a good husband and father someday. I'll provide for my family, but I'll be there for them and not travel so much and miss their activities…

I looked at the name on the top of the essay: Patrick Collins. I've found through years of reading essays that the writer of an essay tells me so much more than what I had asked.

"I made it!" I looked up to see Kyle Goodman. "Just like I told you I would. And I'm not kidding. This is probably the best essay I have ever written. Serious. You're gonna love it."

"Awesome."

"I'm gonna be a sports announcer, and I feel like I show in my paper how a sports announcer is the ultimate American Dream. You'll see what I mean when you read it." Kyle took the stapler from my desk and stapled his cover sheet to his essay. "I've got to go to Mr. Penner's office for a demerit I got yesterday. I'm planning on disputing it." Kyle handed me his essay and ran to the door. "See you, Mrs. Day! Thanks for taking my essay!" He was gone.

"Bye, Kyle."

I'm gonna be a sports announcer.

Wow, just that easy.

He's gonna be a sports announcer.

Just like that. Kyle wanted something, and he spoke as if it were already true. *Gonna be a sports announcer.* Had I ever been that naïve? Or ever that sure that if I wanted to do something in life, I could just go out and do it? I'm gonna be a movie star. I'm gonna be an astronaut. Did I ever think that all of the endless opportunities were out there sitting on a shelf, just waiting for me to decide which one I wanted and then pick it up off of the shelf and check it out like a brand-new library book? Or I could open a box of chocolates—cherry chew; almond; coconut; nougat, whatever that is—and I didn't have to share my box of dreams with anyone. I could just keep tasting the chocolates until I got the exact chocolate dream I wanted. Had I ever thought like that?

You bet I had.

When I lived on the other side of the line, where, ironically, the grass was greener.

Especially in the past few years, I had become increasingly aware of the line. Like the football line that appears out of nowhere like a devious shark on the screen of a football game, "the line" flickers and separates the dreamers from the "dults"—that's what Oliver calls adults, which seems appropriate and depressing at the same time. The dreamers are not aware of the line at all. For those on this side of the line: we resent the line.

Disappointment in the world with a smile on your face. A dult.

This is not how things were supposed to turn out. I was not sup-posed to be divorced at age thirty-two with a little boy and a dog and a mortgage. I was going to be a writer, for heaven's sake. I was going to be happily married and have five kids and a doting husband. We would have a movie night every Friday night, a kid movie finished before 8:30 and a "mom-and-dad" movie for mom and dad, who would hold hands and drink wine while watching our movie after the kids were asleep. That was my dream. It wasn't as if I felt entitled to this dream. It wasn't as if I felt this dream was too complicated, too much to ask for. I didn't think the world owed me. I just thought that if I worked really hard and wanted something, well, then it just happened.

The muck, the muck, the muck.

Get over it. Transcend it and quit your whining.

But the Catty Monster was especially commanding at the end of the day, after my students raced out of the room, stragglers with questions meandered, and then silence reigned. I was an easy target. Tired and alone in room 213. The Catty Monster would slowly slither around my head, usually catching me off guard, and then attack, squeezing my brain with sweet, luscious resentment.

He lied.

Ignore it. Pull away from the Catty Monster.

Too late. The monster had taken over, and I was back in a memory.

He lied.

"I don't think this is going to work out." Jake stood in the door to the bathroom as I was giving Oliver, almost two at the time, a bath. Jake had taken his jacket off and was loosening his tie. We had paid more for that burgundy Louis Vuitton tie than we had for our new garbage disposal. *If I'm going to be a partner, I need to dress like one.* Jake stood there, his blond hair perfect with one perfect piece of hair straying down his forehead. He looked like an advertisement in a *GQ* magazine that women stared at when their husbands weren't around.

"I've got this," I said as I elbowed Atticus back from licking Oliver's face. "You just change and relax. Dinner's in the fridge. I'll heat it up after Oliver's bath." Oliver cooed as he splashed water at Atticus.

"I don't mean the bath."

Oliver grabbed the washcloth from my hand and put it in his mouth. I looked up.

"I mean us. I don't think we're going to work out."

Atticus took the washcloth from Oliver, and Oliver laughed. I said nothing as I tried to get my head around the words coming out of Jake's mouth.

"I've been thinking. I could just stay at the office overnight until I get my own place."

He lied.

I suddenly felt as if I could throw up. I pulled back from the tub and took a breath.

Jake had been working on a big case and spending nights in the office here and there the past few weeks. I'd really seen very little of him since "the case" that was so important had demanded so much of his time and attention. A partner and all, right?

I finally spoke. "What are you talking about? Where is this coming from? We're good. We have this beautiful little boy here. We're building a house. You're probably tired." My voice quivered on the word *tired.*

"I knew it. I knew that the sweet, little, the-glass-is-always-so-heaping-full-I-can't-even-see-reality Annie wouldn't get this. How could I expect you to get this? You can't see that this isn't going to work?"

"Am I missing something? Geez, Jake, is there a woman? Are you—"

"Wow." Usually calm and oh-so-cool Jake slammed his fist on the sink counter. Oliver stopped laughing. Atticus looked at Jake. In a whisper, Jake scolded me. "Can't believe you went there, Annie. I'm going to grab my stuff and head out." Jake moved into the bathroom as he said this. At first, I thought he was leaning in to kiss me, but he moved over to the tub, knelt in front of Oliver and Atticus, and, with hands on both, he leaned in and kissed Oliver. "How are my boys, huh? You guys be good for Mom, OK." I could smell his cologne. Why would his cologne be so strong at seven thirty at night? Jake stood up and looked at me. "I'll let you know when I get settled in the new place. We'll just figure out the details as we go along."

I grabbed each of Jake's arms. "What are you doing, Jake? You're not making any sense." I could feel my voice shake as tears spilled down my face. Oliver started fussing.

"Don't, Annie. It'll be easier in time." (His voice sounded funny, throwing out a phrase he'd never used: "easier in time.")

"But..." My voice cracked. "Oliver? The new house?" (Who plans to build a house with someone and then leaves?) "What about us?"

"You can't just force things, Annie. I won't just stick around when it's not right. I'm not my dad."

Right then and there, on the bathroom floor on a beautiful fall night in 2005, a great big line flickered and then appeared bold and self-righteous, pushing me from the dreamer side of the line.

This was not the chocolate dream I had picked from the box of life. I was officially a *dult*.

He lied.

Jake was a big, fat liar.

"I'm not my dad."

The Catty Monster squeezed more tightly and slowly around my brain.

Jake was exactly like his dad, and I knew at that moment he was having an affair. I surprisingly but correctly suspected Jaymie Shimmer, new lawyer on the team and my now-former friend, as the object of his attention and strange, selfish impulses. I evidently was no longer his sweet, little Annie; only poor, little, pathetic Annie, who didn't have a clue.

Hello, my lovely little Catty Monster. Oh, how you do keep me company and let me wallow in snarky self-pity.

Jake, his dad, and his grandfather were all named Oliver Jameson Day, as if you could never have enough Oliver Jameson Days. Or maybe the parents lacked creativity when the first boy in the next generation was born. Or, most likely, they all shared an egotistical need to continue an arrogant and vain tradition. Who knows? Still, with the Oliver Jameson Day name, Jake had gone by the name Jake when he was little to help avoid confusion with the Chicago Olivers. Actually, his mom called him Jakey. *How can you not love my little Jakey?* The men were all handsome and charismatic. The men were all lawyers. They were all cheaters. And, clearly, all big, fat liars.

His senior year of high school, Jake put a kink in the history chain of the Day men. Jake's dad had wanted Jake to go to University of New

Hampshire in Concord, where he and most men in the Chicago Day family had gone and then stayed for law school. Rebel Jake chose, much to Jake's dad's consternation, to follow a girl to Creighton University in Omaha: Lori. (Always about a woman.) I think her name was Lori or Laura or something like that. Jake broke up with her during Welcome Week of his freshman year. (So many other women, so little time.) Jake and I didn't meet until the end of our junior year; I swear we both knew we would get married after our first date. We married during our senior year of undergrad in a huge, obnoxious wedding—Day style—at Creighton in the fall of 1998.

Jake's father and grandfather were not happy at all, again, when Jake told them that, after graduating from Creighton University's law school, he would not be moving back to Chicago to join the family law firm. After all, he had fallen in love with a little Nebraska gal who had him wrapped around her Omaha finger. I hadn't demanded that he stay. I had just told him that I was not a Chicago-like person.

On the day Oliver was born—this time I ruffled the feathers of the Day roosters—I told Jake that I was fine with naming our baby boy Oliver, but I wanted his middle name to come from my side of the family. It doesn't always have to be about the Day family. Oliver Truett Day broke the chain of Oliver Jameson Days, and hopefully the chain of cheaters and big, fat liars—though that wasn't my original point in picking the middle name. I wanted a piece of my family history to be in our new little baby. Oliver's middle name came from a favorite uncle of my father; the stories he told of his cowboy hero inspired me to name my son after the bigger-than-life Truett McGuire, a man I never met. I loved the sound of it: Truett. Oliver Truett Day will be bigger than life and known as good man. The cheating legacy stops here.

Cheating had been commonplace in the Day family for a long time. The men were so awesome (they thought) that they needed to spread their rooster feathers out into the community. Everyone wanted a piece of them. The women who connected to the Day men needed to be cautious or very patient—and probably pretty stupid—to sign up for the infidelity roller coaster. I learned this after the fact; although, truth be told, I probably always knew it. I was just head over heels in love with Jake.

Once a member of the Day clan, I looked to the other women around the Day men. Jake's mother—Joan Collins meets Florence Henderson (scary combination, by the way)—stood out to me as an amazing woman, if only for her tenacity to dysfunction. While everyone in the room and in all rooms was quite aware of the infidelities of the great Oliver Jameson Day, her own college sweetheart and father of their five perfect children, Victoria Day sat on her great, big, and probably soft and comfortable cloud of denial. Jake said in the early days that there had been lots of women—Leslies, Kathys, a bunch of Susans, and one short-lived fling named Muffy—but by the time Jake got to high school, there was only Bonnie, the firm's secretary, who actually had a child with Jake's father. Oliver, Victoria, and Bonnie (and Jake and his siblings) were all very aware of the infidelities (and their secret sibling) and of the awareness of the situation by all players in the game. A lot of awareness. A heck of a lot of sick, silent awareness.

Hello, we all know. Why is nobody calling it out?

Because that was exactly how my former mother-in-law wanted it. How else could Victoria Day live the life she did? A beautiful, big home in Old Town Chicago and a lake home in Michigan where the family held a talent show each summer with locals on the lake. Expensive trips to Italy and cruises to Alaska, just to get away for a bit. Beautiful clothes and extravagant events. She knew what she was doing. Some people might commend Victoria for her patience, for staying so long with a husband with so many "extracurricular" activities. I always felt sorry for her in the same way that I felt sorry for the rich girl in my fourth-grade class nobody liked since she was such a brat. There is a way to fix it, you know. You're not a victim. You're a big part of the problem.

As I looked down at Patrick Collins's essay and shook my head to shoo the Catty Monster away, I sensed a presence in the doorway and guessed that Kyle had come back to see if I had already read his essay and wanted me to tell him how much I loved it.

I looked up to see the most gorgeous man I have ever seen filling the doorway to room 213. His suit hugged his body in a good way, and his electric smile made me think that he wasn't real. His skin held the deep tan of lifeguards and retired golfers, and he (absolutely) popped against the bland background of a public high school. Tall, dark, and handsome.

Damn.

The eye candy spoke. "You look like you haven't been kissed in a really long time." Coming from a warm, sexy voice, his words enticed and offended me at the same time. And yes, I hadn't been kissed in a long time, unless you counted my cowboy ghost kiss.

"Excuse me?" My voice was deep and scratchy. *Was this guy from the evaluation team?* I wanted to report his inappropriate behavior to his supervisor right after I took one more look at him.

The man walked toward me holding a briefcase and something tiny in his other hand. His eyes were golden, light in the middle and darker around the edges, surrounded by lashes that made me weak. "I know you'll want to try our new Kissers, the best lip gloss invented. These Kissers come in fifty-five flavors that kiss your lips as they heal, glaze, and gloss them." (Glaze and gloss: redundant. I'm silently correcting your grammar.) "This one here is called Smooch Berry, but I have a whole case of most of the other flavors: Smack-Me Melon, Pucker-Up Pumpkin, Karamel Kissing Kousin, Banana Butterfly Kiss, and a few others I can't remember. I'm Trent Kula, your rep from Cheerworld FUN Raising. You must be *the* Annie Day." Trent placed the Kisser on my desk and put his hand out to shake mine.

Smack-Me Melon?

While appreciative of the interruption to my Catty Monster memory, I was torn between swooning and smacking his melon for being so cheesy and smug. I reached out to shake Trent Kula's hand. And, of course, he smelled clean and incredible.

"Let me just pull out the flyer, which will show you all fifty-five pouting flavors, Annie. We're also introducing wacky key chains, though I'm not nearly as excited about them, and, of course, keeping with our 'regulars': wrapping paper and candy. What do you think, Annie?"

I thought I really liked the way he said my name. I cleared my throat. "Looks good."

"Great! Mind if I pull up a chair so we can go over the package we're proposing to your group? I know we meet this coming Wednesday, so I thought we'd go over what I will present to the girls." Trent grabbed a chair, pulled it up to my desk, and sat before I could answer. "I have all of the brochures and order forms for you today, but I'll bring some more with me on the big kickoff meeting. On Wednesday, I'm going to give each of your girls a mini-Kisser as a gift, of course, but we're also hoping for a little product placement in the school—though you didn't hear that from me. This is what I envision. Chelsea Cheerleader is putting on some Makeout Mango lip gloss in study hall, and everyone around her asks, 'Hey, where did you get that?' You see what I'm saying, Annie?"

He said my name again.

"Then everyone will want in on the Kissermania. That's what I'm calling it."

"Kissermania?" I tried to think of something else to say. *Makeout Mango?*

"This year we're asking the girls to get the money up front from the people who order. We ran into some problems last year. Well, I didn't, but the company said they did." Trent loosened his tie and smiled that smile again. "Been with them five months; six this coming week."

"What happened to Greg? The last rep?" This position seemed to have a revolving door concept behind it.

"Not sure, but I've found this company to offer a great platform for groups to have fun while making money." Trent stood up and put his hands in his pockets. The human billboard. Always on. Always selling. Always pushing something at you and throwing out phrases like *You're gonna love it!* As if I've already decided to buy his product. He seemed like a man whose whole life was a billboard. *Let me sell myself. Here*

I am! Would you like to place an order? "On a serious note, so sorry about all the attention the school is getting with your bones."

Maybe Adonis before me was human. "Our bones?"

"And the girl who disappeared."

"Girl?"

"The girl who belongs to the bones. Or would it be the bones belong to the girl? Hey, you're the English teacher." Trent pointed at me with two finger guns.

"What girl?" I stood up.

"The girl identified by the authorities. They just announced it this afternoon. Some girl who went to school here. I can't remember her name, but the news said the dental records sealed the deal. Here, just go ahead and keep this Smooch Berry Kisser. Product placement. Right, right, right!"

I looked at the Smooch Berry Kisser in my hand. I hated lip gloss.

"I have a feeling you're gonna like being kissed," Trent whispered as he grabbed his briefcase.

"OK."

"I'll be back for your meeting next Wednesday. Can't wait to see you again, Annie Day!" The eye candy walked out of my room.

I realized this was first time in a long time that I was looking forward to a Wednesday. And I hated myself for feeling so excited.

5

"Truett's Hat and the Lightning"
Brush, Colorado—July 1979

Rollie

He shoulda been dead.

But that old Truett, he was strong and stubborn and probably a good challenge to God himself.

"When I'm ready to die, I'll die. And I ain't ready."

I'm pretty sure the old man shouted those words to the sky above him as he lay there under his dead horse in a thunderstorm just south of Brush, Colorado, rain pouring down over him, hoping God would hear and take note.

Silver, Truett's favorite horse at the time, had more than likely saved the old rancher's life when the two were struck by lightning. The animal had absorbed most of the jolt of the electrocution, as the beautiful workhorse had fallen on Truett and broken his master's leg, dying immediately right then and there in the back pasture, about a mile from the ranch house. Truett lay there for hours and finally pulled himself from under Silver and crawled the mile back to the Genoa Place. Most men half his age couldn't crawl for a mile with a broken leg after having a jolt of electricity race through their system.

My other uncles told me not to talk about the broken leg. See, Truett didn't care about no silly broken leg when he lost a good friend to Mother Nature. "Don't mention the leg. He'll ignore it if you do."

Uncle Truett had to have been around seventy, almost seventy, that year, but the man still rode every day of his life. You girls were all still little when I went to visit him following the electric-storm accident. I think that was the year Lori was born, Annie. Man, how I wish you and your sisters could have known the man I knew. He was the biggest cowboy ever.

I was always glad I made that trip. I sat with my hero for hours and listened to him talk about the good old days. The memories took me back to family visits to the Genoa Place and one summer that we even lived there. The man was in pain.

"How you doing, Tru?"

"Doing OK. I want to show you something, Rollie, by golly."

Truett showed me the hat he was wearing that day he was struck by lightning out in the south pasture. It looked like a firecracker blew out one side of the hat. He then showed me the shirt where another M-80 blew most of the sleeve out. I saw the charred edges of the burn on the material. He made no mention of the cast on his leg. Neither did I.

"See here, the lightning went through my hat and out of my arm. The rest of it went down to the best horse I've ever owned. Old Silver anchored me. He took the brunt of the charge, and, well, he just fell."

I sat down and waited for Truett to go on.

"The sun was shining all morning long. Who knew that that storm would charge in like it did? But it did."

Truett was working hard to keep it together.

"Just a strange day, that's all."

6

Annie

ennifer Caldwell.

The skull and bone had a name. Mystery Doe was no longer a mystery. She was a dead teenager who had walked the halls of Belmont High School over ten years ago. Mystery Doe was a real person. She was not the boy from Iowa. She was not Becky Kershner, Nadine's editor who never kept in touch. She was Jennifer Caldwell, a different girl entirely.

The parents of Jennifer stepped forward during the investigation the week after the bones had been found to inform authorities that they had never reported their daughter missing in 1998. Their estranged daughter had always been somewhat of a problem child. Out of control. She had usually slept at other people's houses, even in high school. The parents had always just assumed that Jennifer had taken off and lived her ever-random life. When Jennifer's mother proposed that the bones might be her daughter's, investigators went to Jennifer's childhood dentist for dental records.

A match.

Who doesn't worry about a missing daughter? In ten years, they had just said to themselves, "Oh, well, that's just so Jennifer."

(That's just so weird.)

I was in a grumpy mood all Saturday morning wondering how parents could just write off a child. I couldn't imagine moving on with business if I didn't know where Oliver was. Fortunately, my dad was coming over to help me out with a few things around the house. Two plusses for his visit: one, Oliver loved hanging out with his Pappa Rollie, and two, my dad usually took us out for a noon brunch to Smokin' Joe's, a greasy spoon hole-in-the-wall (that would be redundant) a few blocks from my house. Maybe the bacon and country potatoes could take away the bad taste in my mouth about lost daughters who'd been forgotten.

"Ollie, by golly!" my dad shouted as he walked in the back screen door.

Oliver yelled from his bowl of Cheerios, "By golly, Pappa Rollie!" I knew that was the end of the cereal.

"How's my favorite little cowboy?" Roland, my dad and Oliver's hero, was wearing jeans and a T-shirt, which I had not once seen him wear when I was growing up. Suits and khakis. Never jeans. That day on a cool fall morning, my dad had jeans, a tucked-in T-shirt, and white gym shoes that looked a little different than his younger days.

"You look nice, Pappa," I said as I took Oliver's bowl to the sink.

"I am nice," he muttered and knelt down to pet Atticus. "Hey, Cuss, how you doing?"

"Ready for the rodeo, Pappa?" Oliver yelled as he ran upstairs, my dad and I both knew, to put on his red cowboy boots.

"So what do you think, Annie? The backyard's pretty wet."

"I think we redirect, Dad. How about the attic?"

"The attic?" My dad scratched behind Atticus's ears as the old dog leaned into him.

"I know. Sounds weird since there are a million other projects to do around the house, but I'd kind of like to get up there and investigate. I have an idea."

"Let's hear it."

We both could hear Oliver's boots as he held the banister and came down the stairs.

"Let's head up to the attic, cowboy. We're going to check out the territory. So, what are you thinking, Annie?"

"Don't think I'm crazy." My dad raised his eyebrows as he began walking the stairs to the second floor. "I've been hearing what might be bats up in the attic. Or something shuffling around. Kind of like frantic shuffling. Once we figure out the noise thing, I'm thinking I might want to turn the attic into a toy room slash office. I've been setting money aside for this project for a while. It could be really neat." What I really needed was a purpose if I was going to stay in this little old house for-probably-ever. "What do you think?"

"Well, I'm still thinking about bats, raccoons, and a musty old attic."

"Great! Well, then, let's just head up there!"

Atticus struggled up the stairs behind us as we climbed to the second story.

"Hey, Cuss, coming with us?" Leave it to my dad to put a rancher spin on a literary allusion.

On the second floor, we all stopped at a door that opened to the steep, narrow stairway to the attic. "When's the last time you've been up there?"

"Once, maybe, a long time ago."

"Shuffling bats, ya say?"

"Like shuffling, scuffling, every once in a while banging, kind of."

The door creaked open, and a huge wave of a warm, musty smell overtook the four of us.

"Eww!" Oliver shouted. "Skinks like a skunk."

My dad took the first step up. "We're gonna need to find some windows and air out the place. How many years have you been here?"

"Seven years. Almost eight. Never needed to come up here since we stored everything in the basement. Remember, we weren't going to be here that long."

My dad shook his head as he walked up to the top of about fifteen steps with no handrail. I hated to remind him of anything to do with Jake. He usually said—if Oliver was out of hearing distance—"That son of a bitch did you a favor by leaving." And then his mumbling went to a dark place. He also told my mom that he didn't want what's his name—that was what he called Jake—coming into the house. That was why he changed all of the locks on the house after Jake moved out, including the garage. (Earth to Dad. Jake didn't want in the house; he wanted out.) But Roland McGuire, retired two years now, felt productive if he was doing things to protect us from bats, the Belmont Boogie Man who had killed the now-named Mystery Doe, and good ol' what's his name.

One more danger was on my dad's list. Earlier that year, about ten blocks from my house, an eleven-year-old boy and his housekeeper were found dead in their house in the affluent Dundee neighborhood. Dr. Bill Hunter, a professor at Creighton University and the father of the boy, found the two dead when he got home. Neighbors claimed to have seen a man who had parked his car a few blocks away walking toward and then away from the Hunter home. The murder was on my list too, and I had a lock-down routine each night that could only be called obsessive-compulsive.

My dad, Oliver, and I got to the top of the staircase, and we all turned back to see Atticus looking up at us from the second floor. "Hey, Cuss!" my dad yelled. "Don't want to come up?"

Atticus whimpered.

"He probably doesn't like the steep stairs," I said.

Atticus growled.

"He doesn't like something, that's for damn sure. Reminds me of a spooked horse we had back in Brush," Dad said as he reached up to pull a string hanging off of a single light bulb, the only light in the whole attic. "Don't see no bats here." When he was in serious work mode, my dad, one of the smartest men I knew, was sharp and eloquent. But when he was with family, he sometimes fell back into his ranching days as if in his childhood, allowing double negatives and calm cuss words—as he called them—into his speech, sauntering into a drawn-out Colorado drawl that I found endearing.

"Bats?" Oliver asked as he walked to a tall, very narrow window that looked out toward the front yard, probably four feet tall and a foot wide. A sticker tag remained on the corner of the uniquely shaped window, only reinforcing the fact that the window was a slice of something new in this old building.

"Not finding any holes big enough for coons or squirrels...or bats yet." My dad hit his head on the low ceiling. "Son of a bitch."

"Hey, what if we put a skylight in the roof, or maybe two, to bring in some more natural light?" I asked. "Do you think one or two skylights would be good?"

"Not my day to worry about it," my dad mumbled as he pressed against the roof. "Ah, we might have a little problem over here. A little bit of water is getting in through this back window." A wave of his aftershave, Old Spice, overcame me as I moved toward him.

"Fixable?"

"Oh, sure, fixable. But I think we better make a list of all the things we need to fix before you bring carpet and paint up here. Could be quite a few things on that list."

"I see it! What in the hell is this?" Oliver moved toward a dark corner.

"Thanks, Dad," I growled at my dad, who had passed on some colorful expressions to my four-year-old. My dad grinned.

"I found it!"

"Whatcha got there, cowboy?" my dad asked Oliver.

"I found the treasure, Choochoo!" Oliver grunted as he pulled a box from the crawl space. The side of the box sagged, and the words Lux Sunlight Flakes Laundry Soap were blurry but legible on the side of the box. To the left of the words was a washed-out picture of a brunette with dark lips who appeared very excited about the soap.

"You sure did, Ollie, by golly! I haven't seen a box like that in years." My dad helped Oliver move the box under the lightbulb. "My mom used to use this soap."

"Must have been left by the previous owner," I said as I opened the box. The musty smell and my dad's Old Spice were starting to make me feel a little sick. An *Omaha World-Herald* newspaper dated 1948 covered whatever was in the box.

"What's my treasure? Find my treasure..." Oliver said. I picked up the newspaper to reveal old clippings of articles, a few pictures, what looked like documents. "Just a bunch of stupid papers. I thought it was a treasure. You said it was a treasure..." Oliver rarely had temper tantrums, but one ugly fit was brewing as his face reddened. He started stomping his feet and screamed. "Choochoo, where is my treasure?"

"Who's he talking to?"

"Choochoo."

"What the hell's a Choochoo?"

Oliver kicked the wall and wailed as I grabbed him from behind to hold him tight against my body. I moved my head down and pressed my cheek against his. His warm tears smelled like apple juice. Oliver's wails turned to sobs, the sobs to quiet weeping. Atticus barked from the landing below.

"His little friend." I raised one eyebrow.

"He's not little!" Oliver yelled.

"Hey! You're upsetting Atticus when you yell."

"There's no treasure." Oliver sighed.

"But it was fun to find something hidden in that little cave area." I spoke into the crook of Oliver's neck. "Kind of like when we find treasures in your *I Spy* books."

"Yah."

"I got a treasure for you, Ollie, by golly." Dad pulled a coin from his pocket. "I have an old wooden nickel that I carry with me. My uncle Truett gave it to me. Truett gave me one every time he came back from taking the cattle to market. I have quite a few of them." My dad handed Oliver the coin.

"Wooden nickel?" Oliver sniffed as he looked at his treasure.

"I always keep it in my pocket and rub it for luck."

"Is it magical?" Oliver asked.

"Just special, Ollie, by golly."

I heard the telephone in my bedroom ring. I would have let it go, but I was feeling so overheated and nauseated from the smells of the enclosed attic that I thought if I went down to the second level, I might feel better. Dust and Old Spice swarmed in my head as I ran down the stairs and stepped over Atticus to get to the phone.

"Hello." I was breathing hard as I waited for a response.

"Annie?"

It never failed. Anytime I heard his voice, my heart bounced.

"It's Jake." He paused. Why the pause? What did he want me to say? *Hey, Jake. How's it going, Jake? How's the wife? How's the new house that you finished on the lot we bought?* "I wanted to touch base with you on a few things. You have a minute?"

"I do."

"Would it work for Oliver to come with us to the house in Michigan for a family reunion on October twenty-fifth?"

"I think so."

"Great. I'll get you more details when we get closer to the date." Jake hung up.

I stood with the phone in my hand still pressed against my ear. What would I do without Oliver for a week? Who was the strange man I had just spoken with on the other end of the line?

Dad and Oliver came down from the attic. "Who called?"

"A telemarketer."

"Annoying little sons of...Hey, what do you say we go get some grub at Smokin' Joe's."

"Pancakes!" Oliver and his boots moved down the stairs to the main level.

Bacon and potatoes replaced temper tantrums, musty attics, and people you used to be married to but no longer knew. We ate breakfast at Smokin' Joe's and ran from hardware store to hardware store looking for parts and pricing paint and carpet. Oliver was good as gold with his new special wooden nickel in his pocket.

Later that Saturday night, after Oliver was asleep and the house was locked up, I crawled into bed to watch a *Dateline* mystery. "Guilty pleasure" is a mild term for my addiction to "investigative journalism," or, as Jake used to call the shows I devoured, my murder-mission shows. We'd be out eating dinner with other couples, and Jake would throw out, "Annie and those murder-mission shows. I swear, she has a mission. One of these days, if you find me dead in the trunk of a car..." And then he would raise his eyebrows and lean his head toward me. I knew my role in the routine (maybe we were just a routine that wore out its act), and I leaned in toward him and threw out, "No, no, no. I just know how not to kill you. All of those people got caught."

Laughter and drinks clinking. We were so witty.

I fed my craving for *Dateline*, *48 Hours*, and *20/20* (I'd watch any of them) with the lilting and melodic voice of Keith Morrison luring me into the story in his lovely verbal seduction, and I couldn't wait to gorge myself with the twisted storylines of my mental meth. *All those years and they finally caught him; she looked so innocent at first* and BAM: I got my whodunit high.

A new episode.

"Death and the Homecoming Queen."

I was stoked.

"Police had a gun with a bloody fingerprint—and it belonged to the lover of a dead homecoming queen. But everything was not as it seemed."

I snuggled under my covers. Pleasure: guilty. Annie: pathetic. Atticus walked into my room and bumped the box from the attic off of the chair near the end of my bed. Startled, he moved back and then walked to the other side of the bed, sighed, and dropped down. I got up to move the box and decided to look through it as I watched my show. The aroma that billowed out from the box was the smell of another time. I moved the newspaper from the top and dug down to what looked like several photographs, black and white, with ridges all around the photos.

"They were high school sweethearts, but when she was slain, compassion turned to suspicion."

I looked at the young faces of a couple in a photograph from the box. The man and the woman were sitting on the steps of a front porch. The woman had on a casual dress that she pulled in toward her body as she grabbed her knees and tucked her feet under her dress. She was laughing—like right in the middle of an awesome laugh—looking at the camera. She was beautiful. The man was looking at the woman. His face was a blur, as if he were quickly turning to look at her, as though her laughter owned him. He was in love with her. The inscription on the back of the photograph: "Just back from the honeymoon. Lorna and Bill, 1943."

"Now, as a town chooses up sides in this tragic murder, a shocking revelation that no one could have predicted."

I looked at the other pictures to see the couple at different ages and stages in the production of their life. The man must have been the man who had owned this house before we moved in. We had never met him. We had worked only with our realtor and the man's daughter through the process of buying the house.

In almost every photo, the man never looked at the camera. Even in the one with the baby, he was looking down at the baby as the woman looked at the camera. She seemed so full of life. The back of the photo: "Bringing Baby Annette Home, May, 1960." The house behind them was my house.

Atticus sat up and growled.

I put the photos back in the box.

"What's up, Atticus? Bad dream?"

Low, guttural growls struggled from his throat, a gravely purr, as if he were trying not to wake Oliver. I picked up the stack of papers and pictures to put them back into the box.

"It's OK, big guy."

A letter fell out of the pile onto my bed.

"Give to Annette after I die."

The words were written in a beautiful cursive on the outside of the sealed envelope.

"Join us next week for another episode of *Dateline*, when the attractive teacher at a small town college goes missing, and the teacher's pet has blood on his hands. Don't miss it."

I had been so engrossed with the items in the box that I had missed the end of the show.

Give to Annette after I die.

The envelope was barely sealed, hanging on to gluey threads. Annette had never opened the envelope. Annette had never received the envelope. I put the envelope back in the box. I would need to find the number of my realtor to track down the man who had lived in the house before to get this box of treasures to him. Somehow the box had been overlooked in the move.

My sleep was restless that night. I tossed and turned, thinking about the pictures in the box and the ending of the mystery that I had missed. I fell into a deep sleep of bad dreams.

I'm standing at a door of an open garage. I look down to see that I'm wearing an outdated wedding dress and no shoes. It is dark outside and chilly. I know that it's the middle of the night.

I look in the garage and see rows of old folding chairs on the left and right filled with people. I want to see who the people are, but someone is fluffing the back of my dress. I look back to see a young girl in a dirty dress with messy hair who's fixing the train of my dress. I don't know who she is. She smiles and hands me a bouquet of flowers. She nods toward the inside of the garage, where a glowing light is focused on a priest.

I begin to walk down the aisle and look at the people in the rows. They are all either sleeping or dead. Everyone's eyes are closed. I look to the priest again, only this time he has on a white mask, and I realize that I'm not in a garage but in my attic. I can see the tall, narrow window with the price tag behind the priest. I look back to the bridesmaid and the people in the folding chairs, but no one is there. I'm alone in my attic in the middle of the night with a priest in a mask.

I look back at the priest and see that he's pointing toward the niche where Oliver found the box. A silhouette of a tall figure in a cowboy hat emerges from the niche. Mike Sheridan walks toward me. I hear a shuffling, shuffling noise as he approaches.

The priest speaks to Mike. "You may now kiss the bride."

I look at the priest and then back at the tuxedo man, no longer Mike Sheridan. Trent Kula, in a tuxedo and cowboy hat, looks at me.

"You're gonna like being kissed."

The words are clear in the dream, but Trent Kula's mouth doesn't move. He moves toward me to kiss me.

I move to kiss him, and his face turns to pure evil. I can't even begin to describe pure evil.

"Where is your bridesmaid?" the evil screams. "Who loses a bridesmaid? Who doesn't worry about missing a daughter? Where is Jennifer?"

I screamed.

I must have made some kind of noise in my sleep. When I woke from my bad dream, Atticus was sitting up by my bed whimpering. I scratched his ears. I moved covers around and put a pillow over my eyes, and the shuffling sound in the attic and the wind outside quietly serenaded me back to sleep.

7

"Cowboy Cussing"
Summer of 1938

Rollie

"S-s-s-s-on of a bitch!"

He'd say it real fast, with a sharp end to the *ch*. This was usually after he smashed his finger or forgot something important. I guess that wasn't too often. Sometimes Truett had this other real lazy way of saying it, kind of like "So-o-o-o-n bitch."

Now, when he was around ladies, he watched his mouth. Maybe a slip here or there. He respected women. And the women—oh, they did like Truett. He was a tall glass of water with electric-blue eyes that always twinkled. Women wanted to be near him, and men wanted to say they knew him well. I think that most men, myself included, would admit there was just something different about him. They wouldn't say it to him, but they all thought it.

Truett looked so good in 1938, he didn't know he was poor and sure didn't care if someone called those years the Great Depression.

I don't know why they called it great. Nothing great about it. Anyways, at the time, Truett and my mother's other brothers were working a ranch with some farmland about twenty miles southeast of Brush, Colorado. My dad, mom, and I lived with them the summer of '38 because there wasn't any work around. Dad was good with a team and could fix almost anything. I was six years old and wide-eyed about anything going on.

On most afternoons, you could see the clouds rolling in for an afternoon shower. The rain smelled incredible, and the patches of brush perked up and looked five shades of brighter green, like they were thanking the skies for a big glass of water. Swear to God.

I'd always thought that Brush, Colorado was named after the sagebrush, the very thankful and homely plants that were speckled across the "vastness" of the landscape. But no. Jeb, my uncle who was only five or six years older than I was, told me that Brush was actually named after some old cattle pioneer who never even lived in Brush. History books say Mr. Brush actually settled in Greeley, Colorado. Sounded stupid to me back then. Why name a town after a guy who didn't even hang around? Maybe he, like most people, moved down the road hoping to find less sagebrush and more life on the horizon.

Some of the first things I remember in my life, most from that summer, were the smell of old, well-cared-for leather, a good saddle soap rubbed in to make it last longer and stay soft; the creak of a saddle being placed on a horse's back; and one of my uncles taking a seat in that saddle. I can see it clearly. The horse, snorting and prancing, would check to see who would be in command on this ride, himself or one of the uncles.

One day, when my uncles Truett and Emmet, both in their twenties at the time, had nothing better to do—there wasn't a heck of a lot to do out on the ranch after work was done—they tied me dead-man style, stomach on the saddle, hands and feet tied under Old Charley's belly. They led Old Charley up to the house near the kitchen window. See, they knew their sister, my mom, was getting lunch ready for the crew. Truett whispered in the ear of my upside-down head, "If you cuss loud enough and bad enough, we'll turn you loose. But if you don't, we'll turn Old Charley loose in the south pasture." Now, everyone knew that there was no end to the south pasture. At least that's what I was told. You could ride for days and never get to the end. And when you did get to the end, you'd probably fall right off the edge of the earth.

I knew a few cuss words. Learned 'em from the best.

"Damn, damn, damn," I hollered.

"Can't hear ya," Emmet whispered.

"Son of a bitch, damn, damn, damn!" I shouted louder than I'd ever shouted. I didn't want to wander out to the south pasture, dead-man style.

The feet standing by the horse were no longer those of men with cowboy boots. They were the feet of my mom.

My mother knew her brothers, so she only pretended to be mad and scolded them as she swatted them away from me. They laughed all the way to the barn.

I was pretty happy the rest of that day. I knew that my uncles wouldn't tease you if they didn't like you. I also knew that when they gave you a hard time, it was really a test.

The test would be if you could handle it all without sulking.

Well, I guess I passed the test.

Truett and my other uncles were my heroes. I respected how they worked, and I admired how they played.

Kind of liked how they cussed.

8

October 9, 2008

Annie

I hit China Doll in the west parking lot on a chilly October Thursday morning.

I was turning into my parking place when, I swear, a little china doll ran right in front of my car, as if she wanted to be hit.

By the time the ambulance arrived in front of Belmont High School, the sun was slowly beginning to engulf the dark sky, casting long shadows on the parking lot as students hurried up the cement staircase in front of the school, rushing to make the first bell. I stood outside the ambulance as the paramedics spoke with the girl, whom I'd never seen before. In a school of over two thousand students, this girl was one I'd never come across, not even in the hallway.

"Annie?" Judy Haller, the principal of Belmont High School, whispered. "The police are here to question you." Judy squeezed my arm gently as she pointed toward the police car behind the ambulance.

I looked back into the ambulance to see China Girl basking in the attention of the three paramedics. The petite girl sat up straight, dark hair framing her round face with big blue eyes that glowed from her perfect complexion, soft and clear like new china. China Girl blinked; her face barely moved as she looked from paramedic to paramedic.

"Ms. Day?" a tall man with a mustache too big for his face called to me. "I'm Jeff Ahlers. You doing all right, Ms. Day?"

"Just a little shaken up, I guess. I just hit a student."

"Just a few questions, if you don't mind. Did you see Gwendolyn Sparks in the parking spot when you turned in?"

China Girl had a name. "No, no one was there, and then suddenly I heard a thump. I never even saw the girl. I was just parking my car. I feel so bad." I wanted to retract the last statement. I didn't feel bad about parking my car. I do that every day when I work. I felt bad that China Girl was hit.

"So you never saw her."

"No, I'm just being honest. I'm not a careless driver." I shuddered.

"Then what happened?"

"Well, I stopped and got out. I ran to the front of the car. That's when I saw her. She was lying there in front of my car. A bunch of kids gathered around. I had a student run to the office for help."

"Was she bleeding? Crying?"

"No. She was just lying on the ground."

"Was she alert?"

"Yes. I asked her if she was all right. She didn't really answer. I told her we were getting her help."

"At this point," the policeman mumbled, "I don't think Ms. Sparks is pressing charges. We haven't been able to get in touch with her parents."

Pressing charges? Clearly, I had missed the severity of my parking mishap. I was guilty of trying to park my car. I knew I had looked to the parking spot and then turned. Where had this little doll come from? Clearly, she wasn't shattered.

"We'll call you if we have any questions. Here's my card if you need anything." Officer Ahlers forced a smile as he handed me a card.

After I picked up my briefcase, I walked up to the ambulance and peeked into the back carriage. A paramedic spoke into his walkie-talkie. "I think we're going to need to run her back to the hospital to have a few tests done. Purely precautionary…"

China Doll—everything about her was delicate—looked up at me and made eye contact. The expression on her face made my stomach jump. Her big blue eyes, loaded with riddles and agendas, twinkled as her mouth forced a smug pout with a secret.

I got to room 213 about ten minutes before class. Nadine was waiting for me.

"You look like shit," Nadine whispered as she grabbed me.

"Wow, so glad you came by to check on me."

"Seriously, you OK? Judy told me what happened."

"I feel numb right now."

"Well, you better get to feeling yourself because you're up for evaluation."

"The whole school is up for evaluation."

"Not the National Accreditation. District evaluations. Several Sutton sightings this morning. We were talking in the English office, and we're all pretty sure you and Henderson are due. I'm not trying to upset you; I just wanted to give you a heads-up that Dr. Sutton will probably be visiting one of your classes sometime this morning."

"This morning?" I looked down at my pants. Why hadn't I dressed more like a professional English teacher rather than the dumped, pathetic, reckless-parking teacher who wore slacks to work?

"You'll dazzle him. Hey, stop by my room after school. I have something to show you."

I raced into my room praying that the Sutton sightings were just cases of mistaken identity. Standing by my desk was my daily challenge to remain a nice person that semester: Kinkaid O'Neill. Kinkaid was humming.

"Hey, Kinkaid. How're you doing today?"

"I have a very serious problem, Mrs. Day." Red blotches on Kinkaid's face looked as if someone had just slapped his chubby, white cheeks.

"Let's see what I can do to help you out." I looked to the back of the room. Nope, no Dr. Sutton.

"You may not be aware that some of us are taking other, more challenging classes than this one." Kinkaid just didn't get it. "The project you assigned for next week conflicts with my AP Calculus test and an Honors American Government paper. I also work this weekend." He stopped, I assumed, waiting for my shock and dismay at my lack of consideration in assigning my project.

"Sounds like you have a really busy week. I'm sorry, Kinkaid; I can't work around each student's schedule. You can see how that would be difficult to do. I suppose this experience will really prepare you for the challenges of college." I knew the last comment would hit hard since, as a college-bound student, he really had no retort. "Let me know if you need any help." I almost felt bad as Kinkaid walked to his desk. Still no sign of Sutton in my room. Maybe Nadine had just seen someone who looked like Sutton. I pulled out my grade book and set the handouts for the day on my desk.

"Surprise!" Dr. William Sutton stood in the doorway with a gentle, crooked smile. He wore the same gray suit every time he had observed me over the past seven years. His full head of gray hair and his calming blue eyes made Sutton a grandfatherly type. Once more, I wished I hadn't worn slacks.

"Well, hello. How are you today?" I tried to sound pleasantly surprised, which sounded more silly than pleasant.

"Hope you don't mind if I just sneak in the back for a bit?" He said this every time he visited.

"Be my guest." I watched Sutton take the empty seat of Peaches Trumble. Peaches was very adamant about people respecting her bubble. "This here's my bubble, my territory," she told Mike Sheridan with a twinkle in her eye. "Don't you be putting your hands in it. Eighteen inches all round. My bubble." Dr. Sutton was sitting in her bubble.

Maybe Peaches would be absent today.

Most of the seats were filling up quickly. Kids looked back at the man in our room and then at me and then darted to their seats. The students who had settled all looked toward the door. Peaches was standing in the doorway, glaring at Dr. Sutton. She looked at me. Two gigantic orange globes bobbed back and forth, dangling from her ears as she raised one eyebrow and then walked up front to a seat that was open behind Donovan. Donovan gave Peaches the whassup head nod. The bell rang.

"Everyone looks ready for class today."

By now, the students were all very much aware of the grown man in a suit, sitting in a student desk, looking quite out of place.

All the faces in the room looked at me blankly. Had I really hit a girl in the parking lot an hour and a half earlier?

"Yesterday." (Word hint—look at notes from yesterday.) "We talked about the different types of literature in the early days of America. Who would like to start explaining the literary genres I introduced to you yesterday?" The angel faces around me were all blank, very well behaved, and very blank. Come on, Kinkaid and K-Mart. Kinkaid was probably still unhappy with me about the unchanged deadline. Please, K-Mart. You even wrote in your American Dream essay that you wanted to be an English teacher one day.

Hand up: K-Mart scores one for the evaluation.

"Katrina?" I tried not to sound too anxious.

"You told us about Transcendentalism, Romanticism, Realism, and Naturalism."

(OK, sports fans, jump in.) It was only a matter of time before the rest of the Young American Scholars looked in their notebooks to find the answers to my questions. The next twenty-five minutes looked rehearsed and robotic as Dr. Sutton's pen was moving quickly across his evaluation form. My bad dream and China Girl were forgotten as I performed for Sutton.

(Pay no attention to the man behind the curtain.)

"Now let's apply what we know about genres to the Poe short story you read last night. One of my favorites by our buddy Edgar Allan

Poe." Heads around the room looked to Kinkaid and then to Katrina and then to me. "In what genre category would you place 'The Cask of Amontillado'?"

Dr. Sutton's pen stopped.

(Hello, is this mic on?)

"Romanticism." Katrina's voice was soft and timid.

"Very good." The crowd looked bored and uncomfortable. "OK, so Poe's stories are highly emotional and therefore romantic, but not in the way we think of the word 'romantic' today. Strange thing—Poe is considered the father of the short story, even though short stories had been told for centuries and centuries."

"That doesn't make any sense. The Bible was around before Poe. It had a heck of a lot of short stories...and long stories too," LaTrey grumbled. I even welcomed a grumble.

"Good point, but Poe changed the way stories were written. Up until Poe's time, people just told a story in the order of how things happened. Poe wanted to evoke an emotion from his readers; most times he wanted to scare them and put fear in their hearts. What emotion did you feel after reading the story last night?" I was giving them stalling time.

Unanswered questions usually bothered Kinkaid.

A hand, not attached to Katrina St. Martin, rose from the middle of the room. Thank you, Mike Sheridan. Mike Sheridan would lead; others would follow. Dr. Sutton's pen scrawled again.

"Mike, what did you feel at the end of reading 'The Cask of Amontillado'?"

"First of all, Mrs. Day, I've really enjoyed this unit. Poe seems, at least to me, to be a very important figure in American literature."

Mike hadn't read the story.

If Dr. Sutton had not been there, I would have had everyone pull out a sheet of paper and given a pop quiz, a big, fat reading assignment, and a dirty look. They hated dirty looks the most. Under the circumstances, I smiled. "And your emotion?"

"To be honest, Ms. Day." The pen in the back of the room stopped. Everyone looked at Mike. "I felt it wasn't really Poe's best work. I suppose that's because it was written in a very trying time in his life. His wife, mother, and neighbor were all dying of the bubonic plague, and he was struggling, as you know, with a huge drug problem himself." I took a deep breath. Mike had just slaughtered most of the facts from Monday's lecture on Poe's life. "I really cared more for the 'Tell-Tale Heart' and 'The Shadow Before Dawn.'"

Kinkaid cleared his throat.

Two things: first, Mike was clever, as he fell back on "The Tell-Tale Heart," the story that every ninth grader in the district read in a short story unit; and two, I have read every short story by Edgar Allan Poe, and no "The Shadow before Dawn" story exists. The look on Dr. Sutton's face made me realize that wearing pants today was the least of my worries.

"I felt," Mike continued with such sincerity in his big blue eyes that I almost laughed out loud, "that the main character, Alonzo, had no idea what he was in for as the sun rose. I felt sorrow. That's what I felt."

Another hand went up in the row by the door. Arty Elston had a huge grin on his face.

"Arty? Something to add?"

"I guess I felt that last night's story was...a little flat." Such the experts, second hour. "The shadow one was more poignant."

(Last week's vocab word, mispronounced and misused, I think.)

"But in the end, Alonzo's desire to finally grow and try out for a pro baseball team was what made me feel, well, sort of happy for him." From across the room, another hand went up. Of the three, James should have been in Honors English with Kinkaid. James Wu completed the trio.

"James, let's hear some more specific comments on this subject."

"Doom. For me, the overwhelming feeling was the doom." Kinkaid opened his American literature book and began thumbing through pages as he hummed. Donovan, who always seemed to be sleeping as he sat, had a smirk on his face. "Enough about Alonzo. What about Sir

Cunningham? Had Sir Cunningham seen his killer in the light of day, he would never have died such a confused and lonely death."

A confused death? What does that mean? And how exactly do you see a shadow before dawn if it's night?

"Amen," Arty said.

James continued. "Sir Cunningham didn't even know that Eleisha, who suffered from the plague, was his daughter from his secret love. I felt a lot of emotions after reading this amazing short story, but in the end: doom and darkness."

Darkness is not an emotion.

"Eleisha never deserved that," Mike added under his breath.

The short story was starting to sound like a novel, and I was beginning to feel doomed, definitely doomed.

Peaches raised her hand and spoke. "What page are we on? I'm so lost." The bell rang before I could answer.

I gave the class a subtle dirty look. "For tomorrow, be sure to read 'The Fall of the House of Usher.' The pages are on your syllabus."

"Have a great day, Ms. Day," Mike Sheridan said loudly but with a sincere and apologetic smile. "We'll be sure to read." I really wanted to be mad at Mike and my second-hour class, but I was actually grateful that they allowed me to forget about China Doll.

Dr. Sutton sauntered up to me as bodies flew past us like Powerball Ping-Pong balls randomly jutting around one another to get out of the door. "Thanks for letting me join your class today, Annie. This seems like a really nice group. Very motivated."

"Yes. Motivated."

"Wow, they reminded me that I've been out of the classroom much too long. I barely remember some of those stories. I'm heading back to the teachers' dining room to meet with another teacher. I'll just leave my evaluation in your mailbox and make a copy for your department head. Excellent job again." Dr. Sutton gave me a thumbs-up as he headed out the door. I turned around to see Kinkaid waiting for me to acknowledge him.

"Need something, Kinkaid?"

"I'm thinking I need some extra help on this unit. I felt really lost today. Can I come in tomorrow before school for help?"

"Sure. No problem." It was the kind thing to say.

Overwhelming.

That would be the only word to describe the rest of the day. I floated through the remaining classes, trying not to allow my mind to obsess about the accident and the unfortunate evaluation. During eighth hour, Hannah Bixby, my student aide and a former student, filed papers for me as I corrected quizzes.

"Here are a few things that were in your mailbox, Ms. Day. Sorry, I tried not to read them, but they weren't in envelopes." Hannah handed me a paper folded in half from the principal, her neat handwriting, "Please call Officer Ahlers. Judy." The officer's phone number beneath the name was the same as the card he had given me that morning. The other note was scribbled in an angry child's writing in green marker on an index card in all capital letters:

BE CAREFUL.

"I know. Weird, right?" Hannah said. "Don't shoot the messenger! Sorry about your accident, Ms. Day." Hannah smiled as she grabbed her backpack and headed toward the door.

Be careful?

Was someone referring to the China Girl incident? If so, why wouldn't they just talk to me? The China Doll incident seemed like my bad dream, hazy and disturbing. I put both notes in my pocket and started walking to the other end of the building to the journalism room. I needed Nadine.

Coach Edwards and his new assistant coach were walking out of Nadine's room just as I got to the door.

"Annie Day! Have you met the new coach here? Nick, this is Annie Day, a junior English teacher. Taught my nephew."

"Nice to meet you, Nick." I held out my hand to the young, tall man standing next to Coach Edwards.

"Nice to meet you, Annie." Nick's voice was deep and reserved. He had the body of a runner, and his face was exotic, as if God had splashed several nationalities into one face.

"Are you liking it here? We've had a lot going on since you've arrived."

"I do. Still learning the ropes."

"Oh, Annie!" Coach Edwards said suddenly. "Did I hear right? Salzman said he heard you had a little run-in in the parking lot this morning. No pun intended."

Belmont High School had one of the fastest-moving rumor mills in Omaha Public Schools.

"A little girl seemed to come out of nowhere. I'm still a little rattled."

"I'm just glad everyone's OK. We just stopped by to see if Nadine's photographers could stop by before the homecoming game for a few team pictures. I wanted Nick to meet her and the kids who do such a nice job on our paper."

After Coach Edwards and the new assistant left, I looked into Nadine's room, which was buzzing with her little journalism bees. Some bees working on the newspaper. Other bees doing layouts for the yearbook. Donovan Hedder was sitting alone at a table, bent over a big sheet of paper. The room was definitely buzzing.

Nadine was sitting at a table with a student. A strip of paper hung by a long string to the light fixture above the table. Every light in the room had a string and a different quote about procrastination, reminding the journalism classes about the looming deadlines and the temptation to stall.

Procrastination is the thief of time, collar him.

—CHARLES DICKENS

You may delay, but time will not.

—BENJAMIN FRANKLIN

Don't procrastinate.

—MRS. PICKERING

"Hey, Ms. Day!" Nadine got up and rushed toward me. "Come in!"

"You're busy, Nadine. I can connect with you tomorrow."

"Come on in." Nadine grabbed my hand and pulled me to an office connected to the back of the room. "Sit. I've got to show you something." She pulled out a drawer and filed through a pile of pictures. "Are you doing all right?"

"What, you mean after almost killing a student and then almost losing my job? You were right. I was up for my district evaluation this year. Dr. Sutton came to my favorite class on a day when they weren't my favorite class. No one had read, and I was wearing pants…"

"Stop. Did he call you a little firecracker again?"

"Uh, no. But he did give me the thumbs-up on the way out."

Nadine's eyes darted out at her room. "Cripes, my creepy janitor is here. I call him Sketch, obviously not when he's around. I swear he listens in on conversations and does very little cleaning. I found out the reason I get the bad janitors is because my students stay after school and sometimes we even have work nights, so Lyle gets the shift that Doc and the other janitors who've been here for years don't want. Lucky me. See!" Nadine moved her head toward the room.

Lyle was sweeping a corner of the classroom over and over again. His long, stringy hair moved back and forth as he moved back and forth, sweeping the dirt from one area and then back again.

"Maybe he has a crush on you."

"Ew. I think I just threw up in my mouth a little." Nadine pulled out a picture from a drawer. "Found it!" she screamed as she held up an old black-and-white photo. "OK, so I looked through a few yearbooks, but I couldn't find this picture. Then I remembered that we never used the photo because someone found a better shot with more students in it for the layout or something, but anyway..." Nadine came over by me and held out a photograph with three girls sitting on a table in what looked like her journalism room. She pointed to a girl in middle of the picture. "Becky Kershner." Becky was a pretty girl with long blond hair framing her face. The girl held out one hand with the peace sign, the other arm around another girl in the picture.

"Knock, knock, just here to empty your trash." Lyle paraded in and smiled at me. "Don't mind me, ladies."

"What year was this picture taken, Nadine?" I asked, trying to ignore the janitor and still not sure why Nadine was so excited about finding a picture of the girl she had dreamed of at the beginning of the year.

"In 1998. Or maybe the spring of the 1997."

"She's very pretty."

"And smart as a whip. Sharp. You know what I mean."

Lyle walked out of the room and saluted us.

"OK, so why are you showing me this?"

"There." Nadine pointed to the girl to the left of Becky. "Jennifer Caldwell."

"Seriously?"

"I racked my brain after the bones were identified as those of a former Belmont student. The name struck a chord, but I looked through yearbooks before she would have graduated, and the girl was not in one yearbook. Skipped picture day every year. Then I remembered that Becky's little girlfriends, Jenny and Tiffany, used to come and hang out when we had big deadlines."

"Wow."

"I know, right?"

"Do you remember anything about the Caldwell girl?"

"Not much. She wasn't in my class. She and the third girl in the picture just came by every once in a while since Becky was their friend.

Jenny Caldwell was pretty quiet. Not sure if she was into drugs, but she seemed spacey, or maybe uninterested in the whole school thing."

"She was in my dream last night."

"Who?" Nadine set the picture on her desk.

"Jennifer Caldwell. Never met her, but I knew it was her. She was my maid of honor or personal attendant or something. I was in this hideous wedding dress."

"A wedding dream. Tell me more."

"I was in a garage, and all of these people who seemed dead were in the rows on each side of the aisle. Jennifer was helping me with my dress. And then everything changed. I was alone in my attic, and a priest was going to marry me and this cowboy, who then turned evil. It was awful."

"Wedding dreams are supposed to represent new beginnings in your life, but this one seems more about fear."

"OK, so I wasn't going to tell you, but the cowboy was Mike Sheridan, and then he turned into Trent Kula, and then the devil or something worse. I was supposed to kiss him."

"Oh, you were going to leave out the best parts. I see how it is. Mike Sheridan is a student of yours, right?"

"Yep."

"Who is the coola guy?"

"The fundraiser guy."

"Just what is going on in that head of yours? At least your ex didn't make an appearance, unless you count the devil in the end."

I leaned in and lowered my voice. "You have Donovan Hedder in one of your classes? How's he doing?"

"Well, he's not in a class, but Elliot, one of my newspaper editors, sits next to him in some class and happened to see him doodling. Pretty darn good at drawing. We don't have a cartoonist yet this year, and we asked him if he'd show us some of his work. Seems nice. You have him in class?"

"I do. Pretty disconnected, and then he'll write something interesting or do really well on a quiz that everyone struggles with. Can't figure him out."

We both looked out in the room to see that most of the bees had left the hive. Only Lyle, the dubious janitor, and a girl sitting at a computer in the back of the room remained.

"Thanks for being here for me after a bad day, Nadine."

"Tomorrow has to be a better day."

"I have a note to call the officer at the scene this morning. Can you tell I'm putting the phone call off?" I pulled the sheets of paper out of my pocket.

"Just swallow the big frog."

"The big frog?"

"If you have a big bucket of frogs to swallow, swallow the big one first. Get it out of the way, so that the other frogs are no big deal."

"Who swallows frogs?"

"Just do it. Call! You do know your psyche's still pining for your cowboy ghost. Dreams don't lie."

I decided to call Officer Ahlers in my classroom that afternoon before I left to pick up Oliver. How many other frogs were left to swallow, sloshing around in my heavy bucket of a day? Those dang frogs just seemed to get bigger and bigger. After I packed up everything I needed to take home, I pulled out my cell phone and dialed the officer's number.

Several rings.

"Ahlers here."

"Hello, my name is Annie Day."

I heard what sounded like a door shutting in the background.

"Ms. Day, you still there?"

"Yes. Is the girl all right? How were her tests at the hospital?"

"She's just fine. But I have a few more questions for you."

Have we not covered the simple fact that I hit a girl? How many times do we have to rehash the story of the China Doll?

"After you went into the building this morning, a few students came up to me. They say that they saw the incident. I'm not allowed to say their names at this point, but one young gentleman said it appeared Miss Sparks was waiting for you, or waiting for any car to pull into the spot."

"What?"

"Do you know Gwendolyn Sparks, Ms. Day? A former student? In a study hall, perhaps?"

"Honestly, I've never even seen her before today."

"Here's the situation. We were able to get a hold of her father, and he wasn't that interested in pursuing the case. He just wanted to know if Gwendolyn was in any kind of trouble. While the mainstay is that the pedestrian is always right, that's only if the pedestrian is not at fault of some kind."

"I'm not sure I'm following."

"With the situation as it is, I have to ask if you are interested in—"

An incoming call interrupted Officer Ahler's words.

"Sorry. Someone was calling in at the same time."

"I need to ask you if you want to pursue this case."

"You mean if I wanted to press charges?"

"Yes, ma'am."

"Seriously? I can press charges?"

"Yes, ma'am."

"For what?"

"For damages to the car or driver injury."

Ah, there's the rub.

"Wow, this day just turned upside down."

"Between you and me, I felt the little lady was enjoying the attention way too much. I've been thinking about it all day."

"I don't want to press any charges. I'm just relieved that I didn't hurt her." I wanted to dance around my room. I had not shattered China Doll. I felt relief. Great relief, like dumping a big bucket of frogs out a window.

"Are you sure about that? I'm working on the report right now."

"Absolutely sure. Why would someone try to get hit? I just don't get this whole thing."

"Well, that's why I asked you if you knew Ms. Sparks. Sometimes people do things like this to get money or revenge. I'm scratching my head myself on this case."

"I really appreciate your expertise on this whole crazy incident. Do you need anything else from me?"

Like information about crazy notes in green markers?

"No, just be careful parking. It can be a risky thing, you know."

I had one more call before heading to Oliver's daycare. I pulled out the number I had written down a few days earlier from a phone book at home. I would call the real estate agent who had helped us at the closing when Jake and I bought the house several years earlier. I needed to get this box to the man who had sold the house to us. I dialed.

"CBS Homes."

"Uh, yes, this is Annie Day. I'm looking for Terry Lynn Folton."

"Hey, Annie. How's it going?"

(Since you helped us buy a house, it's been pretty busy.)

"It's going great. Still love the house. Strange situation. I just found a box of pretty personal items in my attic that I'm sure belonged to the previous owner. Do you know how I can contact him?"

"Wow. That was a while ago. I think I only worked with the daughter of the owner. I think she was moving him to a home. I can't remember her name. Can I get back to you on that?"

"No worries."

After I hung up, I looked at the note with green, childlike, Magic Marker letters: BE CAREFUL. Maybe the note had been from one of the students who witnessed the accident. I looked down at a missed call. I didn't recognize the number.

I went to voice mail and pushed for my message.

"Hey, Annie Day."

It took me a moment: Trent Kula.

"I missed you in the building today when I delivered the boxes with your cheerleader orders. I just gave them to Twyla. They're all in her room. I'd like to come by sometime this week so we can go over plans for next year. I'll just plan on stopping by your classroom next Friday around three o'clock. Looking forward to it!"

I had never given Mr. Kula my cell number.

He was a schmoozer.

Of course, he wouldn't want Twyla there; I was the business connection, for heaven's sake. She was the smarkler. Remember?

Besides, Trent Kula is so not your type. He represents all that you shake your head at: vanity, lack of depth, agendas minus the sincerity. Just because he's handsome doesn't mean anything. You can look at him (enjoy) and then walk away.

That night, after I put Oliver to bed and corrected thirty-seven tests—and no more, since I was exhausted—I sat by my bed and looked at the note card on my dresser: BE CAREFUL.

Bad day done.

Get over it.

I placed the stack of tests in a folder marked Period Two and noticed a ragged edge of a ripped notebook page sticking out of the uncorrected papers. A cheat sheet? I pulled out the page and found a doodle sheet—pictures and words, no answers to the test. Doodles of stick people and flowers floated around words scribbled on the sheet.

Vote for Obama.

Go green.

YOLO

Your mom goes to college.

Mrs. Day is a boring bitch.

Wow, just when I thought I was done with my bucket of frogs for the day: BAM. I've been called a lot of things; I just can't remember being called a boring bitch before. The sting. Not so much for the bitch reference. I get it. I work with teenagers. Some teenagers just have an Adult Angry Chip that will only dissipate in time, or when they become an adult. Every adult is a naughty word.

The other word burned: boring.

I looked through the pile of unfinished tests to find the test that matched the doodle handwriting. I had a hunch: a girl in Period Two who had missed a good number of days even though we had only been in session about one quarter. On days she was in class, Gina Shatner was not really present; she would either be putting her head down on her desk or—wait for it—doodling.

I found Gina's test. My pseudo-serious, *Dateline* handwriting analysis of the test and the doodle sample made me surmise that, yes, Gina had in fact written the mean memo.

Boring bitch.

Boring.

This tormented teen could not have known the huge raw nerve she hit in me.

Annie Day: boring.

Annie Day is to boring as Jaymie Shimmer is to interesting (a.k.a. not boring).

Analogies, no longer on the SAT, address a clear and necessary relationship between two words.

Annie is to brown as Jaymie is to bright magenta.

Annie is to sloth as Jaymie is to a surprise, adorable puppy on Christmas morning.

Annie is to green-bean casserole as Jaymie is to Brownie Batter Ice Cream.

Jake hated green-bean casserole. He loved Brownie Batter Ice Cream.

I had failed the test.

In 2004, the College Board decided that the juniors and seniors in high school didn't need to see relationships in vocabulary to prove college readiness. Who knew? The naïve high schoolers no longer needed to worry about clear and necessary relationships between words. Personally, I think it wouldn't hurt for those poor groundlings to learn a little something about relationships before they set out into the world. If they had asked me, I would have told SAT royalty to include a great, big, fat section on clear and necessary relationships of the human heart. Might save a few broken relationships that are not so clear and avoid the unnecessary messes made when the whole relationship blows up.

They never asked me.

As I put all of the essays into a folder and crumpled up the offensive evidence, I decided that I would not confront Gina Shatner about her damn doodle sheet. Her opinion of me didn't break my bones or hurt me. *Rise above the muck!* If Miss Shatner showed up to class more often, she might find me more interesting. I could dazzle her with my grammar wizardry and command of the English language. I could help her hone her writing skills.

But.

Maybe Gina had a point.

Clearly, Gina and Jake were not impressed with my simple nature and rhetorical skills.

Maybe a cowboy back in Bailey, Colorado, would have understood my dreams and passion for the written language. Antithesis to Trent Kula, my cowboy ghost had depth and a sincere agenda. I think. Though I would tell no one, my plan this week was to find the phone number of the Park County Records office and research the man who haunted my daydreams.

The shuffling, shuffling from above began as I pulled out my calendar for the next day. Late night was the only time I heard the shuffle noise. Nocturnal animals? Heater issues? Mice that kept late hours? Shuffling cowboy ghosts? I looked at the calendar for the next day off. Today's date, one of the longest days I'd had, jumped off the calendar and mocked me.

October 9.

The anniversary of an (un)wedding day ten years ago.

One last frog to swallow.

Just a slimy, little night cap.

9

Rollie

The months with my uncles on the Genoa Place—well, they were kind of like living in a magical kingdom, only with a hell of a lot more manure.

The summer of 1938: no TV—not even invented yet—but I was in heaven. I never read too much about those fairy-tale kinds of things, but I figured that the world with my uncles out in Brush that summer, far from Denver with no contact with the outside world, was like a land far, far away.

My mom, second oldest to Truett, was the surprise girl in the bunch of brothers: Truett, Emmet, Kenny, Arlan, and Jeb. Their parents, Boone and Sylvia McGuire, had died in a fire trying to save their horses from a burning barn in the middle of the night. That was when my mom was about fifteen, and all six of the McGuire kids then moved to the Genoa Place to live and work for their Uncle Billy, a bachelor cowboy who could use both the help and company running his ranch.

When my mom turned eighteen, she married my dad and moved to Denver. And then I came along. My parents and I would visit Uncle Billy and the boys on holidays, but I'd have to say that I got to know Truett and the other uncles the way I remember them mostly because of those three months that we lived with them.

I guess since I was so much younger than my mother's brothers, I was more like a tagalong. I looked up to those gigantic men as only a six-year-old could. I asked a lot of questions about everything the uncles did.

"Why do you call this old ranch the Genoa Place?" I was following Truett, my favorite uncle, as he fed the horses.

"Hell if I know." Then Truett stopped and reconsidered. "I heard somewhere along the line that 'genoa' was just a fancy way of saying 'general.' I believe that back in the 1860s, when the railroad was moving through this area, the head of the railroad asked General Sherman to protect the men building the railroad from the Indians in the area. There's even a mountain in the Rockies named after him. He actually slept in the room where you sleep."

I told my mom that she was sleeping in the very bed that some old general had slept in, and my mom said that Truett was mistaken The part about the mountain being named after Sherman was true, but he had never slept at the Genoa Place. She claimed that the original owners of the land were the Genoa Family, and, three owners later, the ranchers still give them the credit. The name just stuck.

The main house on the land where over four hundred head of cattle fed was not a mansion by any means. Nothing fancy, but big enough to house us all. The kitchen was the best part, and that summer, Uncle Billy—really my great-uncle—and my mom would get meals ready for all the family in between the work they all did. The noon meal, or dinner, was the main meal of the day. Most of the fellas would get up early and have a big bowl of oatmeal or rice, or a bowl of both. Sometimes supper, the evening meal, would be the same or some sandwiches. But the noon meal was the big meal, and Mom spent most of the morning preparing meat, potatoes, corn, bread and butter, and usually some incredible dessert. When I got bored from playing out by the barn and waiting for the men to come back for a meal, I would help Uncle Billy and Mom with preparing the meals. Those boys could eat. All this worry today about bacon and butter being bad for you. Hell, those men put away more meat and greasy potatoes than anyone I know, and most of them lived past ninety.

I suppose, if you were to look at the Genoa Place from today's point of view, you would just see the worn-down wood on the main house and barn. You would see two outhouses and be disgusted. We saw two outhouses then and thought we were living the dream. Not one, but two outhouses. To be so lucky.

Real cowboys and two outhouses.

From the perspective of a six-year-old boy who didn't come from much, I had died and gone to heaven in 1938.

10

Annie

The order of it all.

Tables lined the Belmont gym in a beautiful maze of order. Oh, the beauty of the order. In about thirty-three minutes, parents of our little groundlings were going to serpentine through the building, eventually forming lines by tables to meet with teachers to either grovel for affirmation of their little masterpieces or beg for bones of hope. *Throw me a bone. What am I going to do with this kid?*

Across the gym, Doc, Avery, and Lyle moved the last of the chairs in the back of the gym so that each teacher had a chair to sit in and two chairs across from that spot. Signs with names of teachers were hung behind the tables, some on packed-away bleachers and some on cement walls. Those names were in alphabetical order, of course, in accordance with that "order-of-it-all" mission.

I think it was the order that drew me into teaching in the first place. I love order. While some adults will remember their time in the school system as imprisoned years of pain and punishment, I remember the structure and the order that lined up all the classes perfectly in beautiful patterns. The order of the school year, the school day, the lesson plans. The order of the seats in a room, the grades in the grade book, the book numbers on the books checked in and out.

Not everyone embraces the order.

Twyla once told me about a student she counseled named Owen. Poor Owen was allergic to school—at least that was how she described his learning challenges. "When Owen walks into this building, he breaks into a sweat. His heart beats quickly. He wants to turn around and run out of the building. This is what he deals with every day he goes to school."

"Sounds like how I feel when I walk into my kitchen."

"Not funny."

"I'm not meaning to be insensitive. I get it. I hate cooking and everything to do with preparing a meal. When I walk into a kitchen, I feel uncomfortable on good days and stressed and anxious on bad days. Women who love to talk about recipes smother me with their words that go on and on: sauté this, easiest thing; just dice some onions; it's so simple, you can't mess this up. Really, then why do I always mess it up?"

I have a kitchen only because it came with the house.

But school. Oh, the order of school.

And just like the order in the school system and the tables in the end-of-first-quarter conferences in the gym, the order of the plans for my life and my dreams for my future were all neatly folded, color-coded, and organized, very organized.

I know now that I had imposed my dreams and the luster of the plans for a beautiful future on Jake. As we fell fast and hard for each other that fall of 1997, I opened up the little corner of my heart and held out those dreams and shared them with Jake. *We'll have it all: a wonderful marriage, five little angel babies. We can go to church every Sunday and make snowmen on snowy days. I don't even care how much money we have, as long as we have a dog and a white picket fence.* I told Jake that I really did like white fences, and not because they were in every description of the perfect American Dream.

I just like white picket fences.

When he loved me, Jake said those dreams were his dreams too, but, as we've already established, Jake is a big, fat liar. I think that much like Owen in a school building and Annie Day in the kitchen, Jake Day soon became uncomfortable in our marriage. So much so that he broke out in an emotional sweat, his heart beating fast, and then he ran out of the marriage right into an affair. Later, in a heated argument about child support, Jake slammed my dreams right back into my face as he screamed, "You and your damn dreams. I swear you're living in an imaginary world with one big, damn white picket fence all around."

"Annie, your table's right here!" Doc yelled across the orderly gym. He pointed to the sign behind the table that read Day. My stomach growled. As Oliver and I had left the house earlier that morning, we were in a bit of a hurry. Oliver had his dry Cheerios in a cup on the way to daycare, and I grabbed a granola bar, took one bite, and then threw it into my big, brown, ugly purse; Oliver called the bag my suitcase.

"Thanks, Doc. I love this corner of the gym."

"I knew that. I kind of lined things up for you." Doc winked and hobbled to the next table.

"Hey, Annie." Avery was moving a big table with Lyle. "Hear you've been causing problems in my parking lot." Avery smiled and showed every crooked tooth in his mouth. A few years earlier, Avery and I got connected when he helped me with a dead battery emergency on a cold, windy afternoon. He jump-started my car, whistling in the cold the whole time. I thanked him and told him that I didn't know what I would have done without his help. Ever since then, he stops when he sees me.

"Maybe I got a little out of control parking my car last week. Everybody's good now. How about you? They let you come in the building now? I thought we had better security than that."

Avery grinned. "Oh, yah, they let me leave my kingdom outside every now and then. Especially when Doc needs help moving tables." Lyle and Doc moved to the other side of the gym to move chairs by other tables.

"OK, so, Miss Annie." Avery spoke in a whisper as he moved toward me. "If I tell you a secret, you've got to promise not to tell anyone."

"Secret? Who keeps secrets around here?"

"If you tell, I'd have to kill you. That's just how it is."

"Sounds pretty serious."

"Found another bone."

"What?"

"Yah, another one."

"You mean on a field? I haven't heard anything in the news."

"That's because it's a secret." Avery's teeth sharpened the s on the word "secret," which sent a silvery shiver up my spine. The bridesmaid Jennifer Caldwell from my dream flashed in my mind.

"Wow. How did you find out about this secret bone, Avery?"

"Because I found it."

"What?" I really was intrigued.

"I found it last week. I was putting away mowing equipment in the storage shed in the far east end of the campus, hoping we wouldn't need to mow again, and I looked down and saw it on the ground near the door to the shed in a big pile of dirt. This one doesn't belong to that Caldwell girl." I thought it was interesting that Avery used the word "belong." Do we still own our bones, even after we're dead?

"How do you know that it's not another one of her bones?"

"Because I found a skull."

"Another skull?"

Another bridesmaid?

"I called Judy right then from the shed. The principal should know. She'd handle this like she did the others. The investigation team told her to touch nothing, just like last time. Only this time the main guy on the team wanted to meet with Judy and me in her office right away. The guy in charge told us that the investigators were choosing to keep this bone quiet. I'm not gonna lie. It shook me up a bit."

"I don't get it. Why don't they want the public to know?"

"Not exactly sure, but they sounded like they think someone's planting these bones."

"Ya think?" Sarcasm aside, someone clearly had an agenda with these remnants of humans.

"They think the 'planter' wants attention, so they're not giving it this time. That's my theory."

"Wow."

"You may not have noticed them, but I know of at least four cars on the grounds every day with people just watching. The team is watching for any other bone planters. Again, my theory."

"I'm not sure if I'm glad or not that you brought me into your world of secrets, Mr. Avery."

"Security's never been so solid. Plus, I got your back." Avery picked up a chair and moved toward the other end of the gym. "Remember, Miss Annie. A secret." He held one finger up to his crooked row of teeth.

I put one finger up to my mouth.

7:53 A.M.

I sat down in the chair in front of the big sign that said DAY. My stomach growled. If I drank water all morning, I could stop the growling and then grab something to eat at lunch. I had to stop thinking about food.

"Ms. Day." A man's voice interrupted my thoughts about eating.

I looked up to see a plump man and plump woman standing in front of my table. "Yes."

"We're Kinkaid O'Neill's mother and father. We're here for our conference." The man spoke as though he had made an appointment. The pudgy woman next to him nodded her head in agreement.

"Yes, please sit down, Mr. and Mrs. O'Neill." Even though conferences technically wouldn't begin for another seven minutes.

"We have some concerns." Concerns before they sat down?

I motioned toward the two chairs on the opposite side of my table.

"I'll go over our concerns, and then we can see how we can resolve these issues." Mr. O'Neill pulled out a piece of paper. Mrs. O'Neill handed him a pen. I sat up straight. "First, the grade Kinkaid has for your class is his lowest. Kinkaid is looking at some big and important schools, and we do not believe that the only non-honors, non-AP class he's taking should be his lowest score."

I looked down at Kinkaid's grade in my records. "Kinkaid has a ninety-five percent in my class."

"That's correct." A red splash covered Mr. O'Neill's cheeks. I swear I heard a humming noise coming from Mrs. O'Neill.

"A ninety-five percent is a very good score. In Period Two, Kinkaid has one of the highest scores."

"But your class is not an honors class. And he's closer to a B than he's ever been...in a non-honors class." Mr. O'Neill said "non-honors" as if he were smelling something from the back of the fridge that had gone bad.

"That's correct."

(Uncooked crescent dough would be the food that this couple before me would be—that is, if Mr. and Mrs. O'Neill were a food. Uncooked, sitting on the counter in a warm room, growing more and more doughy and inedible.)

I was no longer hungry.

"We can't comprehend how Kinkaid would be doing so poorly in a class that's not...well, with honors standards."

(The dough started to glisten in the heat of the room. *Uncookable*, cried the cook!)

"Well, let's take a look. Kinkaid has a hundred percent on every assignment except for an essay."

"Essay? Kinkaid is an excellent writer." Kinkaid's father was starting to give me gas. And I had nothing in my stomach.

"In an essay in which the prompt asked Kinkaid to write about the relevance of transcendentalism in today's society, citing examples for the seven components of transcendentalism they learned in class, he chose not to respond to the assigned prompt."

Mr. and Mrs. O'Neill blinked and said nothing.

"Kinkaid wrote an essay on the problems with communication breakdown in King Arthur's court."

More blinking.

"And that was not what the prompt directed." (And not even a real society.)

"Was it a good essay?" Mr. Kinkaid asked. Mrs. Kinkaid cleared her throat.

"Yes."

"So?"

"Kinkaid received a ninety percent on the essay since he did not respond to the prompt. A ninety percent is still a very good grade."

"Why did he receive such a low grade?"

"A ninety percent is not a low grade. Kinkaid was downgraded because he did not follow directions."

"But it was a good essay."

"I'm a little confused here, Mr. O'Neill. Kinkaid chose not to take Honors or AP English."

"Yes."

"And he has a good grade in my class. His lowest score reflects his choice to not follow directions. Most teachers in college would have placed a failing grade on an assignment that did not follow directions."

Silence from Mr. Doughboy. More humming from the missus.

Mrs. O'Neill stopped humming and finally spoke. "We've had a little problem with Kinkaid's obsession—"

Mr. O'Neill cleared his throat. "Not an obsession."

"Everything…" she said in a shrilly, little voice, "everything he does, he relates it to—"

"Not everything."

"King Arthur. Kinkaid has read everything about King Arthur. He has the new video game…He's obsessed with Camelot and King Arthur and all that knight stuff. It is an obsession." She did not look at her husband as she spoke the last words.

"Mr. and Mrs. O'Neill, Kinkaid is an excellent student. He's doing well in my class. If you think he might like to transfer to an honors class second semester, you can meet with his counselor before you leave today."

No response. (Just gooey dough.)

"I think that's one solution for you. You said you had several concerns?"

Mr. O'Neill cleared his throat and looked at Mrs. O'Neill. "No, I believe we covered it."

"Have a great day!"

I'm happy to say that the biggest frog to swallow in the Douglas County Conference Bucket of Frogs Contest was the first. Swallowed and checked off the list. I took a big gulp of water to ward off growling from my needy stomach and protection from future frogs.

8:25 A.M.

I looked up from the stack of Poe essays I was correcting to see an attractive woman dressed in hospital scrubs, with red lipstick and big blue eyes. A young mother. A smile on her lips. Concern in her eyes. (The flavor of a cherry candy red sour ball. Sweet and then tart. A Cherry Sour.) The striking woman stood in front of the table until I acknowledged her.

"Please have a seat."

"Oh, thank you. You must be Mrs. Day. I knew it when I walked into the gym." (This lady was a little cherry sour ball that makes you want to grab a second one before you finished the first, just to have the sweet and tart sensation again.)

"And you are?"

"Angela. I'm Angela Shatner."

"Gina?"

(Gina *who-thought-I-was-a-boring-bitch* Shatner?)

"Yes, Gina Shatner. I'm looking at her report card here, and...well, it isn't too good." Angela Shatner's hands shook as she held out the report card.

I shuffled through my sheets to find Gina and pulled out a paper with her grade and history of assignments. "Yes, it wasn't a great start. But she's been absent quite a bit, and I think that you can really get behind when you miss a lot of classes. Gina's average is a seventy-two percent, but that reflects many missing assignments more than low grades." (And quite possibly the boredom factor in room 213.)

"She'll be in class from now on. We just got over the hump." Angela Shatner's eyes started to water. "I promise she will be there from now on."

"Has Gina been sick?"

"Well, yes, well...Gina's pregnant." The cherry lips trembled. The blue eyes teared up, looking sour and tart.

I wasn't sure how to respond. I waited for Ms. Shatner to continue.

"We're...she's...Gina's going to have the baby, and then..." Ms. Shatner stopped.

I reached over and touched Angela's hand.

"It's all good," Angela said. "It could always be worse, I told my husband. He's better now...about it all." Angela took a deep breath. "So I'm here to see if Gina could get some extra help. After school or whenever you have time to get her back on track."

"I'd be happy to work with Gina."

"I'll tell Gina. She'll be thrilled."

(I'm not so sure about that.)

"I can talk to Gina next week in class. We'll figure something out."

"Thank you. You've been very nice. Sometimes...sometimes things just don't go the way you think they should go."

(You got that right, Sister Cherry.)

Angela stood up. "Not that I'm a control freak, in the least. I just didn't want her road to be so challenging so early. Thank you for being so nice."

"Hang in there."

"Thank you."

(I could really go for some candy right now.)

9:36 A.M.

A lull.

I talked nonstop from 7:53 to 9:36 a.m. to parents. I enjoyed a lull, realizing that it could pass as soon as it appeared. I looked over the stack of essays that I had picked up from my room before conferences and decided to make some progress in the stack.

Just a paragraph-writing assignment from each of the 180 students.

This essay would not count as one of the ten big essays that would be filed in a student's writing portfolio as evidence of work on writing skills. Students needed to write more than ten samples a year, so I would add a little paragraph assignment whenever I could. Through the years, I've read my share of pretty bad essays. I shivered at the thought of some college professor or office manager reading something one of my angels had written and scoffing, "Who taught this kid to write?" This was a valid fear, since I knew many people in my department, myself included, who would mutter similar cynical and sarcastic sentiments about the writing of the youth passed on to us. What a beautiful cycle of the written word. How in the hell will we ever teach these kids to think and put it on paper with more style than an immature caveman with a bad attitude? Still, I couldn't help but feel personally accountable for each student's abilities, which had actually culminated from the past twelve years of twelve different teachers who had thrown their arms up after looking over bad writing assignments.

So, I would move more quickly through the stack of mini-essays than the five-paragraph essays, which could take almost two weeks.

Prompt: In most of Edgar Allan Poe's short stories, a character is confronted with the challenge of fear and how to handle it. In a paragraph (5–10 sentences) describe a personal fear and how you handle it.

The paragraphs were interesting, entertaining, and at times comical. Edgar Allan Poe was obsessed with and fearful of death and being buried alive. Fears of students ranged from fear of spiders to fear of clowns. And then: flying and dentists and germs, oh my. A few people wrote of their fears of being alone and being judged. Snakes and, of course, death. One young lady wrote about her extreme fear of enclosed spaces and how she almost needed medical attention after her brother locked her in a closet for an hour.

Essay on top: LaTrey Williams.

Overcoming my Greatest Fear

The number-one thing that I'm afraid of would have to be a gun. I'm not that afraid because being shot does not bother me. I know lots of people who have been shot. I'm scared because I can get killed or be paralyzed. I can be put in a coma and never come out. I can also become a vegetable. That would be really bad. I overcome this fear of guns by dreaming about carrying my own gun. Instead of someone smoking me, I will smoke them first. I'm not scared to go to jail. If I die, I die. We all got to go sometime.

Wow.

One for the records.

I reread LaTrey's essay a few times. He did say he dreamed of carrying a gun. Just what was going on in LaTrey Williams's life? All the students come to a room and appear to be all teenagers, like one brand. But I knew that the groundlings who poured into and out of room 213 came from all different spots on the spectrum of home life. I would need to stop by LaTrey's counselor with this essay.

A man cleared his throat and my thoughts. I looked up to see a big man with red hair and a petite blonde smiling at me, grinning like two corgi pups excited for the owner to finally be home.

"You have to be Arty Elston's parents." The skull finder had parents.

"Every conference, hon. Am I right?" The two darted toward the table, and the man pulled out a chair for his wife.

"Uh-huh, sweetie. I think it's 'cause Arty looks so much like me," the woman said and then threw her head back and howled at the irony in her comment.

(Chips and salsa.)

The man put his hand out to shake mine. I could tell you exactly what Arty would look like in about twenty-five years. "We finally get to meet ya. Arty really, really enjoys your class."

"And believe me," the woman said, grabbing the pearls around her neck, "that's a big task. He's never been a fan of English."

"We think"—Arty's dad looked down at Arty's report card—"that the grade he has in your class just might be..."

"His highest grade," Little Salsa added.

They finished each other's sentences.

And didn't even notice.

Guilty-pleasure admission: I want to go to a parent-teacher conference when Oliver is in high school and have "a husband," and we call each other "hon" and finish each other's sentences.

"I really enjoy having Arty in my class as well. He adds so much to class discussion."

"Oh, I bet he does." Arty's dad patted the table several times. "I just bet he does."

"That being said"—Arty's mom touched her pearls again—"what else can he be doing to work in your class? Football will be ending soon, and he'll have more time."

(Really salty corn chips with a big bowl of salsa. You just want to eat them all up.)

"Well, let's see." I pulled out the grade sheet for Arty Elston. "A hundred percent for graded discussions."

"Big surprise!" Arty's dad put his arm around his wife. They both laughed and then looked back at me like two corgi puppies waiting for another treat.

"Eighty-five percent on tests, ninety-one percent on essays, and seventy-seven percent on weekly vocab quizzes."

"Uh-oh." Arty's dad looked at his wife. "Houston, we have a problem."

"I hear that." Arty's mom looked back at me. "We will have a little come-to-Jesus talk with the little angel about those little vocab quizzes. Are they the same day every week?"

"Yes, Friday morning, Period Two. Be there or be square." Corniness by association. (Chips and salsa were starting to rub off on me.)

"Well, we're all over that," Arty's mom stated. "We're all over that."

"Hon, is this the class that he has with Mikey?" Arty's dad asked.

"Yes, yes, yes." Arty's mom looked at me. "Arty and Mike have been best buddies since kindergarten. They claim they're both going to play football for the Huskers when they graduate. Mikey will play college football for sure. I just want to make sure Arty graduates from high school." The two laughed out loud and then stopped and looked at me.

"Arty and Mike are leaders in the classroom. They're positive and hardworking." (When they read the assignment.)

Arty's dad was serious for the first time since he had sat down. "Mikey's dad is pretty much MIA. He was out of the picture before Arty met Mikey. Mikey calls our couch his bed since he's spent more nights than we can count camping out at the Elston home. Mikey doing OK in your class?"

"He's doing fine."

"Great, great, great. The thing about Mikey is that he's a whistle-by-the-graveyard kind of kid. He will make the best of any situation, since his situation isn't the greatest. Uh, well, we don't want to take too much of your time, Ms. Day, but we sure are glad to finally meet you."

Arty's mom stood up. "We'll get on that kiddo to bring those vocabulary scores up."

"Sounds good. Nice to meet you both. Have a great day!"

Arty's dad shook my hand. "We sure are planning on it! Take care now."

As Chips and Salsa walked away, Nadine darted to the seat in front of me. Her spiked hair looked especially spikey, and her bright-purple dress with boots stood out from all the other staff members. "OK, so how's my little brat doing in your class?"

"He's lazy, annoying, and failing. Any questions?"

"Oh, my gosh, these conferences drag on and on. What's new on your side of the gym?" Nadine looked to the gym door. Any sign of a principal or counselor, and she would dart back to her table. I wanted so badly to tell Nadine about the skull secret that Avery had just shared with me, but I wasn't even sure if it was true. If I shared the secret, I was going to make it real.

"Same old, same old. The parents of the kids who are struggling are not showing up, for the most part. Not getting too much correcting done. No news here."

Nadine yawned.

"Am I keeping you up?"

Nadine laughed. "No, didn't sleep too well last night."

"Any dreams to report? My Psychiatrist Is In sign is on."

"Wow, I just remembered one dream right now. Usually, if I don't think about the dreams right away, they're gone. Poof. This dream was good and bad, I guess."

"Let's hear it!"

"OK, so, let me think about this one...I'm walking in an airport. I think it was an airport. I'm with Hank and the boys, only the boys are really little, like preschool age. And anyway, I realize I don't have my suitcase, and I get really worried. I just know that I need to find that suitcase, and so I tell Hank to wait for me as I try to find it. Heck, in real life, I'd make Hank find it...or just go buy new clothes, for heaven's sake. But I left him with the boys by that sign thing. You know, that board that flashes the times of flights coming in and departing? Anyway, I go off and see a door. I open it and go through it."

"Dream doors are always interesting."

"No sign or anything. It was like I knew where I was going. There are stairs beyond the door, so I go down into a huge basement. Like the airport has this big basement, only no one knows about it. And I look at this great big area that seems to go on and on, with a dark, low ceiling. Vacant. And then there she was."

"Who?"

"My mother."

Nadine's mother had died the year before, and during the months before her death, I watched Nadine deflate like an old balloon, slowly drooping to the floor, losing air moment by moment. Her mother was her lifeline, and I struggled to help her, the always strong and I'm-here-to-save-everyone-but-I-don't-ever-need-help Nadine, a deflated balloon. Once the funeral was over, she pounced back up and was back to her normal self: the highest balloon in the room.

"Your mother?"

"She looked beautiful. Amazing. She was the mother I remember from my high school years—young, vivacious, with no stupid cancer."

"Wow." I looked at the door. We were still administratively free.

"I mean, I was just so incredibly excited to see her that I started running toward her. But she shooed me away with her hands like she used to when I got in her way in the kitchen. 'Get, get, get!' That's what she would say and also what she said in my dream. 'Get, get, get!' I told her that I wanted to stay with her. 'Get, get, get back upstairs,' she said. 'Hank and the boys need you. Hurry up now.'"

"And did you go?"

"Well, of course. Everyone obeys Dorothy Wisniscki when she demands something."

"You went back up the stairs?"

"I did. Only I looked down and saw that I was carrying this red suitcase. It looked like the one I had as a kid."

"And?"

"And when I got back to the main area of the airport, I looked for Hank and the boys. And I saw Hank with the boys, only the boys were the age they are now. I told them to come with me to the secret basement. I showed them the door, only this time the door was locked. I just bawled like a baby…and that was the end of the dream. Probably on to another teaching dream where I was naked or drinking a beer in front of a classroom of students…Do you think…"

"Do I think what?"

"I mean, I've always kind of believed it, but now I really think…dead people can communicate through dreams. I mean, I feel like, today, as I'm sitting here talking to you, I'm telling you that I talked to my mom last night."

I had never considered the connection to the dead people you knew. This dream idea was a new one for me. Nadine and I collected dream concepts the way children collect interesting shells, sticks, and other strange treasures and keep them in a shoe box. Dreams are important. We both keep a pen and pad on our nightstands. We both agreed that people in your dreams whom you don't know are really the ghosts that are watching you while you sleep. We had both read somewhere about a legend that says when you can't sleep at night, it's because you're awake in someone else's dream. As I said, we were serious dream collectors.

"I guess I've never thought about it. I've never lost anyone close to—"

"Miss Nadine, you're not in your assigned seat, lady." Doc interrupted my thought.

"Busted!" Nadine threw her head back in laughter. "I better run back to my cage. Annie, want to head to the teachers' lunchroom at break?"

"Would love to, but I need to find my purse, with all the most important pieces of my life in it."

Nadine ran across the gym, like a purple balloon flying in the wind.

"Lost a purse?" Doc asked.

"I swear I set it down when I got here, but I can't find it. An ugly, big brown bag, almost a suitcase. Have you seen it?"

"I haven't, but sometimes the janitors lose judgment when they clean and just throw everything away. Some of the young ones just pick up random items in the hall and throw them out. I'd try the Dumpster down by the loading dock and then work your way back from there, just in case. I think they pick up trash early this afternoon for the week down there. After that, check the office."

NOON

I wanted so badly to head to the teachers' lunchroom for a sandwich. Heck, a stale piece of bread with a swab of peanut butter would be better than crescent dough or cherry tarts, for dang sure. Before food, peace of mind. I needed to find my big brown bag.

How many important items in my life were in that big brown bag? *Let me count the ways.* (1) My cell phone. (2) Oliver's prescription for his ear infection. (3) The half-eaten granola bar that I would love to devour. (4) Phone numbers of nursing homes. I needed to get that box back to the previous owner. (5) The keys to my car and my house. (6) An envelope with five hundred dollars in cash that I needed to drop off at my brother-in-law's office. He was going to start the drywall on the attic in a week. Oh, and (7) The phone number of the county records of Bailey, Colorado. They may just have the key to the mystery of my kissing cowboy ghost. One can always hope.

So, to the dungeon!

I walked down the steps to the bottom floor, the bowels of Belmont, where storage rooms stored forgotten items of Belmont's history and where, when school was in session, the ISS room housed the naughty children. ISS stood for In-School Suspension or, as students called it, Shithead Central. I covered the duty of another English teacher in ISS once or twice. Just a room full kids who had cut class, got caught smoking, fought in the halls, or done some other evil action that warranted sitting in a desk, facing the wall, all day long. Homework assignments and even lunch were delivered to the prisoners, who could not talk or leave except for the two bathroom breaks the group took together, in silence. Truly genius, if you ask me. I would swear to never be bad again after spending a day in Belmont High's Hell. The more severe punishment, out-of-school suspension, was actually a cakewalk compared to the boredom hell that bad students endured.

The long hallway with the ISS room and the storage rooms was dark and narrow, leading to the far-east side of the building: the loading dock.

Please, please be at the loading area waiting for me, I said to my big, brown bag. Please. How many days would I need to teach to cover the five hundred in cash in that stupid bag?

I felt the cool air hit me as I got closer to the end of the long hallway. A sound of laughter erupted and echoed down the hallway. The laughter was of many people, but I couldn't tell where they were. The laughter stopped. A door slammed.

I looked toward the noise of the slammed door.

The laughter erupted again. Like laughter at a dinner party. Male and female laughter sloshing together. Only missing the pinging of wine glasses. The laughter stopped.

I could see the open door to the loading dock, and I walked quickly toward the end of the long hallway. Maybe someone had picked up trash today. What if the bag had been tossed in a trash bin and already hauled away?

The laughter started.

The laughter stopped.

I knew that one of the doors down the hallway was a smoking lounge back in the day before buildings became smoke free. Nadine—Nadine in her smoking years—said that the smokers in the building, who would sneak down for a cigarette during a plan period or even between classes, had camaraderie much like the men who fought battles in the trenches, banished to the basement with their dirty little habit. Even the student smokers could sneak a quick cigarette in a stall in the bathroom or behind the gym, but the teachers were banished, at least until the grounds were smoke free. Nadine finally quit smoking.

The laughter started.

The laughter stopped.

Were teachers eating down here in the dungeon in the old smoking room? Was that the laughter? When I got to the end of the dock, I looked outside. This dock was where the bread trucks and milk trucks would deliver food for the cafeteria. People unloaded items at the dock. People loaded items at the dock. The basement janitor and probably Avery would throw out trash and send unwanted desks and equipment from the dock. Items came in; items went out.

Please don't throw out my bag.

I looked to the far left side of the open area and saw the dump bin, the kind that you see at the end of a driveway when someone's tearing up a basement or tearing down a deck. *A Big Dump. A Quik Dump. Itsgottogo Dumping* services. I stepped up on my toes and looked in the bin. A door opened behind me in the long corridor and then slammed shut.

I looked down the hallway. Nothing.

I looked back at the bin.

The bin was half full.

I laughed out loud.

Jake would make fun of me for my half-full mind-set. I see the positive even in the dump bin. It's not half empty. It's half full of trash. I checked out the bin. The trash in the bin was mostly from trash cans in classrooms: paper, busted folders, full and unneeded notebooks. Only one broken lamp stood out as unpaperlike trash. No big, ugly, brown bag.

The laughter now seemed farther away, so the group of people must be away from the dock area in one of the rooms. Could it be the evaluation team?

The laughter stopped.

I was not going to give up. I decided to head to the main office, which I should have done in the first place. Maybe someone had taken the bag to the front office. As I walked down the hall, I waited for the laughter again. Maybe I could identify the door behind which a midday dinner party was in full force.

No more laughter.

I was heading up the steps, out of the bowels of Belmont, when I heard a slammed door and footsteps running down the hall. Just one set of footsteps. I walked back down and looked down the corridor.

Nothing.

"At this time, we ask that all teachers return to their tables for conferences. Thank you."

I ran as fast as I could up the steps. The main office was just a short turn onto the hallway out of the building. I rushed to the office and pushed the door open.

"Hey, Annie!" the main secretary for the office greeted me. "What can we do for you?"

"Oh, so sorry to barge in like that. I lost an important bag. Has anyone dropped off the biggest, ugliest purse you've ever seen?"

The secretaries giggled like twittering birds. Lois looked around.

"Sorry, Annie. If someone does, we will personally deliver it to you in the gym."

"Thanks so much!"

I darted back to the gym. Parents were wandering around me like lost zombies. From the gym door, I could see a woman with long dark hair sitting at my table. I scoped the room for important-looking officials. I was good. I moved in a straight diagonal line to the table.

"I'm Annie Day. So sorry to keep you waiting."

"No worries." A beautiful woman put her hand out to shake mine. She looked way too young to have a son or daughter in high school. "My name is Sunny Wu. I'm here for James Wu. I'm his sister."

"Sunny, so nice to meet you." I looked through my second-hour folder to find the grade sheet for James. (Sunny Delite. Sweet and smooth.) I took a sip of the water from my water bottle. Must ward off hunger.

"My parents are actually very supportive, but they speak very little... well, no English, really. I just want to see how James is doing and if you need him to be doing anything differently in your class."

"James is a very smart young man."

"Well"—Sunny cleared her throat—"just don't tell him that. Sorry, I didn't mean to sound so sarcastic. James is very bright. He just doesn't want to be in all the upper-level classes. Says he would miss out on all the fun."

"I'm sure he wouldn't call my class 'fun.'"

"Oh, he really likes your class. He says he's learning a lot. I'm sure he is. My parents are worried that he might be a bit lazy. James doesn't have any clue on how doing well in school will serve him well in life...so sorry to go off on that tangent."

"No problem." I handed Sunny the breakdown of James's grade on the computer print-out sheet. "James is actually doing really well. He's on top of all the assignments. Tests are all top scores. Writing is excellent. I wouldn't call him lazy at all. Relaxed, maybe. Yes, James could probably be taking AP English and doing well there."

"Thank you, Ms. Day. That means a lot. If you have any concerns at all about James—any—could you let me know?" Sunny held out a card. In professional font and with a logo:

Sunny Wu
Legal Assistant
Delmar, Delmar and Smith Associates

James's sister worked at the legal firm with *The Jake and Jaymie Show*.

"I work as a legal assistant here. You can call me anytime."

"Thank you, Sunny. Have a nice day."

I was way too tired and hungry to allow the Catty Monster to take over. I watched Sunny Wu walk out of the gym.

Sunny Delite.

A refreshing drink (with maybe a little bit of pulp.)

2:33 P.M.

A little old black woman hobbled across the gym, making a beeline to me, albeit a slow beeline. I looked at my watch. Twenty-seven minutes to go. You can do this. The woman got to my table and looked me straight in the eyes.

"Hello, Miss Day. I'm Louisa Trumble. My granddaughter Peaches is in your English class."

"Please sit down."

"I just need to catch my breath a bit." Louisa set her purse on the table and sat down. "I started out at one o'clock on the bus from north Omaha. I walked from the corner of a hundred and twentieth. So this is where Peaches goes on the bus when she goes to school. What a big, beautiful school. My, she is so blessed."

(Cinnamon toast. That would be the flavor of this conference, the food symbol for this woman before me. Warm cinnamon toast on a chilly, Saturday morning.)

"You rode the bus from north Omaha?"

"Yes, ma'am."

"That must have been quite a ride."

"A very important ride. See, I would love to see Peaches graduate this year. She's repeating this junior English class."

"Peaches is doing very well in my class, Ms. Trumble. She has one of the highest grades. I'm surprised that she didn't pass last year."

"That's why I'm here. You see, Ms. Day, Peaches likes you."

(Add a warm cup of coffee to that toast. Oh, and the morning newspaper.)

"What you don't understand is that Peaches has never talked so much about school. It's Ms. Day says this, and Ms. Day says that. Thoreau this, and Poe that. That girl's talked more about your class this quarter than she's mentioned school through the years."

"Wow."

"And I've always known Peaches was smart. She just...well, didn't want to look too smart since the other kids in our neighborhood would peg her as a sellout. She would do poorly in school, on purpose, if you can imagine such a thing. But now, that girl is talking about college."

"As she should."

"If she goes to college, Ms. Day, Peaches would be the first in our family." Tears filled Louisa Trumble's eyes. "No dad in her life ever. Mom...well, let's just say, she's the indulgent type. Lots of problems. It's just been the two of us for almost five years now. Peaches and her old Nanna."

"You should be very proud of her, Ms. Trumble."

"Oh, I am. The girl lost her confidence in the first year or two here. I told her that she could do anything. Anything she put her mind to. See this here pin." I looked at the pin on the lapel of Louisa Trumble's red coat: a bumblebee, the size of a quarter. White and yellow jewels created the image.

"It's beautiful."

"Oh, it ain't real or nothing. The jewels are fake, but it still cost me more than I could afford the day I got my first paycheck working at Brandeis Department Store. A black lady working at the perfume counter of Brandeis in 1972—something my mother would never have been able to do, so I bought the pin. Know why?"

"Why?"

"Cuz my daddy told me I couldn't do it. 'You'll never amount to anything, girl. Women can't work in this world.'" The old woman before me took the pin off and held it out to me. "Did you know that bumblebees wings are not designed to fly? Scientific fact. Look it up on your World Wide Web." (No one says World Wide Web anymore. Could you be more cinnamony?)

"But…"

"I know. They sure do fly. Don't you tell them they can't fly. Don't tell me I can't work a proper job like any other person can. Just because I'm black or because I'm a woman. I told this to Peaches. When people tell you you can't do something, don't listen. Remember the bee."

"Remember the bee," I repeated. I handed the pin back to Ms. Trumble. "So I want in on this. How can I help? A letter of recommendation?"

"Do you know something about a test? A neighbor of mine said you can't go to college without it."

"Sure. The ACT test is the test Peaches should take."

"Do you think you could guide her or tell her what she needs to do?"

"I'll talk to Peaches on Monday. I can see what she knows and what she needs to do."

"I sure do appreciate that. I just don't know all the rules to the game, you see. I want to set her up..." Tears filled Ms. Trumble's eyes. "Ms. Day, I'm sick. Real sick. Peaches knows, so this ain't no big deal. I haven't been doing so well, you know, health-wise. I just want to get her set up..."

"Say no more. We will get her set up, Ms. Trumble. I promise."

As I watched Ms. Trumble hobble out of the gym, starting her journey to a bus stop to take a bus across town, I noticed half of the tables in the gym were empty of parents and teachers. Quitting time. The last folder I put in my briefcase was the second-hour folder. Two worrisome no-shows: LaTrey (my gun dreamer) and Donovan (my stoner stuck in the nineties.) I had really hoped to meet some authority figure in their lives—grandmother, parent, sister, advocate. Who was standing behind them as they thrashed through their years in high school? I wondered about my China Girl. Did her parents show up today?

"Did you ever get anything to eat?" Nadine yelled from across the gym.

"Nope. Still need to find my damn purse."

"Good luck, girl. Have an awesome weekend!"

My stomach growled as I unlocked my classroom and turned on the light. From the doorway, I saw my big ugly brown purse peeking out from under my desk.

Seriously?

I moved toward my desk to grab my suitcase. I had spent all day worrying and looking for a bag that held important pieces of my life only to find out that I left the damn thing in my room earlier that morning. The strange first quarter of the school year had been stacked with quiet bones, curious unaccidents, evaluations right and left, and mysterious sounds in my attic. So much so that I was forgetting more and more details. The relief in finding the big ugly purse was diluted by my self-disgust.

Get it together, Annie Day.

"Good afternoon, Annie Day." Trent Kula stood in the doorway in jeans and a Creighton Blue Jays pullover, holding a bottled water, looking unbelievable.

I looked at his left hand.

No ring.

"Am I too late?" he asked with a tilt to his head.

I had forgotten that Trent Kula was coming by today. I felt a flush of wooziness that I wish I could blame on the gorgeous man in front of me. I placed one hand on the nearest anchor and leaned against a student desk in the first row. "Not at all. Just getting organized for the weekend." My head was spinning.

"I'm heading to western and central Nebraska for the next few 'fun raisers.' No rest for the wicked, right? I just wanted to touch base about next year and see if we're onboard for another awesome year of raising money for Belmont cheerleaders."

"I'm sure that Twyla will sign on again. Just send us information in the spring…" Trent started to look blurry.

"Thought we might meet with the girls next year before school starts."

"Sounds…"

The room went dark, and I felt my body falling as if it were someone else's body.

I looked up at a beautiful angel.

"Wow, Annie, you don't mess around. You dropped so quick, I thought you were going to smash your face. Crumbled like a house of cards. I don't think I've moved that fast since high school."

"What happened?"

"You fainted, Annie. I guess I didn't know I had that effect on you." Trent smirked, and the smell of cologne and soap took over my senses. "I caught you just in time."

"I fainted?" I sat up.

"Here, drink some of this." He handed me his water bottle. "Maybe we can find you some food or something."

"I have a granola bar in my purse." I stood up. "Whoa." I grabbed the desk again.

"I'll grab your purse."

"I've never fainted before. I'm not sure what that was all about."

"Here." Trent handed me my bag. He was close to me, really close. "Take your time now."

"I'm good. A little embarrassed…OK, so where were we?" I pulled my purse over my arm and picked up my briefcase. "You think starting our fundraiser at the very beginning of the year next year works for you?"

"Actually, I'm not sure if I can wait for the next fundraiser," Trent said, with no humor in his tone. He put his two hands on my arms, I thought to steady me, and then pulled me into his arms. "I need to see you before then." Trent then leaned in and kissed me. His lips were warm and intense on mine, and he pulled me in closer as he embraced me with his hands around my back. He stopped and stepped back. I thought I smelled strawberry. I wanted to laugh.

"I'm so sorry. That was very unprofessional of me. I don't want to look like I took advantage of woman who just fainted."

I grabbed the desk. A man just kissed me in my classroom. (A really, really attractive man.) And all I wanted to do was laugh out loud.

Comical, really. A Harlequin romance, my least favorite type of literature, was playing out in room 213. *He pulled her close to his chest and kissed her against the chalkboard, chalk dust floating in the air and covering the two schoolhouse lovers. Lord, help her if the head schoolmarm caught her in the arms of a local bandit.*

"I apologize. I just couldn't stop myself. I hope you forgive me and agree to go for drinks sometime. I have your number. Just shake your head yes or no, and I'll leave."

Yes was the answer. Trent Kula left the room.

The bandit rode off into the sunset. Chalk dust floated everywhere and landed on the schoolmarm's silky hair.

Room 213 had only whiteboards, no chalkboards. Back from the Wild West to reality.

I finished my granola bar and sat feeling fuzzy for about ten minutes. Shaky from the fall and the kiss, I shook the Harlequin chalk from my imagination, grabbed my big, ugly, brown, and now-annoying bag, and left the building. Walking to my car, I started a list: I would pick Oliver up, and he'd be my little helper as we paid the drywall man and picked up a tarp at Menards. Maybe sandwiches for dinner. I tried to focus on being a mother, a teacher who had just finished conferences, and a manager of the attic project, but I knew that a new title was at hand: a freshly kissed woman. Somebody wanted to kiss me, the formerly unlovable Annie Day. I guess someone in the world—someone really attractive—didn't compare me to a green-bean casserole.

I saw Donovan Hedder walking toward the far end of the parking lot. What was Donovan doing at school on a day off? Before I could speculate on Donovan, something caught my attention. From about twenty feet from my car, I saw it: a small piece of paper under my windshield wiper. I rushed to my car, dropped my bag and briefcase, and pulled the index card from the windshield. In green Magic Marker, all capital letters:

NOT YOUR BUSINESS.

11

Saturday, October 25, 2008

Annie

"I kissed my dog, and I liked it. I hope my toy land don't buy it."

Oliver slaughtered (thankfully) the newest Katie Perry song, which had been playing nonstop during the month of October in 2008. If I changed the radio station, the song would be playing on the next station, so Oliver caught the Katy Perry bug and couldn't seem to shake the song from his head.

Oliver tilted his head, marching around his room. "It felt so wrong, it felt so tight. Don't mean I'm at home tonight."

I put the last pair of socks in his suitcase as Oliver pounded out the no-longer-suggestive lyrics with such fervor that I felt a moment of happiness. I had been brooding all morning about the fact that I would have four days without my little angel. His song about a kiss had me remembering the days when kisses were not so complicated.

I kissed a ghost, and I liked it.

Was I seriously losing it? Had I really been kissed by a ghost? Had I really been kissed by a Kissermania salesman? Maybe my imagination had complicated everything and I had never ever been kissed at all. Maybe, at the end of the day, I was really just *unkissable*.

"And, Mom, I told Atticus and Choochoo to protect you when I'm at Grandma Day's cabin."

"Thanks, buddy."

The "cabin" Oliver was talking about was a $2 million estate on Silver Lake in Genesee County, Michigan. In my years of marriage to Jake, we had spent many vacations with the Day family on Silver Lake. I felt a shudder of jealousy, which dissipated into disgust at the lavish vacations where Jake's parents showed off with gifts and incredible food to their children to assure a loyalty to the Day legacy. Strings attached: everywhere.

"Now remember, I packed you some fruit snacks in this little blue zipper of your backpack here so you can have a little treat on the airplane." Oliver's smile was big as he screamed, "My first plane ride!" His first plane ride without me.

"In the big part of your backpack, you've got your crayons and coloring books. Your *Goodnight Moon* book is here. See?" My voice cracked. Do not cry until he leaves. Repeat. Do not cry.

Oliver threw his arms around my neck. "I'm gonna miss you, Mom. I will pray for you every night."

I took a deep breath. "You're going to have so much fun. Atticus and I'll pray for you too, Oliver."

Atticus barked at the doorbell ringing downstairs. I looked down at my outdated (green-bean casserole) sweat pants and Belmont football sweatshirt. I had a black baseball cap over a ponytail. *It's not a dinner party, ya'll.*

"Daddy!" Oliver yelled as he headed for the stairs. He stopped, ran to the door, cupped his hands over his mouth, and yelled up the attic, "Good-bye, Pappa Rollie. Bye, Uncle Allen!"

"Good-bye, Ollie, by golly," my dad yelled down from the attic. But he would not come down for the exchange with Jake. My brother-in-law Allen and my dad had spent that Saturday morning putting up new drywall on the walls of the attic. I grabbed Oliver's suitcase and followed him down the stairs.

Oliver opened the front door before I could take a big breath.

"Daddy!"

"Oliver! Are you ready for the big trip?" Jake's energy poured through the door like a strong wind. I looked out at Jake's silver BMW with his lovely wife *shimmering* in the front seat.

As soon as the ink had dried on the final divorce papers, Jake and Jaymie (now Shimmer-Day) were married by the justice of the peace. I always wondered how that commitment had gone over with the Chicago Day family. The newly married couple ignored any reaction to the rush and any collateral damage: one broken marriage/family and one broken-off engagement. Jaymie had been engaged to her high school sweetheart when she had landed the job in Omaha. Jeff or Fred had looked for jobs in Omaha once Jaymie got the job at Jake's firm. The fiancé started his new job a week before Jaymie broke off the seven-year relationship and canceled the wedding that was to have been four months from the breakup.

One question: how do you ever feel safe in a relationship that you formed after leaving two other commitments—kind of like sleeping with one eye open to be sure that your new love isn't sleeping with someone else? 'Cause if you cheated with each other on someone else, isn't there a cheating possibility in the new relationship?

Just saying.

"Mommy, Jaymie's going too. Did you see her?"

We all looked to the passenger side of the BMW.

"I did, Oliver." The glare from the bright fall day made me squint as I tried to avoid eye contact.

Jaymie's hand managed a weak wave.

I handed Oliver's suitcase and a smaller bag to Jake. "Oliver needs to take the medicine in this bag twice a day. He's had a cold the last week. Directions are on the bottle."

"Got it." Jake took the bag and suitcase in one hand and took Oliver's hand with the other.

"Wait," Oliver said. "One more kiss, Mom."

Do not cry. Repeat. Do not cry.

"Love you, Oliver."

"I love you too." Oliver ran to the car.

Jake started to follow Oliver and then stopped. Jake waited for more. No kiss here. I had no more.

"Bye."

"Bye."

Awkward.

I shut the door as tears poured down my cheeks. I walked to the phone in the kitchen and took a deep breath. Atticus walked in behind me and whined.

"He'll be back, Atticus. We can do this…"

Next to the phone was a chair with Oliver's bumblebee costume for Halloween. He had tried it on every day for the past week, just to make sure it still fit. I picked up the phone and pulled out a list of numbers from my daily planner. The first number was for Bill Thornton at the Midland Nursing Home in Omaha. This would be the fifth nursing home I had called in the past week. I hadn't heard yet from the realtor, so I just started calling local nursing homes.

I dialed.

"Midland Nursing Home; may I help you?" A chirpy voice sounded pretty excited about her nursing home.

"Uh, yes, my name is Annie Day, and I'm looking for William Thornton. I think he moved about four or five years ago. I'm not family, but I have—"

"Could you spell the last name?"

"T-H-O-R-N-T-O-N."

"We don't have anyone here at this time with that name. Sorry."

Same answer from the previous calls.

I hung up.

There was an urgency to get the box to its owner; I also wanted the task taken off my list. As a list person, I take great pride in crossing off an item when it is bought or completed. The next number on my list to call was the Park County Clerk and Records Office.

I dialed.

OK, Cowboy Ghost. Who are you?

Three rings. My heart was pumping in my chest.

"Park County office; how can I help you?" A scratchy woman's voice wanted to help me. I froze for a moment.

"Hello?"

"Yes, hello. I'm Annie Day from Nebraska, and I'm trying to find a person...I don't actually have his name, but I'm trying to find him..."

"I'm not sure if I can help you if you don't have a name." I'm pretty sure the woman was masking some sarcasm.

Duh.

"Let me rephrase that. So my family was in Bailey, Colorado, this past summer at the Bailey Family Camp, and we stayed in a cabin..." I was sounding more insane and pathetic by the moment.

"Did you try the Bailey Camp? They might be able to help you."

"Well, no, because the person is...dead."

"So you want to find a death certificate? I still can't help you without a name."

"I know this all has to be sounding a little strange..."

No response.

"The cabin I stayed in was haunted, and I believe the ghost that haunts the place is buried in the hill—"

"I'm sorry. Without a name, I cannot help you." The woman had no interest in my story.

"Yes, that makes sense."

I waited for a suggestion.

I guess the voice from Park County had no suggestions for a lunatic from Nebraska.

"Well, thank you...have a nice day."

"You do the same," said the Park County voice.

"We're almost done with drywall," my dad said as he walked into the kitchen. "At least our part. The mudder said he could come next time you have a day off. Just give him some notice."

"Thanks, Dad. I've got lasagna in the oven for you and Allen when you're ready for a lunch break."

"We're on a roll, Annie, but we could use a few more nails. Could you make a run to Home Depot?"

"Just write down the specific type on this index card." List people keep a surplus of index cards. "A nail is a nail to me."

As my dad wrote on the card, I pulled out two plates. "I'll put the plates here, and the garlic bread is cooling, and the forks—"

"Hey now. I know how to get around a kitchen. Not my first rodeo. We'll help ourselves when we're ready."

I pulled out an old jacket from my closet and put it on. "I'll be back soon."

"You gonna wear that?" Dad smiled as he looked at my out-of-style lavender jacket. I think I was pregnant with Oliver the last time I had worn it. Had I actually bought the ugly coat?

"Not a fashion show at the hardware store, last time I checked."

My dad grinned as I headed out the back door to my driveway.

As I pulled out the driveway, my cell phone rang. "Hey!"

"Hey, Annie!" Teri Eckenhoff, my best friend going back to seventh grade, was checking in. "Just making sure you don't back out on us tonight."

In the past few years, I had become notorious for "backing out" at the last minute, which was really just my coping device for adjusting to being "the divorced" friend, my new identity. All of my friends were in good marriages with supportive husbands. I had become "that friend." Now for the beginning of the bad firsts: the first to divorce, first marital failure of the group. (Wow, so soon?) Up until that point, as a kid and a teenager, you look forward to the good firsts. And then, suddenly, you're living the dream, and those good firsts come flying at you like candy from a parade float: the first kiss, the first prom, the first baby, the first house. Catch 'em all! Now that I had crossed over to the land of bad firsts (the first end of a marriage), I felt like hiding out with Keith Morrison on weekend nights and with my dad and brother-in-law in the attic.

"Of course I'll be there." I had seriously considered backing out until Teri's call.

"Awesome! How about Dundee Dell at seven, and then we're all heading down to the Old Market for drinks. Got your sitter lined up?" Terri knew all my go-to outs in the past.

"Yep." I knew I'd cry again if I told her that Oliver was going on his first plane ride without me.

"See you tonight, Annie."

"Thanks, Teri."

I pulled into the Home Depot parking lot with a new attitude. The beautiful fall day with the true, blue skies gave an intimation of winter around the corner with a cold, crisp wind. I had a healthy son, I was healthy, and I was able to renovate my attic. Do not focus on the dropped balls.

Deep breath. No more tears. Transcend the muck.

The muck.

The muck.

The muck.

I walked into the enormous hardware warehouse with a skip in my step.

"You look like you're having an exceptionally good day," an older man with large eyeglasses straight from the eighties and an orange hardware apron said, welcoming me to Home Depot. "Can I help you find anything?"

"Nails would be great."

If you said things like "Nails would be great," then you would start to feel better.

"You'll find every kind of nail in aisle seven."

"Thanks so much!"

(Exclamation point.)

I was feeling better already.

Aisle seven proved to be the epitome (power word) of a nail heaven. I looked for any direction to drywall nails as I put my hand in my jacket's pocket for my index card and pulled out two cards. The top card had folded edges and a list on it in red ink. My writing, not the card my dad had just given me. The card directed:

Bread
Toilet Paper
Parmesan Cheese
Birthday card for Jake
Coffee

Birthday card for Jake

Do not have a meltdown in Home Depot.

I was sobbing by the time the man with eighties glasses found me standing by a shelf of discounted screws.

"Ma'am? Do you need more help?"

I caught my breath before I could look at him. Do I need help? My four-year-old—who has never been on a plane—just left me for four days. I just made a phone call to contact a dead cowboy. Oh, and I almost ran over a student whom I'd never seen before or after, so I'm not even sure she really exists. I'm standing in an aisle at Home Depot, sobbing, with a list from a time when my ex-husband loved me. Something shuffles around my attic every night around ten. I look like a homeless lady with an ugly lavender coat and a baseball cap on, and I can't find any stupid drywall nails.

Yes, I guess you could say that I need help!

I handed the man the index card that my dad had just written on a half hour earlier. I sniffed and took a deep breath.

"Looks like you need one-and-three-eights-inch Blue Ring Drywall nails. You're in luck. We have a whole shelf of 'em over here."

I followed my new Home Depot friend.

"Says here you need two boxes. Here ya go!"

"Thank you."

"You're gonna be all right, ma'am." It was a statement, not a question.

"Sure about that?"

"Yep. Some days, when I'm not having a good day, I just want to find an aisle and have a good cry myself."

I laughed out loud.

"Oh, and here's your little index card. You might need it again. I promise, the day will get better if you just remember one good thing."

The man was heading down the aisle, probably avoiding another meltdown, and I looked down at the grocery list still in my other hand.

One good thing.

Somewhere in another life I was buying a birthday card for Jake Day. Jake's birthday was the fifteenth of October. Today was October 25. This was the first year I had passed the day without thinking about it at all.

That was good.

One good thing.

Baby steps.

That night, when I got home from dinner with my girlfriends, I caught the tail end of *Dateline*. I fell asleep watching Keith Morrison in his jeans and black leather jacket, sharing an enticing preview for the *Dateline* mystery for next week, just a shiny little bait to lure viewers back to their *Dateline* fix. Hours later, the television was still on when I woke to Atticus barking downstairs. I looked at my clock: 1:15 a.m. Atticus barked again and then settled down, but I was wide awake.

Shuffle, shuffle.

The sounds from the attic took over for Atticus. Was it the heater? Now that the renovation had secured the idea that no wild animals were camping in my attic, I was more puzzled than ever by the noises from above.

Shuffle, shuffle. Bam.

I sat up and grabbed my cell phone. I laughed as I thought that maybe I could use it as a weapon to fight off the shufflers. I walked up the staircase to the attic, opened the door, and flashed a light from my phone. Where was Keith Morrison when you needed him? The shuffling stopped. I flashed the light around the room that would soon be the office and playroom for Oliver and me. Tools and toolboxes were set off to the side.

Atticus barked again downstairs.

I walked to the new window at the front of the attic that looked out on the street. Across the street, near a big evergreen tree: movement. The glow of the streetlight behind a tall man cast him in complete darkness. I turned off the light on my phone and stood to the side of the window. Mr. Wagner with his spoiled pug? The figure moved again. No, this body was much taller and broader in the shoulders. He appeared to be looking in the direction of my house.

A ghost?

Atticus barked from downstairs again.

Not a ghost.

The figure turned and moved away from the tree down the street. He crossed the street about two houses down, got into a sedan, and drove away.

Thoughts of the boy and housekeeper that had been killed filled in my brain. My heart pounded as the smell of Old Spice aftershave flooded over me. I ran down to the main floor to the front door. My routine of checking doors each night was borderline OCD. Yes, the door was locked, and Atticus was sitting at the front window, a low growl curled in his throat as he looked out toward the tree.

"You OK, Atticus?"

Atticus sighed and sauntered near the couch and dropped to the floor. I grabbed the throw from the back of the couch. I felt safer near Atticus. I took a deep breath. To keep calm and avoid thinking about the noises in the attic or the shadow man across the street, I started a mental list. I made a mental list of all the reasons that Jake had not wanted to stay married to me. I'm a list person, after all.

Top of the list: *boring.*

Got that.

I would rather read a book than go running. Heck, I even had a fantasy that I could read a book after I fell asleep and bring the book into my dreams with me. How lame is that?

Bet Jaymie never had that fantasy.

I was a horrible cook.

I was a list person.

I wasn't Jaymie.

What if that was all that it came down to: Jake would always have loved Jaymie more, only he hadn't met her before he met me.

As I lay there on my couch, around two in the morning, I analyzed—for the last time, I promised myself—the death of my marriage.

Autopsy of a dead marriage.

I imagined a coroner with a sharp-edged tool of some sort, slicing open the dead marriage, which is lying naked on a cold table: very dead. He takes the edge of the utensil and slices from top to bottom down the middle of the corpse, exposing the organs. He searches with a light for the point of no return. He sees that disease had taken over the marriage and is covering every organ. He sees that the dishonesty and the infidelity has sucked the life from daily communications and dreams from the early days of the marriage. Eventually, resentment and denial clogged the main vessels to the heart. But the ultimate cause of death, the coroner determines, was blunt-force trauma from behind. A veritable sucker punch hit the marriage, once alive. Hadn't seen that coming.

Approximate time of death: no one really knows.

As the coroner sewed up the body and signed his name to the dead marriage certificate, I drifted into a deep self-pity sleep of bad dreams.

I'm standing on the side of a raging creek somewhere in the Colorado Mountains. Suddenly, I'm aware that my dad and Nadine are standing with me. And others too, though I don't know all of the people standing with me in the woods at the edge of the creek. The people all look old and tired.

"Look!" My dad points to the other side, and I notice that the creek is now wider and moving faster.

On the side of the creek is another large crowd. I start to make out a few of the people closest to the opposite edge of the creek: Peaches, Mike Sheridan, LaTrey. I wave to my students, but they don't see me or seem to know me.

"Look," Nadine yells. "Oliver!"

I now see that Peaches is holding Oliver, and Oliver is laughing and looking at the water.

"They're trying to go across," my dad yells. "What the hell are they thinking? The water is too dangerous!"

Arty and James move a boat through the crowd to the water's edge. Peaches gets in with Oliver. Gina is in the boat holding a baby. The group is trying to move the boat into the waters, which are now rapids; the creek is wider than before. People in the crowd are pointing to our side of the creek. They want to come over. But if the boat goes in the water, they will not survive.

"No!" I scream. "Stay there. It's better there. Don't come over here!"

The group begins to move the boat into the water, and a hand touches my back. I look to see the shadow man behind me. I can see the shape of him, but he's all dark.

I scream.

Atticus licked my face as the sun poured into the living room. I looked at my watch: 9:33 a.m. My head hurt from crying so much the day before.

I missed Oliver.

12

"Maribel Winters"
Summer of 1938

Rollie

The first time I saw Maribel Winters, I thought she was a movie star. I'm not saying that my mother or the other women of Brush weren't pretty. They were. But Maribel Winters had a glow about her that made me want to stare at her for a while.

But the thing about Maribel Winters—well, I actually heard a lot about her before the first time I set eyes on her.

We hadn't been at the Genoa Place that long when I realized that the "boys," as my mom called them, would head off to town on the weekends, all dolled up and smelling funny. Their hair was slicked back under their best cowboy hats.

"You look nice," I said to Truett as he looked in the mirror, adjusting his hat.

"I *am* nice, Rollie." Truett winked at me as he walked to the door. "Want to help me start the Model T?"

Truett had an old Model T without a top that wouldn't start without one guy cranking it and the other guy retarding the spark and giving it a little gas with the hand controls. My feet didn't touch the floor. "If you help me start the car, I'll take you in to town with me. Maybe we can find you a pretty girl."

Now, I didn't want no pretty girl, but I thought it might be fun to go into town at night.

"Rollie, by golly, I forgot my hat. You run in and get it, and I'll turn the car around."

By the time I came out, the old car would be heading up the hill. I'd chase after it, and sometimes I'd almost catch him.

The next day the uncles were all clumped together talking and laughing out by the barn, so I walked up to see what was the big deal. I stood by the side of the barn as they smoked and talked about the night before.

"Leave it to Truett. The first new woman to walk into town in how many years, and she walks right up to you. Man, she was a looker," Emmett said to the others.

"She's a lady," Truett corrected.

Maribel Winters was the lady Truett was talking about. I had never seen Truett so happy as the day after he met Maribel Winters.

That night, as I lay in bed trying so hard to go to sleep, I could hear the soft murmur of adult conversation from the other room. See, the walls were thin as paper, but I don't think my mom knew I was still awake. First my mom spoke. She said something about "that new woman in town." The way she said it made me think my mother didn't like Maribel Winters, but the more she talked, I swear she sounded almost like she felt sorry for her.

"She's got skeletons in her closet. That's what I think." My mom said something like that. I had a picture in my head of all these skeletons squished in a dark closet, and I knew I was going to have an even harder time getting to sleep.

A man's voice murmured. I figured it was Uncle Billy. Uncle Billy was really my great uncle Billy, but I didn't know that until I was older. I just thought he was the really old brother. He was actually my grandfather's brother. He said something about Truett needing to mind his own business. "Tru don't need to take care of everybody, especially if they're pretty."

The first time I met the magical Maribel was at the grocery store in Brush.

Mom took Jeb and me with her whenever she went to town. Jeb was the youngest of the uncles, but he was more like a cousin since he was only about five years older than me. Jeb and I spent our free time together, usually doing things we weren't supposed to do. We liked going into town with my mom since she usually let us pick out a piece of candy when we checked out. Bob's wasn't anything like the supermarts we have today. Old Dorothy Manning ran the store, which couldn't have been any bigger than a two-car garage. Wood floor. Bad lighting. Always kind of smelled like something was going bad somewhere in the room. But it was all we had. So once a week, Mom took me into town to grab the "staples," as she called them. I just knew that the afternoon would be long and boring.

Maribel Winters was in the store that day with her son Toby. Toby, fluffy and spoiled, was younger than I was. He ran around the store and touched things he wasn't supposed to. I wondered if he was the skeleton in Maribel's closet. More than Toby, I remember Maribel Winters that day. I thought her name sounded like Christmas and that she looked like an angel. I was only six, but I knew that there was something about her that made people want to move closer to her. To hear her voice. To watch her move. She had long dark hair that I wanted to touch, and she smelled wonderful.

That day in Bob's, as I was waiting for my mom to pay for her box of staples, I looked up and saw that Maribel and Toby were standing next to us in line. Maribel smiled at me and asked me my name. I looked at my mom, and she nodded approval.

"Roland." I wanted to sound older than my six years.

Jeb giggled. Now, no one called me Roland except my mom when she was scolding me, so I don't know why I told Maribel that. Maybe to sound grown-up.

"That's a very nice name," Maribel Winters said. "Toby, this is Roland and—"

"Jebidiah. My name is Jebidiah." Jeb's face got real red. This time I giggled.

"Jebidiah is another nice name."

Toby, who looked about four or five, had the biggest mop of black hair on his head and held tight to his mom as she spoke to us. I wondered where the dad was.

I was so into Maribel Winters that I almost forgot to pick out a piece of candy. Almost. Jeb and I both picked licorice. He picked black, and I picked red.

On the way home from Bob's, I asked my mom what a skeleton in the closet was. She told me that children shouldn't listen in on adult conversations. I wanted to tell her that adults shouldn't talk about things that a kid shouldn't hear. I'll never forget what she told me next.

"Rollie, skeletons in the closet are bad things from the past that you pray will stop haunting you."

I wondered about Maribel Winters' skeletons.

Second Quarter
Skeletons in the Closet

There's a skeleton in everybody's closet
I can think of one or two in my own room
But I would like to introduce them both to you
You'd shake their bony hands and so dispel the gloom.

—"Ghosts That Haunt Me" by Crash Test Dummies

A single dream is more powerful than a thousand realities.

— J. R. R. Tolkien

13

November 10, 2008

Annie

"Sex, sex, sex. Sex is everywhere."

Arty made the provocative announcement as he entered room 213. Students who were in their seats and those entering with Arty snickered and then looked up at me.

I said nothing and hoped that I had misheard Arty, who continued on his inappropriate rant. "Sex, sex, sex, sex." Arty pointed to different students each time he repeated his shock word. Mike and James walked in as Arty pointed to them and continued. "Sex and more sex." Mike shook his head and smirked. Arty looked at me. "I'm just saying, Ms. Day, every person in this school is a product of—"

"We got it, Arty."

"Just think about it. Say you're sitting at a Husker home game, and you just look around at the whole stadium. You've got to be saying to yourself: that's a heck of a lot of sex."

Actually, I had never thought about that before when I had gone to Husker games. Unfortunately, since that remark, I always have.

"OK, Arty sit down," I said as I struggled with the challenge of any teacher in a moment of misbehavior to balance between overreacting and ignoring. Either extreme could create worse results than the uncomfortable moment in a classroom. Need some balance here. Students are looking from you to the culprit and then back to you in anticipation. Just how will you react?

"No disrespect. Just honesty." Arty pointed to Maggie Whitehead as she walked into the doorway. "See! Another one: sex!"

Mortified Maggie rushed to her seat.

"Love the energy. Appreciate the honesty. Need to pull out that imaginary filter, Arty, that should be in front of your mouth. You know, the little voice in your head that says, 'Period-two English is not a place to say sex is everywhere.'"

All students stopped and looked at me. Mike Sheridan could not resist: "Ms. Day. Just where is your filter today?"

"I was just—"

"Uh, filter please." Mike Sheridan shook his head and held a hand out, shutting me out. The room broke into laughter.

"Not how I planned to start class. I guess I have your attention, though. Thank you, Arty."

"Anytime, Ms. Day."

"Everybody, get out your *Gatsby* books, your notebooks, and your filters." I smiled. LaTrey walked in just as the bell rang. Arty looked at him and pointed. "Refrain, Arty. We know."

"Is the test over *Gatsby* tomorrow or Monday?" Cami Halloway asked as she twirled her hair.

"Test is Monday." Cough, cough. It's been on your syllabus all semester. "Your essays are due tomorrow, and tomorrow we'll review for the test. So today we step back. We just finished another great American novel. What do we walk away with after reading F. Scott Fitzgerald's masterpiece? And, more importantly, to help you with those essays you're polishing tonight: Was the title of this book meant as serious or sarcastic?"

The room was still.

"Come on, now." I held up the book. "Fitzgerald didn't just put this title on the finished manuscript because it sounded fun. Actually, he had a plethora—"

"Power word!" Arty shouted.

"This title must be important," I said. "He wanted us to think. So was Gatsby great or not?"

Silence.

I knew they were thinking.

"You all have strong opinions and interesting theories. I know Arty does. So, you don't have to tell me what you think I believe or what I'd like to hear, but you have to back up your point."

Hand up: LaTrey.

I had spoken with LaTrey's counselor shortly after his essay on dreaming about carrying a gun to school. I was glad to have another person aware of his written expression. We were both on LaTrey alert. LaTrey spoke.

"Are you asking if we think Fitzgerald meant it as serious or sarcastic or if we think that the title is serious or sarcastic?"

"I guess since we can't have F. Scott here as our guest speaker today, I'd like to know what you think."

"I see the title as sarcastic. In my opinion, Gatsby was a wimp." Students looked from LaTrey to me.

"Go on."

"I mean, like, his death was his own fault. I don't see why I should feel sorry for a person who was so stupid."

"So why do you think we were supposed to feel sorry for him?"

"The narrator dude went on and on in the end about what a great guy Gatsby was and how he had been 'preyed' on by all the bad people. I'm supposed to admire him just because he was loyal to a stupid dream? That's BS."

Several hands shot up.

"Whoa, LaTrey. Look what you've done. You've inspired us—or fired us up, at least. James, what do you think?"

"I agree," James said. "Gatsby is kind of like the people you hear about today who are always playing the victim. He was obsessed with Daisy, and that ruled his life. She couldn't have cared less about him. She used him. She just liked the attention. The way I see it, all of Gatsby's poor choices brought him to his death in the swimming pool. Just because he was loyal to her doesn't make him a hero or a victim to me. I don't think he was great. I don't even think he was a man."

Arty shouted, "Don't hold back, James. We want to know how you really feel." Students laughed. "Oh, sorry, Ms. Day. Forgot to raise my hand." Arty raised his hand.

"Arty."

"I just think you're all being a little harsh on the guy. Gatsby was a great guy. He threw these huge parties and let anyone come. Anyone. Don't you think that's great?"

James laughed and shook his head. Kinkaid's cheeks grew red.

"So," I asked, "you think the title was serious, Arty?"

"Serious. At least he was loyal to something. Most people I know don't have a mission or whatever. Remember the green light symbolizing hope in the book?" Arty looked to me and raised one eyebrow. "He never gave up hope for getting the girl. Never."

"Always about a woman." The voice came from Donovan. Donovan had on a black Iron Maiden concert shirt. The front read Fear of the Dark Tour. We all looked at the quiet presence in the front seat. Donovan moved his head down when I looked at him. I wondered what color his eyes were. His hair always covered them.

James spoke out loud to Arty. "Daisy was a snob. Unworthy. In the end, Gatsby let everyone down, including himself. The man had no self-respect. Title, sarcastic."

Peaches cleared her throat as she held her hand high.

"Peaches. Serious or sarcastic?"

"Serious. Gatsby was seriously a great man. I felt sorry for him. He didn't know any better. Maybe if he had grown up differently, he would've done it all in a different way. Who's to say? At least he tried."

"OK, so Peaches makes a point about his family of origin. Maybe his upbringing impacted his decision to be committed to Daisy. Do you buy that, James and LaTrey?"

LaTrey shook his head no. James answered. "OK, if you don't see him as accountable, Peaches, that's fine, but I think you could find a lot of people who had bad lives and make good decisions and do good things. Most great people, to me, overcame the things you say destroyed or took advantage of Gatsby. He just isn't a hero to me. Not great."

Cami Halloway raised her hand in the back of the room. "OK, so Gatsby died?"

Peaches sighed. "Girl, read the book."

Katrina raised her hand.

"Something to add, Katrina?"

"I see the title as serious and sarcastic."

"Yay. Whatever, K-Mart," Arty whispered.

"What I mean is that maybe we're supposed to see the difficulty in making it black and white. To box Gatsby up as a hero or not a hero is not so easy when we each have different opinions of the definition of great or hero."

"I think a hero is loyal to himself," Mike Sheridan said without raising his hand.

"Slow clap." Arty teased. "What the hell is that supposed to mean? Oh, sorry, Ms. Day. Lost my filter again."

"Just, Arthur, that a person has to be honest," Mike replied.

"So," I said, "is Gatsby great or not, Mike?" I was curious.

"Not. He was an OK guy, but he wasn't honest, so he wasn't great. He had an agenda with his parties to get Daisy over to his house. He wanted her to see the huge mansion and books he never read so he could take her away from her husband. He did dishonest things to get the money because he was so enamored by her voice."

"OK, let's talk about the voice. As Donovan said, it's always about a woman. What did Gatsby say Daisy's voice was full of? The question will be on the test."

Kinkaid raised his hand and cleared his throat. I wasn't sure whether he or his parents had made that call, but Kinkaid remained in Period Two, room 213, with an inept teacher.

"Kinkaid?"

"Money. Gatsby said her voice was full of money."

"How can a voice sound like money, Kinkaid?"

"Well..." Kinkaid paused. "I think that Gatsby was pretty shallow, and real money enticed him...but Nick also commented on Daisy's voice."

"That's right. What does he say?"

"That Daisy had an indiscreet voice."

"Anyone want to comment on what Kinkaid just said?"

LaTrey's hand went up. I think he was getting into Gatsby.

"LaTrey?"

"She's all bad and corrupt, cheating and lying, and being OK with it." LaTrey sat up with his new idea. "She be like the corruption of the American Dream."

"She be?" I asked.

LaTrey smiled. "Let me rephrase that for you, Ms. Day, oh queen of English. Daisy is the corruption of the American Dream." LaTrey smiled and then added, "She ain't nothing but trouble."

The class laughed.

Arty raised his hand. "I think that Gatsby was kind of unfair to Daisy. Daisy could never have lived up to how high he put her on a pedestal. He was unfair to his dream."

I heard a snicker from the back of the middle row. Everyone looked at Gina, whose pregnancy was still being hidden by oversized sweatshirts. I remembered seeing Gina in the hall the year before. She was the sopho-more "it" girl back then. She was always dressed in the nicest clothes. Her hair always looked as though she had gotten up two hours before school to style it. This year: sweatshirts and ponytails, minus makeup.

Mike Sheridan raised one eyebrow and turned to the seat two desks behind him. "Something funny, Miss Shatner? Would you like to share it with the rest of the class?"

Gina rolled her eyes. "Nope."

"It's all right, Gina," I said. "Everybody has been pretty blunt up to this point. What made you laugh?" I tried to encourage without alienating the person who found me boring.

"It's just a stupid love story. More like a soap opera than a classic..." Gina looked to the door to room 213.

All of the students looked to the door. Coach Edwards stood in the doorway, his new assistant Nick standing behind him.

"Look." Arty pointed. "Another one."

I glared at Arty.

"Another what, Elston?" Coach Edwards asked.

"Another...great American...leader, sir. We're studying about American leaders." Arty grinned, and the rest of the students smirked and shuffled in their seats.

"Got that right, Elston. Ms. Day, I'm afraid I'm going to need to borrow Sheridan, Elston, and Wu." (Oh, my.) "Just for about five minutes. We're moving a few things in the weight room after the football season, and I knew all three were in your second hour. Just for five minutes. I promise."

I looked to the three. "If you three would be so kind as to help Coach Edwards."

James, Arty, and Mike walked to the fronts of their rows and then to the door. Mike turned back to the room and shouted, "Mike Sheridan, number forty-five on the roster, number one in your hearts. Yes! Thank you very much, ladies and gentlemen."

"Sheridan, get out here," Coach Edwards yelled from the hallway.

"OK, so where were we?" I turned back to the class.

"Gina was throwing shade at Gatsby." LaTrey winked at Gina. Gina tried to hide a smile.

"Hey!" Cami Halloway yelled out and stood up. "I'm so creeped out."

"What? A spider?" LaTrey asked. "I love spiders."

Cami pointed to her book and showed Peaches.

"Wow," Peaches said in a tone so quiet I almost did not hear her. "Jenny Caldwell. 1997."

"I'm reading the book that was checked out by that dead girl." Cami shook her hands as if she had just touched poison.

Just when we had all pushed aside the bones from the daily interactions at Belmont High School, the darned things kept reminding us of their existence: *we're here, and we're not leaving.*

"I heard that they found another bone," Phil Timmerman said.

"Did not," Cami scolded. "They never said that."

"If by *they* you mean the media, you're right. I just heard a rumor. That's all I said." Phil scowled at Cami.

I walked to the closet and pulled a *Great Gatsby* book from my cabinet. "If you're uncomfortable, I'll trade you books."

"What do you think about the bones, Ms. Day?" LaTrey asked.

LaTrey was putting me on the spot. I'd rather talk about Daisy's indiscreet voice or sex.

"I don't know what to think." I was honest.

I always am.

That night Trent Kula and I had our first date.

If that's what you want to call it.

Two weeks after our first kiss in room 213, we finally connected. I'd spent more time that evening than I ever had picking out clothes to wear on the alleged date. I hadn't been out with a man in years. Most of my closet was teacher-y clothes. I found a black sweater that Jake had always liked, and I wore that sweater with a pair of jeans and fun earrings.

I decided to meet Trent Kula at the bar rather than have him pick me up at my house—for several reasons:

A. I wasn't ready for Oliver to see me dating (was I really dating?).

B. I wasn't ready to open my private Annie world to a person I wasn't sure I even liked.

C. I wasn't sure Trent Kula was a real person (the kiss may have been just a silly daydream in my classroom). So you can't have an imaginary person pick you up for a date.

D. All of the above.

D is the answer.

When I walked into Saddle Creek Bar, I scanned the room. Leaning against the bar, Trent, in a gray fitted sweater and jeans, looked like the clothed version of the guy on all those romance novels—remember, I hate romance novels—wrapping his arms around some exhausted, needy vixen on the steamy cover of a book called something like *Until the Edge of Darkness*. When he looked over at the door to the bar, he smiled (still not sure he was real) with a sexy flash of all those beautiful white teeth (not sure they were real), stood up, and moved toward me.

"Annie Day! You came. I thought for a moment that you weren't going to show. Thought maybe I scared you away—you know, when I... sit down, sit down. The waitress said she'd get us a table when you got here. You look—well, amazing."

We ordered drinks and traded light remarks about the fundraiser finale. Orders were in, and Kissermania was in the books. Belmont High lips were now glossier than ever, and I couldn't have been happier about the end of the fun-raising agenda. The girls had made enough money to buy the pink pompons for Breast Cancer Awareness month and donate some to the cause. Done.

Big checkmark.

Oliver and a failed first effort at marriage were not brought up in conversation. I just wanted to be a woman on a date—not a single parent English teacher. The title just reeks of green-bean casserole with too much mushroom soup.

We walked to the parking lot following our date, which, by the way, turned out to be real. Trent followed me to my car and then surprised me by getting in on the passenger side.

"I'd like to start seeing you."

"Well, I'm right here." Funny, literal joke.

"I mean, I want to do this again." Trent moved toward me.

"Sounds good to me." Trent was going to kiss me.

Until I married Jake, I maintained a personal contract, something I called a kissing contract. I wasn't shallow or easy. I would kiss a guy only if I felt emotionally connected with him. A kiss meant something.

No kissing contract with Kula.

Trent moved in for the kiss.

We kissed.

For a really long time.

I had forgotten how much I liked kissing.

I threw my kissing contract out the car window when I decided—carpe diem—kiss if I want to. Was it wrong to want to meet again, if only for the kissing? Was I using Trent Kula? Was he using me?

Only thing that I knew for sure: I liked kissing.

I never told anyone that I had met with Trent. I even told my little babysitter, a fourteen-year-old neighbor girl, that I was running errands. I was becoming quite the little truth enhancer. I technically wasn't lying if I withheld information or enhanced the truth. I was running a kissing errand. It wasn't a lie.

"Oliver was perfect!" Ellie said as I handed her money. "We hung out with Choochoo all night. Oh, and he knows every word to *Horton Hears a Who.*"

"I do too. When you read the book every night ten times—"

Bam!

Something on the floor above had hit the floor to make the loud sound.

"Sounds like someone is still up," I said. "Thank you so much for helping me out tonight."

I paid Ellie and watched her walk across the street to her house. She waved and went in. I locked the doors (and checked the locks three times each) and walked up to the second floor. I looked in on Oliver. He was sound asleep. He was warm as I kissed his forehead. I walked to my room to see the big box from the attic on the floor and most of its contents poured over my bedroom floor. I began putting pictures, newspaper clippings, and documents back into the box, and then I noticed the envelope again, the seal so loose that it appeared to be open.

That night I fell into a deep sleep and dreamed of the dark.

In the dark.
On my knees.
Crawling.
Frantic.
I can't find what I need. I can't find what I'm looking for.

14

November 17, 2008

Annie

"Momma had a baby, and its head fell off." Mike Sheridan's song entered the room before he did.

"Say what?" Cami Halloway said as she sat down.

"Didn't you ever take a dandelion as a kid and pop off the top?"

"Well, yah." Cami moved her pen to her mouth as she spoke.

"You'd take the dandelion and sing, 'Momma had a baby, and its head popped off.' And right when you sing 'pop,' you just pop the top of the dandelion off."

"No. That's horrible."

"OK, so what did you do as a child, Cami?"

"Well, I used to have a voice talking about my life—you know, like I was a celebrity, and the voice would talk about what I was doing all day."

Mike raised his eyebrows and looked at me and then stared at Cami.

Cami continued. "You know, like, 'Cami knew that picking the right outfit for her slumber party would determine just what kind of a night she might have.' Or 'Cami was nervous that her parents would hear her come in late.' Didn't you do that?"

"Nope, I never did that. Were these voices in your head from outer space?"

"No, silly. I was narrating my life. Only it felt like it was someone else."

"I'm silly?" Mike raised one eyebrow and sat down as more kids poured into room 213.

Mike Sheridan looked at Peaches. "Nice purple planets, Peaches."

Peaches realized Mike was talking about her earrings. "They not planets. They snowflakes, Einstein." I saw a quick smirk on her face as she sat down and sighed.

"Snowflakes? You got gypped. Just saying." Mike pulled out his vocab words.

LaTrey leaned over to Mike. "Hey, Sheridan, what does 'staunch' mean? I can't read my own handwriting." I was curious how LaTrey could use a word he didn't know in a sentence.

"You got to be kidding me, man. 'Staunch' is easy. It's just the past tense of stench." (Staunch is not a verb.) "In a sentence: You staunched so bad in our car that we kicked you out on the side of road. Staunch."

"Thanks, man." LaTrey went back to studying.

Peaches shook her head, her snowflakes rocking around her head.

"OK, following the power-word quiz, I'm going to introduce our next novel, John Steinbeck's *Of Mice and Men*. While I'm taking roll, look over your words."

James Wu was the last to walk in. "I'm late because I had to write a sentence for each of your power words in my biology class."

"Oh, please don't tell me you do your English assignments in other classes."

"Oh, sorry. I won't tell you that again. These sentences kind of feel like busy work. No offense. Why do we have to write these sentences?"

"None taken. In answer to your question: A, the main reason you need to write weekly sentences is because I'm the queen of this king-dom. And since I'm queen, you do as I tell you. B, writing a sentence using a word in context, correctly, reinforces your memory of the word.

It also helps me to see if you know what the word means and how to use it. C, studying vocab this year will come in handy when most of you take the ACT or SAT and in college. Any more questions?"

"Oh, yah. About the queen thing. How does that all work out?" James asked. Students smiled and laughed.

"Well, in room 213, I'm the queen, and it's pretty much all about me, and I'll tell you when you're wrong. I decide the book, the discussion for the test, and when we will work on grammar. Oh, and everyone must be nice in my kingdom."

James sat down grinning. "What if we all get tired of you being the queen and want a different queen?"

"Very good question, Mr. Wu. Back to A: I'm the queen and will tell you that you're wrong. You're wrong. Any more questions, my little groundlings?"

"Nope. You pretty much covered it all." James would get a 100 percent on the quiz, even if he didn't study.

I marked my attendance sheet and then looked up. Every face was looking at me. Period Two was perfect.

Following the weekly vocabulary quiz, students handed them up to the first seat in each row. "OK, Phil and LaTrey, would you be so lovely as to come up here and hand out a paperback book to each member of the class? I'll pass around a sheet where I'd like you to sign your name and your book number."

Teaching a really great class is like being on an imaginary island away from the harsh realities of the world. That day on Island 213—an island over which I was queen—I got to avoid the random mysterious bones in the world, the noises in my attic, a china girl who may or may not exist, and the shimmery woman my former American Dream was married to. On my island, we got to do what I loved to do: talk about great literature and have fun.

"OK, so notebooks out, and pencils ready? It's going to come at you all fast and furious. Before we can talk about John Steinbeck and his classic *Of Mice and Men*, we need to talk about the title. Everyone write the word 'allusion' in your notebooks." I went to the dry-erase board and wrote the word: "allusion."

You could almost see the steam from the pens.

"This is not the illusion from magic. This is allusion with an *a*, which basically means referring to something. So the title of the novel is a literary allusion, and those in the viewing audience who are well read catch the allusion."

I handed out a copy of the poem "To a Mouse" by the Scottish poet Robert Burns.

After we read the poem, Arty said loud enough for all to hear, "Well, that's four minutes of my life I will never get back."

The class laughed.

"I don't have a clue what the poem was even about. Translation, please!"

"OK, so the poem was famous over two hundred years ago, and it was written in a Scottish twist to the language."

"And," Mike Sheridan added, raising one eyebrow, "it was written to a mouse."

"*The best laid plans of mice and men often go awry*," I repeated the line from the poem. "The poet realizes that he is no different than the mouse. The farmer just plowed over the mouse nest. He realizes that the mouse worked hard to build his nest, and it was destroyed in an instant. He too works hard, and a storm could ruin his crop. The best-laid plans, or the plans that you've put a lot of thought, time, and energy into—well, they sometimes don't go the way you thought they would. The best laid plans… of mice and men."

"That's it?" Mike asked.

"Haven't you ever heard anybody say, after it rains on a parade or a person's project falls apart, 'Oh, well, the best-laid plans'?"

"Nope."

"I get it." Peaches said. "This poem is basically about life."

"Right, Peaches." I went on. "OK, so I understand your cynicism. A mouse and a dead Scottish poet: Why should you care? Because what

Burns is talking about is your life. He's talking about the guy who finally has the guts to ask a girl to prom and then finds out she was already asked. Or you have studied really hard for a test, only to find out you studied the wrong chapter."

"Or you go out on the field to win state, and Bellevue West gets in your way," James Wu said.

"In this novel, George and Lennie, the two main characters, in the Great Depression, have a dream of getting their own place to 'live off the fat of the land.' In the meantime, they go from ranch to ranch to do odds and ends or temporary work until they have enough money to get their own place."

"Spoiler alert!" Mike said. "They don't get their own place. Sorry, Ms. Day. I'm just guessing."

"The point is that Steinbeck implies that dreams are important if life is going to be meaningful. Dreams give people purpose and bring them together in shared dreams, even if the dreams are not realized."

Cami raised her hand and stood up.

"Cami? You have something to add or ask?"

"Well, I'm not sure if this has anything to do with the mouse poem… or American Dreams. OK, sometimes I feel like, well, I know a lot about the life of Fergie—you know, the singer—and I know all about her ups and downs, and I've probably read everything about her life. But, what I mean is that I feel like I really know her. Like she's a good friend of mine. Like I can relate to her and she knows me. Does that make sense?"

"Uh," Arty said, "in a word: no."

"Are you suggesting," I said, struggling to mend the unmendable, "that Fergie has some best laid-plans that didn't work out and that things still turned out pretty good for her?"

Cami paused. "Yah, I really do think that's what I meant."

"OK, so when you're an adult and you're at dinner party sometime in the future, and someone throws out the title of the book we're about to read—*Of Mice and Men*—you have that little literary allusion to the poem 'To a Mouse' that will entertain the room."

"Wait!" LaTrey said. "If any of you ever see me standing at a dinner party where people are talking about poems 'to a mouse,' you can just shoot me in the head because my life would suck."

I could only smile at LaTrey.

The bell rang.

Gina Shatner was already sitting in a desk in the back of the room after the last bell rang. She looked tired.

"Hey, Gina. How's it going?"

That awkward moment when the girl (who called you a boring bitch) and you are alone in the classroom that usually has about thirty-eight other people in it to buffer you.

"OK, I guess. Still not sure what we're doing here." Gina pulled the sleeves of her sweatshirt over her hands.

"Well, your mom wants you to get caught up with the missing assignments and tests you missed in the first quarter."

"Cool. I guess."

"Do you mind moving up to this first desk so I can pull up another desk, and we can work together."

Hannah, my aide, came in as Gina walked toward the front of the room.

"Need anything, Ms. D?" I had never seen Hannah in a bad mood.

"Actually, I'm caught up today."

"Cool beans! See ya!"

As Hannah disappeared from the room, Peaches appeared. She stopped at the doorway and looked at Gina and then looked at me.

"Double duty today, Peaches. Come on in." Peaches and I had already met the week before to start working her prep plan for the ACT test in December.

"What's she doing here?" Peaches asked.

"She's doing some catch-up work." I handed Peaches an ACT test. "Work wherever you want in the room, and we'll go over your answers when Gina is writing her essay."

That was Day One.

Day one of the many that Peaches, Gina, and I worked after school together.

The routine was bumpy at first, but in time, we became a smooth machine. I set Peaches up with a timed ACT practice test, and then I worked with Gina on her missing assignments. When Peaches finished her test, we would go over the missed questions while Gina worked on her missing essays.

What a group of misfits.

Gina: A donkey on the edge.

Gina was emotionally fragile and prone to meltdowns in the midst of vocabulary quizzes. The once-popular and borderline-stuck-up teenager was now a pregnant donkey on the edge of a temperamental cliff and wanted to disappear from high school.

Peaches: A single thread.

Peaches was hanging by a thread. That thread would be a grandmother who may not be around much longer. Peaches told me that Ms. Trumble's trip to the conference in October had been one of her last days before she was homebound. She was now in hospice care. The thread was wearing thin, and Peaches was hanging in there.

Me: The brazenly banished, boring bitch. (Let's sprinkle a little alliteration on this image.)

I completed the Misfit Trio.

On Day One of the Island of Misfit Toys, Doc was already sweeping the back of the room before we noticed him.

"Hey, Doc," I said.

"Don't mind me. I don't want to disturb all the hard work going on in here."

"Ladies, this is Doc. Doc, this is Gina and Peaches."

"Hey, ladies."

Peaches and Gina mumbled lackluster greetings to the friendly janitor.

"Are you limping, Doc?" I asked.

"Just a bit. Nothing big. Just another rubber-band episode."

"Rubber-band episode?" I asked.

"Probably have a few of them a day. The big ones in my life—well, they were big. Setbacks." Doc stopped and took out his handkerchief and blew his nose. Peaches and Gina did not seem annoyed but rather curious. "You know how you pull a rubber band out to shoot it?"

We all nodded our heads yes.

"Well, you need to pull it back to get it to go forward in its trajectory."

Peaches and Gina looked at me.

"Power word, ladies. Trajectory. Path you take. Usually flying off in a different direction."

Doc continued. "Well, this little pain in my leg is just a little rubber band episode, just holding me back so that I give it a rest. The pain is shooting me forward in the direction I'm supposed to go—listen to the pain. When my wife died, well, I thought that was the worst thing ever. Pulled me back so far, I couldn't find a reason to get up in the morning. But one day I got up and just shot forward. That was the day that OPS offered me the job here back in '99. Got me up each morning. Hell, this is where I'm supposed to be…so sorry I said hell, ladies."

"Hell, cussing doesn't offend me," Peaches said with a grin.

Doc laughed out loud.

Day One: three rubber bands, pulled tightly back.

On my way out of the building, I poked my head into the office of Mary Claire Forbes, the counselor assigned to Peaches. She was alone.

"Busy?" I asked.

"Come on in. I was meaning to get a note to you today. Got a little busy after three o'clock. We're good to go." Mary Claire gave me thumbs-up.

"Peaches is registered?"

"Yep."

I had given Mary Claire a check for the fee, and she sat with Peaches before school a few days earlier to get her signed up to take the ACT.

"She's going to take the exam at a school closer to her house, so she can walk there that morning. I'm not sure what you did with that one, but I've been trying to tell that girl for the past four years that she was college material. Thank God for the good stories on days when I hear way too many bad stories...don't get me started."

"Well, not to drop any more on you, but I wanted to touch base on LaTrey Williams."

"Oh, yes, LaTrey. How could you not love the grumpy old man inside a kid."

"A tough read at first. Now I'm really enjoying him."

"Well, if you only knew the story behind that one. LaTrey is a ward of the state. He gets himself up and gets himself here without any adult encouraging him. He's an emancipated minor. Fingers crossed that we get that one to graduate..."

"LaTrey is in good spirits every day. He did mention a gun again today, jokingly...Something like shoot me in the head with a gun if I ever talk about English at a party as an adult."

Mary Claire laughed out loud.

"What?" I asked. "You think he was just saying what everyone in the room was thinking?" I smiled.

"Just keep me updated."

"Absolutely. I...I know this sounds nosy, and they may not even be students you counsel, but I have questions on two other students."

"Shoot. I'll tell you what I can."

"Do you have Gwendolyn Sparks in your group of students you work with?"

"Uh, yes. Is she a student of yours?"

"No. She was...she was the girl that I hit in the parking lot back in October. I've never seen her before or since that day. I just wondered about her."

"Well, she's not here much, for one. And she's not passing any of her classes, though you didn't hear that from me. Mom's not in the picture; Dad is but shouldn't be. Not a stellar home life...all I got on her. You said two students?"

"Donovan Hedder. What do you know about him?"

"Never heard of him." Mary Claire cleared her throat. "If I do, I'll let you know."

By the time I got to the parking lot, only a few cars speckled the west and east lots. I saw a man sitting in a an old, dark-blue Ford Taurus, a car I had seen in the lot every day as I walked to my car. The man avoided eye contact with me.

Are you one of the good guys protecting us?

Or are you the one who is scaring us with all of these bones?

15

November 29, 2008

Annie

*B*ecause I could not stop for Death, He kindly stopped for me.
The light was green, but my car sat idle as a pageant of cars with headlights on passed through the intersection at twelve fifteen on an overcast Saturday, the pace slow and steady in the rhythm of a slow, rocking wave on a lazy afternoon.

"Damn it," I mumbled. I had a list of places to get to before Oliver's birthday party with my family. Everyone was coming by for pizza and cake and a celebration of a four-year-old turning five at six o'clock, and I knew this little kink in my agenda chain would throw my perfect schedule off. A funeral procession was not on my list. Oliver and I were almost to Costco when a parade of slow cars reminded us that people die even when others are celebrating another year of life.

"The light's green, Mom." The voice from the backseat was serious and polite.

"You're right. We're waiting on a parade."

"Parade? How come no one's throwing candy?"

"Not sure…"

Because I could not stop for Death, He kindly stopped for me.
The Carriage held but just Ourselves—
And Immortality.
"Just a reminder…"
(Not going to live forever.)
"A what? Look, a police guy on a motorcycle. Cool."

I had had a professor in college who taught an American poetry class and spent half a class on Emily Dickinson's poem about death. Dr. Pincer (we called him Pincher, since his nostrils pinched together when he became animated) told us that the poem "Because I Could Not Stop for Death" reveals Dickinson's calm acceptance of death.

The poem put chills up my nineteen-year-old spine at the time.

I didn't agree with Dr. Pincher's assessment of the poem. The first two lines spoke to me as a reminder: *I'm here.*

Because I could not stop for Death, He kindly stopped for me.

"Green car, blue car, white car, 'nother white car." Oliver was enjoying the parade.

I rarely think of death, especially death personified. When I hear of tragic accidents or deaths of family members or friends, I quickly push the thoughts out of my head; I just can't handle it. So death kindly reminds me, on occasion, that I'm not in control and that death is very much a part of life, whether I want to think about it or not. I'd been reminded by Death, ever so kindly, with several random bones in recent months and a funeral procession that Saturday in November.

The last car of the procession was a red truck. Oliver loved red trucks. Let's all try to find the silver lining in this death procession. "Look, mom! A red truck!"

"Awesome!" I said as I unbuckled Oliver in the parking lot of Costco. "Just for your birthday."

"You're getting me a red truck for my birthday?"

"Maybe when you're old enough to drive." I pulled out my Costco membership card and took a deep breath as we walked into the behemoth warehouse.

"OK." Oliver put his hand in mine.

I gave the Costco card to Oliver, and at the entrance he held the card up to the card checker, who smiled at Oliver and then at me. I held tightly to Oliver's hand as we walked toward the back of the enormous store for one item only. Is that even possible? One item from Costco? Yep. We were picking up a cake and nothing else.

The year before, I had attempted to make a homemade cake that was supposed to look like Barney, the lovable dinosaur. It looked like a purple blizzard with two dripping black eyes. I'm hoping that Oliver has no memory of the cake, as I will hide all pictures that could be evidence. As for 2008, there would be no pictures in photo albums that Oliver looks at as an adult and might say, "Oh, and here is a picture of a birthday cake in the shape of a red truck my mom made back in 2008. She was an amazing baker."

(That story would be fiction.)

My eyes looked to the back of the store. I had to look over the heads of the Costco zombies who moved like a convention of oblivious and spatially challenged androids standing in the middle of the aisle eating samples and looking around, unaware of a woman needing to walk down the aisle to get a cake at the back of the store. In the midst of the zombies, carrying a case of bottled water down the main aisle of the store, was Nick Stander, the new assistant football coach, whom five different teachers had tried to set me up with in recent months. I pulled Oliver's hand toward the electronics aisle. Even without my ugly lavender coat, I still could pass for a bag lady that day.

"I thought we were picking up my cake."

"I thought we'd take a look at a vacuum while we're here." I peeked around the aisle as Nick walked by.

"I don't want to look at a vacuum."

Nick walked toward a woman and child near the book aisle.

"What else do we need?" I overheard Nick ask the attractive woman with a baseball hat and blond ponytail. The toddler in the cart was a perfect blend of the two.

The woman looked over a list. "Oh, almost forgot. We need lettuce. It's back in the corner room."

"On it." Nick turned around and walked back to the area of the store where I needed to pick up my cake.

Nick Stander was married—at least he looked married.

If Nick Stander was married, why was everybody trying to set me up with him?

"I said," Oliver huffed, "I don't want to look at a vacuum."

"Don't you think this is a nice vacuum?" I said, stalling.

"No."

Once Nick got back to the cart with the woman and boy, I moved toward the area to pick up our cake. "Maybe you're right, Oliver. We don't need a vacuum today."

Cake in hand, we walked through the zombies to the front of the store.

"When we get home, can I have a party with my guys?"

"Sure." I handed my Costco card to the man at our checkout station.

"A cake!" the tall man with big teeth said to both Oliver and me. "That cake for you, big guy?"

"Yes." Oliver gave the man a serious look. Oliver had been versed on the warnings of Stranger Danger.

"Me and my girlfriend got a cake for her friend's birthday."

(Subjective case pronoun when pronoun is used as subject: my girlfriend and I.)

"Me and my girlfriend have a party to go to. Maybe we'll take a cake tonight."

(Personal pronoun for "I" or "me" is always second when placed with another noun or pronoun: my girlfriend and I.)

I smiled as I paid for the cake. "Sounds like a good idea."

I looked for the door to exit the giant store.

An hour later, after all errands were run, Oliver sat on the dining room floor holding court with a stuffed animal Horton of *Horton Hears a Who*; Smurfy, a Spiderman action figure; and Elf on a Shelf. The "guys" were in a circle, each with a *Horton Hears a Who* paper plate in front of him, which would no longer be used for the birthday party. Oliver was having more fun having an imaginary birthday party with his guys—as he called them—than he would when all of my family came over for pizza and cake in a few hours. Atticus sat about two feet from the party. Far enough that he didn't have to be part of the party and close enough so that he knew what Oliver was doing.

"It's actually Choochoo's birthday too, Mom. Did you know that?" Oliver's hands always moved in the air as he spoke, as if puppets were on his fingers.

"I think you told me that."

"He's sitting right here." Oliver showed me a plate that did not have a stuffed animal or action figure next to it. "Right next to Elf on the Shelf."

My sister had given him the Elf on the Shelf kit the year before for his birthday. We never filled out any adoption papers or named the elf. I found the whole concept of the elf moving around my house at night and spying on Oliver to see if he was behaving a little creepy. Evidently, Oliver did too. We read the book that came with the elf once and never again. He was just glad to have another guy to join his little adventures around the house.

"Well, we're actually having a birthday/Christmas party since the tree is up. Oh, the weather outside is frightful." Oliver sang a song we had been singing all day. "Let it snow, let it..."

The doorbell interrupted the little living room party, and Atticus barked and limped to the door. The party was not for another three hours. I opened the door to see Jake wearing a navy-blue overcoat and a smile bigger than his legal firm.

"Surprise!"

Yes, this was a surprise. Jake had not called to say he was stopping by.

"Hey! Is the little man here? I want to give him his present on his actual birthday."

Oliver came running. "Daddy!"

"I know we're celebrating next week with Grandpa and Grandma Day, but I've got something for you on the big day. Stay right there. Oh, and close your eyes, buddy."

"Surprise!" Jaymie appeared with a red bicycle with a big blue bow. *Another surprise.*

"A bike?" Oliver hollered.

A bike? Really? My present for Oliver: Royal Rescue, a bridge-building logic game. A big green-bean casseroley type of gift from Mom, a gift designed to develop spatial reasoning abilities and stretch a player's logical thinking skills. Damn, I should have reconsidered getting Oliver a red truck, with a bow.

Jaymie moved the shiny bike into the center of my living room.

"Well, we've got to get going. We have a really busy schedule today." Jake looked at Jaymie. Jaymie shimmered and smiled. "We're heading to the travel agency to plan our trip to Jamaica. I'll need to get you dates."

As abruptly as they had entered with the birthday surprise of red bikes, that darn cologne and the shimmering wife rushed out of the house. *The Jake and Jaymie Show* left for their busy day, leaving behind a little boy who wanted to ride the bike in the house but who was denied that fun. Oliver was mad at me until his party.

Love surprises.

Several hours later, the house was filled with my family, laughing and wishing Oliver a happy birthday. Oliver had insisted that I invite our next-door neighbors Nora and Fred and their spoiled pug. Oliver was the star of the night and was energized by the attention. Two hours after the party started, Oliver's face was red and his eyes glazed with weariness. Nora and Fred were leaving when Oliver came up and gave them each a big hug. "Thank you for the Thomas the Train books. I love Thomas the Train." I was so proud of my gracious little host.

"You bet, Oliver. You'll probably be reading those books yourself soon. You're smart as a whip."

"As a whip." Oliver liked to repeat new expressions after he heard them, almost as if he were tasting them. "As a whip." Oliver then ran back to the dining room, where my mom and dad were picking up wrapping paper and trying to get everyone to have another piece of cake.

"Thanks so much for coming," I repeated.

"Wouldn't have missed it," Fred said as Miss Elsie squirmed in his arms.

"Oh, I almost forgot, before you go. Do you know how I can get hold of the man who owned this house before...me?"

Nora and Fred looked at each other and frowned.

"Bill. I think Bill was his first name. Does that sound right?" I asked.

Fred looked at Nora. "I'm going to take Miss Elsie out for her evening walk. Thanks for the lovely party, Annie."

After Fred left, Nora looked at me. "Annie, Bill died."

"I knew he was pretty old. I think his daughter was at the closing for the house. When did he die?"

"Well, actually...he died the night before they moved him and his stuff out of your place."

"Oh, my gosh..."

"Those last months...heck, that last year, when they were selling the house, Bill went downhill. Lorna had been gone for almost ten years by then. Annette, their daughter, was at the house every day, helping him and getting the house ready to be sold."

"How did he die?"

"Well, we're not sure. He was so confused in the end. The night he died, the Trainers were outside, and they heard a crash from the attic window and looked up to see Bill there. They called nine one one right away."

"The attic window?"

"When the paramedics came, they didn't even have to break in... Bill had forgotten to lock the doors...it was probably a blessing. Fred was always afraid he was going to burn the place down making dinner...Well, when all the neighbors gathered in the street as they took

Bill away, one paramedic told Fred that Bill had torn the whole attic up and then had taken a chair or a small table or something and threw it through the window like he was trying to get out. Poor thing was just so confused in the end…they think it was a heart attack."

"Wow."

"He was supposed to move to a nursing home…I know that's not what they call them these days…but Annette was setting him up in a place where he would have more care. Why do you ask?"

"Well, we found a box up in the attic. Pictures, documents, and stuff that I'm pretty sure Annette would want. Do you keep in touch with her?"

"Only Christmas cards. I'm sure that the address on our Christmas list is for an address in Olathe, Kansas. Sorry that Fred left like he did, Annie. He just misses Bill. It was so hard to see how things ended for him…"

"I cannot imagine how hard that must have been. Is there any way you can get me Annette's address? I think she would want it."

"Sure. I'll get it to you, Annie. It was a real nice party."

After the party was over, I held Oliver's hand as we walked up the stairs to his room. My family left shouting (for the umpteenth time) happy birthday to a freshly five-year-old boy. I felt Oliver tug at my hand as he whined, "I don't want to go to bed. I want to have another party with all my guys," he whimpered as I opened a drawer to get his *Horton Hears a Who* pajamas. "I want to have another party." Oliver picked up his Smurf stuffed animal and Spiderman action figure from a pile in the corner of his room. "Hey, where's Elf on a Shelf?"

In less than ten seconds, Oliver went into meltdown mode. I could feel it before I could see it. His cheeks turned red, and his mouth clenched as tears poured down his face. "Where's Elf on a Shelf? Where's Elf on a Shelf? I can't have a party without him." I moved toward him to help him. Then the kicking began. I felt a strong kick to my calf as I grabbed Oliver, and I hugged him and wondered why I always had to do this alone.

"We're good." I held Oliver tightly as he threw his pajamas to the floor. I moved him toward his bed, hugging and restraining him.

"No, we're not good!" he yelled. "We're not good. I bet Choochoo stole Elf on a Shelf."

I pulled Oliver down with me to lie down on the bed. I whispered as I brushed my hand softly on his head, "Oh, the weather outside is frightful, but my dear…" I slowed down the movement of my hand rubbing the side of his head as I sang more softly. "Let it snow, let it snow, let it snow…"

Oliver was out. I moved his body, still in his clothes, so I could pull his covers back. I placed Oliver's head on his pillow, took off his glasses, kissed him, and covered him.

Before I turned off Oliver's light, I looked to the pile of "guys" that had been to his birthday/Christmas party on the living room floor earlier that day.

Where was that damn Elf on a Shelf?

Postmeltdown and postlockdown, I grabbed my cell phone and headed to my room. I had a text:

Need to see you soon. Can you meet tonight?

Ah, the Trent Dilemma.

On the one side: a beautiful man who made me feel not unappealing.

On the other side: a hole in the future, as far as I could see.

Recently, I had found Trent to be more and more emotionally needy each time we met. We'd met four times since our kiss in room 213. And we did the same thing: I spent way too much time picking out something fun to wear, we met at an obscure bar, we split an appetizer and had one drink, and then we would kiss in my car, fogging up the windows, and that was it. The last date, he mentioned something that made me nervous. He thought it was time that we take it to the next level. He must have sensed my hesitation.

Take it to the next level? Like go on real dates where people might see us? Like introduce each other to our families and friends? Like let him know that I had a son? Like inform him that I had been married before, and the first guy didn't want to stick around?

Just what was the next level?

I was just fine with kissing status, with no background.

So was I using him?

Probably. If the definition of using someone is spending time with that person but not wanting a future, then I was. I had always scoffed at the users of the world. Why give another person hope? Why lead someone on?

Because I was enjoying myself. The kiss was a just a kiss. Not a promise. Not a contract.

And what about Trent? Was he using me?

I texted back:

Not tonight. Maybe later this week.

Send.

What a bland text. I was relieved that we never talked on the phone.

Ding.

Not sure I can wait. Need your kisses.

Ew.

I liked Trent's kisses but did not like statements like "Need your kisses."

Will let you know when. Stack of papers to correct. Good night.

Send.

Ding.

Not a good night without you.

Ew.

I didn't want to think about what I wanted in a relationship after my long day, which had started with a funeral procession. The fun factor had not been present for me during a day of celebration. My ex had won the Look who Got Oliver the Best Gift Contest. I found out that a man may or may not have died in my attic. My son just had a major postbirthday meltdown. My shin hurt, and a freakish elf was lost in my house, perhaps waiting to pounce on my dreams. Oh, and I had just received several texts that ended my day with nausea.

I looked over to see Atticus standing near my bed looking at me. He moved his chin down to rest on the bed, his nose touching my arm.

(If dogs could talk, what would this saintly retriever, who knew me more than anyone in the world, say?)

Other than that, Mrs. Lincoln, did you enjoy the play?

My cell phone dinged again. I ignored it.

The shuffling sounds started up in the attic. I ignored them.

16

"Skeletons in the Closet"
The Summer of 1938

Rollie

Skeletons in the closet.

In time—once I figured out what my mom meant about those skeletons—I heard enough stories about Ms. Maribel Winters's skeletons to keep my brain busy late at night. I lay on my cot in the small room I shared with my parents and battled visions in my head that I just couldn't unsee.

I can't hear so well today, but I heard plenty from the adult conversations about Maribel Winters that summer—and no two stories seemed connected.

Uncle Emmett told some other ranchers that he had heard that Maribel had gone to be a star in a picture show and gotten pregnant by the director, who was already married. Toby was the secret affair baby.

Some big lady in a flowered dress who talked too loud told her other big friend outside of the church on Sunday that Maribel had been a lady of the night—didn't know what that meant, but it sounded mysterious—and had to run from a town in California before the law caught up with her.

Dorothy from Bob's Groceries told the delivery guy that Maribel Winters was just a fake name and that Maribel's real name was Trixie LaMay. Newspapers said LaMay had killed her abusive husband with an ax while he slept, fled from Oklahoma, and come to Colorado to start a new life.

One closet with a heck of a lot of skeletons.

The story mom told Uncle Billy is the one I chose to believe, though I wished they were all just big lies. I heard my mom telling Billy that Maribel's sister, the woman who was letting Maribel and Toby stay with them, said that Maribel's husband in Texas had almost beat her to death, so she took her son and slowly traveled town by town, getting work here and there, hiding from the alcoholic abuser. She finally made it to Colorado and was trying to lie low.

In a small town during the Great Depression with not too much going on, Maribel gave Brush, Colorado, something to talk about.

17

Annie

"Boo! Did I scare you? It kind of looked like I scared you there." Lyle appeared to have washed his hair and tucked his shirt in, which looked comical on him. I could hear Nadine narrating the scene: "You can put lipstick on a pig; it's still a pig."

"No, I saw you there." I stapled the last few handouts before class started.

"Well, I was just in the area and thought I'd check in."

"OK." The hair on the back of my neck was standing straight out.

"Just want to make sure you're still behavin'."

"Yep."

The bell rang.

"Well, you have yourself a good one, Mrs. Day."

Kids moved into the room on either side of Lyle; the greased-up pig looked a little overwhelmed by the teenager ambush. I prayed that Lyle would not come and see me again, alone. He slithered out into the hallway through the bodies pouring into the room.

"Wow, Ms. Day," Mike Sheridan said as Lyle left. "Can I just say that you could do so much better."

"All set for the final next week?" I changed the subject quickly.

"I am. Have to be honest, though." Students moved in quickly. Most sat down and opened notebooks. "Got a little distracted last night. Back-to-back Christmas specials on ABC Family. I'm like, you're killing me. *Holiday in Handcuffs* and then *The Santa Clause*. A two-fer-one. Doesn't make it easy during finals week."

"Seriously?" K-Mart, who usually remained quiet during silly banter, was joining the preclass discussion. "You still watch Christmas specials?"

"Whoa, K-Mart. Why the sass? Of course I do. I've been counting down the days to Christmas on ABC Family. It's dope."

James spoke while still looking over his notes. "You do all realize that Mike had a portal to Halloween Town in the back of his closet until seventh grade."

"Still do," Mike said with a grin. "You guys are just jealous. My dilemma next week is that the night before the English test, the movie with the snow globe...can't remember the name...is on."

"*Snowglobe*," Katrina said.

"That's what I said."

"No, the name of the show is just that: *Snowglobe*."

"So you do like the Christmas shows, K-Mart." Mike pointed to Katrina.

"I haven't seen them in years."

"It might do you good if you watched a few of them now. I know they're cheesy, but I'm not gonna lie. Sometimes I just find myself in the mood for a little back-to-the-classics cheese. This is the best time of the year."

"Now that you're all seated and thinking of Christmas specials, I want you to shift gears and get out the study guide for the first-semester final I gave you last week." Period Two complied as I continued. "I want to help you to prepare for a final. The study guide is helpful, but how can I help you study for the next test better?"

A hand went up. Arty smiled.

"Arty?"

"I'm just thinking that an omelet chef or waffle bar in in our study halls might help. Just throwing it out. I know I'd study better and be more prepared for finals."

The class laughed. "I'll send that one to the principal for consideration. Not sure it will pass. Love the energy, though."

Katrina raised her hand.

"Katrina?"

"Do you know when our final grades will be posted online?"

"I usually post my final grades the last day of finals."

"You'll have all of our tests corrected by then?" Arty asked. "Our history teacher takes forever to correct our tests."

"I don't leave until I'm done correcting them the last day." For sanity's sake, I finished the tests so I could get home and enjoy my break with Oliver.

"Wow. How do you get done so fast?"

"Not my first rodeo," I said as I caught a smile from Donovan, the gentle giant slouched in the seat in front of me.

"Why do we even waste time taking finals?" The voice came from Phil Timmerman, in the back of the room. "I mean, seriously, how is reading *The Great Gatsby* and memorizing the characters and themes going to make me a better doctor or businessman someday? Why do we even need to study English?"

"That's because Ms. Day here," LaTrey said, "is the queen. Don't you remember? And don't forget that dinner party."

Phil continued. "Memorizing vocabulary. Knowing what a participle phrase is. Why? And why do we take time to read all this literature from all these dead guys?"

Students looked at Phil and then at me.

"Valid questions, Phil."

"And?" Mike Sheridan prompted, his arms folded over his chest.

"And...let's just take it piece by piece. Let's start with the grammar. Phil, let's say you're a doctor someday. You're going to be communicating daily with staff and patients, and often that communication will be through e-mail. Would you want to be that one doctor who communicates poorly? Or the doctor everyone cringes at as they read all of the mistakes in his e-mails to the staff? I mean, it's great to speak casually or *slangish* with your friends, but you'll need some skills to write well."

"Can I get an amen?" Arty yelled and clapped. "Give her the point."

"And," I continued, "the same would go for vocabulary. I call them 'power words' because stronger vocabulary gives you integrity. Others will find merit in what you have to say. And the literature—"

"The dead guys," Phil interrupted.

"The dead people from literature that we study are relevant. I always look at literature as studying the personal side of history. In your history class this year, you are reading about what happened, in general. In this class, we're connecting to those people from the different eras. And it's almost as if they're speaking from the grave…They may be a hundred or two hundred years away from us, but they're just like us."

"But!" James wanted to get in his two cents worth. "Why are those dead guys worth studying for a final more than, say, our Belmont bones, the people whose bones have been showing up on athletic fields?"

"Because our Belmont bones ain't talking; that's why," Peaches said.

"Ain't," Kinkaid mumbled, "ain't a word."

"Is it, Ms. Day? Is 'ain't' a word?" Arty asked.

"Yes, it is, but it's probably the most stigmatized word in the language. Enough stalling for one day. Now, let's turn to the last page of your study guide. I have a checklist you can use as you study for my final." I looked over at Mike Sheridan, who didn't have his study guide out yet. "Are you with me, Mike? You ready to review for the final?"

"Not my first rodeo, Ms. Day." Mike winked as he pulled out his study guide.

That night, a Friday night when I knew that not one of my students, not even K-Mart, would be worrying about the final I was giving the next week, Ellie, my little junior high babysitter, came over with her backpack and a smile bigger than puberty to watch Oliver while I went to the Belmont High staff holiday party. The football coach and his wife usually hosted the party every year the weekend before the last week of school for the semester.

"Wow, Ellie. You brought your backpack? I'm impressed." Oliver tried to pick up Ellie's backpack.

"Well, once Oliver goes down, I want to start studying for my finals." Ellie was definitely on the other side of the river from me, full of hope sprinkled with good intentions, void of disappointment and emotional accidents.

"I wish my students were that devoted. I won't be too late, and Oliver can stay up a little later tonight."

"Yes!" Oliver cheered as he gave up on the heavy backpack and went over to hold Ellie's hand.

"I brought a few games too, Oliver. I thought we could play them after you eat your dinner."

Even though I had left dinner for Ellie and Oliver to heat up, I had not eaten. So after I picked up a bottle of wine for the host couple, I ran into the Bagel Bin to grab a little something to keep me from stuffing myself on appetizers at the party.

"Lame on lame." The nice-looking young man behind the bagel counter smiled as he spoke to me. His name tag read Jason.

I looked behind me. No one was there.

"Lame on lame. Plain cream cheese on a plain bagel, untoasted. Isn't that what you usually order? You can't get more lame than that."

I laughed as I pulled out my wallet. "Yep. You have my order right."

"Didn't you used to be a teacher at Belmont High School?"

"Still am. Pretty lame, right?"

"Plead the fifth."

I paid and took my bagel out to my car to sit—just sit and take a breath. I started the car, took my lame bagel out of the bag, and took a big bite.

Could I be more lame?

I took another bite as I listened to the rhythm of the windshield wipers teasing me: Loser, so lame. Loser, so lame.

I looked beyond my windshield wipers. The beautiful snow was coming down in gigantic flakes, and the headlights of cars as the night took over the city reflected on those flakes. A beautiful snow. I took a big bite of my bagel. I decided right then and there that I would work harder at no longer being known by the bagel kid for my lame order. I would try new things. I would no longer be lame. I pulled a little wine bag from the backseat that I had brought from home and put the wine bottle in the bag. I grabbed a pen from my purse to sign the card on the bag.

Merry Christmas! Annie Day

I took one last bite of my bagel and started the car. I looked up to see a license plate on an old gold van; it read TAG 250. A beautiful woman with short dark hair got out of the car. She opened the van to help a little girl, about five years old, a smaller version of the woman, jump out of the van. The little girl stopped, looked up at the huge snowflakes floating around her, and stuck her tongue out. On the driver's side of TAG 250, the father appeared to be helping another child out of the car. His back to me, he held the little boy, maybe a year, up in the air and then pulled him back. The child laughed and hugged his father's neck. The scene tugged at my ever-so-lame heart.

The American Dream.

The little scene reminded me once again that I had failed in attaining that dream. *At Christmas time we can take the kids with us as we run errands before the holidays get too hectic. Let's grab bagels before we head to the mall.* This little family had no way of knowing that they had hit the jackpot. They had it all.

The father put a hat on the boy and then turned to shut the van door: Trent Kula.

Trent Kula. (And yes, I'm being redundant.)

Trent Kula.

The illusion of the American Dream.

The corruption of the American Dream.

My stomach buckled. I had been dating a married man, and the thought made me want to throw up my lame bagel in my lame car and cry about my lame life. Sure, I hadn't shared specifics in my life, such as having a son or having been married before. That was part of the fun. I could pretend to be normal. But he had spared me a few important details: a wife and two kids.

Could he be *more* lame?

Could I be more lame?

I got to the Christmas party at 1027 West Cherry Plaza late.

On purpose.

In and out. Make an appearance. And then go home and sulk about my Trent Kula discovery.

Single people love going to parties (heavy sarcasm) where people bring spouses and significant others. Do you not have a significant other in your life? *I do, but he has a 7:45 bedtime. You got a problem with that? Oh, and I used to have secret dates with a married man, but let's not count that.*

I walked into Coach Edwards's beautiful home after I shook the snow from my coat. Cassie Edwards, the effervescent wife of Coach Edwards, stood at the door. Her red sweater sparkled, and her teeth were whiter than the snow. "Hey, Annie, let me take your coat."

"Thanks for having the holiday party again." I handed her my gift bag with a bottle of wine.

"We love having staff over. Please, grab a plate in the dining room."

I searched the house for any sign of Nadine. I would talk to her for a while and then head home to pout about the fact that I had been romantically duped. I would give no hint of my rattled mood. While I'd much rather be in my pajamas watching Christmas specials with Oliver, I didn't want to become the teacher who doesn't go to teacher events and then complains about the staff not being unified.

In the main room, near the fireplace, Nadine and her husband, Hank, waved to me. As I got closer, I could see Nadine's red face and her glazed eyes. Hank gave me a she's-had-a-bit-too-much-to-drink look.

"Annie, you got here. I was afraid you'd chicken out on us." Nadine moved toward me and gave me a big hug. Nadine was not a hugger. She smelled like peppermint. "Where the hell have you been?"

"Running errands and had a hard time leaving Oliver with the sitter."

"Liar." Nadine stepped back and grabbed a drink from the mantel and tapped the side of her glass. "Is this thing on?" She spoke into the glass. "Testing: one, two, three…"

Hank shook his head. "Evidently the Coach Edwards makes a mean sleigh-ride jingle-jangle juice: peppermint something with a little more than something. Nadine never knew she liked sleigh rides so much."

"Not Nadine," Nadine slurred. "Buddy Pickle-Pants. My elf name." She pulled out a piece of paper from her pocket. "OK, so my yearbook staff was reading everyone's elf name as we worked on our first-semester deadline today. Just follow this chart." I had never seen Nadine in the state she was in, which at the moment wasn't Nebraska. Nadine had always been to me the picture of self-control. Maybe a peppermint sleigh ride was just what she needed after a busy semester. "OK, so all you have to do is take the first letter of your name and the month you were born and look at this little chart, and, so Annie, your elf name would be…Perky Plum-Pants."

I laughed.

A laugh felt good in lieu of the recent encounter with a secret man I'd been dating. See the good, see the silver lining: you were eventually going to end things anyway.

"And Hank here…" Nadine put her arms around her husband. "Hank is…tell her, Hank."

"Tootsie Sweet-Buns." Hank smiled and toasted the air. "I guess that would be Officer Tootsie Sweet-Buns at your service." Hank was an Omaha policeman and one of the nicest guys I knew.

I laughed again. I hadn't laughed a lot with Trent. Wonder what his elf name would be: Naughty Liar-Pants?

"Isn't it perfect? Isn't it a perfect elf name for my little elf husband?" Nadine's ornament earrings bobbed back and forth as she shook her head.

Hank interrupted. "How's that attic project going? Nadine told me you and your dad were working on some project."

"And she's also going to start dating the new assistant football coach too..." Nadine slurred.

Hank looked at me. I shook my head no. We both smiled.

"Oh, wait, there's another chart." Nadine pulled her finger to lips. "Shhh, this one I didn't hear about from my students."

"Another one? But we already had so much fun already with the elf chart."

"I don't have a piece of paper, but that's OK. It's right here." Nadine pointed to the side of her head. "The Stripper Name Chart is in my head."

"What?" Hank said. "I guess I should be a little concerned..."

"OK, so you take the name of your first childhood pet and the name of the first street you lived on, and, even if those two things don't sound inappropriate alone, you'll be surprised how bad they sound when you put them together. They make the perfect name for you if you decide to become a stripper. You first, Hank. First pet?"

"What if I don't want a stripper name?" Hank pouted.

"Oh, but you'll think it's funny. Childhood pet—go!"

"And I have no choice on this...OK, Chipper."

"Name of first street...this is going to be good."

"Happy Hollow."

"Hah, see! Chipper Happy Hollow...do you not just love that?" The staff of Belmont High School was celebrating the holiday around us while Nadine, Hank, and I had our own little party. "OK, Annie, you're up. First pet?"

"Ok, a little nervous here...Prudence."

"First street."

"Parker."

"Oh my gosh! Prudence Parker," Nadine spit. "That's crazy! Prudence Parker!" Nadine shouted my stripper name. "That's perfect."

"Look at you with the perfect stripper name," Hank said.

"Could I just stay with the elf name? I don't want to be Prudence Parker."

Hank tried to be the voice of reason. "Perky Plum-Pants sounds even more like a stripper name."

Terrence Bromberg, a quiet history teacher with whom I had never once had a conversation, moved toward us from across the living room with a frantic glaze in his eyes, I suspect more from the sleigh-ride drinks than the holiday spirit. What I knew was that Nadine found the history department fixture pompous and annoying.

"Oh no," Nadine said. "Here comes trouble. Wonder what Bromberg's elf name…"

"Ladies, ladies, ladies…"

"Guess that makes me a lady," Hank mumbled and grinned at me.

"Relax, Chipper," I whispered.

"I need to tell you English teachers about the article I just read. Absolutely fascinating." Terrence wore short-sleeved work shirts and ties to school every day. His tie was crooked that night, and I wanted to reach out and fix it. "Hamlet. The skull. Have you heard?"

Nadine wasted no time. "Sure, uh, let's see…Hamlet…heck of a guy; has some problems, though; stumbles upon his childhood jester Yorick being unburied. Reflects on mortality as he holds the skull. Read it in the paper yesterday. 'Looking Death in the Face,' film at eleven…"

"So you read the article?"

"Terrence, I read the play. Your point?"

"The article was about the real skull used in the Stratford-upon-Avon showing of *Hamlet* the past few months. Fascinating, really. A fake skull is typically used in the scene on stage. This year, in England, a man donated his skull, which he specifically donated in his will to be used in the play."

"That's disgusting," Hank grumbled.

"He actually donated it in his will years ago. The donor was a pianist named Andre Tchaikowsky, who died in 1982 and wanted it to be used onstage for all these years, and finally—Tchaikowsky, not to be confused with Tchaikovsky, the great pianist whose overture-fantasia 'Hamlet,' inspired by Shakespeare's *Hamlet*—"

"Wait!" Nadine leaned one arm against a chair and held the other one up. "I object. Are you making this up, Ter-Bear?"

Terrence put his hand over his crooked tie and heart. "Scout's honor. The cast tried to keep it a secret this past fall until the lead guy let the cat out of the bag. Or the skull out of the play, as it were."

"As it were," Nadine said and giggled. She never would have taunted Terrence without the help of her sleigh rides.

Chipper Hank said, "If I may—"

"If I may," Nadine said.

Hank continued. "Is that even legal? Using a human skull in a play? I'm sure there's a—"

"With or without any legal stipulations, the RSC confirmed that they're not using the skull anymore, despite the dead guy's wishes. Turns out, audiences were also a bit creeped out after they found out. Nonetheless, the representative of the skull owner was 'disappointed' by the decision." A puddle of spit sat at the side of Terrence's mouth. He needed to stop talking and swallow.

"Nonetheless..." Nadine mumbled.

Note to self:

If I ever decide to write a play for Broadway, I'd like to explore the uncharted waters of uptight high school teachers letting their guard down when the sleigh rides flow.

Tipsy Teachers.

The New York Times says, "Annie Day hits one out of the park in Tipsy Teachers. *Elf names? Stripper names? Who knew our old English and history teachers could be clever. You'll never be able to look at your high school teachers in the same way after watching* Tipsy Teachers. *Inappropriate fun at its best. We laughed; we cried."*

"And you read this where?" I asked. I was curious how I had never read anything about the Hamlet skull.

"In the *Daily Telegraph*, a British newspaper. I read it online after a friend of mine e-mailed me about the whole incredible story."

"Alas, poor Yorick." Nadine held her cup up and toasted the absent skull. "You know, Shakespeare was pretty clever. Here's a scene where Hamlet realizes that a lowly jester and a king, who in life were in different social levels, were both going to die. Death is the great equalizer—the simple jester and the bones of the great king, when dead, are both just that: dead and bones…"

"I thought you two would find it fascinating, you know, since you're English teachers, and, well, the skull thing being timely, in lieu of our bones…" Terrence swallowed. Finally.

Our bones. The Belmont Bones.

The past several months and the unfortunate attention to the findings on our campus had forced the Belmont community to identify with our bones. Our Belmont Bones. Even other schools made note of that sinister identity as they held up posters at football games in our stadium that announced We're Stomping through the Belmont Boneyard or Make no Bones about It—We're Here to Win. Really morbid if you sat down for five minutes and thought about it. But I suppose joking about death is what you call a good, old-fashioned coping mechanism—compartmentalizing. Let's put this horrific idea of death—and the fact that we will all die—in a box and ignore it.

If you can't laugh, you'll go crazy thinking about the fact that some people had died, and, well, someone was playing with their bones and teasing our community with their deaths. That was what it felt like. You want to mess with us, we can handle it: we'll joke about it. Though still macabre, joking was better than facing the idea of someone moving bones around to threaten us.

"But, in other news," Terrence continued. "My daughter Eileen—remember, Nadine? You had her in class. She graduated from SLU last year and just got a job as an underwear model…but not like the Victoria's Secret kind. Like the JCPenney Sunday ads section. Leslie and I couldn't be more proud."

I looked at Nadine, who was ready to say something she might regret in the teachers' lunchroom on Monday. I tried to save the moment. "Terrence, could you show me where I can get one of the sleigh rides?"

"Oh, right over in the kitchen, right by the...oh, hey, Mark...could you excuse me for a sec?" Terrence moved toward the kitchen, where Mark was monitoring the sleigh-ride table. Next to Mark was Nick Stander, the new coach. I hoped that Nadine wouldn't see him and make a big deal about setting us up. I didn't have the heart to tell her that I had seen him with what looked like a wife in Costco. It would break her little Buddy Pickle-Pants heart.

"Oh, hey, Terrence!" Nadine shouted across the crowded room. "What's the name of your first pet?"

Hank placed his arm on Nadine's arm and whispered, "We probably need to head home. I've got to run into work for a bit in the morning." I would have to wonder for the rest of my life what Terrence Bromberg's stripper name was.

Nadine's head moved down into her hands. When she brought her head up, she looked me straight in the eyes. "How'm I gonna get through Christmas without her, Annie?"

I looked at Hank.

He mouthed, *her mom.* Talking about the great equalizer, death, in Hamlet had Nadine reflecting on her own mother's death.

"My first Christmas without her..." Madonna's version of "Santa Baby" was playing around us with the voices of teachers venting and sharing end-of-semester stories.

The dramatic sighting of my freshly ex-yet-married-boyfriend and my weekly episodes of *The Jake and Jaymie Show* seemed trivial and petty when compared to the load that Nadine had been carrying the past year as she juggled caring for her sick mother and then burying her. I knew from my years at Belmont that Nadine and her mother had been best friends.

"You were so good to her." I could think of nothing else to say.

"I just...miss her." Nadine wiped her tears as Hank held her coat out for her. Beyond Nadine and Hank, Nick Stander moved toward the door to leave. He stopped and shook Coach Edwards's hand and then left the house.

Are you heading home to your wife, Mr. Stander? To your sister? What are you hiding?

Seems like everyone's hiding something these days.

"We'll need to get together over break," Hank said as he put his own coat on. Nadine started walking toward the door. "Thanks for understanding this unusual little evening, Annie."

"Hey, you can call me Perky Plum-Pants, if you want," I said as I pulled out my car keys from my pocket.

"Only if you promise never to call me Chipper Happy Hollow. Deal?"

"Deal." The three of us walked to the front door, leaving the tipsy teachers and their holiday cheer.

Coach Edwards said to us, "Careful on the drive home. Snow's really starting to come down."

Hank and Nadine's car was just on the curb in front of the house. "Want us to drive you to your car, Annie?"

"I'm just a little farther down. See you Monday, Nadine."

"See you, Annie." Nadine sniffed.

The beauty of the snow coming down was illuminated by the street-lights. My problems were little. I just needed a little perspective slap in the face every now and then. Thanks to Nadine, I decided that I was going to have an awesome weekend with my little Oliver and his sidekick Atticus. As I unlocked my door, I looked up, and something or someone moved by a car several houses from where I was parked. A figure, looked like a man, moved to open his door and got in. From the silhouette, I did not see who it was, but the man, who appeared to be looking at me, did not acknowledge me.

I drove home, paid my sitter, and settled into my bedroom.

Before I crawled into bed that night, I turned the TV on for company. The commercial playing was a Christmas jewelry commercial. A man held a package with a big red bow and smiled an extra-cheesy smile at a beautiful woman walking into the room. She saw the present and opened the box and pulled out a heart necklace and then kissed the man.

Can you have more cheese?

Every kiss begins with Kay.

I wondered if the cheese man on the commercial had any secrets from the woman he was kissing.

My phone buzzed as a text came in from Trent. I picked it up from my side table and read:

Thinking of you.

I was disgusted.

I set the phone down. I decided life would be easier if I just went back to my relationship with my cowboy ghost, my good and hardworking, and probably very honest, cowboy ghost.

My *Dateline* Cowboy, Keith Morrison, was serenading me from my TV set. I didn't need Trent Kula. Keith stood against the backdrop of a barn and squinted. He looked straight at me and beckoned: "It looked to be an open and shut case...clear as day...but if that were true, we wouldn't be telling you this story, now, would we?"

My phone buzzed again.

I decided to swallow the big frog and reply, quick and short and honest: *I need to stop seeing you.*

Nothing more.

As I finished my date with my *Dateline* Cowboy, I turned out the lights. As soon as my head hit the pillow, the attic shuffling began. My last thoughts before I slept that night were of Terrence Bromberg's crooked tie and the man standing by his car after the party.

That night I had rambling, strange dreams.

About a king and his jester.

And a crazy elf.

18

"The Cowboy Code"
The Summer of 1938

Rollie

Well, that summer alone, I bet I had my ears cut off at least a hundred times.

"First I'll cut your right ear off, and then I'll cut off your left." Truett did love to torment me. He'd yell, "Rollie, get over here!"

Now, I'd do just about anything that Truett asked me to do. Truett would grab me and then get my head down between his knees where I couldn't see anything. His knees held my head down tightly, and I could hear him get his knife out and open it. I'd holler for my mom, and she would be off in the kitchen doing dishes. She knew the routine. She'd say nothing. I think she was laughing.

Ever so slowly, Truett moved. I could feel the blade on my ear, and I could feel the blood run down my neck. It didn't hurt as much as I thought it would. But maybe ears don't hurt all that much.

When Truett finally let me loose, I'd run to the mirror by the front door and see if my ears were gone. They were both still there.

When I got older, I watched as he cut off the ears of my younger cousins, and I could see that he had a handkerchief with warm water. And the knife he used? Well, it was just his thumbnails. He'd wink at me as my cousins wailed.

I winked back.

I think Truett could see I was anxious to be a part of it all, the cowboy world. He told me I could have Old Charley, a horse about thirty years old or so. I'm pretty sure he bought me a kid saddle, and he showed me how to put it on Old Charley and loosely cinch it. Truett even drew me up a bill of sale. Wonder where that piece of paper went. I'd give $1,000 for that bill of sale today. With Charley, I got a clear rule: don't run him, or he will die.

One day, as I was riding him to the old barn, Old Charley started to trot. I think it was even a little boring for him, walking around all day. I reined in, but he probably trotted a hundred more feet. That night, when Truett came in, I told him what had happened, stammering and practically bawling. "It's OK if Charley wants to trot, even if he's tired, but we just won't run him."

I took turns tagging after one uncle, then the other, asking questions about all the things they did. I guess you could say I could be annoying. I could always tell if it was a good question or a bad one. They didn't answer the bad ones. You had to be careful about the answers you got from Truett, though. Sometimes he would not completely tell the truth, and sometimes he just flat out fibbed. If Emmett was around, he'd scold Truett and then grin as he walked away.

Sometimes he lied.

Truett was a good liar.

During the weeks that we stayed at the Genoa Place, I'd start my day by looking out the window for some sign of one of the uncles working around the corrals. "Stay close to the fence, and don't get in the way." Sometimes, when the uncles were branding or doctoring cattle, they would call me over and have me hold the head. I'd get a lot of advice as I lay down the head of a yearling calf: "Don't let go, or Emmett will get killed," Truett would say. "Ear him down if he starts to get up," another would add. "Keep his nose up."

All of the comments were rules that I stored away for future use. There were a lot of rules:

1. Keep your reins in your left hand.
2. Sit straight. You won't get tired, and you look better.
3. Keep tight reins, or the horse will be boss.
4. Take good care of your rope; stretch it out once in a while.
5. Check your cinch after you've ridden a few minutes. A horse will swell up when you saddle him.
6. Don't gallop or run your horse without a reason.
7. If you're not going to use him for a while, either unsaddle or loosen the cinch and take the bit out of his mouth.
8. Never expect a new horse to like it when you groom him. Be gentle and respectful while grooming your horse.

But I knew the other rules of cowboys, the ones that were never spoken, the ones about life. Every cowboy on the Genoa Place knew the code, from where I stood. There was a Cowboy Code, and I can tell you that from all the rules I learned from my uncles, the rules of the Cowboy Code have served me best in life.

1) Treat children and animals with the same respect as you would your mama.
2) Be real good to your mama.
3) If you think you've worked as hard as you can, work harder.
4) Give a hand to the less fortunate.
5) Leave the workplace in better condition than when you got there.
6) Don't take crap from bullies.
7) If you can't take a joke, who needs ya.
8) A good laugh can fix any problem.

9) Try not to cuss in front of ladies.
10) Don't lie unless you're being polite, telling a really good story, or teasing a relative.
11) Don't complain.
12) Ever.
13) At the end of the day, be good with God.
14) Just don't talk too much about it.

My uncles lived by the code.
The summer of 1938.
I watched.
I learned.

19

Annie

I'm not sure what the etiquette is for kicking out imaginary friends, but I was so close to calling the National Imaginary Friend Hotline at 6:42 a.m. on a Wednesday that I needed to put myself in timeout.

Choochoo had crossed the line.

My patience was being challenged as I felt a nonstop annoyance with a not-even-real person named Choochoo and with a man I barely knew who pushed lip gloss to cheerleaders for a living. The Trent Kula Factor and the Choochoo Factor came together that cold morning in December to create the perfect storm.

"Choochoo says he doesn't want me to go to school today." Oliver was sleepy as he spooned a mouthful of Cheerios into his mouth. He was dressed in a red sweater with a snowman woven into the wool. Daycare, or "school," had always been Oliver's favorite time of the day.

"Well, Choochoo needs to worry more about Choochoo and less about Oliver." My words, loud and clipped, were out of my mouth, filled with rage.

Oliver tilted his head as his lips pouted. His big blue eyes fogged over with tears behind his crooked glasses.

"I'm sorry, Oliver." I got up and hugged him from behind. "I guess I'm just a little frustrated with Choochoo right now. I'm not upset with you. You have your Christmas concert today and tonight. You wouldn't want to miss that, would you?"

I felt bad for my seething resentment of an imaginary friend who had made us late to church most Sunday mornings, moved Oliver's books around the house, and told Oliver that broccoli wasn't a real food.

"Choochoo doesn't like you."

My cell phone dropped to the floor. I had just texted Annette Graham in Olathe, Kansas, regarding the box. Nora had given me the correct address and phone number for Annette a few days earlier. Inappropriate Catholic guilt or a small house with barely enough room for my own boxes had me chomping at the bit to hand off the treasure box with the interesting letter. I had left a message as Oliver and I had been eating breakfast. I was beginning to think that Annette was just an imaginary friend since I was having such a hard time contacting her.

Imaginary friends help some children handle changes. For others, their make-believe friends or creatures are simply whimsical. Whatever purpose an imaginary friend serves and whatever form one takes, fantasy friends point toward a productive imagination that's more likely to belong to a child who is firstborn or one with no siblings.

I had read several articles on imaginary friends over the past several months. Psychologists from all different articles sounded off about the good, the bad, and the ugly of make-believe friends. The bottom line was that the annoying bonus friend would soon just fade away as maturity and development moved a child on to the next phase. Oliver was five, a typical age for children with imaginary friends. He was also an only child who was super adept at playing alone, all common traits of children who have an imaginary pal. The main suggestions to parents: don't worry, and don't react.

Which I had just done over breakfast.

Choochoo didn't like me? What universe was Choochoo living in, anyway?

Don't answer.

I looked behind the coffee table to find my briefcase full of essays and tests. I walked toward the coat closet to get my coat as Oliver was pulling his coat out. "What do you want for dinner tonight? Maybe we can make breakfast for dinner."

"Yes!" Oliver jumped up and down. He held out his hand for a high five. I complied.

"Yes!" I shouted.

"I'm Oliver True, and how do you do. Oliver True, and how do you do..." Oliver sang as he skipped toward the back door and grabbed his little backpack.

Just like that, Choochoo was no longer a part of our conversation.

"I can't wait for my program. I'm in the front row," Oliver said as Atticus came in the door.

"I can't wait!" I said as I grabbed my keys.

The rest of the day was uneventful, and I was grateful. An end-of-the-semester lull meant that teenagers were just going through the motions with winter break on the horizon. While elementary school kids were excited and energetic before break, high school students were complacent and tired.

Eight periods.

Day done.

Gina Shatner sat slumped down in the first seat of the middle row. The empty room wrapped the two of us in that end-of-the-school-day relief. I wiped the dry-erase board as I broke the silence.

"I guess we can focus on finals now. Gina, if you get an eighty percent on your final, you'll pass the semester. I don't see that being any problem. What do you think?"

Gina shrugged.

Gina was still at the point in her pregnancy where students around her held expressions that questioned, *Is she pregnant, or did she just put on some extra pounds?* Their faces spoke of reactions to Gina's transformation from va-va-voom cheerleader to pretty darn close to my homeless lady in Home Depot look. Tears flooded Gina's big green eyes as she looked up at me. "I can't do this anymore."

"Well, we could always work on that last essay you need to do," I said. "We don't have to study for finals today."

"I can't do this." Gina spread her arms out to the room. She pulled her hair away from her face and wiped her pregnant tears on her oversized sweatshirt. "I can't see him in the hall and know that he doesn't care for me."

I said nothing but must have looked like a giant question mark.

"Jason Monahan," Gina yelled. "I can't take seeing his face in the halls anymore. I'm dying here. Can't anyone see I'm dying? You have no idea how I'm feeling."

First of all: wow, a whole heck of a lot of drama.

Second: you really think I don't know about rejection and pain and seeing a lost love on a regular basis, as if some bully were kicking sand in your face, again and again? Gina and I had more in common than I had thought.

"That would be frustrating." Statement to Gina: safe and honest.

"He loved me sophomore year. He really did. Jason said he loved me. I was a cheerleader. He was the quarterback. He used to say that we were the perfect couple." Gina ran her fingers through her hair again, her tears pouring stronger than ever. "That's what he told me."

"What you crying about, girl?" Peaches Trumble stood in the doorway.

The Afternoon Club was complete. For the most part, conversation was pleasant in a my-toothache-doesn't-hurt-as-bad kind of way. I still knew that Gina didn't particularly like me, and I still (even though I wanted to be bigger than that) resented the boring factor that Gina might still see in me.

Gina sniffed. "Life."

"Oh, don't you even get me started, girl."

"I see him every day," Gina cried. "I mean, I'm walking down the hall today…and there he is, ten feet from my locker, flirting with Hillary Volk."

"You're just a hot mess, girl. Don't have time to listen to any stories of immature, self-absorbed men. So, just when is this baby due?"

And there it was: the truth.

Even I had not talked to Gina about her pregnancy, only about getting her "caught up."

"May. Sometime in May. I can't even think about that." Gina sniffed.

"You keeping the baby or putting it up for adoption?" Peaches asked.

"Not sure." Gina's sobs again filled the room, and Peaches and I moved in unison, like a life-saving machine toward the dying patient. We got to Gina at the same time, and we both stopped and stood near her: that awkward moment when you're not sure if hugging would send someone into another crying episode.

Peaches sat down in the chair of the desk next to Gina. I leaned back against my desk.

"I'm not ready to be a mom. This poor kid didn't ask to be here…" Gina sobbed and then looked up at me. "Is it tough being a single mom, Ms. Day?"

And there it was: another truth.

I had pretended to be an invisible elephant. The elephant had been called out.

"Well, sure…"

I hadn't written down "single parent" on my goals in high school when a jubilant counselor encouraged us to think about what we wanted to be when we grew up. Gina's question put me in a delicate spot. I didn't want to be accused of giving advice to students, especially a pregnant one who was deciding the fate of her unborn child. "My situation is very different from yours…I think you have to do what's best for Gina, and only you know what that is."

"I'm not stupid." Gina screamed. Her voice bounced off every corner of room 213, trying to find a place to settle. She looked at me.

"I know that," I said.

"I mean it. I'm not stupid. I mean, earlier when I was flunking your class, that wasn't me. I was in Honors English both freshman and sophomore years."

"You were stupid enough to get pregnant from a jerk," Peaches said as she pulled out books from her backpack.

Gina and I stopped and stared at Peaches.

Peaches looked up. "What?" Peaches flashed a big smile, the first smile I'd witnessed from this anomaly before us. "Just trying to lighten things up around here. Way too serious."

Gina smiled, the first smile I'd witnessed from this former beauty queen.

"You would be stupid," Peaches continued, "if you let this guy or situation hold you back or control you. I'm not kidding about that."

Gina sniffed. I cleared my throat.

"You're bigger than that." The number of words coming from Peaches was more than all of the words she had said the past semester. "This is not the end of the world. Girl, I've known so many pregnant teens in my life that screwed it all up, my own mom included. Peaches. The woman named a baby Peaches Alabama Tremble, OK? I'm not embarrassed to be named after a fruit...but Alabama? We have no connections to Alabama. My mom had never even visited Alabama. She had to be high on her ever-comforting meth to name a baby after an irrelevant state. Why couldn't she have named me Mary or Marie...didn't happen. I guess when you're high all the time, you can't name a child anything normal...it wouldn't make sense. The rest of the women in my life—not counting my grandma—are making fun of me right now for wanting to go to college. Now, that's messed up. My cousin is my age and has three babies. She can't even take care of them. Stupid women everywhere. You're not stupid..."

"I'm not," Gina said again and then looked at me. "I'm not stupid."

"She's not stupid," Peaches repeated.

"I know that." I stopped there since I sensed Gina was venting rather than attacking.

Gina looked down at her folded hands in her lap. "My family thinks the Shatners have to be so smart. My dad is a doctor. My mom works as a surgical nurse. One brother is in law school, the other premed. And then..." The waterworks started up again. "Me: the pregnant girl who ruined my dad's perfect, practical, and professional plan. My dad didn't talk to me for two weeks after my mom told him I was pregnant. How does a pregnant teenager figure into that perfect plan?"

Peaches started to speak, but Gina continued. "And my girlfriends, well—who used to be my girlfriends—they said they'd stick by me through this whole thing, but..." Gina threw her hands in the air. "Do you see them anywhere?"

Peaches and I did not answer.

"No, I certainly don't." Gina was on a roll. "They moved on as if we haven't been friends since kindergarten. We were all going to be in one another's weddings. We were going to have babies together...Do you see them? Do you see those friends?"

Peaches raised her hand.

"What?" Gina screamed.

"Is that a rhetorical question, or do you really want us to answer? I mean, since you keep asking if we see those girls, 'cause I sure don't see the girls. That is, if you want an answer. They ain't here...I mean...the girls sure ain't backing you."

Gina sniffed.

"What I do see," Peaches continued, "is a short teacher obsessed with the American dream and a big black girl here who just may be the first to even go to college in her messed-up family, listening to your sorry story. That's what I see."

A loud sound echoed in the hallway outside of my door. At first, I thought the sound had been a student slamming a locker shut, but the noise continued in a pounding rhythm. A girl screamed and then laughed. Gina, Peaches, and I all moved toward the door.

Slam, slam, slam.

"Stop it!" A male voice screamed right before we got to the door.

Down the hallway, in front of the doorway that led to the stairway that led to the in-school suspension room and the loading dock, two tall male students and a small female silhouette stood in silence and looked at us.

"Everything all right?" I called out in my most concerned, teacher-like voice.

"We're good," one male voice replied.

"You OK, girl?" Peaches asked the short figure, whom I soon discerned as China Girl: Gwendolyn Sparks. I hadn't seen China Girl since the accident a few months back. We walked toward the group.

"Sure." Her voice was soft and sweet and at odds with the clothes and makeup. Her big eyes, strongly adorned with makeup, blinked from her pure skin. China Doll was dressed tightly like an open invitation: *I'm available and need your love. Oh, and while you're at it, look at my cleavage.* I recognized one of the students as a boy who had been in my study hall the previous year. China Girl, with her perfect but posed pout on her lips, leaned into him as he put his hand in her back jean pocket.

"Sounded like someone was getting hurt," I said. We stopped right in front of the three.

"Nope. We good." The second boy took China Girl's arm. "Just heading down to the loading dock. We helping Lyle with some work."

"Gwendolyn?" I asked. China Girl looked shocked that I knew her name. "Are you sure you're all right?"

She nodded her head yes and tilted her head toward the student with his hand in her pocket.

"We already said we OK," the second male said, annoyed and rushed as he opened the door to the stairwell down to the floor below. "Come on."

The three moved through the doorway quickly. Laughter ricocheted in the stairwell corridor after the door slammed.

"Wow," Peaches mumbled. "That was sketch."

"And did you see the girl's purse? What high school girl can afford a purse like that? That was a Prada bag, easily two thousand dollars. Even if it was a knock-off, it wasn't cheap."

We all turned and walked back to my room. Gina's tears forgotten for the moment, we all reflected on the bizarre scene we had just witnessed. I could not get my head around my confusion with that China Girl.

"Weird," Peaches mumbled.

"I know, right?" Gina said.

"I remembered why I stopped by, Ms. Day." Peaches said. "I took the ACT last week. Of course, I wore my lucky bee pin my Nanna gave to me."

"Oh my gosh, I forgot to ask. How do you think it went?"

We got to the door and moved into room 213. Gina went to her backpack and pulled out a notebook and sat in the front desk. I guessed we would be reviewing for the final.

"I thought it went well. A little bummed. A kid in my first hour class told me something that ruined my whole day. Man, did you know that that Cami chick got a thirty on her ACT? That just scorches me. Some of the things that come out of that girl's mouth make me wonder...and then she goes and gets a thirty on the ACT."

"Peaches, I know you did well. We scored your practice tests, and unless you blacked out during the ACT, I can't imagine you did poorly."

"Well, I don't know how long I have to wait to see...I have to send everything off to colleges. I can't afford to go to college."

"You're going to college, Peaches. You'll be fine." I knew how bright Peaches was and how little money her grandma had. Between financial aid and scholarships, Peaches was on a new trajectory. (Power word.)

"Do you want to study for the final with us?" Gina's voice was kind and different from the self-absorbed negative tone that we'd grown accustomed to.

"I guess. As long as I'm here. Just don't be stupid or anything like that."

Gina laughed.

"'Cause that would be *redundant*. Power word," Peaches continued. "Since you've said it like a million times."

That night I sat alone at the Rainbow Factory Preschool Christmas program. The auditorium was packed with coats and hats and families of the little angels on the stage. Cold air, exhaustion, and parental pride permeated the air above the packed folding chairs. My parents had gone to the afternoon program so that Oliver could have someone at each program. That night I sat alone.

I was getting used to the singular lifestyle. Single parent. Solo. Not such a bad gig. My comfort with the singular lifestyle had not happened overnight. I had loved being married. I had loved having a husband stand next to me in church, in the grocery story, in life. The days, months, and years had been solid training for this solo journey. The Solo Annie was more comfortable in 2008 than immediately after Jake left.

I had been watching the couple sitting in front of me since I sat down before the program. A purse and coats sat on the chair in between the man, whose hair stuck out on all sides of his head, and his wife. He had his arm around the chair to his left, which supported a boy who looked to be about eight years old. The woman on the other side of the middle chair looked exhausted as she bounced a fussy, toddling little girl. Not once during the program did the husband and wife speak to each other. They were simply coexisting in their endless state of fatigue.

On the other end of the couples spectrum, the couple to the left of me bickered before the program and grumbled in snippets.

"You said you brought the video recorder," the thin man grumbled to his short and fluffy wife.

She ignored him.

"Can you hear me?"

"I'm not doing this."

Everyone around looked toward the couple.

"Really? So that's what we're going to do. Got it...loud and clear."

The voices of the singing children washed out the angry whispers of the couple to my left, but their tension simmered throughout the hour of holiday singing. The state of alone was feeling better and better. I looked up to see Oliver in a reindeer hat singing loudly with the other children. He looked happy.

A head on a man four rows ahead of me caught my attention.

I knew that head.

I looked at the back of Jake's head. I knew that the brain in that head thought that Patrick on SpongeBob was hilarious and sounded even funnier when he tried to imitate him. I once watched that head eat five bowls of Fruity Pebbles in one sitting. I knew that the head I was looking at had been cracked when he was eight after jumping off the high board and hitting the side of the pool. I consoled that head as it lay in my lap, crying to me once when it felt overwhelmed with the bar exam.

But now, I was not so sure of the head. I didn't know what that head had had for breakfast today or what he thought about the weather. I didn't know *what dreams may come* into such a head. It was really just another head in the crowd.

To the right of Jake's head was a head of full, dark, and beautiful hair. The head drooped down. Jake leaned in. Jaymie pulled away. *The Jake and Jaymie Show* appeared to be struggling with a technical difficulty. I remember times in my marriage to Mr. Oliver Jameson Day, even before the ever-shimmering Jaymie, wondering who the woman was whom Jake talked to at a party (and forgot to introduce to me) or who had texted him late at night when business should be done for the day. You kind of wonder those things when you're married to a man who loves women. Believe me, Jake always reassured me and even sometimes scolded me for even suggesting it, but—and there's no denying it—Jake loved women.

While a feeling of smug pettiness could have easily been my reaction to the unpleasant Christmas program exchange between my ex-friend and ex-husband, I felt sorrow and relief. I felt sorry for both Jake and Jaymie. I felt relief that, at least on that night, I was sitting alone with no tension, just holding a green program. No weird texts from a narcissistic man telling me he misses my kisses.

Just me, stress free.

Miss Nancy, the director of the Rainbow Factory preschool, stood up at the microphone in front of the children layered on tiered shelves like icing on a gingerbread house. Her voice filled the room. "We're so happy that so many family members could be here tonight for our special Christmas program. Aren't we, kids?" Miss Nancy turned to the students, four-and-five-year-old children dressed as snowflakes, reindeer, and elves.

"Ho, ho, ho!" The children said in unison and put their right hands up in a cheer on the last "ho." Tired parents smiled and laughed. In the front row, Oliver smiled as the construction paper antlers on his head tilted to the side. The lighting on the children made them look angelic, while the rest of the room was dark.

"Well, I guess there's your answer. We hope the voices of the angels behind me bring joy into your hearts tonight with the songs in our program. We hope to cheerfully entertain you!"

To cheerfully entertain?

Uh oh. Miss Nancy just split an infinitive, and I was probably the only person in the room who noticed.

An infinitive: the word "to" plus a verb.

To entertain.

To sing.

To marry.

Let's go ahead and split that infinitive by putting an adverb between the word "to" and the verb.

To cheerfully entertain.

That's right. Let's put an adverb in between the word "to" and the verb. Let's break up that infinitive. Let's rattle the entire grammatical world.

Long ago, splitting infinitives was considered poor grammar. How do you tell the difference between a good writer and a bad writer? Well, the good writers place adverbs after the phrase, the then-considered-more-effective approach to the verbal phrase.

To marry naively.

The bad writers would wedge that adverb right in the middle of the infinitive phrase.

To naively marry.

In the history of grammar, around the time that color televisions replaced black-and-white televisions, the world became more accepting of a split infinitive. You could just turn on that color TV and hear a voice call to you from the *Star Trek* universe: to *boldly* go where no one has gone before. *To boldly go?*

Oh no, he didn't.

In time, about the time I started teaching English, most writers would just mumble under their breaths regarding the split-infinitive dilemma: get over it. Most strong writers would even suggest that a split infinitive could be interesting; it might just add a little zippy something to an otherwise drab sentence. The old adage that good writers can break rules applied here, and then some.

Just like with marriages.

As time went on, split or broken marriages (a result of people marrying naively) were more acceptable; it was OK for kids to have parents who "split up," just as the English language community accepted split infinitives.

I looked around the room at all the split infinitives: the chair between the husband and wife, the tension between the couple next to me. I thought about Jake and his not-so-shimmering-tonight wife. Just what gets in the way of a good marriage? What splits the union, abruptly and slowly over time?

Several rows ahead of me, as the children began singing an effervescent round of "Up on the Housetop," Jaymie stood up and wiggled through the row of tired parents. She darted to the door of the auditorium and left. Jake's head sat alone for the remainder of the program. I wondered what that head was thinking.

The auditorium lights went on after the last song, and parents began to grab purses and coats.

"Well, are we going home or getting dinner? Which is it?" The woman next to me nagged her husband.

"Whatever you want. That's what we do anyway." The tired husband put a hat on the boy next to him.

I moved away from the negative energy and looked up at the stage for Oliver. I saw Jake hugging him, so I waited for the two to have time together. Oliver looked up and saw me.

"Mom! Did you see me? Did you hear me? I was in the front row!"

"I did. You were awesome!"

Jake gave Oliver one last hug and mumbled a hello to me and then a good-bye to us both. He left through the same door that Jaymie had exited.

"Did you see me?" Oliver wrapped his arms around me.

"I did. Did you have fun?" I held out Oliver's coat for him to move into.

"I did. We worked real hard in practice. Where did Jaymie go? Hey, look!" Oliver held up the wooden nickel that my dad had given him. "My pocket. That's where it was. I thought I lost it. Good thing I had it tonight. It helped me to sing the best I could."

"Yes, it did. Do you want me to hold onto your wooden nickel so you don't lose it again?"

Oliver handed his lucky token to me and yawned. I looked down at the piece of wood fashioned into the shape of a large quarter. On one side, the "nickel" read Wooden Nickel and had a picture of a bison on it. The other side read Medicine Bow on the top and Wyoming on the bottom. In the middle were the words "When you call me that, smile."

I took the wooden nickel and placed it in my purse.

"We better head home before Atticus thinks we forgot about him."

As I put on Oliver's hat, I looked up to see a couple hugging their little girl. The two bent down together, and the man put one arm around the little girl and one hand on the back of the woman.

Even though you can split an infinitive phrase, that doesn't mean you have to.

That night, after Oliver was asleep and the house was in lockdown mode, I went over my list for the next day in my bedroom, the news playing on my small television, the volume on low. A little annoying thought that had been rattling around in my head all night settled and announced itself: Why would Lyle the janitor need help?

Gwendolyn Sparks and the two boys with her were heading down to the dock to help Lyle. In a private school, students sometimes had jobs at the school to help with tuition. I had student taught at a Catholic school years earlier, and I knew of students who mowed the lawn, cleaned rooms, and worked in the front office. Their hours at work shaved money off tuition. Belmont High School was a public school. Why would students help the janitor?

"And the letters to Santa keep pouring into the post office this year."

I looked up at the news story. The camera had captured hundreds of envelopes with letters to Santa pouring into a large bin at the local post office.

"We just hope Santa's pen has enough ink to answer all of these letters. Back to you, Rob."

The letters reminded me of the single envelope sitting in a box, now on the floor of my bedroom next to my dresser. I could see the letter from where I sat on my bed. I wanted to read that letter, but I knew it was private and clearly marked for Annette only.

What I knew: a letter to Annette with the seal loose but unopened sat in a box in my room.

What I did not know: who wrote the letter and what content in that letter was so important that Annette could not read it until the writer was dead.

Talk about fodder for an episode of *Dateline*. I should contact Keith with the proposed storyline. I was dying to read the letter.

Maybe if I had a sign that it was all right to read the letter, I could just peek in and read it quickly, once. After all, Annette had not read the letter yet, and she was still sending Christmas cards to Nora and Fred. That meant that the letter wasn't a matter of life or death. Right?

A sign.

And then, as if in answer to my quirky request, Atticus hobbled into my room with a dead Elf on a Shelf. I couldn't remember the last time that Atticus had something in his mouth. No longer a pup, Atticus had long ago pushed aside the ways of immature puppies, no longer jumping on people or chewing on shoes or doggie toys, and had grown into a mature dog that slept and sighed for the most part. That was why I was shocked to see him carrying the demon-like Christmas toy into the room, its face disfigured by canine teeth. Atticus walked into the room and up to me and sat with the gift for me: a sign.

I took it as a sign.

For several reasons, I felt better at that point. First, I was no longer wondering if a ghost in my attic had stolen the freakish elf, an elf that Oliver had not mentioned once since his birthday meltdown. Second, I was amused by the fact that my elderly dog agreed with my attitude toward a holiday marketing ploy gone wrong. So he stood, with his offering to his master, as if I had shot the elf in the sky and Atticus had run out in a field to retrieve it.

"Good boy, Atticus." I took the soggy and mutilated gnome from his mouth and looked at my sign. Somehow, when I had asked for a sign to read the mysterious letter, my dog came with my answer, albeit dead and mushy. I patted my obedient dog's head and put the elf in my trash can. I placed the small trash can on my dresser to remind myself to throw the impish clump in the trash can outside the next morning when I let Atticus out and before I woke Oliver.

I saw the letter on top of the pictures and documents, winking at me like a secret. I picked up the envelope and looked at it for the hundredth time. *Give to Annette after I die.* I took the letter back to my bed and sat down. The paper was so worn and thin, I could see the ink of the handwritten letter inside. The slight movement of the letter pulled the last thread of the seal. With the tips of my fingers, I slowly pulled the single sheet from the envelope. My eyes moved across a sheet to the most beautiful cursive handwriting I had ever seen.

Atticus slumped on the floor and sighed. His work was done.

"My dear Annette," I read.

For some reason, my eyes went immediately to the name at the bottom of the letter.

"Love, Mom."

"June 7, 1982."

"Lorna."

Bill's wife, Annette's mother, the writer of this letter, Lorna, had been dead for almost twenty-seven years. Annette was maybe twenty-two when she lost her mother. I couldn't imagine losing my own mother when I was twenty-two. Lorna's bones were buried somewhere out in this world in a grave next to her husband, who had joined her a few years ago. Buried bones calling out. Somewhere out in the night, the bones lay restless.

A soft voice heard only on paper: Lorna.

My dear Annette,

By the time you read these words, I will be gone. Know that my greatest regret is not having enough time in the world to be with you. My second greatest regret is not telling you earlier about your adoption. The day you found the papers and were so angry was probably the worst day of my life. I understand your anger. What you may not understand is that I was protecting you.

The year you were born, I had a student at UNO who was pregnant. She confided in me that she would be missing a class, since she was going to get an abortion. Your father and I had tried for so many years to have a baby with no luck. I felt an overwhelming sense that the baby in that young lady was our child. I felt that I was saving you.

Professionally and personally, I made mistakes. I should never have approached the young lady with my proposal, but I did. I could have gotten fired for inappropriate relations with a student. Your father and I still made her the offer. We agreed to pay for her prenatal care and pay her a good amount of money if she allowed us to keep the baby. She was a lost soul who could use the money, so she agreed. Her one demand was that we never contact her again. She did not want the baby to ever know who or where she was. We complied.

After seeing your anger this past year about us not telling you about the adoption, I knew, and I was right, that you would be even angrier that we would not give you information about your birth mother. This past year, my cancer and your absence in my life have been the lowest point I can remember.

I've come to realize that my commitment to you is more important than my promise to that young woman.

Please know that I love you more than life. I'm so sorry.

Love,
Mom
June 7, 1982

Your birth mother's name is Sandra Wellington. She was born in Grand Island, Nebraska. I think she moved out of Omaha shortly after you were born. She was 19 the year you were born. That's all I know.

A powerful, beautiful voice from the grave, only the person who was intended to be on the listening end of the message had never read the words I had just read. I needed to get the letter and box to Annette.

The shuffling began.

The dreaming began.

Oliver and I are standing at the bottom of the stairs that lead up to my attic. I can see a silhouette of a man at the top of the stairs.

Oliver and I walk slowly up. We don't know if that man knows we're behind him.

We're in the attic.

No lights are on. The only light is coming from the moon outside the front window.

Oliver sees Atticus by the window and runs toward him.

I see the man to my left. He's frantic.

"Where is it?" he screams.

I can see the face of the man. It's Nick Stander, the new assistant football coach.

"Why are you here?"

"Where is it?" Nick screams to himself as he slams the wall.

"Where is what?"

Nick picks up a chair and runs toward the window where Atticus and Oliver are standing. Nick is running to the window with the chair as if he doesn't even see them.

I scream.

Oliver stood by my bed and rubbed my back. "You just had a bad dream, Mom."

"Did I wake you up, Oliver?"

"That's OK." Oliver continued rubbing my back. Atticus stood next to him.

"Do you want to crawl in?" I said.

"Sure."

Oliver got into bed, and I covered him up.

"Mom?"

"Yes."

"I'm sorry that Choochoo was so mean to you today."

"I love you, Oliver."

I rubbed Oliver's back until we both fell asleep.

Second Semester
Third Quarter
Whistling Past the Graveyard

SIR LANCELOT: Look, my liege!
[trumpets]
ARTHUR: Camelot!
SIR GALAHAD: Camelot!
LANCELOT: Camelot!
PATSY: It's only a model.

—Monty Python, Monty Python and
the Holy Grail

20

January 12, 2009

Annie

Five below zero.

Not cold enough for a cancellation but cold enough to make the city miserable as its drivers grumbled in their cars on the way to work on Monday morning.

I sat in my classroom on one of the coldest mornings that school year with a huge pile of essays in front of me. Oliver and I had gone over to my parents' house the Sunday evening before for chili and cornbread. Oliver brought his backpack and favorite books, since he was going to have a sleepover with my parents. They planned to keep him all day until I was done with my workday. I got to work at 6:30 a.m. and had been plowing through the pile until I hit a wall. Blame it on the lack of sleep or the essay exhaustion, but I absolutely hit a wall.

I may have been looking down at an essay with a red pen in hand, but I wasn't correcting any essay. I was thinking about Sam Piccolo, my first true love. I'm not sure how he popped into my head, but here he was: Sam Piccolo.

Sam was golden.

Long before lying ex-husbands and cheating fund-raiser men, there was only Sam: a tan, tall, and muscular boy from my neighborhood with blond hair and green eyes that took my junior high breath away. The summer before I was in seventh grade and before Sam Piccolo was in the eighth grade, we spent every day together. We weren't alone. Never. We hung out with the neighbor kids, and usually one or two of my sisters were there, but I spent almost every waking moment of that summer with Sam. I was very Sam aware: aware that his shoulders were getting broader, aware of the way he tilted his head when he smiled, aware of his big green eyes against his tan face, aware of his spiky blond hair that was brittle and beautiful from the chlorine of the neighborhood pool, aware of every single word that came out of his mouth. I just wasn't sure if he even noticed me.

One random evening, toward the end of the summer, Sam and I were the only ones walking toward the corner of Parker Street and Robertson Drive. That was where everyone usually met after dinner. We usually played a game of kick the can or ghosts in the graveyard or maybe even kickball, but that night Sam and I were the only summer kids on the corner.

"Annie-Bannanie!" That was what he called me. "You're getting browner than a berry."

He noticed me.

"Spent the whole day at the pool." I tried to sound uninterested.

"I know. Saw you there." Sam was bending over to pick up something he saw on the sidewalk. "Hey, you wanna head down to the 7-Eleven on Dodge?" My mom didn't like me going to the gas station on Dodge without my older sisters. "I have a few bucks. We can get a Slurpee. My treat."

"Sure." No girl—I repeat, no girl, including my mom—standing in my flip-flops in front of Sam Piccolo at the moment would have said no to his green eyes and his almost-like-a-date proposal.

"Let's go!"

We walked down Robertson Drive to Dodge, close to each other but not touching each other. I hoped my parents wouldn't drive by, and I hoped any girl in my class would be in a car and see me walking alone with Sam. I was in heaven. We both ordered a blueberry Slurpee with a silly straw, Sam paid, I thanked him, and we slowly walked out of the 7-Eleven.

"Wanna head over to the empty lot by the Methodist church?" Another place I was not allowed to go, even with my older sisters.

"Sure."

"We can just finish our Slurpees as the sun goes down."

Sam had about a bazillion buddies in our neighborhood. Had he intentionally met me to be with me alone?

"Sounds cool."

Sam and I walked from 7-Eleven to the empty lot, and I pinched the side of my leg. I might just be dreaming. Was I dreaming? I felt the pinch. As we walked, Sam's arm touched mine, and about a million little nerve endings came to life.

"Where do you want to sit?" Sam asked me. I could barely see the field as the glow of the most beautiful sunset I had ever seen overtook me.

"Anywhere. Have you been here before?" I had not.

"Whenever I can get away at this time…or the time that sun decides to set. It changes all the time, you know. Every day, after the twenty-third of June, the days get shorter and shorter. So the sun sets earlier and earlier. Kind of cool. Don't you think?"

"It's amazing!" The beauty of the endless colored sky, combined with the sexual energy that Sam gave off unknowingly, caught my breath.

"Now, watch the clouds above us. If you stare at the clouds long enough, they start to look like things you know. The challenge is that the clouds are moving all the time. See there, a truck. Do you see it?"

"I see it!"

"And see there, a knight on a horse."

"Cool."

"But what you can't see is that beautiful damsel in distress that he's going to rescue at the nearby 7-Eleven."

I laughed out loud.

"I really like you, Annie."

"What?"

"I know you're just a sixth grader, but I really like you." Sam stopped and then took a big sip from his straw.

Two weeks after our sunset date, my dreams shattered.

"My dad got a promotion, and we're moving to Philadelphia in a month." Sam cleared his throat and blinked his eyes. I was trying to remember where Philadelphia was. I was never very good at geography, probably because I was always reading fiction, stories about unreal places and made-up people. Where was Philadelphia? Was it close to Nebraska?

Sam took my hand. "We can keep in touch. You know, with letters and stuff."

We did write letters, a handful. Sam wrote about all of the new places he'd been to and the people he'd met. He said he had run to the top of the steps at the place where Rocky did in the movie. I wrote about all the neighbor kids and told him funny stories about everyone and that I'd seen *Dirty Dancing* three times in the theater. And then the letters stopped, and we both moved on in very separate lives, moving farther and farther from the empty lot and the clouds of 1987.

Through the years, I've found myself wondering whatever happened to Sam Piccolo. Sure, I could look him up on Facebook, but I don't have a Facebook. And then, what if I found out he was no longer beautiful and happy? And what if I found a picture of him bald—no beautiful, brittle, pool-kissed hair? What if I found out that he had had an affair on his wife? He would no longer be my golden boy. No, Sam remained in my memory only.

Frozen polarization.

Sam would remain frozen in time, and I would not allow him to grow up and make mistakes and break hearts or lie to loved ones. I didn't want to know that his resume lacked parallel structure or that he said he did *good* on things instead of *well*. Sam would remain in my memory only. Sam was forever golden.

"Ms. Day! Catcha."

A loud voice interrupted my golden daydream. It was gone, like a cloud that changes form right before your eyes.

Kyle I'm-gonna-be-a-sportscaster Goodman stood in my doorway. "I'm the bird; you're the worm…The early bird catches the…"

"Worm? Good morning, Kyle."

"Man, it's crazy out there!" Kyle darted toward my desk and then sat on the edge.

"I know, below zero, yet we're still here." Teachers like days off of school more than the students. "Who said you could sit on my desk?"

"No, not the weather." Kyle stayed on my desk and picked up my stapler. "The cop cars. Probably four or five of 'em. You're out of staples."

"What cop cars?" I had seen no police cars when I walked into school forty-five minutes earlier.

"Well, I think they're trying to be sneaky. No lights or sirens, and they parked on the far west lot near the pool, but I know why they're here."

"You do? Are you like a detective or something?" I was curious why police would come to Belmont High School on a cold, early Monday morning.

"More bones."

No media had reported the secret second skull that Avery had told me about at conferences back in October, so other than the two bones reported at the beginning of the year, Omaha had backed off from the mystery bones as a daily discussion.

"And you know this because…" I put my pen down.

"I just ran into my sister by the gym. I have to bring her to swim practice every day…that's why I get here so early; the early bird…anyway, practice was canceled after Mallory Talcott opened her locker in the locker room before practice—found a skull and another bone and, evidently…" Kyle made bunny-ear quotation marks with his fingers to encase the word "evidently." "Evidently a ton of dirt. My sister said that Mallory's locker was practically packed with dirt, and uh, the skull and the other bone."

"This morning?"

"Yep, and you know girls can be so dramatic. Screaming and crying and lots of drama." Kyle put the stapler down and stood up.

"In the school?"

"In her locker."

"Wow."

"I know, right? Creepy." Another set of bunny ears around the word "creepy," and Kyle headed out the door.

By noon, the official news of the locker bones was on social media and the noon news. Because students were involved, word of the skull and bone in the locker could not be concealed by the investigators. Kids were talking about the creepy incident with the girls' swim team all day. The story about the invasive gesture was creepier than the sounds from my attic, *The Jake and Jaymie Show*, and Choochoo's sassy attitude mixed together. The news was creepier than the three texts I had ignored the night before from Mr. Kissermaniac.

Hello? I'm confused?

Ignore.

I need to see you.

Ignore.

I miss your kisses.

Creepy. (Bunny ears in the air.)

After I witnessed his marriage and family in the Bagel Bin parking lot, I went radio silent. But so did he. What with Christmas and family and legal commitments as they were. But as soon as the Kissermaniac got out of family-vacation mode, he was texting me regularly. The only thing that creeped me out more than the bothersome texts were the bothersome Belmont bones.

Whoever was planting the Belmont bones had just crossed a line. The bone planter meant business when he or she or they or it walked into our building with more of the morbid, tormenting bait. The intentional and blatant display of human remains was offensive and disturbing.

By three o'clock, the afternoon sleep monster was crouching on my head. A nap would have been heavenly, but I looked out at thirty-eight desks and a cold floor and realized that I needed to attack the last stack of essays before I picked up Oliver.

"You look tired, Annie Day." Doc's voice soothed me and brightened the room. "Long day?"

"How'd you guess?" I smiled. "But wasn't it a long day for everyone. More bones. Doc, this is crazy. Do you know anything?"

"The forensic people and some other pretty serious faces are the same team from back in August."

"Do you think a bunch of teenagers are having fun scaring people? Do you think there is a point to all of this? Will there be an end?"

"Only thing that I keep tossing around is that these are real bones. Human remains. A person died and decomposed, and then a live person took those bones for people to find. That much is very clear. Real people."

"I know."

"Been here long enough that I can tell you when we used to have fun with scary stories of bones." Doc took a deep breath after he spoke. He looked as if he had had a long day too.

"Fun?"

"Well, the whole story about Samuel J. Belmont being buried under the big *B* on the floor of the entrance to the school."

"What?"

"Well, it's not true, but the stories about it go into detail of the ghost of the old superintendent of the Omaha Public Schools back in the fifties whom they named this school after. Kids used to tell all sorts of stories about strange noises in the hallway. Voices coming from empty hallways. Lockers slamming with no one around. Boy, they loved scaring one another. It was all pretty innocent. But these are real bones. Not funny at all."

"No."

"Just don't be staying here late and walking to your car alone, Annie Day. Promise me that."

"I promise."

"Hey!" Hannah Bixby stood in the doorway. "Did you all have a great break?"

"I did." I pulled out a packet for Hannah. "Could you run this poetry packet down to Ms. Lannon. Could you smile and tell her that Ms. Day needs a hundred and eighty copies. I don't need them until the end of January, but it's a pretty big packet."

"Got it!"

Hannah almost knocked over Gina Shatner as she turned to leave. "Oh, my bad, sorry, Gina."

"No worries." I had not seen Gina since before the winter break, and she looked different. A glow around her face and the smile on her face, especially her green eyes, made Gina Shatner beautiful. No ponytail that day. Gina's hair was combed and possibly curled. I think I saw a little makeup framing her eyes. Gina smiled.

"I was a little worried when I didn't see you in class. Everything all right?"

"I'm good. Hi, Doc. Sorry I missed your class, Ms. Day, but I had a doctor's appointment." Gina was clearly pregnant and not just fluffy. Her hand was on her growing baby bump.

"How was the appointment?"

"Great." Gina smiled and sat in the desk in front of me. With our catch-up sessions, Gina had finished the first semester with a B-minus. I was banking on her acing the second semester. "Is it all right if I still come in after school? My locker is near all my old friends, and I thought if I came here right away and sat awhile, I could miss the drama in the halls…if that's OK with you."

"Absolutely."

Doc moved his cart toward the door. "You ladies have a good night. Remember what I said, Annie Day."

"You bet, Doc. Tell Alice hi for me."

"You bet." Doc forced his cart through the door, the wheels squeaking as he moved down the hall.

"It's a boy."

"What?"

"The baby in me is a boy."

"You found out today?"

"We did. My mom was with me." A vision of the cherry bomb with the red lipstick at conferences popped into my head.

"Oh, no, look who's showing." Peaches filled the doorway with her frame. Her blue sparkly earrings shook back and forth as she grinned at Gina.

"And," I said, "Gina has some news today, Peaches."

"Well, you better have a signed excuse for missing class today." Peaches walked toward my desk and handed me the FASFA forms that we would be working on. "You had us worried."

"It's a boy!"

"No way."

"Way. A tiny little boy is in me. And I have other news."

"More news?" I asked.

"I think I've decided on the parents. I have it down to two couples, but I'm pretty sure I know which ones I'll pick."

"What are you talking about?" Peaches sat down next to Gina.

"The adoptive parents."

"You get to pick the parents? Get out." Peaches shook her head. "You're going to know the parents of your baby."

"Well, he's not my baby. I'm just the messenger, or the stork." Gina smiled. "I'm a stork!"

"Wow," Peaches whispered. "I just can't get my head around that. You giving up the baby and picking the parents."

"Yes," I added. "I have a friend who openly adopted her son. The birth mother sends cards on birthdays and Christmas. It is actually a pretty neat thing."

"Can you change your mind?" Peaches asked Gina. "I mean..."

"That's OK, Peaches. I get what you mean. I've been working with Simone, a really cool lady at Catholic Charities who counsels me. She helps me with the whole mental and emotional stuff. I feel good about this. It's been up and down. Mostly up lately. I feel like I'm responsible for this little boy...it's a boy! And I want him to have an awesome life. I mean, he didn't ask for this situation..."

"I think my nieces and nephews would have been better off if my cousin had done what you're doing. My cousin is all messed up, and she just keeps getting pregnant. What you're doing is good. Most girls like you..."

"Like me?" Gina asked.

"Never mind. I just think it's cool."

"Most girls like me," Gina said, "would have the 'thing' taken care of early on, never carried the baby in the first place. You don't see a lot of my friends carrying babies, do you?"

"OK, are we doing the rhetorical question thing again?" Peaches asked.

Gina stood up and rubbed her belly again. "I think we're pretty tired. Baby Boy and I are going home to take a nap. You look pretty tired too, Peaches."

I looked at Peaches. We were all tired, but the white in Peaches's eyes was red.

"You all right?" I asked Peaches.

"My whacko cousin came home all methed out again late last night. Let's just say she put up a good fight. I had to get her to a place where she could get clean. Again. Grandma and I are taking care of three little boys. I can't get to college soon enough to be able to help her little kids get out of their situation. And my grandma has such a hard time with it all." Peaches stood up and pointed to the forms she had given to me.

"Do you think you could look over the notes from my counselor and help me with this on Monday, Ms. Day?"

"Sure."

"How do you do it?" Gina stood up and looked at Peaches. "Every day?"

"How do you do it, girl? You carrying a load there yourself. Getting bigger every day!"

"I know, right."

"Well"—I picked up my stacks and my purse—"why don't we all walk out together?"

Walking out of Belmont High School with Gina and Peaches after an especially long day, I smiled when I thought of Oliver at my parents'. The dark, overcast skies wrapping around the dreary cold of a Nebraska January day would not put a damper on my warm spirit. I would go to pick him up, and Mom would have dinner waiting for me. I would act all surprised but sit down with them and enjoy a warm meal that I hadn't cooked and then take a happy boy home. How do single parents without support get through the long days? I was blessed.

A perky woman ruined my blessed moment.

Down at the bottom of the main staircase in front of the school stood a mob of students looking to a perky woman in an aqua suit, perfect brown hair encasing her perfect, perky face. The woman moved a microphone toward a student; her cameraman, positioned behind, followed her every movement.

"Does the news of more bones found now inside of your school disturb you at all?"

The student in front of her kept his hands in his pockets as he looked at the cameraman and then at the lady.

(Are you kidding me? Does the news disturb you? What a stupid question to ask. Let me ask you a question, lady. What do you think the answer is going to be? Do you think some old lady will be sitting on the edge of her plaid davenport watching your little snippet at six o'clock

215

tonight, wondering what a sixteen-year-old is going to say in response to your stupid question?)

"Uh, well, yah, I'm kind of freaked out by it all." Visible clouds came from the mouth of the student in the cold air. While the thermometer read below zero, most of the students in the huddle wore sweatshirts and nothing more. The student rubbed his nose and looked around at the other students for support.

"Do you feel that the administration is handling the incident well?" Perky reporter tilted her head and smiled. One more item on the creepy list: smiling reporters with stupid questions.

"Uh, I guess. I don't really know what they're doing."

Perky reporter turned to the camera with the mob of teenagers behind her, all looking at the camera like lost orphans. "Concern at Belmont High School regarding this morning's discovery of a human skull and bone in a student locker this time. We'll have why one parent is up in arms about the delay in notification of this shocking incident. Stay tuned for our ten o'clock report with more on more bones at Belmont High School. Live from Belmont High School, I'm Sasha Melbourne. Back to you, John."

Aqua and perky Sasha gleamed as the cameraman signaled that she was done. She then dropped the gleam and walked away from the student mob without so much as a thank-you to the lost orphans huddled behind her. The orphans stood for a moment and then wandered out in all different directions.

"Do you have the addresses of the parents with you?" Sasha patted her hair.

"Yep."

The cameraman and perky reporter moved toward a car in the parking lot, pleased with their manipulative act of turning a frightening story at our school into an "Administration Ignoring Its Bones" feature, leaving the orphans behind. I guess the news of the bones was not enough for a feature story. The unfounded insinuation that the administration wasn't doing enough in the continuing saga of the mysteriously appearing bones implied that there was a school district protocol in place somewhere about handling the bones of dead people showing up on a school campus and that Belmont High School leaders had been remiss in addressing those bones. Sasha and her sidekick felt the need to kick up the dust on reaction to the news and present a story as immature as drama that I've witnessed in the high school halls.

"There's the late bus. See you two." Peaches walked down the stairs to her bus.

"It's going to be hard napping after that reporter…she bugged me… Bye, Ms. Day!" Gina walked down the stairs in the opposite direction.

My cheeks stung as I ran to my car. I struggled to open the door with my stiffening fingers. I turned on the heat and sat for a moment while the car warmed up.

Does the news of more bones found inside of your school disturb you at all?

Yes, Perky Aqua, we're all disturbed.

Are you happy now, Sasha?

We're all very, very disturbed.

Put that on your ten o'clock news.

As I drove past the school marquee on the edge of the campus, I read the large black letters with a distress that could only be assuaged by a home-cooked meal (not prepared by me). I read the words "Welcome Back from Brake."

Brake?

Seriously?

All kinds of wrong displayed on a busy street for the world to see at the high school that was already battling bad bone notoriety and feeling very disturbed at the moment.

21

"Ghosts in the South Pasture"
Summer of 1938

Rollie

"**B**usier than a one-legged man in an ass-kicking contest. Get your butts to the barn."

Truett needed Jeb and me to go help him with some dirty work in the far end of the south pasture. I had never been to the far end of the pasture yet. Most of the time, my mom wouldn't let me go any farther than the barn and the space in between the house and the gate and wanted me doing the little chores around the main house, but Truett ran it past his sister, and I was allowed to go on the adventure that day.

I had no idea what we would be doing, but I felt like a real rancher heading out with Truett and Jeb. I was on Saratoga, Truett's horse then, with Truett, and Jeb was riding Old Charley. It felt like we'd been riding forever when Truett pointed to a big old tree that looked out of place. I knew the tree because the uncles had talked about it. If they said "the tree," we all knew which tree they were talking about: the tree at the end of the south pasture.

"That tree marks the beginning of the end of the earth, Rollie."

About twenty feet high, the tree looked like a big umbrella trying its hardest to shade the massive area out there in the middle of nowhere. The branches reached up and out and seemed hungry for the sky. Now that I think about it, I wonder how a tree could grow to be that big and no other trees grew around it. It was almost as if that tree was a survivor of a bad catastrophe, and it stood alone in its raw stubbornness. It looked pretty lonely.

"Hey, are we going to make it back in time for dinner?" Jeb always worried about food.

"Not my day to worry about it," Truett mumbled as he looked off to the horizon. Truett always said this when he really wasn't listening to you.

"Well, I don't want to get too hungry and be starving by the time—"

"Rollie, watch how Old Charley gets spooked as we get closer to the south pasture." Truett grinned as we moved closer to the tree on the horizon that grew bigger as we got closer.

"You're gonna love this!" Jeb wanted to make sure I knew that he had witnessed the spooking of Charley.

As we got closer to the tree in the south pasture, Old Charley started snorting and rearing. Jeb was still able to handle him, but Old Charley was clearly agitated.

"Why doesn't he like the south pasture?" I asked.

"I think he senses all the ghosts from the Sand Creek Massacre. The surviving Cheyenne Indians came north after the attack and hid in the prairie on their way up to Cheyenne almost seventy years ago. So many of them died along the way. All those gold rushers felt entitled to their land. The sons a bitches..."

"Ghosts?" My voice squeaked. I had always suspected there was a ghost in the outhouse.

Truett laughed a belly laugh at my expense but never did answer my question. Truett and Jeb stopped their horses and grabbed shovels from a bag that he had pulled from the side of Saratoga's saddle. Both Truett and Jeb just let the horses wander. No need to tie them up, and really nothing to tie them to except the tree. Truett said the horses knew where their dinner came from.

"Over there." Truett pointed to an area and then handed me the smaller shovel. "Start digging."

Over there was to the left of a pile of bones. I shivered when I thought of the ghosts that were spooking Old Charley. I started digging, and I had already figured if I asked questions, Truett would just laugh at me. Jeb started digging with me, and I looked up at Jeb and raised my eyebrows.

"It was a cow," Jeb said dryly.

I was getting pretty grumpy about being the dumb kid, but I did feel better that we weren't digging a grave for the bones of a Cheyenne ghost.

"We usually have more than one carcass a year." Truett said as he moved dirt. "I'll check that area beyond the tree, but I think you're in luck, boys. Only one dead cow so far."

"Luck?" I said.

"Hey now, better than a poke in the eye with a jagged stick." Truett walked beyond the tree.

Jeb rolled his eyes and muttered, "Just watch out for rattlesnakes as you dig…"

"Looks like the only one, fellas." Truett whistled a tune I couldn't decipher.

"I'm just glad," Jeb said, "that this one is all bones. I hate when they still have hair and skin. Makes me gag. Guess we're lucky again."

"How'd he die?" I asked.

Truett stopped whistling. "More than likely, this one got lost or overheated last summer. Or she found herself a heavy alfalfa patch and just overate. She probably got sick and fell away from the herd. After she died, she just filled up with gas like a big cow balloon, and then the son of a bitch just exploded. Boom!"

Jeb laughed as he dug deeper.

Poor cow. Out there in the heat, blowing up with gas and then exploding all over. Then all by himself in the far end of the south pasture in the wind and the snow. Right near the lonely tree. And then down to just bones. Bones that had walked this earth and breathed the air only a year earlier.

Lonely bones.

"That's a damn lie," I said.

"No lie, Rollie. Happens every year, boy. I've actually come across 'em when they're all blown up on their back, their legs straight up in the air. We need to bury them since the other cows won't graze near them. We waste all this fine grass for feeding if the dead don't get taken care of. Almost like those cows can smell the death and don't want anything to do with it."

"So we just bury the bones, and that fixes it?"

"For the most part."

We finished digging in silence, and Truett and Jeb moved the bones to the grave as I watched. I was glad we were giving the poor cow a proper burial. I wasn't going to let Truett know that I felt sad for the cow. Most of the uncles didn't see cows the way they saw horses or dogs. You give a name to a dog or horse. A cow was just their livelihood. A cow was a cow. No names for cows. When Truett smelled cow manure, he'd yell, "Mmmmm…just smells like money!"

"So the cow exploding is not a lie," I said. "But the ghosts spookin' Old Charley—well, that's a lie." Over those months at the ranch, I picked up on the fact that half of everything a cowboy said was just a big lie. Stories were for entertaining, so let the lies fly.

Truett never answered my question but offered me advice. "You tell a lie long enough, Rollie, pretty soon it becomes your truth."

"What the hell is that supposed to mean?" I asked.

Truett motioned for Jeb and me to start pushing the dirt over the grave. We finished, and Truett whistled for Saratoga and Old Charley, who had wandered over by the lonely tree.

As we packed up the saddles with the shovels, Truett stopped and turned into a big, boring adult. "Now I'm gonna tell you boys a few things you should never do, and you better hear me out. Never go out to the south pasture alone. This one's not about ghosts, Rollie. It's about safety. Well, you already know what happened to this here cow. And never head past that lone tree or go near the South Platte River at all. If I ever hear otherwise, I'll tan both of your hides. Never wear your dirty work boots into town...and oh, and never take a wooden nickel as real money. You'll just have 'sucker' written all over your face if you do."

"Who do you think you are, Tru?" Jeb said. His arms were crossed, and his face was sour. "You're not God."

"Didn't say I was. Just wanted to make sure you guys make good choices is all."

More than fifteen years between the two, the brothers could not have been more different. With no parents, I could see where Truett felt it was his job to watch out for Jeb.

"Well, just remember. You're not my dad."

"Never said I was."

We rode back to the ranch in silence. I was glad that we only found one dead cow.

Just lucky, I guess.

22

February 4, 2009

Annie

"Can you smell that?" Mike Sheridan shouted as he walked into the room. He stopped and took another deep breath.

Arty moved in quickly behind him. "Wasn't me."

"No, the smell of signing day. Across the country today, amazing high school athletes are signing letters of intent to college teams. I love signing day."

"And next year," Arty continued, "Me and Mikey will be welcoming Coach Bo Pelini to Belmont High School. He'll hand us each a pen and show us the line to sign."

"Me and Mikey?" I grumbled as I took roll.

"No, me and Mikey," Arty said. "You can't play football, Ms. Day. No offense. But you're a pretty darn good English teacher."

"Evidently not," I said. "I was referring to your grammar. *Mike and I* will be welcoming Coach Pelini."

"Coach Pelini will be asking us to sign for the Huskers. I haven't decided what I'm going to wear." Mike's blue eyes sparkled as he spoke.

"You'll be lucky if you walk on," LaTrey Williams teased.

James had heard the tail end of the discussion. "You two will be lucky if you get student tickets."

"We can always dream," Arty said.

"OK, groundlings, until next year's signing day, let's get back to the business of helping Arty with his English, shall we?" I took my stack of poetry packets and handed them out.

"Why do you always call us groundlings?" LaTrey asked as he opened his packet.

"You remember reading *Romeo and Juliet* in freshman English?"

LaTrey shrugged. "How am supposed to remember something I learned two years ago?"

"Well, in the background of Shakespeare, you learned about the Globe Theater…ringing any bells yet? When the townspeople came to watch Shakespeare's plays, the common people had to sit in the pit, the cheapest part of the theater. Five hundred people crammed together in the heat. They were called 'groundlings' and sometimes even called 'stinkards,' for obvious reasons."

"So you think we stink?" Arty asked.

"OK, my stalling groundlings, you should each have a poetry packet on your desk. This packet will become your new best friend for the next few weeks, so please bring it with you to class each day."

Katrina raised her hand.

"Katrina?"

"Are we going to be tested over everything in the packet?"

"No."

The class cheered.

"But!"

The class groaned.

"You will be graded for taking notes from student poetry presentations. You'll also be graded for collecting a poem, writing samples of literary devices, and giving a presentation to the class on your poem, the literary devices used in that poem, and the background of the poet."

"What!" Phil Timmerman yelled. Donovan grimaced in front of me.

"My goal is not to persuade you all to be poets or even make all of you poetry lovers, although that might accidently happen if you're not careful. My goal is to have you walk away from this unit and have a greater appreciation for poetry and what goes into writing a poem."

Mike Sheridan raised his hand.

"Mike?"

"Can we bring in a song?"

"Yes, but I'll give extra credit to students who choose published poems rather than songs."

Mike raised his hand again.

"Mr. Sheridan."

"I say we make a rule that the poems we pick cannot be written to a mouse. Is everyone with me on this one?"

The class cheered.

"I'm fine with that...no poems to mice. Although the best laid plans..."

"Uh, Ms. Day. We said no mice."

"Got it."

"What about what we think the poem is about?" This time Peaches was curious. "I mean, can the poem just mean what we think it means?"

"Absolutely, Peaches. I also want you to research what others have said about the poem or song and what it means."

"That's fair."

"Well, let me put it this way. The poem is yours. When you read a poem, it is your poem."

"I own a poem?" Arty asked.

"Yes, in the sense that the poet may have meant one thing with the poem, but you see it differently. The poem is what you see it as. My supervising teacher, who had taught in the early sixties, said that Robert Frost was kind of a big deal back then. His poem 'Stopping by the Woods on a Snowy Evening' seems like a simple poem of a guy on a sled led by horses heading home on a snowy evening, case closed, right?"

"Sure," Mike Sheridan said, speaking for the class.

"Anyway, my supervising teacher and a colleague had an ongoing argument about the poem. Many other people—and this was before you could Google things on the Internet—felt that the poem was about a person contemplating suicide, and that the lovely, dark, and deep woods were death, and that the person in the poem wanted to stop and go into the woods rather than take the long ride home."

"And you're telling us this to make us feel good about poetry?" Arty asked.

"The two decided to write a letter to Robert Frost because that's what people did before e-mail and Facebook and because Robert Frost was still alive. In the letter, they asked Mr. Frost what the poem meant."

"I'm dying," Mike Sheridan sarcastically screeched. "Tell us what Mr. Frost said."

"He sent back a copy of the poem."

"Cool..." I barely heard the quiet word from Donovan right in front of me.

"When it comes to poetry, you don't need to know all the hidden things, like in the man behind the curtain..."

"What curtain?" LaTrey asked. "I thought he was looking at the woods."

"It was an allusion to the *Wizard of Oz*. 'Pay no attention to the man behind the curtain...'"

Hand up: Cami Halloway.

"Yes, Cami?"

"I'm, like, so lost. Did the Frost poet guy ever answer your two older lady friend mentor people?"

Arty swung around and opened his mouth wide and looking bug-eyed at Cami.

"I have a question."

"Kinkaid?"

"Does our poem need to be an American poem?"

I had already guessed that Kinkaid would find a poem about Camelot or King Arthur or something from his crazy medieval obsession.

"You can bring in an American poem, a British poem, lyrics of a song today. Heck, you can even bring in a poem you've written."

Kinkaid's mouth curled into a crooked smile.

"Good poetry is good poetry, whatever country it comes from. Now please turn to page three: literary devices. Are you with me?"

Audible and inaudible replies.

"So you think some poet just threw a bunch of words on a page? Oh, so much more went into the making of the poem or the song. Some poems use rhyming as a device, and some use no rhyme but depend on the length of the line. See the first device on page three: alliteration. 'Peter Piper picked a peck of pickled peppers.' Repeating the initial sound for effect—in this case, a silly effect."

Pens flew in room 213 as I lectured.

Hand up: Arty.

"Yes, Arthur?"

"What if I decide to write a poem about the bloodcurdling, bad Belmont bones that burn like a burr in my brawny brain? See what I did there?" Arty said. "Alliteration for effect."

"Bad effect," James said.

I spoke. "Let's say, for the sake of my sanity, we sidestep scripting stanzas about skulls and sad stories. See what I did there?"

The Belmont bones had not been cooperative as the forensic teams had struggled over the recent weeks to connect the dots of the bones and the dirt and the consistent target of the ghastly terrorism. "Bones are the last opportunity that people have to say what their lives were like," said Earl Rohrig, the forensic team lead that the *Omaha World-Herald* interviewed. "Written into your bones are the things you do frequently, the injuries you endured, your sex, your age, and the cause of your demise." The public was growing impatient for answers, and the interview gave us little more than a pontification of what we could all find on any episode of CSI.

Tell us why these bones are here, already. Tell us who these people are.

Rohrig added that the salient soil in each case was all from the same area. Experts just needed to the find that area. The samples of soil had been sent to several test sites. What the team did know about that soil was that the evidence of quicklime throughout the samples suggested that someone was hoping that the evidence would just go away. Rohrig said, "The use of lime is common in many forensics cases dealing with clandestine burials due to its well-known capability to remove the identity of the dead and extinguish the remains. In this case, we were lucky to see bones that were not destroyed. More than likely the quicklime was to hide the smell of the decomposing bones from anyone in the area."

In other words, we had little info but more anguish surrounding our Belmont bones.

We were all still disturbed.

And because of our anguish, I didn't want students writing poems about the bones, even alliterative masterpieces.

"OK, so similes are next on our list. What's a simile?"

Hand up: Kinkaid.

"Kinkaid?"

"Would you like a definition of a simile or example?" I knew he had both in his arsenal.

"Why not both."

"A simile is figure of speech in which two unlike things are plainly compared to each other: He's as strong as an ox or she's sly as a fox."

"Perfect, Kinkaid. I should have you get up here and finish the lesson."

Kinkaid's face turned red. He moved his glasses up on his nose and hummed.

"Anyone else?"

This lesson is full of promise and fun like shiny lips with special Kisser gloss.

"Ooh!" Arty waved his hand.

"You again?" I grinned.

"I have another one of your thing-a-majiggas. Arty hates writing similes like a really good-looking, athletic young man who hates writing stupid, silly similes. I like that one." Arty gloated.

James cleared his throat.

"James, I bet you have a good one."

"Think so. Arty is bad at grammar, like, whatever."

Donovan chuckled, a quiet, low laugh.

"Now let's compare two unlike things with each other, and then let's extend them. A single simile is all right. An extended simile is oh much more interesting."

Hand up: Peaches. "Say what?"

"Let's make the comparison and then add another sentence related to the comparison. Example: 'All the world's a stage, and all the men and women merely players; They have their exits and their entrances; And one man in his time plays many parts.'"

Peaches smiled. "I get it. How about...A bad attitude is like a flat tire. You can't get anywhere until you change it."

"Exactly, Peaches. Anyone else getting this?"

Hand up: Mike.

"Go!"

"Signing day is like Christmas. OK, here comes the extension: Bo Pelini is the Santa Claus of my signing-day Christmas. That work?"

"Works for me."

Hand up: Arty.

"Arty."

"My ex-girlfriend is like Frankenstein. When I see her monster face, I'm scared to death."

"Wrong and wrong. One, Arty, we aren't going to demean people here. I'm assuming the ex-girlfriend is fictitious."

"Yes, ma'am. What you said."

"And two...do you think that Frankenstein is a monster?"

"Yes, ma'am. With a green, ugly face...like my, uh, fictitious ex-girlfriend."

"I want everyone to write this down now and never forget it: Frankenstein is not the monster."

James cleared his throat. "I thought we were studying poetry."

"Just a side step here, from a very frustrated teacher. Repeat after me: Frankenstein is *not* the monster."

"Frankenstein is *not* the monster." The grins from the students as they spoke were like jewels in the sky.

"Frankenstein," I continued, "was the doctor who made the monster. For all we know, Frankenstein was a very good-looking man."

"Wait!" LaTrey shouted. "What is the name of the monster? I mean, we always call him Frankenstein. That's what it says on the names of movies and shit...I mean stuff. Sorry, Ms. Day."

"Forgiven, LaTrey. You've been duped by the world. The monster is called the monster. The monster wasn't so bad—just neglected. The doctor who brought him to life is Frankenstein. You'll learn about him next year in British literature."

"Do you feel better now, Ms. Day?" Mike Sheridan asked.

"Much."

"Are you happy?" Arty asked. "Like a fish in water?"

"Like a monster with a name?" James asked.

"Like a student skipping poetry class?" The voice came from LaTrey.

"My apologies for that digression. Back to your similes."

"Well," Mike said, "as long as we're having so much fun with words, we do happen to have a coach we know—not saying any names—who likes to do funny things with similes...I'm not sure he means to..."

"Yeah, we do. Like 'You guys need to hear me out; if the shoe fits, pay attention to it,'" James said.

The class laughed.

"That's called a mixed metaphor or simile. Like 'I wouldn't be caught dead there with a ten-foot pole.' Anyone else?"

"It's as easy as falling off a piece of cake." The voice: Gina Shatner.

"It's time to step up to the plate and lay your cards on the table." James Wu wanted in.

"We'll tackle that bridge when we get to it." Arty added.

"I have a lot of black sheep in my closet." Peaches may have had the best one.

"I'm a poet," Arty said, "and I know it."

All eyes of my groundlings left me and moved to the door. I looked to the door to room 213 and saw a China Doll standing with a pretty pout and a piece of paper.

"Can I help you?"

"I think so." A forced British accent encased each word. "Isn't this room two thirteen?" Gwendolyn Sparks puckered her red lips and looked around the room. Her cleavage, unfortunately, was the next thing to catch my attention, so I'm sure Period Two saw the same exposure. Her chest was full and on display, *like the ancient exhibits at a museum that wanted everyone to come and stare at them and then the teacher made them all leave since the display was inappropriate.*

That kind of display.

"Yes, it is." And yes, we're full. And no, I did not want the girl whom I almost ran over in my class.

"This is for you." China Girl handed me a sheet. The skin still pure, the walk still full of need for attention, but not in a Cami Halloway kind of way.

"Maggie Whitehead's gone today. You can take her seat; we'll need to figure out where to get another desk by tomorrow."

Arty pointed to the seat in front of him with a grin bigger than Gwendolyn's cleavage. Gwendolyn smiled at him and twirled around and settled into her seat.

"Gwendolyn," I said, "Here's a poetry packet, and can you see me after class to pick up a semester syllabus. OK, groundlings, so where were we?"

"I believe," Arty said, "We were talking about me, Ms. Day, and my career as a great American poet."

"Ah, yes, the know-it poet. Why don't you all turn to page three in your poetry packets. This little packet will become your new best friend in the next two weeks."

As much as I enjoy poetry, I have found teaching a full day of poetry about as much fun as a root canal minus the laughing gas and a color-blind person playing Twister combined. That much fun.

I found two notes in my mail slot in the teacher's workroom.

1. A note from the paint store: "Call Shari at Elementary Paint. Your paint is ready."
2. A note from Delmar, Delmar and Smith (Jake's law firm; pause): "Please call Sunny Wu about James."

The firm. What are the odds that I have a concerned sister of a student working at my ex-husband's firm? Pretty good odds in Omaha, Nebraska.

I called Sunny Wu on my way to pick up Oliver. She answered on the first ring.

"Delmar, Delmar and Smith; how can I help you?"

"Hello, Miss Wu. This is Annie Day. I have a message to call you."

"Oh! Right. Thanks for getting back to me so soon. I just wanted to check with you to see how James is doing."

"He's doing great."

"After he got his report card, I think I persuaded him to take a few honors classes. I just wanted to give you a heads-up that he'll be asking for your signature to move up to Honors English next year. Is that something you would approve?"

"Absolutely." James would miss his partners in crime.

"Great. I'll let him know."

Sunny Wu either had not made the connection or was playing it professional-like.

Oliver and I had a date night. We went to a five thirty showing of *Kung Fu Panda* at the Dollar Theater and had hot dogs and popcorn for dinner. Oliver said it was the best night ever. That night I had a hard time falling asleep, but once I was asleep, my dreams changed channels all night long.

I'm waiting tables in a very dark restaurant and taking an order from a big group of mean people. I go to the kitchen to put the order in, and...

I'm teaching a class, but I have nothing ready to teach. I can see that the students are getting restless. They start laughing at me, and I look down to see that I'm still in my pajamas, and then...

I'm walking by a swimming pool, and I see Sam Piccolo on the other side of the pool. He sees me but ignores me. I call out to him, and I see...

Frankenstein. The doctor is calling to me. "I will fix you. Come with me. Come down this hallway, and I..."

I'm walking down a hallway and suddenly remember that I didn't get the food to the table of mean people. I look for a door and can't find one. I'm worried that I won't be able to get the food back to the mean people, and...

Crying and crying. I'm running barefoot outside toward a big tree, set off by itself. I hear voices crying. The night is dark and cold, and the voices keep crying to me...Come find us.

Come find us.

23

"The Gun"
Summer of 1938

Rollie

married another, the devil's grandmother,
And I wisht I was single again, again;
  I wisht I was single again.
Jeb stood in the back of Truett's red pickup and sang at the top of his lungs. My mom didn't care much for the song. I had heard the uncles singing the song when they were being silly or sitting out in the barn with a few beers. The lyrics about an abusive relationship didn't match the lighthearted, silly melody. I guess that was what made it funny.

Jeb took off his hat and held it against his heart.
She beat me, she banged me, and threatened to hang me,
And I wisht I was single again.
"Aren't you supposed to be helping Truett out in the field?" There were some benefits to having to stay on the main ranch near my mom. I got a break from Jeb every once in a while. "Well?"

"Well what?" Jeb looked down at me.

"Well, why are you singing so loud in Truett's pickup when you're supposed to be helping him out in the field?"

Jeb put his hat back on. The heat was something fierce that day. "'Cause when Truett gets back from the field, me and you are going with him and Emmett into town."

"Without my mom?" I asked.

"Yes." My mother's voice was right behind me. "Without your mom. You'll be fine. Wear this hat, Rollie. The heat is going to get worse."

"Where are we going?" I asked Mom, not Jeb.

"You and Jeb are going to run a few errands with Tru and Em. We're having pot roast for dinner. You will be back in time." Mom walked back to the main house.

"What happened?"

"First off, Truett is madder than hell at those two knuckleheads."

"Come on, Jeb. Who?" Jeb knew how to drag out a story like no one else.

"Kenny and Arlan."

"Uncle Kenny and Uncle Arlan?"

"Yep. The bad brothers. Truett had to go into town late last night to pull their sorry asses out of Boone's."

Boone's was a bar. My mother always frowned when her brothers talked about trips into town to Boone's.

"Late last night, long after you was asleep, he yelled across the bar to them and then threw them both in the back of this pickup and drove them back to the Genoa Place."

"So he's tired."

"Oh, he's more than tired. Arlan and Kenny decided, after quite a few beers, that they didn't want to be ranchers or 'cowboys' no more. Said they wanted to go to Denver and become bankers or doctors. So while Tru was driving 'em back, they threw the saddles that were in the back of this pickup out on the long dirt road between Brush and here, singing real loud the whole time. Truett didn't know the saddles were gone until morning."

"The saddles that were ready to be taken in to Willy's for some rigging replacements this morning?" Jeb and I had carried four saddles from the barn to the pickup yesterday.

"Yep. Just threw the sons a bitches over the side the pickup on the way home as they hooted and hollered and sang 'Wisht I was single again,' again."

"They lost the saddles?"

"Oh, no. Truett discovered the missing saddles early this morning and pulled their sorry asses out of bed before the sun came up." If Jeb said "sorry asses" one more time, I was gonna kick his sorry ass. "He made them drive out until they found the saddles early this morning and then take them into Willy's to be fixed. They were both sicker than dogs but more than happy to comply. He has them working out at the ranch today. And that's why Truett ain't too happy today."

"Oh." I looked out on the trail for Truett. "So, we're really goin' into town?"

"Yep. Get in." Truett was behind me as he spoke. Uncle Emmett headed to the passenger side of the pickup. Truett wasn't his regular funny cowboy self. He wasn't laughing or winking any eyes; that's for sure.

I jumped into the back of the pickup with Jeb as he raised his eyebrows and flashed a told-you-so grin.

"Hey, Tru," Jeb said, smirking. "Where's Kenny and Arlan?"

Emmett yelled back, "Don't ask."

Truett drove off to Brush. The dusty, bumpy ride threw Jeb and me around in the back of the pickup, and I thought I was going to throw up off the side of the pickup if the ride took much longer. We got to Brush, and Truett drove to the hardware store and told Jeb and me to just hang tight while he Emmett went in to get a few things. Clouds were starting to roll in above us. The typical midafternoon rain was a welcome relief to the heat we'd felt all morning.

"The hardware store? Are you kidding me? That's our little errand?" Jeb pouted. "I'd rather be back at the Genoa Place."

"Maybe this isn't our whole errand."

"It better not be."

It was a good thing the uncles came out of the hardware store before I killed Jeb. Man, that kid could complain and talk and talk and complain. Truett and Emmet had a few boards that they put in between Jeb and me.

"Scoot aside, but you two keep this stuff from rattling as we drive to the house." Truett was stern but direct.

"Where we going, Tru?" Jeb asked his oldest brother.

"You ask too many questions. Don't let the boards rattle."

We drove to the far side of town to a house I'd never seen before. The overgrown yard and the worn paint on the side of the house made me wonder if anyone lived there. We sat in the pickup as Truett and Emmet came around to pull out the boards and nails. A larger woman stood in the doorway and waved to Truett. I realized that she was Roslyn Granger from church.

"You're too kind to be doing this. We're so relieved that Daddy won't be getting up on the roof."

"No problem at all!" Truett's voice was in charming mode.

"Heard we might get some rain," the woman said as she took off her apron and patted her hair. "Will that be a problem?"

"Not at all, ma'am." Truett winked. Sure wasn't the same Truett who had driven us into town.

A little boy ran from the back of the house, and a woman stood behind him. "Toby, be polite now."

Maribel Winters looked radiant. Her dark hair was pulled back, and she wore a blue dress that made her eyes look like blue jewels.

"It looks like you brought some help today." Maribel looked at Jeb and me. I felt all goofy in my stomach, but not from the drive into town. I looked over to see Truett looking at Maribel. He grinned a crooked smile and tipped his hat.

"Sure appreciative." The voice came from an old man behind the screen door. I guessed that must have been Daddy. He moved slowly through the screen door with a cane and stood out on the porch. There was no way in hell that Daddy could have gotten up on that roof. I was pretty sure that Bob from Bob's Grocer wasn't selling any green bananas to this old coot.

"Could have done it myself, but the girls said that you was coming by."

"We were coming into town anyway." Lie. "We didn't have anything else to do." Another lie.

Both the good kind of lies.

"We think that the squirrels keep getting in somewhere on the roof," Roslyn said. "I know when the next heavy rain comes, we could have problems."

"We'll get up there and take a look," Emmet said as he pulled the ladder from the pickup.

"Your daddy would be so proud of you and your brothers."

"We're happy to help. I brought some young, strong muscles to help." Truett tilted his head toward Jeb and me. Jeb rolled his eyes.

"I got me both my girls back home. I couldn't be happier." Gravel filled the old man's voice.

That was when a giant light bulb went off in my little six-year-old brain. Maribel's sister was Roslyn Granger. All I can say is that God must have been working on another project the day Roslyn was born, because she sure didn't look like Maribel.

"We should be done fixing the patches on the roof in about an hour. Does that work for you ladies?"

"Toby, why don't you take the boys out on the porch for a soda? They have to be parched from the ride in from their ranch." Maribel smiled at me.

"Sure!" Toby yelled. "Come on!" He ran to the back porch before Maribel finished her request.

Jeb was already running with Toby. I turned to Truett to make sure it was all right with him and if he needed our help. My eye caught Truett looking at Maribel and Maribel looking at Truett. I may have been six, but I wasn't stupid. I don't think that Truett was here just to fix a roof, and I don't think Jeb and I came along because we were really good with tools, 'cause we weren't. I ran to the porch.

"We have two flavors." Toby boasted. Pounding noises from the roof rained down on us. "Orange and root beer." Toby sounded as if he were the four-year-old expert and friends with the Soda Pop King himself. I had never had a soda pop in my brief life, thus far, and I'm pretty sure it was Jeb's first carbonated adventure. After an eternity, Jeb picked orange and I picked root beer. Toby showed us how to take the lid off the top of the bottle with a little gizmo.

Where do I begin?

The foam, the fizz in my nostrils, the bubbles, the huge belch after my first gulp?

I was hooked.

"Come on!" Toby was running into the house to a small room with a bed covered with an old quilt. "This my room."

"You have a room by yourself?" Jeb asked.

"Well, with my mom. C'mon, sit down."

Jeb sat with Toby on the bed, and they both took big gulps from their big bottles of bubbles. I went the window seat across from the two and sat on the edge with my new favorite thing in the world: a bottle of effervescent happiness. I moved back to get more of my backside on the window seat, and I bumped into something hard.

"Come on. Let's go. We've got the biggest tree swing in all of Brush."

Flies didn't settle on the boy. Jeb followed Toby to the backyard.

Before I followed the boys, I looked back at the dress covering the hard thing that I had bumped into when I sat down. What I found ruined my day: a gun.

My first thought was that I probably shouldn't be sitting on a lady's dress in her bedroom and that I didn't want Truett to find out. My second thought was that if I had sat directly on the gun, I could have blown my private parts off. And my third thought was a blurry and scary confusion about why a lady would need a gun. I never told a soul about the gun. Since that day in Brush in 1938, I have always understood the expression "Ignorance is bliss."

Guns in Brush were usually about one thing only: keeping the herd safe. Rattlesnakes, skunks, and coyotes were more of a threat to my uncles than rustlers out on the range. Cattle rustlers weren't as common as they used to be, but they did still exist back then. But ranchers mostly carried guns more to protect their herds and their land. I know most ranchers would shoot a wolf on sight if it got near their cattle. And, as strange as it sounds, cattle can kill ranchers. I've heard the uncles talking about stories of other ranchers out working cattle alone and getting trampled or gored to death by a herd. Guns might have saved their lives.

Truett used to preach to me when I asked him why he had a rifle in the windows of the pickup when he was checking cattle and fields or carrying a side arm out to the far pasture. "Guns are not a weapon, Rollie. The weapon is your brain, if you use it. The gun is just a tool."

I wondered why Maribel Winters had a tool. She wasn't taking care of any cattle that I knew of.

The pounding of the hammers on the roof, the anguish I felt finding the gun that day, and the carbonated mass in my stomach brought everything to the forefront. I ran from the room to the backyard, where Jeb was pushing Toby on the tree swing. I ran behind another tree and threw up my first root beer. I stood up, wiped my face, and came around the tree as if nothing had happened. Jeb, Toby, and I played out back until the rain started coming down hard. We sat on the porch, where Truett and Emmett found us after they finished their job on the roof.

"Come on, you two knuckleheads," Emmett called. "We need to get back to the Genoa Place so your momma don't get mad at us for making you late for dinner."

As we crawled into the cab with Emmett and Truett, the Colorado rain poured over the top of the pickup, a calming rain that made my unsettling discovery and unsettled stomach feel a little bit better. The wet earth smelled calm and safe.

Roslyn and Maribel waved from the porch. We all waved back. Toby was throwing rocks off the porch into the rain. Daddy sat on a rocking chair in the corner of the front porch.

"Those boards should keep that rain out plenty good. Don't ya think, Tru?" Emmett asked.

"Uh huh," Truett said.

"She sure is pretty," Jeb said.

"Yep," Emmett replied.

Truett said nothing.

I fell asleep in the cab on the ride back to the Genoa Place, the rain pouring down the whole ride home.

When I crawled into bed that night, I thought about the day. My first soda pop. And whether Jeb could see it or not, I knew that Truett liked Maribel and Maribel liked Truett. I wasn't stupid. I struggled to sleep, maybe because of the nap I had taken on the way home but mostly because of a picture I couldn't get out of my head.

I tried to get the thought out of my head, but I couldn't: Maribel Winters had a gun.

24

Annie

"Bring out your dead."

Arty's voice carried through the crowded halls, booming over the students heading to second hour that cold morning in February.

"Bring out your dead."

The second voice: James.

"Marco?" Arty yelled.

"YOLO!" James replied.

"Marco!" James yelled as he entered the room. Two of the three amigos stood in the front of the classroom and looked at me. They had what appeared to be volleyball kneepads on their heads.

"Polo?" I replied.

"Aw, come on, Ms. Day. You're supposed to say YOLO." Arty's red hair stuck out of the top of the kneepad turned hat.

"When I was a kid, we answered 'Polo.' What's a YOLO anyway?" I asked.

Arty's eyes were squished together with the tightness of the kneepads. "You only live once. Keep up, keep up."

Donovan strolled into the room, that day in an oversize AC/DC concert T-shirt. He put his fist up and walked to his seat.

"That's what I'm talking about, Donovan, my man. We must stand together. United!" Arty shouted.

Peaches walked in and raised one eyebrow. "What's with the kneepads on your heads?"

"In a word, Peaches, or power word: solidarity," James said as he put his fist in the air. "We stand here today in support of our dear Mike Sheridan down in in-school suspension. We stand behind our man."

"Your man," Peaches said, "got himself in trouble…and the kneepads on your heads unite you how?"

"OK, unite to your seats," I said.

"So what did Mike Sheridan do?" Cami Halloway asked.

"Officer down!" Arty said.

"Officer down…in ISS," James echoed. "Repeat," he said into his imaginary walkie-talkie.

"He made Mr. Conway mad," Arty said. "And no, we can't make Mr. Conway mad. I swear that man is the human version of skid marks in my underwear—"

"You could be joining Mike. Be nice, Arty," I said as I started taking roll. "I'm sure that Mr. Conway had a good reason for writing Mike up."

Cami stood up. "Am I ever going to hear what Mike did?"

"Well," James explained, "Mr. Conway spoke to the junior class at an assembly about planning for college. Weren't you there, Cami?"

"Orthodontist appointment."

James continued. "Mr. Conway told the class that they should be thinking ahead to college, even though we're just lowly juniors. And, well, Mike mumbled under his breath, 'Your mom goes to college.' And you should have seen Mr. Conway just flip."

"His toupee almost flipped off his head," Arty added.

"I'm not following." I stopped taking roll.

"The line is from *Napoleon Dynamite*," said Arty.

"I don't even know what that means."

"It's a movie."

"If it isn't animated or put out by Disney, I haven't seen it. I still don't get what the problem is. And why you're all standing behind your man."

"Look," James said, "Mike was just trying to be funny. Kids have done way worse things and have not even been called out. Mr. Conway was just in a bad mood, and Mike is the victim in this whole thing."

"Last year, when I skipped English…" Arty said. "English was really boring last year, Ms. Day. No offense to you. I spent a day down in ISS with all the real criminals. You know, smokers and fighters. There are things you see in ISS that you just never can unsee. The witch in charge down there…well, she turned me into a newt."

The class was silent.

"I got better."

Arty and James almost fell out of their chairs howling.

"OK," I said, "so we all know you spend way too much time watching Monty Python reruns. Good for you. Now take the kneepads off of your heads and get out your notebooks. We're going to finish our poetry presentations."

"*Monty Python and the Holy Grail* was the best, by far," Arty said.

"By far," James agreed.

"OK, so who's Monty Python?" Cami asked, sounding more annoyed.

"Not who. What," Arty said. "Only the greatest comedy troupe ever. They do a lot of skits about the King Arthur days."

Kinkaid wrote something down in his notebook.

"Well"—I could linger for a while—"your little Holy Grail comedy troupe is actually fascinating on several levels."

"How so, Ms. Day?" Arty feigned great interest (in the great interest of stalling.)

"Well, tell the class what the Holy Grail is, boys."

"The holy cup that Jesus had at the last supper," James said.

"And," I added, "the search for the Holy Grail is a universal theme of searching for a higher meaning in a life full of struggles…Hello?"

"Transcendentalism," Peaches said quietly.

"Oh no," Arty yelled. "She's going to ruin Monty Python with transcendentalism."

"Not Monty Python, Arty. The Holy Grail story. Do you think your comedians were the first to address the quest for the Holy Grail?"

"I'd like to think so..."

"The quest for the Holy Grail is kind of like a symbol for King Arthur's search for redemption and peacetime. He established the Round Table and tried to be a good king, but he didn't feel it was enough on earth, so he searched for something higher and deeper."

"All I know is Monty Python," Arty said, "is funnier than...*Napoleon Dynamite.*"

"Enough stalling," I said. "We need to finish our poetry presentations we've been doing for the last week. Do I have any volunteers for our last day?"

Hand up: Kinkaid.

"Give us what you've got, Kinkaid." I took my stack of evaluation forms and moved to an empty desk in the back of the room.

A strange air of calm surrounded Kinkaid as he cleared his throat, took a deep breath, and spoke. "For my poetry presentation, I have chosen the poem 'The Lady of Shalott' by Lord Alfred Tennyson."

"Lady of Shalott? I bet she's hot!" Arty whispered loud enough for everyone to hear.

Kinkaid stopped and looked out at all of the students. "Another coincidence with the whole..." Kinkaid looked down at his notes and read, "Monty Python thing is that my poem is about the land of Camelot, the mythical yet legendary castle associated with the also mythical King Arthur."

"Wait! What?" Arty asked before raising his hand. "OK, sorry..."

"You have a question, Arty?" Kinkaid asked.

"I mean, Kinkaid, are you really telling me that the King Arthur thing is all made up? I thought King Arthur was a real dude."

Kinkaid looked at me and then answered Arty. "Yes. King Arthur, as far as experts can find, did not exist."

"OK, King Arthur isn't real. I kind of feel like I just heard that there's no Easter Bunny. But Camelot exists, right? I think my aunt lived near Camelot when she lived in London."

"Not possible. Camelot is also mythical."

"You're sure?"

"Very. Now some literary sources claim that Camelot, if it did exist, would be south of England."

"Maybe it's buried," LaTrey said.

"Not likely," Kinkaid said. "For the most part, Camelot is the idea of a perfect society. The name Camelot summons visions of knights governing a beautiful world of peace and justice, beauty and goodness."

"Sounds like heaven," LaTrey said. "I bet your Camelot is the star on Ms. Day's picture she made us draw of transcendentalism...you know, for the fake people in that fake world."

"Mythical," Kinkaid said, correcting him.

"Yet, strangely, there are a ton of stories out there," James said, "about a man and place that don't exist."

"Right," Kinkaid said. "It's actually fascinating. Before I read my poem, I wanted to give a short lesson on the Knights of the Round Table and their code...if that's all right with you, Ms. Day."

"Of course," I said.

"Bring it on!" Arty was sincere.

Kinkaid took a stack of papers and began passing them out to the rows.

"King Arthur represents a man who was the epitome of good against evil," Kinkaid began. "Light against darkness and the struggle between what is right and that which is wrong. What I've handed you all is the list of directives on the Knight's Code of Chivalry and the vows of the knighthood. You'll note that the list includes such directives as to protect the weak and defenseless, to live by honor and for glory, and to respect the honor of women, to name a few."

Kinkaid read the entire poem, longer than most, in a strong, confident voice that held the room captive. During the last lines of the poem, Kinkaid seemed to be in a trance.

But Lancelot mused a little space;
He said, "She has a lovely face;
God in his mercy lend her grace,
The Lady of Shalott.

Most of the second-hour students went for the extra credit and chose a poem over a song. I upped the ante when I offered double extra credit for students who came to me for an assigned poem, one that I thought would be a good poem to present—that is, my favorite poems. The past several days had been packed with great presentations.

James Wu impressed us with a great background and reading of "Ozymandias" by Percy Bysshe Shelley. My recommendation.

Donovan Hedder shocked me with a beautiful presentation of Dylan Thomas's "Do Not Go Gentle into that Good Night." He mumbled quietly before he sat down, "It's about a dude whose dad is dying, and, um, the dude tells his dad to fight the good fight."

Our dearly beloved prisoner LaTrey found 'like a gob of similes and metaphors' in Langston Hughes's poem "What Happens to a Dream Deferred." Again, my recommendation.

"The Road Less Traveled" by Robert Frost made total sense for Arty's choice. His own selection.

Cami Halloway even stepped it up when she read Edna St. Vincent Millay's "Well I Have Lost You," one of my all-time favorites. I hadn't even recommended it.

Mike Sheridan, who had presented before his day in the dungeon, threw me for a loop when he picked "Death, Be Not Proud," a poem that's scolding Death as if a person (duh, personification), and the voice in the poem tells Death to just back off and quit acting so noble.

I looked over my list to see who had not yet presented: Peaches and Gwendolyn Sparks. Because Ms. Sparks's seat was empty, I called out, "Peaches, it's show time."

Peaches stood up.

Peaches was a presence.

When she stood up, she was taller than any male student in the classroom. The intimidation factor was gone for me, as I found her tender core endearing. That day, Peaches had feather earrings that were also a prop for her poetry presentation.

"Your poem title, Peaches?"

"'Hope Is the Thing with Feathers' by Emily Dickinson."

"And why did you pick this particular poem?"

"Well," Peaches said, grinning, "Ms. Day told me about Emily Dickinson, so I looked her up, and, well, Emily Dickinson, turns out, is pretty cool. She seemed a little...weird at first. Most of her poems were published after her death. She used to hide poems around her house, in sugar bowls and other strange places. After she died, some other people found the poems and then, uh, published them. The more I read her poems, the more cool she got. And, well, she does some strange stuff with punctuation, and her poems are pretty short..."

Peaches stopped again.

"I looked through all her poems, and, well, I picked this one."

'Hope' is the thing with feathers—
That perches in the soul—
And sings the tune without the words—
And never stops—at all—
And sweetest—in the Gale—is heard—
And sore must be the storm—
That could abash the little Bird
That kept so many warm—
I've heard it in the chillest land—
And on the strangest Sea—
Yet, never, in Extremity,
It asked a crumb—of Me.

Silence.
And then clapping.

"The feather earrings were a nice touch." Arty winked at Peaches. The white teeth in Peaches's mouth had never looked so white.

The class looked to the door.

The emotional temperature of the room dropped fifty degrees.

Gwendolyn Sparks stood in the doorway and smiled as if the applause had been for her grand entrance. She was late for the third time that week alone. No cleavage today, but a very tight and short dress with tights and boots.

"Thanks, Peaches. Hello, Gwendolyn."

"I had to talk to my counselor for a while." She smiled as she handed me her pass.

"You're just in time to do your presentation of your poem."

"Well, I hadn't planned on it. I had to talk to my counselor, remember?"

"As it turns out, you're the only person left to present, and I'm starting a new unit tomorrow."

"I wasn't planning on it…"

"We've been doing presentations for four days, so I'm pretty sure you should have planned on it. We'll wait for you to get your poem."

The China Doll's face was flushed as she moved to put her books on her desk. She put her purse in the chair and walked to the front of the room with no paper.

"You have your poem memorized, Ms. Sparks?" I asked.

"I do."

"Title?"

"My poem is the song 'The Sweetest Girl.'" China Doll wasn't going for the extra-credit points, I guess.

"The poet?"

"Poet?"

"Writer of the song."

"I'm not sure. The singers are Lil Wayne and Niia." Hushed laughter as students looked to Gwendolyn and then to me.

"That's not the poem that you wrote on the sheet at the beginning of the unit."

"No, it isn't."

"Why did you pick this poem?"

"Because I just liked it, I guess. Should I begin?"

"Sure."

I had never heard the song before, and I knew I was taking a risk in allowing her to share the lyrics. Shock more than curiosity kept me from stopping China Girl from saying words and phrases that implied prostitution with pimps. Gwendolyn said the last line of the terrible song and looked at me with a smug grin that spoke volumes: You asked for it.

Students looked at me.

"Thank you. So what does the poem mean to you, Gwendolyn?" I spoke in deliberate syllables.

"It's about a girl a guy used to know…and then she changes."

"Anything else?"

"I think the guy is sad. You know…that she changed."

"Literary devices."

"What?"

"We've been studying literary devices for two and half weeks, and you were supposed to find at least three literary devices in your poem."

"I don't know."

"Alliteration, similes, metaphors, rhyme?"

"I don't think so."

"OK, so if you'd like to take a seat, I'm going to collect all the poetry packets from each of you before you leave today."

Gwendolyn remained standing in the front of the classroom.

"You can sit down, Gwendolyn."

Gwendolyn, no longer smiling, walked slowly to her seat.

No one was looking at her.

Later, at lunchtime, I scrambled.

I needed to call the carpet installers for the attic project during my lunch, so I knew that I needed to hurry down to ISS with Mike Sheridan and Erica Truman's assignments for my class that day. ISS. The plan is always to get the work to ISS students before school, but I was late.

I walked to the ISS room, which was about halfway down the hallway. I looked in the small window on the door of ISS to see Dirk Meyers, the track coach / sometimes health teacher, reading the sports page with his feet on the desk. Dirk's dark, thick hair shocked out in different directions as he lost himself in the sports section of the newspaper. He was known for wearing Belmont sweatshirts, khakis, and white tennis shoes every day. I opened the door. Dirk sat up and threw the newspaper on the desk. The warm, packed room smelled like body odor and disgrace. Each desk that faced the three walls of the rectangular room had a body in it, most with his or her head down.

"Heads up, people!" Dirk shouted as if he had control of the room. "Hello, Ms. Day. You've got work for which of my little rock stars?"

"Mike Sheridan and Erica Truman." The room appeared unmoved. Two heads turned to me. Mike smiled and waved, and Erica opened her eyes. I moved to Erica first, since she was closer to the front.

"Hey, Erica. How are you doing?" I whispered. I couldn't think of one reason why Erica would be in ISS.

A meek smile was her reply.

"We're finishing the poetry unit, so be sure to do the last two worksheets and then send them up. Also, could you send up your sentences for vocabulary and the grammar worksheet when you finish them?"

Meek smile and a nod.

"Take care."

I moved toward Mike and noticed he was reading *Into the Wild* by Jon Krackeneir, the true story of a young man who attempted to live a life like Thoreau after walking away from opportunities.

"You know I couldn't go the whole day without seeing you, Ms. D."

"Ditto," I whispered.

"You and Erica," I said loudly enough for her to hear, "can send up notes with questions if you have them. You two, be good." I gave a sappy thumbs-up to both and moved back toward the front of the room.

Dirk was standing with his hands in his pockets. I got the feeling that he was trying to impress me with his ISS authoritarian skills.

Not working.

"Mr. Carmichael!" Dirk said in a loud and deep voice, both hands on his khaki hips. "I can see the ear plugs. Give me your iPod. Now! Are we going to have a problem today?"

"No." A mumble came from the also-unimpressed teen prisoner.

"People, in ten minutes, we will take a bathroom break, and in a half hour, lunch will be brought down. Anyone got a problem with that?"

The spongy, uninterested faces looked back at Dirk. One boy rolled his eyes. A stifled laugh came from the back of the room.

"Something funny?" Dirk shook his wayward locks.

No one responded.

"I thought so." Dirk looked at me and spoke as if from a poorly written script. "Thank you, Ms. Day, for stopping by. You have yourself a good one."

"You too."

I opened the door and shut it as I suppressed a laugh. I pulled out my phone to see if I had received any calls yet about the carpet installation. I stood in the hall as I read the text: *We can install the carpet on Saturday morning. Does that work for you?*

I texted my reply: *Works for me. What time do...*

A door creaked down toward the dock. A man I had never seen holding a purse and a sweater held the arm of a smaller person with a hoodie covering his or her head; the two moved out into the hall. The smaller figure walked toward the dock as the man went to lock the door. He paused and looked up to see me. A look of horror on his face, he moved toward the hoodie person and pushed the person to the dock and then outside.

I didn't know whether I should run into the ISS room and ask Dirk the Questionable Room Monitor to help chase the bad guys or run upstairs or do nothing. I wasn't even sure what I would be reporting. My teacher fog from the poetry unit had me questioning what I had just seen. My feet were frozen, and I stood until Lyle the Questionable Janitor moved a bin full of boxes from the outside dock. He moved in with force and stopped.

"Oh, hey there, Mrs. Day." Lyle flipped his greasy hair to the side and cocked his head to the side. "It's downright frigid out there." He moved his head toward the door leading out to the dock.

I was still trying to discern what I had just witnessed.

"What ya gonna do? It's February, am I right? I like to call February the f-month, if you know what I mean." Lyle laughed until he hacked and then spit in the bin.

"Yah." I pretended to look in my purse for keys or perhaps some words to reply to the snake before me.

Lyle's phone rang. I shook the fog from my head as I hurried to my next class. As I moved quickly the opposite direction, I overheard Lyle's short, firm response. "Got it...I said, I got it."

The day moved on like a lesson on similes, full of poor communication yet brimming with hope. I was going to be early picking up Oliver, and I smiled at the thought of his Tweety Bird face. A notecard on the dashboard caught my eye. Another index card with big, capitalized letters in green marker:

BACK OFF BITCH. WE'RE WATCHING.

The note was actually inside my car.

In my car.

In.

My.

Car.

The audacity.

I opened the door and looked out over the parking lot.

I looked down at the card in my hand and read the green words again. *Back Off Bitch.*

Seriously? Direct address needs a comma.

Example: Back Off, Bitch.

Where is the comma, Bully?

I'm silently correcting your grammar, Bully. And, by the way, I've been called worse. At least you didn't use the "boring" word. How dare you get inside my car.

I looked out at the parking lot. Had the person who had been planting the bones been the same person singling me out? Was the person nearby? Screening the parking lot, I suddenly felt empowered as I mentally threatened the bully:

I'm silently correcting your grammar, (note the comma) Bully.

25

Rollie

C al Winters came to Brush in the middle of the summer with an ego bigger than Texas.

And ranchers in Colorado don't like Texas and really don't like men with big egos. So, if the story of Maribel's husband getting killed in Oklahoma was true, I guess the son of a bitch didn't know he was dead.

The first time I saw Cal Winters, I was sitting on a fence near the front gate when I looked up and saw a man riding a big black horse onto the Genoa Place property. "You live here, boy?" Cal Winters looked at the barn as he talked down to me. Cal was a big man and almost as good-looking as Truett.

"Yes, sir."

"Well, go get your daddy now."

I didn't like the guy from the get-go. Who died and made him boss of me? I wanted to tell him where he could shove it, but I knew he could take me.

"Now!" he yelled.

"Yes, sir."

I knew my dad was out on the far properties with the uncles and would be coming in for the noon meal soon. I didn't know how to tell this mean man at the gate my daddy wasn't here, so I did what any six-year-old cowpoke like me would do: I went and got my mom.

Mom looked concerned as she peered out the window. She dried her hands on her front apron as she walked out to the gate. I tried to keep up with her pace as I followed her.

"Can I help you?"

Now, I knew my mom pretty well. I did spend most of my time with her. She was always kind and warm to people when she spoke. Her curt words to the man at the gate did not sound like my mom.

"Well, I bet you can," Cal said as he got off his horse. I didn't like the sound of his words. I didn't like the way Cal looked at my mom.

"The ranchers on this property will be back shortly. What do you need?" Mom looked past Cal to the horizon.

"Well, see, I'm new here in town." Cal tilted his hat and grinned. I could tell that he was used to women reacting differently to him than my mom was. "I'm here to see if I can find any work. Been looking around Brush, and there don't seem to be too many opportunities." Cal dragged out the word "opportunities" with a Southern drawl. I moved in closer to my mom, maybe to protect her, maybe for her to protect me.

"The men should be back within the hour."

"Well, I'll wait, then."

I sure as hell hoped my mom wasn't going to invite this son of a bitch into the house. Usually, mom would ask a perfect stranger to join the noon meal. Cal was anything but perfect.

"You can wait here."

That was all she said. She turned around without as much as a "have a good one" or "take care of yourself." She just marched straight back to the main house. I marched behind her. When I think back to that moment, I now know Mom was probably scared to death. We had never had a big, strange man come to the ranch while the men were out working. We had always felt so safe out on our tumbleweed island, far from other people. Traffic was scarce, and this man could have easily hurt both of us, and no one would have heard us scream.

"Well, I guess that's what I'll do, then." Cal's words were full of sarcasm as he yelled at my mom as we walked back to the house.

I sat by the kitchen window for what felt like an eternity. I spotted the uncles and my dad far out on the property. They looked like little ants marching toward a biscuit. "They're coming," I whispered real loud.

"Thank you, Rollie." I heard relief in my mom's voice. She walked up to me and stood behind me with her hands on my shoulders. We both stood in the window and watched the tiny little ants on the horizon get bigger and bigger as they moved toward the main house. Cal saw them too. The men picked up the pace when they must have noticed a big man on a horse at the gate. Jeb was on a smaller horse in the rear. He was the last one to get to the front gate.

Truett was the first to engage with the stranger, who would soon have a name: Cal Winters. Truett got off his horse and walked up to Cal.

"Can I go?" I asked my mom. I wanted so badly to hear what the men were saying.

"You stay right here with me, Rollie." Mom looked out the window as she spoke.

I could see Cal talking to Truett as he pointed to the barn and then out to the pasture. Truett stood still with his hands on his hips. The other uncles and my dad stayed on their horses behind him. I was mad as hell that Jeb got to hear what was going on.

Cal finally quit talking, and I could see Truett tilt his head and then shake it with a no. Truett walked toward the house with a huge scowl on his face. What I remember most about that day is that Truett never shook Cal's hand—not when he met him, not when he was done talking to him.

I know it now, I knew it then. There is nothing more sincere than a cowboy handshake. Unlike politicians or even most people today, a cowboy still makes a deal with a handshake, and his word is his promise. A cowboy does not make hasty choices because the wrong decision can be the difference between life and death for him, his horse, and those he works with. A handshake seals a deal.

Guess there was no deal.

Cal Winters got on his horse and rode back to Brush.

The uncles and my dad took the horses back to the barn. Truett came into the house and looked at my mom.

"Sorry that man came here when we were gone, Edith." Truett took off his hat and put it on the mantel. "I told him not to come out here again. We have no need for him."

"Hungry, Truett?" I asked. I was holding a stack of plates.

"Sure am, Rollie, by golly."

"Who is he, Tru?" Mom looked worried.

"Trouble. Nothing but." Truett went to wash his hands as the other men and Jeb took over the room.

My job every day was to set the table for the daily meals. Because my mom and I had been glued to the window with the strange interruption of the day, I had not set the table. The men all came in at once, and no one seemed to notice me hurrying around the table with plates and silverware. They were all taking off hats and mumbling about the incident.

"The guy had nerve," Emmett said. "I'll say that much."

"Never seen that one before," Kenny said. "Wonder where he came from?"

All the uncles stopped and stared at Kenny.

"Didn't you hear his name?" Jeb asked. "Winters?"

"Geez, even a kid figured that one out." Emmett scooped a big helping of potatoes onto his plate.

"Winters? Like Ms. Maribel Winters?" Kenny asked. "Ya think that's her brother?"

All the uncles stopped and stared at Kenny again.

"Come on, Kenny," Jeb said. "Did you crawl out from under a rock?"

"You think he's what Ms. Winters has been running and hiding from?" Emmett asked, but all the men looked at Truett.

Truett shook his head as he chewed his food. He didn't shake it yes or no. He just shook it, kind of like he was taking it all in.

"You handled that guy real well, Tru," Arlan said.

"Not my first rodeo." Truett stood up and looked at my mom. "You outdid yourself again, Edith." He walked to get his hat from the mantel and head back out to work.

Truett knew who Cal Winters was: a bad man who had finally found his wife, Maribel Winters.

The real question was: Did Cal know who Truett was?

26

March 6, 2009

Annie

"OK, so if Willy Loman didn't die the death of a salesman, why is the play called *Death of a Salesman*?" Maggie Whitehead tilted her head. "I just don't get it."

"Irony."

I thought the words had come from my mouth, but I had not spoken. The students in room 213 all turned and looked at Gina Shatner, the no-longer-dubiously-pregnant girl in the last seat of row three.

"Willy Loman was following the wrong dream the whole story." Gina looked down as she spoke, as if she were talking to herself. "He should have worked on a farm and done something with his hands, but he got this idea in his head that he wanted to be like..." The room was quiet as Gina tried to recall the name of the man who had died the death of a salesman.

"Dave Singleman." This time the voice came from the front of the room, right under my nose. Donovan looked shocked that the words had come out of his mouth.

Wow, a two-fer-one: two students who never participate join in at the same time. I wanted to encourage them both.

"Right and right. Gina, the title is absolutely ironic. Like you said, Willy Loman was obsessed with something he could never be and was loyal to the wrong dream. And Donovan, Dave Singleman did die the death of a salesman. So, Donovan, what does it mean to die the death of a salesman, at least to Willy Loman?"

Donovan continued in a deep whisper. "Uh, he was popular and successful...and, even though he was an old dude, hundreds showed up at his funeral."

"So," I said, "what does that mean to Willy?"

Donovan's pain was palpable. "The American Dream?"

"Say it loud. Be proud, Donovan." Arty shouted.

We might as well have held a spotlight on Donovan. His tall and manly body squirmed in his chair. A low, steady, yet still quiet voice proclaimed, "The American Dream."

Hand up: James.

"James?"

"Except Willy was kind of the corruption of the American Dream—a liar and a cheater. And his son followed in his footsteps."

"Great point, James."

"Even a blind squirrel finds an acorn every once in a while," Mike said.

"Speaking of liars and cheaters..." Cami curled her side hair with her finger. "Everyone's talking about it."

"It?" I asked.

"The cheater you caught."

"Yah, I heard about that kid from period four. Everybody's talking about it," added Mike Sheridan.

Belmont students were all talking about Teddy Bogard, the notorious cheating bandit in my other class; he had boasted to students and teachers alike that he was uncatchable.

Well, I caught him.

"I guess I just looked into his eyes and knew that he was cheating."

"Your what hurts?" Mike Sheridan asked.

"My what—"

"Ignore him, Ms. Day," James said. "That's just something stupid that Mike says when he can't hear you or he needs you to repeat something."

"Well," I repeated, "I just looked into his eyes and knew. Try this sometime, when you're trying to catch a cheater. Ask him about the thing he's lying about and see which way his eyes move when he's thinking about the answer."

"Your what hurts?" Mike asked again.

"Watch the eyes. If the person looks up to his left, he's trying to recall a memory. If he looks up to the right—the creative side of his brain—he's trying to create something, a story, a lie."

That's my story, and I'm sticking to it.

"Shut up!" Cami said.

"It's true." (What was true was that I had read the theory somewhere in my life.)

"And you just told him he was lying, and he caved?" Arty was curious.

"Yep."

The true story behind Cheating Teddy is a very different one than the story I told my second-hour class. Truth be told: Teachers don't like discovering cheaters. But when we do catch a cheater, we have to punish the cheaters. We just do.

The true story of Teddy Bogard: I never even saw his eyes.

I was sitting in my planning period, innocently planning the next few days, and a pimply freshman walked into the English office and handed me a note. I opened the note and read: "Teddy Bogard wrote notes on his arm. He's in your class following my study hall. Robert Homan." In a school as big as Belmont High School, I hardly knew Robert Homan, but we teachers are in the trenches together, battling hormonal creatures, and though we may not know one another, we're on the same side. We must fight together.

So I caught Teddy Bogard.

With the help of chemistry teacher Robert Homan.

The day I busted Teddy Bogard, I asked him if he could help me lift something. Truly, I won't lie. I enjoyed that Teddy had no clue that I was on to his lying game. I walked him out to the hall and stopped. I looked up to Teddy (only in stature; he was six feet four) and said, "Would you do me a favor, Teddy?"

"Sure, Ms. D."

"Will you lift up your sleeves?"

The expression on Teddy's face made my day, and I felt horrible for that—for about one minute. Teddy moved his sleeves up both arms. The vocabulary words were revealed.

"Whoa! How could you know that?"

"An easy little vocab quiz. Really?"

"I was only going to use the...arm, if I needed it. I can barely see through my sleeve..."

"No more cheating."

"Yes, ma'am."

"A zero today."

"Yes, ma'am."

I have had my share of cheaters through the years.

I've known cheaters and liars.

I am a liar.

Peaches came into my room after school with a smile bigger than Teddy Bogard's bad reputation.

"Well," Gina said, "what's with the cheesy grin?"

"This!" She handed the paper to me. I read the letter aloud.

Dear Peaches Trumble,

We're happy to inform you that you have been chosen for the Mary of the Holly Hill Scholarship Program to College of Saint Mary. This scholarship program will excuse you from *paying tuition fees, hostel fees, and library charges. You'll also be awarded with a monthly stipend of $200.*

Your scholarship may be extended to the next year, for four years, depending upon your performance in the first-year examinations. Please find the enclosed document, which will give all the details.

Congratulations,

Karen Cornwell

"What!" Gina stood up and waddled over to Peaches and hugged her. "You're incredible."

"They say my essay sealed the deal." Peaches looked at me. "Thanks for your help, Ms. Day."

"Does your grandma know?"

Peaches stopped smiling and moved to sit down at the desk. "I'm taking the bus to the hospital to show her this afternoon. She's not doing too well, but she'll be pleased…"

"Now you're going to be able to help your cousin's boys."

"Just like you're helping Baby Boy."

Gina rubbed her stomach. "He's been kicking a lot today…" Gina looked down at her belly and said, "Should we tell them our good news, Baby Boy?"

"You better," Peaches warned.

"Well, Tavish and David Kolterman are her new parents." Gina stopped and took a breath. "My parents and I met them last night. I guess I was drawn to the mother's name, which it turns out is a family name…I prayed about it…and then when I met them…" Tears filled Gina's eyes. "I just knew."

"You OK?" I asked.

"I'm awesome," Gina sobbed. "Seriously, these are good tears."

"Sure about that?" Peaches whispered.

"I want this little boy to have the best life. Tavish and David— well, they're like the greatest couple who have been trying to have a baby for so long...and they have a home, and he has a great job...and Tavish will stay home with..." Gina rubbed her stomach as her green eyes melted.

"He'll be so happy." I added.

Gina took a deep breath and wiped her tears. "Don't think I'm sad...I'm just hormonal. I cry all the time. I just know in my heart the Koltermans will protect Baby Boy's dreams."

The March winds blew hard against my car as I started the engine and looked around for any runaway China Girls. The good news from both Peaches and Gina had made my day. I didn't have big news like a scholarship or a new parents epiphany, but I did have a few little nuggets of good news that Winnie the Pooh March day.

The attic project was really starting to come together—almost done. Oliver hadn't had a tantrum in months. The sound in the attic no longer bothered me. And Jaymie Shimmer didn't really bother me anymore, that much. Cheerleaders, they still bothered me, but tryouts would be over soon. I had really gotten better at managing my Jake expectations. He was a big fat liar, after all. I guess I was getting really good at managing my expectations and catching liars.

I looked across the parking lot. All of my little nuggets of good news, all of my little baby steps away from feeling lost, all of my good days layered on good days helped to soften the little pit in the center of my chest that I couldn't ignore: someone was out there. A person out there was messing with my head, hoping to what? Make me feel unsettled? It was working. I looked out at cars to see if people were looking at me.

TRK 311.

A black jeep, license plate TRK 311, became Track (as in tracking down people), and 311 stood for the band 311, a band from Omaha that Jake loved. One of our first dates was at a 311 concert.

OK, Tracking down 311, are you a good jeep or a bad jeep?

Two rows over: LYL 402.

A man sat in a green sedan. License LYL 402 became Loyal for the two most important people in my life. Loyal for (0) Two. Loyal for Oliver and…Atticus.

A snazzy red car was two parking spots to the left of my car. Couldn't tell you the type. Money. Vanity plates.

IMKARMA.

What goes around comes around.

Kind of funny: a car goes around and comes around.

Karma's a bitch.

A shout-out to the parking lot: *Who is watching me? Who is writing me notes?*

I looked down at my phone.

Missed call.

Message.

I pushed Play on the message and set the phone on speaker to hear the message from a number I didn't recognize.

"Hi, Annie Day. This is Annette Graham. I'm so sorry for not getting back to you sooner. I want you to know that my husband and I will be in Omaha in early May for a conference, and I wondered if we could stop by and get the box you mentioned in your message. We'll call before we do. Looking forward to seeing the old house. Have a great day."

I pulled out of my parking spot and moved out of the lot to the main street in front of Belmont High School. The project in the attic would be done by May, so I guessed the timing was good. I also wanted the pressure of the letter off my heart. Annette may not have been in any hurry, but I felt the urgency of the secret letter.

I am sure everyone carries secrets in life. For me, the burden of the letter felt heavier as the months flew by.

Teddy Bogard may have been a cheater.

And Jake may have been a big, fat liar.

But I was a secret holder. I knew a secret that I no longer wanted to carry alone.

27

"The Meeting"
Summer of 1938

Rollie

al knew.

Couldn't have been more than a week, and talk around Brush was that Cal Winters knew that Truett had been spending time around his wife while he was away. I was a witness to an exchange between the two men that could confirm the word on the street: Cal knew, and he was not happy.

I remember the day as starting out in a good way. Probably the best morning of that summer. Uncle Billy had told Truett and the boys to take the day off. The scorching heat was dangerous even at the early hours of that morning, so the uncles, who usually spent long days out on the ranch, got to take it easy.

"Mind if I take Rollie here with me to groom the horses?" Truett asked my mom as I was picking up the breakfast dishes. I pretended not to hear, but my heart pounded.

"Go on, Rollie. I'll finish up the dishes."

We walked to the barn, and Truett didn't say a thing. Once we hit the cool of the dirt floor, I felt the calming of the horses around me. They trusted Truett.

"You always take good care of your horses, Rollie. That's in the Bible somewhere; I'm sure of it." Truett walked up to Ruby's stall first. A soft nicker blew from the nose of the old workhorse; she shook her head in delight.

"Good ol' Ruby." Truett wooed her and moved his own head up to Ruby's large head. His face touched hers. "You're such a good girl." Truett grabbed a rope and tied a quick-release knot and connected the rope to the side of the stall. "Just in case, Ruby. Just in case."

"Why you tying her? She ain't gonna run." I stood close but, as always, asked a lot of questions.

"It actually calms her down a bit. See, I tied a quick release so that if she did scare and buck, she could break free. We just need her to stand still while we clean her up."

I'd been in the barn before when the uncles were grooming horses, but I knew that Truett wanted to teach me. He always liked to teach. "Lots of reasons for grooming your horses, Rollie. I like to check the horse over, for scratches or any health problems. Ya got to check for loose or missing horseshoes. Ya got to comb their manes. They won't admit it, but the horses like their coats looking pretty."

Truett brushed out Ruby's coat with the currycomb to remove all of her loose hair. He moved the brush in a circular motion over her muscles, and she blew an approving wind of air through her huge nostrils. "That's right, Ruby. It's all good."

Truett handed me the curry brush. "Now you work on her while I look at the hooves of Whiskey and Chief." Truett moved to the bin with the other equipment for the horses. "Main reason you groom your horses is to let them know that they can trust you. The time here this morning is as helpful to us as it is to their health and pretty hair."

Whiskey whinnied as Truett walked by his stall.

"That's what I'm talking about, Whiskey." Truett laughed. "When they trust us, we can handle them better when they're on duty out on the ranch. These are some really good horses."

I brushed the side of Ruby, mimicking the circular motion Truett had used on her. Ruby's big brown eye stared at me as she pulled her head back. Hell, she knew I didn't know what I was doing.

"Damn!"

Truett's voice, though low and quiet, startled a few horses. Emmett's horse, Dakota, whinnied. "Sorry about that, ladies and gentleman. Rollie, it looks like we have ourselves a bit of a problem. Can't find the Dandy brush anywhere."

"Do we really need the brush?"

"Not the end of the world, but we've got the time. Go tell your momma you're going in to town and meet me at the pickup."

Uncle Billy had made the right call with giving everyone the day off. By the time we got to Bernie's Horse Tack and Supplies, the scorching heat had made the ride in from the Genoa Place unbearable, and I almost had Truett pull over so I could throw up my breakfast. I held tight, and a slight breeze calmed my stomach as we hit the turn where you could see the buildings in town. I took a deep breath and pulled it together.

The cool of the dark horse-supply store felt like a big glass of water. I loved the smell of the store; it smelled like a perfect saddle. Bernie heard the bell above the door and came out from a back room.

"Tru, see you brought the little guy with you today." Bernie, who needed his mustache trimmed and his hair cut, evidently never had kids, or he would have known better than to call any boy little.

"Rollie ain't little, or I wouldn't have picked him to help groom our horses. We did run into a bit of problem when I couldn't find any good Dandy brushes. Need a few of 'em."

"Let's see what I got here." Bernie whistled as he looked on a back shelf. "Ain't throwing any more saddles out of trucks, eh, Tru?" Bernie laughed at his own joke.

"Still not funny, Bernie. Probably never will be."

"Here, I knew we had a few good ones left. Want any of these?" Bernie showed Truett four or five Dandy brushes.

The bell above the store rang as the door opened again. Cal Winters stood in the doorway with a wicked grin and the door wide open.

"Shut the door, would ya?" Bernie yelled to Cal. "Keep the heat and the flies out of my store." I couldn't tell if Bernie knew who he was or was just yelling at a customer.

Cal shut the door and leaned against a shelf. His hair looked messy and dirty. The man who staggered into Bernie's shop looked different from the man who had come to ask for work at the Genoa Place the day he bullied me. His shirt untucked, Cal Winters looked bad and no longer handsome.

"Thought I saw your truck out front." Cal looked at Truett.

Truett ignored Cal.

We hadn't invited him to our meeting.

"I think I'll take three of 'em. Throw in a few peppermint sticks, and we'll be good to go. Thanks, Bernie." Truett knew I had gotten a sour stomach on the ride into town. The peppermint calmed the nausea.

"Peppermint sticks?" Cal teased. "Well, all the girls in town like peppermint sticks. Is that how you woo 'em, Truett?"

Truett ignored Cal.

"Ya need something, Cal?" Bernie did know Cal. Cal stumbled toward the main counter. "Shit, it's before noon, and you're...I got no work for you here. Told you that before. If you ain't buying, you best be flying. Now go on."

"I ain't going nowhere." Cal no longer grinned. "I asked you a question, Mr. Truett McGuire. You got a hearing problem or something? I asked you how you woo the ladies."

The perfect day was about to turn into one of the worst days of the summer.

"Heard you loud and clear." Truett did not look at Cal as he pulled out money to pay for the brushes and candy.

"Then you better look at me when I talk to you, boy," Cal spit as he yelled.

In the second before Truett answered, I realized that I hadn't seen Maribel and Toby at church since Cal had come to town. I guessed that Cal Winters was not the church-going sort.

"Like Bernie said," Truett said as he put his money away, "You best be going."

"Look at me when you talk to me, dammit. I said look at me!" Cal moved toward us, and a spray of sweet and sweaty odor moved over me. I stood between Cal and Truett, trembling.

"Get the hell out of here, Cal." Truett's voice was calm, but this time he looked straight into Cal's eyes. I looked up at Truett. He put his hand on my shoulder, and I immediately felt calm. "Go on now."

Cal Winters then stood straight up, looked into Truett's eyes, and moved his finger into Truett's chest. "Stay away from her, you hear me? Stay away from her, you son of a bitch."

Almost as if a snap of reality hit Cal, he looked down at me and shook his head. Cal turned around and stumbled out of the store, holding to shelves and counters and walls as he moved toward the door.

"What's wrong with Mr. Winters?" I asked.

Bernie answered. "That man is trouble, son. That's what's wrong with him. Here's your bag, Tru. I threw in the candy for free." Bernie handed Truett the bag of brushes and peppermints.

Truett and I drove back to the Genoa Place. I sucked on the peppermint stick the whole way. I went with Truett to finish grooming the horses, but there would be no more lessons and stories from Truett.

As I said, Cal Winters ruined the perfect day.

Cal knew.

28

March 19, 2009

Annie

"Ever hear the one about the dyslexic that walked into a bra?" Mike Sheridan threw the question out to students walking into class.

Most students stopped and waited.

"That's it. That's the joke, people. Get it? The dyslexic walked into a bra...not a bar, like most jokes—three guys who walk into a...oh, man, never mind."

Katrina St. Martin giggled. Peaches smiled.

"Thank you, ladies!" Mike yelled. "I'll be here all week."

"That was bad..." Peaches added.

"I'm not bad, but bad people run from me." Mike smiled.

"And the jokes just keep coming," I said as I took attendance.

"Wow, Ms. Day. You're kind of gussied up today. You look nice," Mike said.

"I am nice."

"Ha, good one. Are you dressing up for Period Two?"

"Yep, just for Period Two." I was wearing a skirt and sweater that I usually reserved for parent-teacher conferences.

Actually, I was dressed up for a meeting in my eighth-hour plan period with an unhappy father of a girl who hadn't made cheerleading. Hell hath no fury like the father whose daughter was spurned by the cheerleading moderators. Twyla was out of town, so she handed the cheerleading baton to me. I needed to tell the unhappy father that his daughter was a great cheerleader (she had cheered the year before) but that the scores on her teacher evaluations were low because of low grades, so she hadn't made the team. I thought I should dress up to look professional before the attack—plus, it was my birthday.

Kind of a big day.

After all, a girl doesn't turn thirty every day.

No big deal to be a single mom at an age at which I thought I'd be happily married and growing a family. No big deal to be thirty and receiving strange and bullying notes from an anonymous stalker; maybe the note stalker was a student who was mad about a grade. After spending a day turning thirty and talking to my "unhappy dad," I planned to go meet with Avery, my grounds-crew buddy, to share my concerns about my note stalker.

"I know you're all sad to come to the end of the book we've been reading for the past few weeks." The students all took out their notebooks without me even prompting.

"How many times would you say you've read *To Kill a Mockingbird*, Ms. Day?" Arty asked. "I can barely get through a book once."

"I can't even tell you. I bought my first copy at a garage sale when I was in fifth grade."

The first day of the unit, earlier that month, LaTrey had wondered if the book should be called *To Grill a Mockingbird* or *Tequila Mockingbird*—again, not my first rodeo.

"First, let me guess." LaTrey was holding his book and grinning. "It's written by a dead dude about a dead dude who was all mad about the corruption of the American Dream."

"Not even close. Written by a woman, still alive, who wrote my favorite book, so no making fun."

"Are you going to try to make us believe that your crazy obsession with the American Dream and the transcendental stuff fits with this book?" LaTrey looked at Arty. "You just know she will."

"Absolutely. Wouldn't want to disappoint. Let's start with my obsession with the American Dream. Your thoughts?"

Silence.

"Anyone? Bueller?"

Hand up: Kinkaid.

"Thank you. Help me out, Kinkaid."

"Well, *To Kill a Mockingbird* is nothing like *Death of a Salesman.*"

"Thank God," Arty mumbled.

"I mean, even if they do both kind of address the American Dream." Kinkaid cleared his throat. "In *Death of a Salesman,* Willy Loman is all wrapped up in the promise of the dream and not so much about working to get there…"

"Awesome," I said. "Keep going."

"On the other end of the spectrum, Harper Lee's ideas about the American Dream are quite different from Willy's. Throughout *To Kill a Mockingbird*, the courage and determination alone of the characters show that…well, that's kind of what the dream is about. How you get there."

"Exactly, Kinkaid. *Death of a Salesman* is the 'how not to go' for the American Dream—in other words, the corruption of the dream. And *To Kill a Mockingbird* holds up the true American Dream, the purity of it."

"Amen." Mike was no longer joking.

"OK, now everyone turn to the last page of the book. Love, love this passage. You've got little Scout, who's telling you the story, escorting Boo Radley home. For the first time, this little girl gets to see the world from Boo's porch, or his perspective. Throughout the book, the children were obsessed with the scary story behind Boo Radley, and it turns out that he cared for those kids. Cared enough to save their lives."

"Are you crying, Ms. Day?" Arty asked.

"I'm not crying. I just love this passage."

"You're for sure crying," Mike said.

"Am not."

From behind Mike Sheridan, I could see a hand up.

"Gina?"

"I think that the book stresses that you never really know a person."

I wondered if she was thinking of her ex-boyfriend, me, or the person planting bones at Belmont.

Gina continued. "Like Atticus said, you never really know a man until you stand in his shoes and walk around in them. So the person who seems scary and evil could be protecting you, a.k.a. Boo Radley. And the person you trust could be...not good."

"Go on," Mike Sheridan said. "We're curious, Ms. Shatner. Just who is naughty, and who is nice? Who's naughty?"

"Well, maybe some characters from your made-up Edgar Allan Poe short story."

"Ouch!" Mike said. "Methinks the woman doth protest too much."

"Hey, leave her alone, Sheridan," LaTrey said. "Don't worry, Gina. If you start to have contraptions, I can get you to the hospital."

"Thanks, LaTrey." Gina blushed. "It's contractions."

"Wow, LaTrey," Mike said as he held his fingers close together. "You were this close."

"OK, so what about the transcendentalism?" LaTrey was like a dog with a bone. "I don't see any transcendentalism in this one."

"Well, love is a transcendental experience. Remember when Jem loved his dad even though he was frustrated that he couldn't play football like the other younger dads. Jem transcends his frustration and loves his dad."

"OK. Love is transcendental..."

"Oh," I added, "and you can't forget the ultimate transcendental experience: death."

"Death?"

"Well, in the book, when Tom Robinson is killed. What we know is that through death, Tom Robinson transcends his physical body. The bars he was going to be living behind in prison would no longer lock him up. He no longer lived in a world where a community would send a black man to jail for helping a white woman...I didn't want him to be killed either, but the experience of death is transcendental, and Tom Robinson rose above his physical body and all of the muck when he died."

We used the rest of class time to go over the study guide for the test the next day. The bell startled us all, as we were engrossed in the story and its themes.

"Bye, Ms. Day," Arty said as he left. "Please tell me you're not going home to read this book again and then cry yourself to sleep."

"I just might."

I looked over to my right. LaTrey was standing next to my desk. He was waiting for students to leave before he made eye contact.

"Need something, LaTrey?"

"Well, I was just wondering, if...well, my book has a big rip on the back cover, and the corners look like someone dropped the book in water...I'm not sure if you'd want another kid to read it next year...in this condition. I know we're supposed to hand our books in tomorrow before we take the test..."

"Why don't you just keep that copy, LaTrey. It's in pretty bad shape." I knew my department head was ordering more *To Kill a Mockingbird* books for the next school year.

"I mean, if that works. I just—"

"Good luck studying, LaTrey."

"Thanks, Ms. Day."

The talk with the unhappy father eighth hour went well, for the most part. I got the feeling that Daddy was used to fixing things for his little girl, and in this case, the little girl probably had a daddy coming home with a sermon on grades.

I did add unhappy father to the list of potential note stalkers. You never know.

So after the man with the best-laid plans to fix things left, I handed Hannah a pile of tests and essays that she could file in student folders while I ran a quick errand.

"Do you need anything run off?" she asked.

"I think I'm pretty set for the next week. Just the folders, if you don't mind. I may or may not be back here before the bell rings. Thanks."

"You bet. Have a good one, Ms. Day."

I grabbed my sweater as I left the room. I walked down the east hallway, which led to a door that took students out to a garden. I opened the door to the back terrace and felt the cold of the early spring day. I shivered as I rushed toward the shed on the far end of the campus, where I knew Avery would be.

I had told no one up to that point about the three notes, all of them on note cards, all written in the same messy handwriting with the same green marker, all with the same menacing tone. I wanted to tell Avery that I was keeping the cards as evidence—evidence of what, I wasn't sure. I wanted to share my secret with him. After all, Avery had shared the secret with me about the skull found around the fall conferences. I wanted him to be an extra set of eyes for someone who seemed to feel the need to taunt me with cryptic, unsettling messages.

I ran from the garden to the far end of the campus.

I shivered as I knocked on the shed door.

"It's open," a voice that sounded like Avery yelled to me.

"Damn, I should have worn my coat," I grumbled. The wind blew me into the shed and the door slammed shut.

"Wow, Annie Day. I do believe that I just heard you use profanity. Sounds pretty funny coming from little old you."

"Sorry about that. Do you have a minute, Avery?" It had not occurred to me that I could have been more considerate in making an appointment with the grounds crew manager. His time was as important as anyone else's.

"No worries. I'm just writing down a few notes about the tools that seem to go missing every year. I need to let Sheila in the front office know that I'm ordering more so that—"

"Sheila Cromberg is back? Didn't she just leave last spring, to work with her son or something?"

"Sheila left to work with her brother."

"Oh."

"Well, she left to go help her brother with his palm reading or psychic or fortune teller business, but I guess things tanked, so she decided to come back."

"Should have seen that coming."

"Seen what?"

"Avery, they should have seen that coming! If her brother was a psychic and he could tell the future, he should have been able to see in the future that the business wouldn't work out. Should have seen it coming?"

Avery's head went back as he howled. His teeth jutted out and mocked me. "Should have seen it coming. What a hoot." Avery howled again. "Shoot, that's even funnier than hearing you swear, Annie Day."

I leaned back against a table near the door, and my hand touched a lunch sack. As soon as I touched the sack, I felt a wave of nausea rush over me.

"You OK?"

"Whoa. I just got hit with a sick stick."

"You'll never believe what's in that bag."

"Your lunch from last week?" I tried to sound silly. The shed felt warm and strange.

"I knew things were too quiet for too long."

"Don't tell me." The room was getting warmer by the minute.

"Nope, not another bone. But I do think whoever's organizing our little bone scavenger hunt may have planted this as well."

"This?"

Avery put on gloves and picked up the bag. "I need to go meet with Judy in her office, just like last time, to get the 'evidence' to the right people." Avery opened the bag and held it under the light.

I looked in the crumpled bag and saw mostly dirt. I looked at Avery and tilted my head.

"Here." Avery moved the dirt around and then moved toward the light until I could see a necklace. The word *Tiffany* was anchored by each side of the chain. The cursive of the word *Tiffany* was fashioned to look like the necklace made popular by the show *Sex in the City*. The main character, Carrie, wore one in the show; this necklace, however, did not look like the real gold in her necklace. Parts of the finish were rubbed off and dark.

"Wow."

"See, not a bone, but I found it in my toolbox. It was showcased like someone wanted to make damn sure that I found it. Dirt covered my tools—and I keep this place pretty clean—but the necklace was laid right on top of the dirt like a jewel in a display case. Not even sure if this necklace is connected. Just creeped me out, so I called Judy right away."

"When did you find it?" The room started spinning.

"Just this morning. I wonder how many bones and items we need to find before the police figure this out...it's sad, really." The "fun" of the investigation was gone from Avery's face. "Oh, what were you going to ask me?"

"Well...you haven't seen anyone near my car, have you?" I needed to leave the enclosed area before I threw up on Avery. I moved toward the door.

"No, ma'am. Did something happen?" Avery stood up and looked angry. "Did somebody hurt you?"

"No, no...nothing like that. I just, well, it feels like...I don't know. Could you keep an eye out, I mean, if you're around my car or room? I'm sorry to just barge in like..."

"I got your back, Annie Day. No more cussing now."

I opened the door. "Thanks, Avery."

The fresh air hit my face, and I ran to the school building.

I crawled into bed that night after reading to Oliver, tucking him in, and locking doors. I looked over at the three index cards on my dresser top and shuddered.

Green marker.

Three index cards.

Be careful.

Not your business.

Back off bitch.

I still didn't feel that great, but I did feel old.

My voice mail had entertained me earlier in the evening, with several members of my family singing off-tune versions of "Happy Birthday." My mom's message reminded me that the family was going to have a dinner on Sunday to celebrate my thirty years.

Thirty.

It's really just a number. Not a big deal.

Technically, the date noted the fact that I had, in fact, lived thirty-one years on this planet, but you tell me I'm thirty.

OK.

Thirty.

No big deal.

But it was significant.

At least to this English teacher.

In *The Great Gatsby*, Nick Caraway, the narrator, remembers that the day is his thirtieth birthday in the middle of a drunken party with people he hardly knows. We English teachers tell our students that Nick's epiphany is symbolic of the end of the Roaring Twenties, the wild and crazy decade that idolized debauchery and the "purposeless splendor" of the superficial and selfish individuals who didn't worry about tomorrow.

But then comes the end of the twenties. The thirties. The Great Depression. The stock market crashing.

The end of fun.

I had been to five surprise parties in the past six months for my girlfriends who had turned thirty. Husbands celebrate their wives and throw parties, and the world knows that their wives are loved. I was fine without the party. I just couldn't get over the "end of fun" factor. Or the world, as you knew it, will never be the same because—drum roll—you're thirty.

I finished my birthday pity party as I turned on my TV. My mystery shows were Friday and Saturday affairs, but every once in a while I could find an episode of *48 Hours* or *20/20* on the more obscure channels late at night during the week. Where are you, Keith Morrison? Where are you in your jeans and black jacket leaning against a fence, taking in the mystery? What I wouldn't give to have a birthday episode with Keith crooning, "Ah, so the story went cold, at least for a while, but then (dramatic pause for effect) that's what everyone thought..."

I stopped on a channel: *To Sir with Love*.

Not a murder mystery, but even better.

I fell asleep with the TV on during the credits of *To Sir with Love*, my lost thoughts deciphering who in my world was naughty or nice.

The ground is cold.

My feet are bare, so the ground feels like ice as I walk alone in the frigid, dark night. It is late, very late. I look at the horizon, at a big, lonely tree.

"Come find us..."

Several voices cry out to me. They're sad and frantic. I know they're calling to me. I know this for sure. I run toward the tree. That's where the voices seem to be coming from.

"Come find us. We're here. We've waited."

I run even though my feet hurt on the uneven, cold ground beneath me.

"Come find us."

I run faster to get to the tree, to get to the voices. I stop at the tree and find nothing but the tree.

"Find us..." The sad voices, louder than ever, are beneath me, under the cold ground.

Suddenly I'm underground. I'm crying with the other voices. We need for someone to hear us. We hear someone walking above us. We know someone is looking for us.

"Please! Please, come find us! Don't stop looking for us."

Fourth Quarter
Lonely Bones

I learned this, at least, by my experiment:
that, if one advances confidently in the direction
of his dreams, and endeavors to live the life
which he has imagined,
he will meet with a success unexpected in
common hours.

—Henry David Thoreau, Walden

29

Annie

$\mathcal{S}$ pring had sprung.

Oliver and I counted nine different sets of birds chirping from the time we left our house to the time we got to his daycare. The trees were budding. The world smelled like spring.

So why was I so grumpy by the time I got to the school building?

Because I had heard three different songs on three different stations, each with grammatical errors in the lyrics, on the drive into work after dropping Oliver off at daycare. I will spend the rest of my day convincing teenagers who listen to the same songs on the way to school that most of the language they hear on TV, radio, and social media is basically slaughtered.

Lady Gaga was not helping the cause that year. I wanted to scream back into the radio: Seriously? *You and me could write a bad grammatical romance*. My grammar grumpiness was compounded by the groggy grip my dreaming tree dream had on me all morning. Dreaming Tree Dream. That was what I had started calling my recurring dream. Exactly the same. Every night. The dark night, the cold ground beneath me, the voices crying for me to find them. The tree.

Period Two would help me shake the grogginess.

"So which are you, Ms. Day?" Arty asked as he walked into the classroom. "Team Edward or Team Jacob? Some go for the handsome and intelligent vampire type who can read people's minds, while others go after the *werewolfy* man who represents warmth and the down-to-earth fantasy…and, let's not forget, the complications of a mixed relationship. And you would be?"

"I think this has something to do with the characters in that *Twilight* movie, right?"

Phil Timmerman always had to put in his two cents' worth. "Are you kidding me, Elston? That *Twilight* stuff is so 2008."

"Oh, yah, well…" Arty was trying hard to create a comeback. I'm pretty sure he was looking up to his right. "You still do dance routines in your basement to *High School Musical* songs."

"I think that you don't need to vote for either team, Ms. Day," LaTrey grumbled.

"Why thank you, LaTrey. While everyone is trying to decide vampire or wolf team, get out your thesis sheets and topic permission slip forms. Why should I not vote for either?" I asked. Most of the kids were seated and opening backpacks and folders.

"I think you'd be better off voting for Team Skull Scavenger." The kids all stopped and looked at LaTrey. "No disrespect to the dead, but if you're going for annoying and scary, which is what the vampire and werewolf stuff is all about to me, you might as well pick the Skull Scavenger."

The Skull Scavenger was the latest twist in the rumor mill regarding our campus terrorism; evidence was filling social media and graffiti on doors of bathroom stalls. How do you talk about a person or an evil entity all the time without giving "it" a name? The kids had christened the person who was planting bones on our campus with a name: School Skull Scavenger. Most days the kids just said Scavenger for short.

"I'm just saying," LaTrey continued, "that wolves, vampires, skull planters...they're all creepy and annoying. Again, no disrespect to those who are no longer with us, just dissing the stupid movies."

"No longer with us?" James seemed to be talking to himself.

"I thought 'the dead' was starting to sound..." LaTrey said.

"Creepy?" Arty said.

"What would you *prefer* to say?" LaTrey asked.

"Passed away?" Arty offered.

"People who have crossed over," Cami called out.

"Is this one of your thingies for poems?" Arty asked me.

"Yep. Figure of speech: euphemism. Just when you thought you knew all of the literary devices or figures of speech—boom: another one. 'Euphemism' is just a nice way of saying something unpleasant. And death is unpleasant."

"A lot of things are unpleasant," Peaches added.

"Right. And a euphemism is just what you need to soften the speech to avoid offending someone."

"OK," Cami said, "so a euphemism is just being politically correct?"

"In a way...yes." I hesitated. "To avoid being blunt or offensive, we say something nicer or less harsh at least. Most people feel uncomfortable talking about using the restroom—which, by the way, is also a euphemism. So people say things like, 'I need to powder my nose.'"

"Oh," Arty shouted. "I know another one...making your bladder gladder."

"I've got one," Mike Sheridan added. "I've got to go see a man about a horse." Mike spoke in a cowboy twang.

Hand up: Kinkaid.

"Yes, Kinkaid."

"So your euphemism device is really just a lie?"

"Two things: first, it's not my euphemism...and second, yes, it is a white lie. Not deceitful or conniving as much as a lie that softens the blow...and avoids hurting someone's feelings..."

Mike Sheridan said, "You're basically telling us that lying is good?"

"No, no, no...please tell the truth. Lying is not good, but there are times when telling the truth is harsh. Our world is inundated with euphemisms every day. We have Wellness Centers instead of Buildings Where You Take Sick People. We call old people seasoned or experienced people. We call bratty children, kids with challenging behavior."

"Short people"—Mike Sheridan looked at Gina and cleared his throat—"are vertically challenged."

"Or fun sized." Gina smiled.

"Think about it," I said. "A world without euphemisms would, yes, be more honest, but it would also be a rougher world."

Hand up: James.

"James?"

"Do we have homework tonight?"

"Yes, it's on the syllabus."

"Are you lying, like a nice lie, like we really don't have homework?"

"Nope, that's the truth."

Hand up: Arty.

"Arthur?"

"We wish you were a better liar. You should really work on that."

Oh, if he only knew.

I needed Nadine.

I had seen little of Nadine in the weeks of March. She was busy. I was busy. But that groggy day, I needed Nadine. My Dreaming Tree now haunting me in the daytime; I needed to bounce off my thoughts with the best dream swapper I knew.

I walked down the hall to Nadine's room after school, and a creepy thought—creepier than Team Jacob and Team Edward combined—occurred to me: what if my grammatically challenged green-marker-note-writer was also the Skull Scavenger? Weird things had been taking place across the grounds of Belmont High School throughout the past school year.

I stood in the door of the journalism room and looked in.

Nadine turned to a boy at the table. "If you like the sound of your copy, I'm fine with it...if anything, you might get a quote from one of the coaches. Annie! Come on in."

"You look busy..."

"Pull up a chair, Annie. Let's get caught up. Oh, Jackie, don't forget to take one more picture of the ladies in the front office. And make it a fun one. OK, Annie, I've got scoop."

"Well, big surprise."

"You know Lenora in the Science Department?"

"Yes."

"Well, it turns out that her husband left her."

"Yes, Nadine, we all knew that. Didn't that happen before winter break? And that's not really scoop since we've already established that husbands leave wives. Hello? You need better scoop."

"No, wait, listen."

"OK."

"Remember that Lenora was putting her new husband though med school?"

"Yes. Still not scoop."

"Well, it turns out that he wasn't going to med school. At all. Ever."

"Wow."

"Wow is right. Turns out for three years he was getting up every morning. Lenora was making him breakfast, and...he was going to the casinos and to the bar, and anywhere other than the place where people go to become doctors...but he would always take a backpack, like he was heading off to class, and then just spend all her money. She didn't have a clue."

"Wow. For three years?"

"Yah, so way worse than your story..."

"And poor Lenora, coming here to teach every day and believing in her husband and his dreams..."

"And I get credit for real scoop, right?"

"Pretty much. It's just so sad."

"Yah, right. You and Lenora are such smart women, Annie...How'd you make such stupid decisions?"

Most of the students were gone for the day. I could hear one kid in the back room moving chairs.

"I swear, a journalism teacher knows more about the school than anyone. Just sit and work on something and listen. Anyway, these two juniors today were talking about Dr. McDreamy and Dr. McSteamy."

"From *Grey's Anatomy*?"

"No, from Belmont. The kids have labeled the new assistant football coach Dr. McDreamy. What's his name? He helps with the winter conditioning?"

"Nick Stander," I said dryly. Nadine knew his name. She was leading up to something with her story.

"And they're calling that lip-gloss guy who did the cheerleading fund raising Dr. McSteamy."

"Really?" I would call that one Dr. McSchemey, or, even better, Dr. McToxins-in-my-bloodstreamy.

"Yep."

"You got a point?"

"Nope. Just that it's pretty amazing that we have all these attractive men crawling around our school and...are you OK?"

"I guess I'm not sleeping well and...weird dreams. Let's just say I don't feel myself today."

"Weird dreams?"

"Well, dream. One dream over and over the past week. You know how you call a dream that sticks with you dream residue? Well, I have a dream I can't shake."

"Cool! A recurring dream...the doctor is in...wait, one minute. Brittney, don't forget to pick up the pictures that Elliot took of the drama club. Deadline, tomorrow. OK, so shoot!" Nadine looked at me and smiled.

"So I keep dreaming about a tree."

"Ooops, I almost fell asleep there. A tree?" Nadine frowned. "That's no fun."

"And voices crying; I'm not sure from where. That's the weird part of it all. I don't remember much else. Just a tree, far off. I feel like I need to get to it. Every night this past week. What do trees mean in dreams?"

"Let's Google it." The red of Nadine's nail polish shimmered as she typed on her computer.

"You mean to tell me that you look this stuff up on the Internet?"

I guess I had Googled my ghost; the concept actually sounded inappropriate. Googling ghosts could make you go blind.

"When I'm stuck, I do. Some of the info is crap. Some stuff is interesting...OK, here's something: trees are messengers. They represent a person, a spiritual being, and one who provides insight and understanding to a worthy explorer."

"OK, but my tree feels bad. Dark. Sad."

"Wait, single tree...No, this all sounds good, like good health, strength, and protection from evil.... something, something...full of foliage and has a huge and healthy root system denotes longevity, wisdom, and tapping in to a source of life that has witnessed many centuries of change...maybe you're misinterpreting this bad stuff. Maybe the tree, Annie, is trying to get you out of your rut."

"I'm in a rut?"

"Seriously, you don't know that you're in a rut. Girl, you need to get out and start living. Maybe dating again...just saying."

"You mean the doctors in the building. Steamy and Dreamy?"

"OK, well, if you're going to be picky. Hank works with this great guy—"

"Stop. I'm not in a rut."

"Whatever. Oh, look..." Nadine looked at her screen. "It says here that a tree dream occurring over several nights is telling you that you're in a rut and need to start dating again..." A crooked smile appeared on Nadine's face. "Fascinating!"

"OK, you're not helping with the dream...and there's something else."

"Hope it's more exciting than tree dreams."

"Do you believe ghosts of people you don't know can—"

"Wait. Are you still dreaming about your cowboy ghost in the mountains?"

"Well, strange as this may sound, I think I have another ghost, only this one is closer to home, in my attic."

"Another ghost. Girl, you're just a little ghost magnet."

"Nadine, I hear shuffling up there late at night. Only when I'm alone and...thinking."

"A ghost in the attic. Kind of sounds like a kid's story with fun illustrations. *There's a Ghost in My Attic*. Or *Give a Ghost a Cookie*."

"What kind of info do you have on ghosts? As a kid, the scariest thing for me was the alleged ghost on *Scooby-Doo*. But now, my ghosts haunt my head more than anything."

"Well, mostly, ghosts are just spirits stuck. Kind of like a craving is holding them down here—a craving for revenge, to fix something—that craving is keeping them drawn to the world they can't go back to. tramp souls—I like to call them—like bums on trains, not where they're supposed to be. But sometimes..."

"Sometimes what?"

"Sometimes evil spirits—not the souls of those that have passed, but true evil—can mess with people. Take on the forms of innocent—"

"OK, so why are you telling me this? Thank you for making me feel worse."

"No, I'm just saying, don't invite them in. If this spirit is trying to connect with you, that's one thing. But don't be pulling out the Ouija board or conducting séances in the attic."

"Never. I didn't sign up for this. Why am I hearing the bumping and shuffling and...feeling something around me? Weird."

"Maybe because you're so vulnerable now. It's like we all have this emotional radio, and you have a really strong frequency right now. They're tuning in; that's for sure."

"I feel sad for them. Those poor tramp souls."

"Don't feel bad, Annie. They're unaware of time, so the cowboy ghost that you feel so bad for doesn't even know that a hundred and fifty years have passed. It's like that *Groundhog Day* movie where the guy wakes up and each day is the same. In his case, taking care of people. He doesn't feel trapped. Frustrated, maybe. He has no clue."

"OK, so..."

"Have you ever had experiences like this in your life? Like when you were younger?"

"No direct experience, but I do remember a weird thing when I first started teaching in Fremont. I lived in this big, old beautiful white house on the street in town that was the golden mile. My house had been converted into apartments. Five of them, in fact. I was able to rent the only updated apartment. New carpet, new drapes, new paint."

"Cool."

"The not-cool thing, though I didn't know it at the time, was that I was going to be the only tenant, at least at first. It filled up a few months later. So I was all by myself in this great big house."

"Wow."

"It didn't bother me. I was twenty-two at the time. Fresh out of college, ready to take on the world. My parents had just moved me into my second-story, 'adorable' apartment."

"And?"

"When my parents were leaving, my dad looked at my door and scowled. He said, 'This door is as thin as paper. I don't like it.' My mom tried to shush him up. This was where I would be living the next year. Why dwell on it right then, right?"

"Right."

"So they leave. I go to bed, feeling very independent, I might add. And then..."

"Then?"

"I dreamed that night that the apartment was on fire. And I ran to the door to get out, but I couldn't get out because flames were everywhere. I saw my mom and dad on the stairs; they were both reaching up to me since the fire was only in my apartment. They couldn't help me."

"And?"

"End of dream. You know how that works. Dreams always start in the middle. *In medias res*...You don't have a beginning. You don't have an ending. The next day I just figured the dream—which had felt so real—had come about since my dad was so worried about the door."

"OK, so what does this story have to do with ghosts?"

"Flash forward a year later. I moved out of that apartment into a newer one. At a lunch break for one of our teacher days, I gave Sister Mary Margaret a ride to the café where all the teachers were meeting for lunch."

"Still not seeing a connection."

"We had to drive down the street of the old house with the apartments, and I happened to tell Sister Mary Margaret that I used to live in that apartment. And then Sister Mary Margaret said that back in the seventies, a chemistry professor from Midland College lived there and died in a fire. And then I connected the dots and realized that my apartment was the only remodeled one. The one upstairs."

"Wow."

"But I didn't see the ghost. I was the ghost."

Nadine said nothing.

"I felt that panic of being in a fire. And now, in my tree dream, I feel so sad and panicky...and I know I'm in a real place, near a real tree. The details of the tree are so real, so specific, so consistent each time I dream."

"So you have a window open somewhere. Not in your dreams...in your soul. Some spirits must know that you have an open window. I'm just guessing."

"A window?"

"You may sense, you know, the dead around you...the sad spirits that are lost...like your cowboy. I'm not sure about the tree. I honestly don't know what that's about."

"I'm not sure I like having this window open. How do I shut this window?"

"I don't think you can."

30

Rollie

*M*y dad left for Denver in early August of the summer of 1938 to look for work. Mom said that once the cooler weather came, there would be little work for him to do on the Genoa Place. Uncle Billy said we were welcome to stay on the Genoa Place come fall, just with no paycheck.

"You'll be starting school in the fall too, Rollie," my mom told me whenever I started fussing about leaving the Genoa Place. "We need to get back to Denver."

I had mixed emotions about it all. School sounded like a pain in the neck: sitting in desks and writing letters. I sure would miss the uncles and the sagebrush.

"You'll make friends and learn so many wonderful things," my mom said as she cleaned the potatoes for the noon meal. "I think you're gonna like school."

Funny thing is that back then I wanted to stay on the Genoa Place forever and grow up to be just like my uncles. As I look back, I can see that world differently, and I now know that the glamour of the attitude of my uncles and their sure-fire humor was pretty much masking the loneliness and the hard life of the men who live out on the range, day to day.

I just didn't know that back then.

Mom and I rode with Truett into Brush the Sunday after my dad left for Denver. The other uncles were in another pickup behind us as we headed off to church. Truett said nothing the whole ride into town. He was quiet most days after Cal Winters came to town, and I couldn't blame him one bit. Cal Winters ruined everything. Hard to believe one person could change the temperature of a town, but I swear that summer, after that mean man walked into Brush, everything felt wrong.

We filled two pews near the back of the church, and I pretended to pray as we waited for the service to begin. I was tucked in between my mom and Truett, and I squinted my eyes tightly while some old, fat woman stood at the front of the church with the organ playing behind her and sang "In the Garden" in a key I'm pretty sure that song had never been sung in.

I come to the garden alone,
While the dew is still on the roses.

Jeb, who was in the pew behind me, leaned forward and whispered in my ear, "I think there's a reason why she's alone in the garden."

At first my laugh was not noticeable, but I soon got to giggling and shaking so hard, I couldn't stop. I didn't make a sound, but my body trembled, and I could hardly breathe. My mom touched my knee and gave me her stern look. And then mom looked toward the aisle. I stopped laughing and looked up.

Roslyn, Maribel, and Toby walked up the aisle toward the front of the church. I watched the three bodies huddled together, moving like one machine past our pew. I prayed that they wouldn't look at us. I looked back. No Cal. Maybe he was off in a garden walking alone. More than likely, staggering in the garden. He sure wasn't in church.

And He walks with me, and He talks with me,
And He tells me I am His own…

I watched Toby squirming through the service, moving left and right like a firefly in a jar. Truett watched Maribel. After the last hymn was sung, we sat as the people poured out of their pews. Maribel walked with her head down as she passed our pew. Toby leaned into her and would not leave her side. We all saw it at the same time: Maribel's right eye was black, purple, and swollen. Her left arm was held close to her in a sling, which she covered with a shawl.

After Maribel passed our pew, Truett stood up and started to move toward her.

"That son of a bitch!" he shouted.

Emmett and Arlan held him back and pushed him back down to the pew. Anyone who might have still been in the church heard the outburst of my uncle.

And I'm pretty sure God and everyone else knew exactly who he was talking about.

31

Annie

"Did you all know that eighty-seven percent of all statistics are made up on the spot?"

James Wu threw out his clever little question to anyone who would listen as he walked into room 213. Hands in his pockets, his backpack thrown over to one side, James Wu grinned as he walked to his seat at the far side of the room. The funny little question sounded more like something Arty or Mike would ask.

"Oh, I get it. Made up on the spot. Like you just did there. Funny." LaTrey was sitting at his desk looking over notes.

"And did you also know that today is Shakespeare's birthday and death day? Pretty cool, huh?" James was on a roll.

"Pretty awful." Kinkaid grumbled. Most of the kids were in the room scattering to their seats.

"Pretty awesome," Arty said. "Like a two-fer-one. Shakespeare didn't know that every year he was celebrating his birthday, he was also celebrating his death day."

Kinkaid shook his head as he pulled out his notes.

"Is that true, Ms. Day? Did Shakespeare really die on his birthday?" Cami asked.

"Records state that he did, but we can't really trust the record keeping from that era. Sometimes people just wrote down the dates of when people were buried instead of the day they died, or they recorded dates that they thought they died because they didn't have calendars. Even birthdates are questionable, since people were more concerned about surviving than writing down dates. Probably pretty random."

"How can you be too busy to write down when a baby is born or a person dies?" Cami asked.

"Accuracy of dates was not a priority to people who were fighting the plague and syphilis. Shakespeare didn't have a choice, but he was living in questionably the worst place and time in history. London was overcrowded and rat-infested. They actually closed down the Globe Theater for a while due to the plague. We can't be certain of either Shakespeare's birthday or death day, even though I've always found the double-day scenario interesting too, James."

"Kind of like Amber Harris," LaTrey said.

"How in the world are Shakespeare's records anything like Amber Harris?" Kinkaid's tone was dripping with aggravation.

Amber Harris was a twelve-year-old Omaha girl whose murder had been in the news the past several weeks. She had attended junior high school several blocks from Belmont and was last seen getting off a school bus in November of 2005. In spring of 2006, authorities had positively identified her remains, which had been found in Hummel Park in north Omaha. Jurors were probably listening to the case against accused murderer Roy Ellis as we sat in my classroom that day.

"We don't know her death date either. We just know the day that they found her body. We'll never know her official date of death." LaTrey wasn't rattled by Kinkaid's mood.

"Same for our Belmont bones," Arty said, "even though we do know who the dead people are. Do you think we'll ever find out who killed our Belmont bones, Ms. Day?"

A week earlier, authorities had identified the skull found at the beginning of the semester as that of thirty-two-year-old waitress Peggy Medina. So Mystery Doe Number Two, a.k.a. Locker Room Skull, now had a name and a history. The week following the day that Peggy Medina's skull had been discovered in a locker before swim practice back in February, the administration held a meeting with teachers led by a crisis expert. The first words that our expert said after being introduced were, "I have worked with crisis situations in the school district for over fifteen years, and I will say this much: I have never had a situation like this."

(What? School skulls are unusual? We, as the Belmont community, had grown to associate the two words, almost like a cheer. I say "school"; you say "skull." SCHOOL-SKULL-SCHOOL-SKULL! Go team, go!)

The expert's advice to the staff the day of our in-service back in February was not that different from any other crisis situation in a school. "Make counselors aware of any students who may seem to be suffering more than others." "Let students talk about the crisis in the classroom if they feel the need." "Be the adult in the room to guide the discussion." We were also directed to not let kids get too fixated on the issue.

"Mrs. Jenkins said that she knew the family of the last skull identified. She was so sad," Cami said.

"Wow, that's too bad." I wasn't sure if Mrs. Jenkins should have shared that piece of information. I shared little of my personal life with my students, and I had never shared with anyone—since Lyle had asked me to keep a secret—that there were actually three skulls found. The football practice field skull had been identified as Jennifer Caldwell. The locker room skull had only recently been identified as Perkin's waitress Peggy Medina. The skull that Lyle had found in his shed, the one that had not been released to the media, had yet to be identified.

"Yah, I know, right?" Mike said. "Remember when Mrs. Jenkins got so mad at you that she yelled, 'If you don't stop doing that, I'm going to ask you to stop doing that again.' Classic Jenkins."

"What was I doing that made her so mad?"

"You got up and said something like 'This is my impression of Coach Edwards impersonating Keith Richards singing Lady Gaga's 'Poker Face,' and she got so red in the face…"

"OK, my stalling groundlings. You do have a major research paper due in two and a half weeks, so get out your notecards so I can explain how I want you to keep track of the information you find to support your thesis statements. Up until this point, you've all done pretty well at playing the parrot, memorizing and spitting back. And because you're going out into the world soon, you need to start thinking critically."

"Thus, the research paper," grumbled Kinkaid.

"And what you all must remember is that you've all gotten by, up until this point, with just your good looks and charm…"

"It's worked for us up to this point," James said, grinning once again.

"Juniors in high school, in my opinion, sit in a unique place in the universe…five or six years ago, you were playing outside in the summers, playing Barbie dolls, building forts. Five or six from now, you'll all more than likely be out in the world in jobs and making a difference in this world. No other age is as close to both worlds as juniors in high school. A research paper is not a book report. For Phil back there."

Phil Timmerman sat up straight.

"Phil's topic is the Civil War. Phil's not writing a report about what happened in the Civil War. He's going to write about how many people have different views about what started the Civil War. And Phil is writing, in lieu of all the other opinions, that the Civil War was kicked off by…" I looked at Phil.

"Manure, population, and states' rights." Phil smiled.

"That stinks…" Arty mumbled.

"And our little joke-teller James is writing his paper on the mass murders, which we all know hit too close to home last year."

On December 5, 2007, nineteen-year-old Robert Hawkins had taken his own life after killing eight people and wounding sixteen others in a deadly rampage in Von Maur, a store in a mall about five minutes from Belmont High School. An Omaha gunman killed eight people and then shot himself. A suicide note reportedly read, "Now I'll be famous."

"I don't need James to write a report on what happened that day in Von Maur last year before the holidays. I already know what happened. It was horrible. Most of the country knows. And in the case of his paper, it's not a case of whether you agree or disagree with what happened that day. What I want James to do is think."

"When does he not?" Mike said.

"James is not going to say: mass murder, good or bad, yes or no. We all know that mass murders are bad. James decided to take the angle of the role the media plays in repeated mass murders. That the media often gives too much attention to the events. Katrina is not doing a book report on the attack on America on September eleventh, 2001. Katrina is going to address the negative impact the incident had on the travel industry. Kinkaid is researching early medieval history and legend with a Camelot twist. Donovan here," I said as Donovan squirmed, "is taking on the Bermuda Triangle and the issue of whether or not planes, boats, and people have really been lost in a mysterious zone some- where between Florida, Puerto Rico, and Bermuda. Who is attacking or taking these people? Is it aliens, a strange magnetic field in the bottom of the ocean, or a gigantic hoax? Which is it, Donovan?"

"Guess you'll just have to read the paper and find out." One corner of Donovan's mouth curled up into a half smile. Donovan Hedder was as mysterious as the Bermuda Triangle and possibly as deep as the ocean that stole the lost souls from the world.

The intercom came on in my room. The static noise was soon replaced by a voice.

"Ms. Day?" I knew that voice as Angie Lourdes, a secretary in the main office.

"Yes?"

"This is your plan period, right?" The office usually didn't call us by way of the intercom.

"No, I'm actually sitting here with thirty-four other people working on research papers."

"Help!" Arty screamed. "We're being held captive by a crazy English teacher." The class laughed at Arty's high-pitched squeal.

"Uh, well," Angie said. "We're sending down a substitute teacher to take over your class. Everything is fine…"

My heart dropped.

"But Oliver's daycare called to say that he cracked his head open. Repeat, he's fine. They just need you to come and get him to the hospital…Aemon Phillips is the person who is on his way to take over your class…Are you there?"

"Yes, I'm here. Thanks for the message, Angie."

"Sorry, Annie…Aemon will be there shortly."

Mike Sheridan stood up. "Don't panic, Ms. Day. I cracked my head open, and it was no big deal."

"No worries, Ms. Day," Arty said. "I've cracked my head open five times. I can show you all the stitches. See here…" Arty tilted his head and moved back his red hair form his forehead.

"I knew I could count on Period Two to help me feel better. Be good for the sub."

Aemon Phillips stood in the doorway.

I handed Aemon my sub folder. "All of my classes are working on notecards, but if it looks like people need more to do, I have grammar worksheets in this folder."

The class groaned.

"Oh, one more thing to add," Arty said to me as I got my purse and keys. "Now we can add one more thing that happened on this day in history. Looks like your son joins Shakespeare on interesting things happening on this day in history."

"Put it in the record, Arty." I yelled to the class as I left, "Be good!"

By the time I arrived at Oliver's daycare, I had calmed down. He's going to get hurt, I told myself. This will not be the only time he will need to get medical help for an injury. Do not be that mom who falls apart during the tough times.

The daycare workers were awesome. The hospital staff was great. Oliver was in a pretty good mood, and I secretly thought he was enjoying all the attention he was getting. We went through the Burger King drive-thru on the way home. He was happiest when he got home to Atticus, and Atticus carefully sniffed at his stitches.

The excitement of the day wore us all out. Oliver fell asleep as we read *Horton Hears a Who*. I corrected no papers and turned in early.

Knocking, knocking.

No shuffling from above.

Knocking, more knocking from below.

My heart was beating as I woke out of a deep sleep. The knocking sounded as if it was at the front door. I looked at my alarm clock and saw 4:27 a.m.

A man's voice was yelling. I couldn't make out what he was saying. Atticus moved down the steps at a pace I had not seen in years. He growled a quiet, low growl that sounded as if it was sitting in the back of his throat. I panicked. I had a child and no one, other than an elderly golden retriever with arthritis, to protect me.

Bam, bam, bam.

I crept down each step. The third step creaked. I stood on a step where I could see the small window in the door. I had my cell phone in hand in case I needed to dial 911. I got to the landing and could make out a man standing at the door, pounding now.

"Annie, it's Jake. Open up."

I got to the door and looked out. I wasn't afraid. I was annoyed.

I unlocked the door and opened it.

"What do you need? Oliver's sleeping." Atticus continued his low growl.

A shower of vodka and cold night air hit me as I opened the door and Jake brushed in. He grabbed me. "Annie, I need you." His cologne, a brand I had bought him when we first got married, overcame me. He shut the door and grabbed my hands and pulled me on to the couch. Atticus stopped barking, but he stayed nearby.

"What's wrong, Jake?"

"I've been thinking…I've been thinking…"

"You've been drinking. You need to go now. I have to work in two hours, Oliver is sleeping…"

"No, no, no, just listen. I've been horrible. I've been wrong." Jake moved his hands up and down my arms. "I know that. You never deserved all the selfish, mean things I've done and said. I'm taking you back."

I said nothing.

"I know…this is crazy, right…but it's so, so right. I'm taking you back, my sweet, little Annie."

The scene that had played over and over in my head as I lay in my bed countless nights imagining Jake begging me to be together again was playing out in my living room—only this time, in real life, and I was disgusted.

"You need to go."

Jake grabbed my hand "Are you not hearing me, Annie? I'm taking you back."

The arrogance mixed with vodka and Omni cologne slapped me into the most anger I had felt in years.

I stood up. "You have a wife to go home to. Now go home," I whispered as loud as I could. Atticus growled.

"But…I don't get it."

"You think I'm that pathetic, Jake? While you've gone on these past three years to live your life, do you think I've just been waiting?"

"What about your little picket fence and all of our little angel babies? Our home?"

"This is not our home. This is my home, and I need you to get out of it."

"You were right, Annie. This corporate world I'm in and all the parties and…this…" Jake stood up and threw his hands out to the room. "This is pure."

Atticus sighed and flopped to the floor.

"Jaymie," I said, only this time I didn't whisper. "You have a wife. Now go home to her. She should never know that you were here." Right then, Jaymie had no idea where her husband was. My guess: I wasn't his first conquest. I felt sorry for Jaymie for a moment, and then the moment was gone. She had signed up for this.

"Jaymie and I..." Jake shook his head and looked down. "We just..."

"Stop. I don't want to know one detail of your relationship with her. Just go figure your life out." I pointed to the door as I walked away from the couch. "Please."

"But...listen...I had an epiphany, Annie." Jake's slur on the word "epiphany" was comical, and I thought I could actually laugh out loud, and that laughter might just feel awesome. "Listen to me...Your dream to have this..." Jake threw his hands up and looked around the room. "This simple life. This pure life. It's good."

"You're making no sense."

"I want it all back. I'm taking you back."

I laughed.

"I thought you'd be happy, my sweet little Annie."

"Jake, I'm not your sweet little Annie, and, sorry to break it to you, but you are not the center of my universe."

Jake looked slapped.

"I have no desire to have you back in my world. For God's sake, even your wording—do you not hear it? I've lived my life since you left, and I like it. Oliver and I are doing better than ever. No, I'm not taking you back, Jake Day."

"But you always said I was your dream. I was the answer to your dreams."

"I was wrong about the dream, Jake."

"The dream is good."

"The dream is good. But I was wrong about you and the dream. I was wrong. And that's OK. We did have a really neat kid through it all."

"You said I was your knight in shining armor." I had actually said those words? "You said that...you said..." Jake spit on the last word.

"People say a lot of things that they really just want to be true. Every day, people speak of dreams like they're realities."

"We can still make those things real."

"No, Jake, you can't. We're divorced, remember? I forced you into my dream in the beginning. You...well, you are who you are, and you do the things you do." Jake squinted his eyes in confusion. I knew he would never change. "Go get yourself sober and work on your marriage."

Jake shook his head.

"I'm calling a cab for you. You're on your own to get back and pick up your car. Oh...Oliver cracked his head open. Three stitches. He thinks the stitches are pretty cool."

Jake sat on the couch as I called the cab. Once the cab arrived, I turned to him. "Jaymie should never know you stopped by."

I watched Jake walk to the cab. He looked handsome and pathetic.

I felt sorry for him.

32

"The Incident at Wind Hill"
End of the Summer of 1938

Rollie

We needed rain something fierce. The dust on the road was dreadful as we drove home from church the day we saw Maribel looking the way she did. I couldn't stop thinking of her swollen, purple face around an eye that was merely a slit. No one talked as we made our way home for supper.

When we got to the Genoa Place, we ate the noon meal, once again with hardly a word, aside from a "Pass the peas" or "Good meal again, Edith." All the uncles disappeared after lunch as I helped mom with the dishes. Sunday afternoons were for napping, so it didn't surprise me none that the men all took off. Once Mom and I were alone, I cleared my throat.

"Mom?"

"Hmmm…"

"It was Mr. Winters who hurt Maribel, right?" I felt I was inching into adult territory, where my mom never liked me to wander. It was still a time when most kids were not allowed to join adult conversations, but I figured she was the only one in the room, and I wanted to have a conversation with her. I wasn't technically interrupting an adult conversation, just talking about a very adult problem.

"We don't know that for sure, Rollie. And this is something you shouldn't worry about." My mom handed me a plate to dry.

"Why can't the sheriff just put Cal Winters in jail? Everyone in town knows he's a bad guy." I dried the plate and stacked it on the pile of plates I had already dried.

"Rollie, you don't know what Mr. Winters has done or had not done. Just because you don't like a person, doesn't mean you can assume—"

"Do you think he hurt her?"

My mom stopped but said nothing.

"If the sheriff can't do anything, why can't we?" I asked. "We could just go and get Maribel and Toby, and they could stay here with us. And all of us together could protect them. If that bully ever came around here, we could all take Cal on."

"It's more complicated than that, Rollie."

"But what if he hurts Miss Maribel so bad that he kills her? I mean, her face was beat up bad. Wouldn't we be part to blame since we weren't doing anything?"

My mom looked at me. "Rollie, listen to me. In strange situations... like this one...helping might be like putting your hand in to stop a dog from attacking a cat."

"So you do think he hurt Maribel?"

"I have no idea, Rollie. But if he did hurt her, we can understand now why she was hiding from him...if that's what she was doing."

"Only Cal found her."

"And now, it's really none of our business." Mom handed me the last plate. "No more talking about it, ya hear. Only makes the uncles angry."

"Yes, ma'am."

"I don't want your heart to carry this problem. It's an adult problem. Everything will be all right...Now go find Jeb, and you two find yourselves something to do. Go on."

Something to do.

Easier said than done. We didn't have swimming pools. We didn't have parks with swing sets. We didn't have a television on the Genoa Place. We just had our imaginations. And that sometimes got us into trouble.

I changed out of my uncomfortable church clothes and ran out to the barn. Jeb was already out of his church clothes and feeding the horses.

"Whatcha doing?" I yelled as I walked toward the barn.

"Nothing. But I have an idea."

Most days, after we finished up in the barn, Jeb and I would try to find our own fun when we could. You can only build forts with corncobs for so long, and then you could go crazy. I would go along with anything he said. He was eleven, after all. An eleven-year-old hanging out with a six-almost-seven-year-old—probably because no one else was around—was kind of a big deal.

Jeb looked around and then said in a quiet voice, "Want to head to Wind Hill?"

I had never been to Wind Hill. My mom said that it was a heck of lot of fuss about a place that she didn't want me anywhere near. I knew we had to ride a horse or drive a car, so I didn't know exactly what Jeb had in mind, but since I didn't have any other commitments, and because Truett was napping and my mom was in the house, I said yep.

Jeb and I were going somewhere we weren't supposed to go. And I was pretty excited about it all. Truett had warned us not to go beyond the tree on the end of the south pasture without supervision, but it was the end of the summer, and I would now have a fun story to share with my buddies back in Denver.

We rode Old Charley out to Wind Hill.

Charley was older and calmer and more patient with boys, I guess. I held tight to Jeb as I sat behind him. Charley didn't move too quickly, so it took us about forever to get to the tree on the south pasture. A long ride on Old Charley was a stomachache waiting to happen. Just when I was going to tell Jeb to turn around, I saw the cliffs that jutted out over the South Platte River.

Jeb pointed as he yelled back to me. "We'll leave Charley down here and head up. You still OK with this?"

"Hell, yes," I yelled back to him. I did have a momentary guilt pit in my stomach but then took a deep breath and laughed.

Good news was the wind was picking up. The whole point of going to Wind Hill—based on all the cowboy stories or lies I had heard—was that the wind was the only thing that kept you from falling off the cliff. I looked down. I took a breath. I didn't want to throw up in front of Jeb.

Jeb grinned. "Let's do this."

"Have you ever done this before?"

"Oh, tons of times," Jeb lied.

Once we got to the highest point of the bluff overlooking the river, I stopped and looked out. The view was one of the most beautiful in the area. While the rest of Brush was vast and tired looking, the view from the cliff showcased trees and rocks on the horizon. The great sky protecting the land was both beautiful and scary at the same time. As if the world just went on and on and on, and it was breathtaking. I felt like how God must feel when he looks down at his creation. Proud.

"Now we just get as close to the edge of the cliff, like this." Jeb moved the tips of his work boots just over the edge of the rock cliff. "And then…." Jeb stopped.

"And then what? Shit, you don't know what you're doing." Cussing gave me a jolt of confidence. If Jeb did this, I had to do this.

"And then, we just wait."

"Wait?"

"Wait for the wind, dumb shit."

More confidence cussing.

I moved closer to the edge. Jeb and I both stood there as if we were waiting for a train.

"And put your arms out…like this…I think."

"Ya think?"

"Here it comes it. Hear it?"

A howling like I've never heard before took over the valley below. Like a lonely ghost crying for someone, anyone. And then, all at once, the wind took over and pushed against our bodies.

"Now! Lean."

Jeb and I both leaned into the wind pushing against us, our bodies leaning out toward the valley below. I felt the wind hard on my face. It was strange to think that air was holding me up. I felt as if I were flying. The howling and the pressure made me forget that I was a kid. I could hear Jeb laughing or crying or something, and then something grabbed me and pulled me back. Jeb and I fell to the ground.

"What in the hell?"

Truett was screaming at Jeb and me as we looked up from the ground. It was then I saw that Jeb had been crying. Howling like a baby.

"What in the hell were you thinking?"

I tried to say something.

"Jeb, you know better than that. You could have fallen down to your death, boy. And taking Roland with ya? What the hell were you thinking?" Spit sprayed from Truett's mouth.

I sat up and felt my face. It hurt where the wind had blown against it.

"I wasn't thinking," Jeb wailed. He was all slobbery, tears and snot all over his face as he cried. I wanted to make fun of him. I knew he'd be razzing me if I were bawling. We found out later, when Truett retold the story over and over again, that Jeb was actually starting to fall forward when the wind backed down and that Truett pulled us both back before he fell. "I-I-I wasn't thinking."

"Roland, your mom is worried sick. Good thing Billy warned me that he saw you all heading out in this direction when he did. He said you were just two specks on the horizon, but he was pretty sure it was you two. I just got in the pickup and headed this way. This is worse than when you took turns seeing how long you could hold on to that electric fence. I ought to smack both your heads together and see if I can knock some sense into ya."

"Sorry, Tru," Jeb blubbered.

"You ruined my nap, you little sons a bitches." Truett tilted his head as we walked back to get Charley. Our little sneaky game was not what he needed after what he had witnessed in church.

And then—I started laughing. I don't know why. I just couldn't stop. Between Jeb bawling and Truett looking funny being mad and wanting to smack our heads together and, I guess, the adrenaline from almost falling down that cliff, I laughed harder than I've ever laughed.

Truett no longer looked mad. Jeb stopped crying and wiped his eyes and started to laugh. A little smile crawled onto Truett's face. "Get yourselves together, and we'll head back to the house."

I rode in the pickup with Truett, and Jeb rode Charley behind us. We didn't say anything on the long ride home.

33

Saint Deroin—Indian Cave State Park

Indian Cave. Cemetery of a Saint. You'll find the bodies by the tree.
The Omaha Police Department reported the phone call coming in to their main office at 11:10 on Friday morning, April 24. Of course, Ricky Dupree, the officer who first heard the message, immediately thought what every person who heard that message thought: the Belmont bones.

Maybe Officer Dupree thought of the Belmont bones because of the plural on the body count. Maybe he thought of the bones because the Belmont bones kept popping up in the news, and by this point in the investigation, it was clear to even the most naive ninth graders in Belmont and any high school that the bones had been intentionally placed on the grounds to get attention. Well, the whole city of Omaha was paying attention, so the police department suspected that the mysterious Indian Cave message was just another freakish clue in the game that was starting to wear down the nerves of the department and of the people of Omaha watching the news from the safety of their homes.

The anonymous call, traced back to a disposable TracFone sold at a local Omaha Walmart, gave the police this haunting message: "Indian Cave. Cemetery of a Saint. You'll find the bodies by the tree." The voice of the caller was that of a man, whispering to the receiver, his tone intense and grave.

Officer Ricky Dupree worked with Officer Kelly Tramper on the task of researching and decoding the voice mail, which the two played over and over again. Their chief directed the two to "work on it" while he made a heads-up call to the team lead of the men investigating the Belmont bones. Kelly Tramper Googled "Indian," "Cave," "Saint," and "Tree" and found that a park in Richardson County in southwest Nebraska kept popping up.

With 3,052 rugged acres bordering the mighty Missouri River, Indian Cave is a pristine area devoted to camping, hiking and backpacking, picnicking, nature, and wilderness activities.

And possibly a good place to bury bodies.

Indian Cave State Park, near the lowest point in the state on the Missouri River and including words that matched the cryptic message, "Indian" and "Cave," in the name, was at least a place to start.

"The park is near an old ghost town. Saint Deroin," Kelly told Ricky as she scrolled through the information. "Although the man whose name graced the town was by no means a saint. The trader Joseph Deroin and his wife set up a trading post there around 1850."

"So how'd 'Saint' show up in the name?" Ricky asked.

"Looks like the guy thought he would boost traffic to the area with a name similar to Saint Joseph and Saint Louis. The town died a miserable death when the Burlington Railroad was built in 1903. Besides the Indian Cave State Park, the only other ghostly remnant of the town is a schoolhouse and Saint Deroin Cemetery."

"Wonder how many trees are in that graveyard," Ricky asked.

So the police department in Omaha called the Richardson County sheriff's department and asked them to go to check the area of Indian Cave State Park.

For the tree.

Not a tree, mind you: *the* tree.

Indian Cave. Cemetery of a Saint. You'll find the bodies by the tree.

The tree.

Strangely specific and yet oddly vague.

The oxymoronic message left a great deal unsaid, but Officers Gage Dalton and John Weller had nothing else to do the afternoon that they received the call from Omaha, so they decided to drive to Indian Cave State Park—if the Indian Cave in Richardson County was the Indian Cave that the caller was talking about—to find the tree and then look for some bodies. Officers Dalton and Weller finished their coffee and then drove from Falls City, Nebraska, north to Indian Cave State Park with no clue that their day would soon be turned upside down.

The tree.

At the north edge of the cemetery stood a big tree by itself, tall and solid, as if it were a survivor of a great tragedy that had left no other survivors. The fact that the tree was set off on its own caught the attention of Officers Dalton and Weller, so, without talking, the two men started walking in the direction the tree. Fifteen feet from the tree, both men slowed down, and again without speaking, stopped. At the base of the tree, on the far side from the men, several piles of dirt littered the shaded ground. The two men walked closer to the tree and saw that a shovel was lying between two of the piles.

The tree?

By the time the two men got to the piles of dirt, the bones in one open grave were visible, exposed and disturbing.

"We called the officer from Omaha. He told us to stay there and touch nothing. The hair on the back of my neck stood on end for the rest of the day," Officer Dalton later told a reporter. "I didn't eat anything for twenty-four hours."

Almost two hours later, an entire team of men and women in two trucks had taken over the area around the tree in Saint Deroin Cemetery in Indian Cave State Park. The beautiful weather lay as a backdrop in contrast to the tension yet relief of the men and women infiltrating the ground by the tree. The tree was surrounded by a swarm of officials with good intentions, but you know what they say about good intentions.

They pave the road to hell. Not a lot of saints in hell.

By the time the Omaha investigation team got to Saint Deroin Cemetery, reporters, both local and from surrounding states, were panting like watchdogs at the edge of the cemetery. Good old Dalton and Weller were guarding the cemetery, giving a brief report and then protecting the scene throughout the remainder of the day.

Two hours south of Omaha, the whispering roots in the very deep, silty soil near Indian Cave in Richardson County were no longer whispering. The bones had been there through ten long winters, waiting for a proper burial.

In 2008, with the help of a phone call from a mysterious man in Omaha, Nebraska, the bones had been heard.

(Keith Morrison's calming voice laced the backdrop of the scene in Saint Deroin: *Was the story over? Oh, not even close.*)

34

"My Seventh Birthday"
August 27, 1938

Rollie

I turned seven in late August in the summer of 1938.

I felt like I had grown a lot that summer. Mom said I was taller. I had done chores on the Genoa Place that most seven-year-olds I knew had never done. Seven felt big and responsible and a hell of a lot like maybe being ten.

Birthdays back then—well, they weren't a big deal. No big parties or nothing like today. You never wanted to act like you thought so. Mostly, my mom said happy birthday to me when I woke up and when I went to bed. For my seventh birthday, Mom was making me a special dessert.

"Now scoot outside, Rollie. I don't want you to see what I'm making. Go on."

I ran out the door as it slammed shut. Mom yelled through the screen, "Stay away from Wind Hill, ya hear!"

I was dreaming about the peach cobbler that I hoped my mother was making as I hung upside down on the post out by the front gate.

Since the incident at Wind Hill, Jeb and I were restricted from anything fun and dangerous. From my upside-down perspective, I saw an old black Plymouth driving up our long road. I knew the car. Everyone did.

Sheriff Stoltenberg.

Only two reasons why Sheriff would be heading out to our place on a Saturday morning: he had received an invitation to dinner or he was delivering bad news.

Mom usually told me about dinner guests, and I wondered if it was a surprise for my birthday. Didn't sound right. I barely knew Sheriff Stoltenberg, aside from the fact that Jeb elbowed me anytime he drove or walked near us and whispered, "He's coming to take you away."

"Hey there, little shaver. Your mommy or daddy home?"

"My mom is. I'll take you to the house." Sheriff Stoltenberg was a larger man with a big, unkempt mustache and a tendency to call boys little shavers. I would never have wanted him to come to my birthday dinner.

Mom must have heard the car, since I could see her in the doorway with a towel in one hand and a spoon in the other.

"Hey, Ed. How's the new grandbaby?" my mom called out.

"Growing like a weed. Prettiest little baby in Morgan County." Sheriff Stoltenberg called out to Uncle Billy, who joined my mom in the doorway as he walked toward the house.

"Can I get you an iced tea, Ed?" If my mother was concerned, she sure didn't show it.

"That'd be nice." Sheriff Stoltenberg took off his hat as he walked through the door. I walked in behind him, trying to make myself invisible to my mom.

"Rollie, go on now."

Rather than head back out of the house, I ran into the room where my cot was next to the bed my parents slept in. I kept the door open a bit.

"Hey, Billy."

Either Uncle Billy did not reply or he did so quietly that my big ears could not hear. The room was quiet. I heard the ice in the iced-tea glasses clinking from the other room.

"What you need, Ed?" Uncle Billy growled.

"Truett on the grounds?"

"He's not," my mom said. "Is there a problem, Ed?"

Sheriff Stoltenberg cleared his throat. "Well, hope not. Unfortunately, Cal Winters was found dead early this morning, just about three miles outside Morgan County. His horse was nearby, almost waiting for him to get up."

I held my breath so that my shock could not be heard in the other room. Cal Winters was dead. My body was buzzing with excitement and fear.

"Dead?" That voice was Billy's.

"And drunk. Dead drunk…"

It was quiet for a bit, or maybe I missed out on a few words.

"What's this got to do with Truett?" Mom sounded concerned now.

"We just need to know where Truett is, Edith. We have Ms. Winters and the boy down at the station in Brush. They're safe."

Safe from what? The big, bad bully was dead.

"I wish I could tell you. He could be working out in the field. Right, Billy?"

"Could be. Don't know. He's an adult, for God's sake. He don't report to us, Ed."

"I know, Billy. It would just make things a heck of a lot easier if we knew where he was. That's all. We're on your side…"

At least that was what it sounded like: *We're on your side.* Whatever that meant. I was freshly seven, but I couldn't figure out what we'd all be taking sides for.

The clinking of ice and the clearing of throats and finally: words.

"Your boys were all in town at Boone's last night, Billy." This time Sheriff Stoltenberg wasn't using the small-talk tone.

"Aware of that, Ed." Uncle Billy's tone was still stern.

"Were you aware that there was a scuffle of sorts?" Sheriff Stoltenberg coughed. Sounded like a fake cough to me.

"What do ya need, Ed? Speak your piece and go on."

"I need to ask Truett a few questions. That's all. And maybe talk to your other boys. And then I'll be on my way. Truett and Cal got into it last night. Wasn't a pleasant exchange, by any means. We got plenty of witnesses. Truett's brothers included. We just need to get all our stories straight. Cross our *t*'s and dot our *i*'s. Maybe Truett and your boys could shed some light on what happened…"

The creaky screen door opened, and I didn't know if I should pray for it to be Truett or not.

"Hey."

The voice belonged to Emmett.

"Hey, Emmett."

"Sheriff."

"Got a few questions…uh, about the night, about last night. You got a minute?"

"I got a minute." His voice was still coming from near the front door.

"We need to hear from as many witnesses as possible. What happened last night? At Boone's?"

A long silence took over the room. I wanted to cough so badly. Just when I thought that Emmett was refusing to answer the sheriff, he spoke.

"Well, everyone was having a real nice time until Cal Winters showed up, three sheets to the wind. Most people go to bars to drink. Looks like he's been doing plenty of that all over town since he hit the streets of Brush."

"And then what happened?"

"Sit down, Em." My mother's voice was soft.

I don't know if Emmett sat or not, but he answered Sheriff Stoltenberg. "Cal walked right up to Truett and spit in his face."

"And?"

"And what? Truett said nothing, did nothing. The spit just rolled down his face. And then…Cal yelled at Truett to mind his own business. He was about two inches from his face."

"Then what?"

"Truett left."

The room was quiet. I swallowed and squinted my eyes.

Emmett added, "And then Cal followed him."

"And none of you went to help your brother? Did anyone follow the two men?"

"Nope. Isn't that what the other witnesses told you?"

"It is."

The room was quiet. The ice must have melted in all of the glasses. The smell of burnt cobbler filled the room.

"Oh..." my mom's voice said as I heard her rush to the kitchen.

Cal had followed Truett. And now Cal Winters was dead.

I heard the front door open.

"Truett. Whatcha got there?" my mom called out. I heard a baby lamb bawling and hollering.

"It's a bum lamb. The brood ewe finally went into labor last night."

More mumbling, and then I heard my name.

"Rollie. Come on out."

When I walked into the main room of the house, the first thing I saw was blood all over Truett's hands.

"Hey, cowboy. Found a friend for ya." Truett ignored everyone in the room except me. The bum lamb in his arms started bawling, and I wanted to laugh out loud.

"Sir?"

Truett laughed. "No need to 'sir' me, Rollie, just 'cause the sheriff is here. I saved this baby last night from dying out on the range by itself. Its mamma was in labor all night. A real rough delivery...Mamma didn't make it." He winced as he held the wild baby from breaking loose and running around the house.

I didn't know why he was telling me the story of the orphan lamb or why Mom didn't squawk when he brought it in the house. My eyes kept landing on the blood on his hands.

"Rollie, this little guy is gonna need someone who's responsible to take care of him. Your uncles and I are busy all day, so I thought you'd be the best man for the job."

"Yes, sir...uh, Truett. Do you want me to take him now?"

"I'll go with you, Rollie," Truett said. "We'll get him out to the barn and get him settled for tonight. You might even need to sleep with him a few nights."

"Truett?" Sheriff Stoltenberg would not be ignored.

Truett turned and looked at the man on the couch, holding a glass of dead iced tea.

"Truett, are you aware that Cal Winters is dead?" Sweat dripped down the sides of the sheriff's fat face.

Truett stopped and stared at the large official from Brush in our living room. He said nothing.

"Where'd you go after you left Boone's last evening? We have to ask, Tru."

"I went home, Ed. Heard this orphan's momma crying as I drove onto the place. Billy was with me most of the night."

Sheriff wanted this over and done. He was sweating.

"You need anything else, Ed?" Truett asked. "It's Rollie's birthday, and, well, he needs to learn how to take care of this kid." I knew my mom would not allow me to take a lamb into the city when we left for Denver.

"I think..." Sheriff Stoltenberg set down his glass and pulled out a handkerchief to wipe his face. "I think I have everything I need...Happy birthday, little shaver."

"Thank you, sir."

"Come on, Rollie, by golly. Meet your new pet." Truett was calm and cool as he walked me to the barn.

In the barn, Truett had already filled an old beer bottle with milk and placed a nipple on the nozzle. He showed me how to hold it tightly as the little feller went at it. After we fed the baby its first bottle, he turned to me and said. "Happy Birthday, Rollie. You're a good kid."

When I look back on that day, I don't know if Truett was calm because he was innocent or because he knew that Maribel and Toby were safe. I just know he was calm and awfully focused on that orphaned lamb.

I felt good about being seven. But it wasn't all cobbler and whistles and fun. I felt good about being a whole year older, but turning seven had its sad parts.

I'm not gonna lie.

35

Annie

Remains of Five Bodies Found in Southeastern Nebraska
The headline on the front page of the *Omaha World-Herald* jolted me awake as I drank my Saturday-morning cup of coffee in bed before Oliver woke up. Everyone had been talking about the news, tangled with rumors of the bodies found in Indian Cave Park the day before. The news had provided the city of Omaha with a strange (albeit speculative) sense of relief. Death should not bring relief, in most cases, but in that school year, the discovery of the five bodies, with a few skulls and bones missing, was not like most cases.

The picture alongside the article was of several faces of men and women working under a tree down in Indian Cave Park. Their faces were more of the story than the article, which basically stretched the headline as best it could. The expressions on the faces read loud and clear: *We're doing our jobs, but we're pretty freaked out at the moment. After all, we did just find five bodies under a tree.*

People all over the city reading the same article and looking at the same picture that morning were speculating, just as I was, that the bodies were connected to the bones that had been sprinkled on our campus for the past two semesters. The writer of the article implied the fact with subtle words: "Authorities are not saying that the bones found in Richardson County are linked to the Belmont bones but are investigating a possible connection. Authorities are also not saying who tipped the force off to search the area in southeast Nebraska."

Why had the bones been buried where they had been and then later moved to Belmont High School? To torment the innocent? I'm sure I wasn't the only one with those questions in mind.

The phone rang.

It was probably my dad. He was heading over that afternoon to help me move some of the tools and equipment down from the attic.

"Annie?"

My dad's voice on the other end of the line was tinny and tired.

"Dad? Everything OK?"

"Toby died, Annie. Mom and I are heading out to Colorado for the funeral tomorrow. Wasn't sure if you and the boy would want to go."

I searched the synapses of my brain: Toby? I had a Toby in fourth hour; I knew a guy named Toby who worked at Vanity Insanity, a place where I got my hair cut—and then it hit me: Toby McGuire, Truett's son. Of all the cowboy stories my dad shared, the one I enjoyed most was the love story of the uncle Oliver was named after, Truett, and Miss Maribel Winters. Following the death of her husband, Truett and Maribel married, Truett raising Toby as his own son, even giving him his last name.

"So sorry, Dad. When's the funeral?" Oliver ran into my room and jumped on my bed. Atticus sat up from the end of the bed and came to get his chin rubbed by Oliver.

"Monday. Know it's short notice. Your sisters have already left early to see relatives. Mom and I are leaving tomorrow afternoon. You and the boy are welcome to join us."

I would not be going to a cowboy funeral for the man who had died. I would go for my cowboy father. If he was asking me, I would be there for him.

"We're in." I would need to call a sub and set up some lesson plans, but I had taken only two sick days that year, when Oliver had a bug. "We'll pack and be ready whenever."

"We'll call you with details, Annie...thanks..."

I hung up and set my coffee on the nightstand.

"Morning, Mom." Oliver crawled in under the covers to cuddle.

"Morning, Oliver. You win the sleeping-beauty award today."

"Yep. Did I sleep longer than Atticus?"

"Think so. We need to pack for a trip."

"So we're not going to work with Pappa Rollie in the attic? I told Choochoo we were working in the attic. He won't be happy."

"Nope. Getting ready for a trip."

"I'm not excited about telling him...hey! Look what I found." Oliver reached under the covers and pulled out his wooden nickel. He had lost it for the hundredth time a few weeks earlier. We had lost that wooden nickel more times than I could count. Oliver would fret and pout, and then, mysteriously, the damn thing would reappear, and Oliver exclaimed the magic of it all. We had just found a piece of wood, but I would ride the magic train if it made Oliver feel good about it.

"It's a miracle!" Oliver shouted as he held out the wooden nickel to Atticus. Atticus sniffed it and sighed.

"I think the miracle is that you haven't rubbed those stitches out."

"But the snitches itches. Those are rhyming words."

Choochoo forgotten, wooden nickel found, life good.

(Parallel structure.)

The drive to Colorado was uneventful and relaxing, and I realized how much I needed to just sit and read books to my son for six straight hours. Oliver and I sat in the backseat of my dad's car, Mom and Dad in the front seat staring off toward Colorado. Once I had set my little sitter up with instructions to feed and let out Atticus, I too looked toward

Colorado, time away from drunk ex-husbands, annoying notes from strangers, and unearthed dead bodies. It would be nice to get away.

"Still all right to head to my sister's after the funeral luncheon?" my mom mumbled to my dad.

"Yep," Dad mumbled back. "We can stay the night there and head back on Tuesday morning."

Rain tapped on the windshield as we crossed the Colorado state line, and the soothing rhythm of the windshield wipers rocked Oliver to sleep about an hour before we got to Morgan County. We arrived in Brush late Sunday evening at an Econo Lodge outside of town, a motel that I'm pretty sure didn't exist in the summer of 1938. I carried the tired body of Oliver into our room, and we all settled in.

Monday morning brought sunshine and warm air to the flat vastness that is the South Platte River valley enveloping Brush. The beauty of the day and the promise of adventure zapped renewed energy into my five-year-old's body, and Oliver ran to the car after breakfast and shouted, "So where is the fun real?"

Fun real?

Oliver, new to the language, had never heard the word "funeral" before and really didn't know where we were going. I thought the drive to the church would be a good time to brief Oliver on the strange traditions of death.

"*Funeral.* We're actually going to a church for what people call a funeral." I clicked Oliver's seatbelt. Mom and Dad sat quietly in the front seat. "A person who Pappa Rollie grew up with died."

"Died?"

"He was sick...and well, he had a great life, and we're going to a church to...talk about his life and celebrate the fact that he gets to go to heaven."

"Oh."

Nothing like zapping the "fun" out of funeral.

The short drive to the small church in Brush was just enough time to allow the revelation of the strange adult traditions of death to deflate the pure and innocent energy of a child.

"There she is," my dad said, more to himself than to his riders. "She's still standing."

"Who?" Oliver asked.

"The church, Ollie, by golly. Ain't she beautiful?" The hint of a drawl embraced the word "beautiful."

"The church is a girl?" Oliver asked as I unbuckled him.

"She is to Pappa Rollie," I answered.

The old church was smaller than I had imagined from my dad's stories about Brush. Several men and women walked up the front stairs to the door, men with cowboy hats, women in scarves. I felt as if I had stepped out of the car into a time long ago. Men took hats off as they entered, and my parents, son, and I walked up the steps into the timeless chapel. The sun poured through the windows onto the pews. I had never been to a funeral for a cowboy, and I'm glad to say that I had the blessed opportunity.

It was simple.

It was pure.

A picture of a young man standing by a horse was on the cover of the funeral program. He looked to be about twenty or so. The black-and-white picture made me smile.

"Is that the dead man?" Oliver whispered, and several heads turned to smile at the innocent question.

I shook my head as a woman by an old piano at the front of the church started singing "To the Garden." I looked down at the photo again. The cowboy with his horse was not the roly-poly kid from the stories my dad shared about Toby; the kid who moved to Brush, Colorado, in 1938 had grown to be a genuine cowboy. I opened the program and found a poem.

The Hoss
I bless the hoss from hoof to head—
From head to hoof, and tale to mane!—
I bless the hoss, as I have said,
From head to hoof, and back again!

I love my God the first of all,
Then Him that perished on the cross,
And next, my wife,—and then I fall
Down on my knees and love the hoss.

The simple ceremony was enough to send a cowboy off to heaven, and the words of "To the Garden" rang in my head the rest of the day. A hand touched my dad's shoulder after the service ended, and I looked back to see a tall man lean in to my dad.

"Who the hell let this guy in?"

My dad turned and smiled and shook the man's hand. "Sons a bitches. Jeb, did you get old." The ornery young uncle was an old man.

"How'd your girls get to be so perty when you're so ugly?" The tall cowboy looked at Oliver. "You were pretty darn good in church, young man."

Oliver cleared his throat. "It wasn't easy."

Cowboy Jeb howled in laughter at Oliver's response and then winked at me as my dad called my sisters to the pew and introduced us all, gleaming as his two worlds collided. My sisters all headed back to Omaha with their families as I, tethered to my parents, waited outside the church for the next destination, the luncheon put together by the church ladies.

"You've got options, Annie," my dad said to me as the crowd sauntered out of the junior high cafeteria where the luncheon was held. "Go with Aunt Mary Jo and mom back to Mary Jo's place, or go with me to the Genoa Place and then head to Mary Jo's…"

I had to see the ranch that had housed the *Day Cal Came to Town*, *The Day the Uncles Got Drunk and threw Saddles Out of the Pickup*, and *The Incident at Wind Hill*.

"Genoa Place. No brainer. Where'd you get the hat?"

My dad took the cowboy hat off of his head and turned it to the side; charred material and a big hole were unmistakable. "Toby's daughter said Toby wanted me to have it. It's the hat ol' Tru was wearing when he was hit by lightning." Dad put the hat back on.

"Just follow us. Don't you get lost, now." Jeb winked at us as he yelled to my dad. He and a small boy I had not seen at the funeral got into a blue suburban.

The road to the Genoa Place was exactly as my dad had described it in about a million stories: winding, long, barren, yet inviting at the same time. The Genoa Place, however, was a ghostly image of a time no longer. Abandoned and faded, the buildings on the place appeared on the horizon and grew as we drove closer. The main house was off to the right, where I had envisioned it. The barn was much farther from the main house than in my mental pictures of my dad's childhood. Of the two outhouses, only one remained standing. No one lived on the place, but local ranchers rented the land to fatten their cattle. The summer of 1938 flickered like the wick of a cheap, tired candle. No vivid colors. Nothing defined. Still, the slow and ghostly sizzling of another time entirely was a teasing spark between the main buildings and the horizon. Genoa Place was a ghost ranch.

The two cars stopped, and two little boys jumped out of them to run out onto the abandoned grounds. Dad had reminded me on the drive there that Jeb was the last of the generation of McGuire men of 1938. Jeb looked good for his age, and the smile lines around his eyes looked similar to my dad's.

"Charley Horse, no throwing, now, you got that," Jeb yelled out to his grandson, a feisty little shaver who was exactly like his name, a sassy pain in the butt. The cowboy boots, the tilted hat, the cocky smile: Charley Horse may have been four years old, but he was the real deal and a bit intimidating to Oliver, who stared with big round eyes at the crazy kid who couldn't sit still. The wind blew a sad, wounded breath upon us as the boys ran up to the front gate and climbed up on it. That same wind had blown on my dad seventy years ago as he hung on the same gate. I looked beyond the boys and saw it.

The tree.

"Hey, Jeb," I said. "Is that the tree that marks the end of the south pasture and the beginning of the end of the earth?"

Jeb howled again, a beautiful laughter. "How the hell did you...has your daddy been sharing stories?"

"That tree looks exactly the same as it did way back," my dad said as Charley Horse threw a stick at the barn.

"That's also the tree where Truett died. Remember that story, Rollie?"

"I've heard it a few times."

"I haven't." I thought I had heard them all.

"What year did Truett die?" Jeb looked down and asked himself.

"The year that Oliver was born," my dad said. "I couldn't make it since we had a new baby around the time. What year was Ollie born?"

I looked up to see Oliver following Charley Horse running around the barn. "Two thousand three."

"Two thousand three? Seems like yesterday." Jeb went into full-story mode, as if the scene was playing out in front of him. "Clear as day, I remember Truett's horse Bonnie wandering by the barn before lunch. And, well, Bonnie and Truett were inseparable by that time. See, Truett was well into his nineties then, and he mostly did little odds and ends around the place. So Toby and I tied up Bonnie, got in the old Chevy pickup, and went looking for him. We saw him sitting with his back against the tree on the edge of the south pasture. Looked like he was sleeping, like he was dreaming away. We both yelled for him as we got closer to the tree. The old man didn't budge. The drive to Denver was, let's just say, eventful. The rain was pouring down, so we put Truett in the front cab. The truck drove into a ditch...ran out of gas...and we almost got in an accident once we hit the Denver traffic. The Denver doctor pronounced him dead in the hospital. I think Toby's son asked the doctor, 'You sure about that? See, it wasn't on his agenda for the day.'"

"Five years ago?" I asked again.

"Yah, and the place was pretty run down by then, and the young sons and grandsons had gone off to college or bought their own ranches.

After Tru was gone, we all moved into town. We rent the property out to a guy over the hill whose cattle feed on the land."

"Truett was kind of like that tree out on the edge of the earth, in the south pasture, all alone and surviving so long. He finally said to God, 'OK, now I'm ready.'"

Oliver and Charley ran up to the three of us.

"The whole town came to his funeral," Jeb said. "Standing room only."

"Well, I'm glad the son of a bitch is dead." Charley sounded as comfortable with the phrase "son of a bitch" as most five-year-olds are with juice boxes.

"What the..." Jeb looked rattled. "We weren't talking about Toby. Why would you be glad he's dead?" Jeb was clearly not offended by the cussing from Charley Horse.

"Now don't scold him, Jeb." My dad had a grin as he spoke. "Did Toby cut off your ears, Charley?"

"Every time I saw him." Charley threw a rock at the gate.

"Truett taught Toby well." My dad smiled.

"Truett?" Oliver jumped in. "That's my name, or one of my names. Right, Mom?"

"Yep."

As we all walked back to our cars, Jeb looked down at Charley Horse. "Hey, didn't your momma tell you not to wear the good boots out to the Genoa Place? I heard her tell you that, now."

Charley looked up at his grandfather, squinted, and tilted his head. "Not my day to worry about it."

The drive up into the mountains to my aunt's house took us longer than I remembered. When we passed the turn-off to my aunt's house, I knew where my dad was heading. I didn't say a word as we drove up to a locked gate at the entrance to the Bailey Campgrounds.

"Hey!" Oliver said from the backseat. "I know this place."

Only eight months earlier, my mother's family members had filled the area with activity and noise, in contrast to the abandoned grounds in front of us. A last-minute sign read: Closed til Spring (message: vague with improper word usage.) A gust of wind blew in, and Oliver laughed as he got out of the car. "I'm gonna fly with the wind."

Oliver ran around the gate as Dad and I walked up to the sign. I saw the big A-frame where everyone had gathered for dinners and at night at the family reunion eight months earlier. I looked over to the hill with all of the little cabins jutting out of the big hill like gingerbread houses on a holiday cake. One cabin stood out as bigger and more majestic: our cabin. I looked over at the hill just to the left of the house. No grave marker anywhere. A man buried with no grave marker? Maybe the whole thing was just an interesting story to keep the summer guests talking.

My dad cleared his throat. "We could go into town and ask around. See if someone can let us in."

"For what?" I felt silly.

Why the obsession over the past year? Did I think that if we drove back here, my cowboy ghost would come out to greet me? Just sweep me up in his arms and tell me that he missed me? I couldn't be the only one who had felt something with that kiss. "I'm good." I started back to the car. "Come on, Oliver."

"I thought we were going in there." Oliver threw a rock toward the cabin at the base of the hill.

"Not today, Oliver. Looks like it's closed, buddy. Head back to the car. See how fast you can run." Then he turned to me. "If it makes you feel any better, Annie, I met your cowboy."

I stopped and looked at my dad. He was looking at our cabin.

"What?"

"Didn't see him. Just heard him. He scolded me."

"Who scolded you?" The wind blew my hair all around. I heard a wind chime.

"Your damn ghost." Even my dad called him my ghost.

My cowboy ghost.

I couldn't believe what I was hearing. I wanted to hug my dad and strangle him at the same time. Validation: I'm not crazy.

"The damn nerve of that son of a bitch...he came in the night and told me to stop snoring. Just roll over, he whispered. Thought it was Peggy's husband. All the son-in-laws had been giving me a hard time about my snoring. Said I was keeping everyone up at night. Got a little old, if you ask me."

"Are you serious, Dad?"

"I asked Allen the last morning. By then, he was the only man staying in the cabin. Everyone else had left."

"Asked him what?"

"I asked him if he had tapped my shoulder in the night...and told me to roll over; I was snoring too loud. He just gave me a strange look. That was the end of that."

"Why didn't you tell me?"

"At first I wasn't sure it happened or if it was the same...ghost or whatever that you experienced. Later, I wanted you to move on. I think you wanted to help him. There ain't no helping a ghost."

"I'm mad at you, Dad." I looked down and kicked the dirt.

"Sorry, Annie."

"I'm such a fool. I'm not sure what I wanted. I felt a connection, and I just thought...who is this man or remains of a man? What was his story? I wanted to come back and let him know it was OK."

"What was OK?"

"Broken dreams. To have broken dreams. I mean, obviously, his life didn't turn out how he planned. In my head, there was a man who went for the gold, literally, and wanted to bring it home to his family...and then he died."

"That's right. He died, Annie. Truett died. Toby died. Everyone dies."

"But for some reason, this man is stuck. Like he has all of the muck in the way, and he can't move on. Or he doesn't know he's dead. He just tries to take care of everyone."

"Like you."

"I don't know about that. The poor man roams a house over and over to protect everyone, to cover children and tell old men not to snore so loudly and..." I felt a burning in my throat.

"And?"

"And to console a rejected woman who felt unlovable." I cried into my hands. I didn't want Oliver to know I was crying.

My dad cleared his throat.

"He's real, Dad." I sniffed.

"Hell, I met the son of a bitch."

"I can't help him to move on. I can't get him over the muck. I can't get him to heaven. I can't save him."

"Annie, somehow you got it in your head somewhere along the way—maybe 'cause you're a teacher; maybe 'cause you're you—you think that you can fix everything, that you can save everyone. You can't save the world, Annie, and that's OK."

A whisper of wind chimes called from the old cabin.

"I want to go in!" Oliver was hanging on the end of the locked gate. "I want to go in the house of the big man."

"What man, buddy?" I asked as I gently pulled him from the rusty gate.

"The big man in charge."

"Do you remember a man, Oliver?"

"He works for the place. He lives in that house. Right, Mom?"

I looked at my dad. "Yah, he works there, bud."

"But the place is locked up, Ollie, by golly," my dad added. "See, they're only open in the summertime."

"Can we get McDonald's on the way home? You said we could get McDonald's on the trip."

"I think we could find one, Ollie, by golly."

We walked back to the car, and another gust of wind overtook us. I put on my sunglasses as Oliver ran to the car.

36

A Bad Ring

"A bad ring. Under your nose."
The second phone message to the Omaha Police Department was again intense, but this time also frantic. Techies were able to trace the call back to a landline, inconsistent with the first message. The message, sent as a warning, came from Belmont High School.

A bad ring. Under your nose.

Two agents in street clothes—now the FBI was involved—drove to Belmont High School to join other undercover officers in efforts to find the ring, only this one was nothing like the ring in *The Lord of the Rings*.

Under your nose?

Belmont High School, authorities assumed. The caller had to have known that authorities had been staking out the grounds ever since the skull on the football field had been found.

Right before the first message led them to Indian Cave, officials had already made the connection with the unique soil found in three areas of Nebraska. The greatest amount of the soil was in the Indian Cave area.

A bad ring?

Was it taking place at the school? An operation of sorts. If so, the investigation had led them to nothing except more bones. Drugs had, of course, been a consideration. And while the visual of a teenager with a nose ring did cross his mind, Officer Kelly knew the voice saying those words was not goofing around.

A bad ring under your nose.

37

"Life after Cal Winters"
End of the Summer of 1938

Rollie

Brush was quiet in the days that followed the death of Cal Winters. My mother always said, "If you can't say nothing nice, don't say nothing at all."

So it was almost as though the son of a bitch had never lived. Poof— he was gone, and that was that.

Of course, there was the talk. Quiet stories like serpentine snakes slithered through discussions about what had happened that night.

The man had died from a gunshot wound to the head. Did he kill himself? Did he walk out of that bar that night so distraught with himself, a man with no job, a wife who no longer loved him, a town that saw him as a drunk bully?

Could we give him that much credit?

Beyond that, the talk was even quieter: Could the unthinkable have happened?

No CSI unit in Brush, Colorado, in 1938 like the ones you see on your Friday-night TV. If Truett said that the blood on his hands was from the dead mother of the bum lamb, well then, that was what it was. No lie detectors in Brush, Colorado, at least. No forensic unit came in with Q-tips or DNA kits to test the facts. No fingerprints were taken at the scene of the crime, for all I know. I guess the sheriff's grunt men just put Cal Winters's dead body in the back of the pickup and walked Cal's horse back in to town. So when the sheriff found Cal Winters dead outside of town and his horse wandering nearby, the sheriff declared the son of a bitch died after a bender. The investigation included a few questions here and there. And then it was done.

I saw Maribel and Toby shortly after the death of Cal Winters. They were in church a few pews ahead of us that next Sunday. They were sitting with Maribel's sister. Toby wasn't squirming. Maribel barely moved.

I wondered if they might be mourning the death of Cal or sending prayers of thanksgiving to God that their nightmare was over.

In the quiet of the night, when I couldn't stop my thoughts from going there, I wondered about that night. I always believed that if Truett had anything to do with the death of Cal Winters, it had to have been in self-defense. All we knew back then was that a really bad guy was dead, and Truett wasn't fessing up to anything. If Cal Winters hadn't died that night, he might have caused a few more deaths in the years to come.

In time, Truett began courting Maribel. No one was surprised or judgmental. He took Maribel and Toby to church, and the three would head out to the Genoa Place for lunch after. I took Toby out to the fenced-in area, where my lamb, Shadow, would chase us around. My mom had named the orphaned lamb Shadow since it followed me all around the ranch.

At the end of the summer of 1938, my dad got a job back in Denver. We packed up all our stuff to head back. Mom said I couldn't take the lamb to the city, so I left it with Jeb, who said he really didn't want no silly, annoying lamb. It all worked out when Truett married Maribel, and

Maribel and Toby moved to the Genoa Place. So Toby took over my duties with Shadow.

Not all fairy tales end with that "happily ever after" line. Maribel got real sick a few years later. My mom said it was cancer or a tumor or something. Back then, we didn't always know. By the time Maribel knew she was sick, well, it was just too damn late. That was what Jeb told me. Truett found his true love, and, well, then the woman of his dreams just died. Truett raised Toby as his own, and when we visited, you would have thought Truett was Toby's dad from day one.

Like I always said, Truett was a good man.

38

May 8, 2009—8:37 a.m.

Annie

"Does that just blow your mind?"

Twyla twirled her hair as her mind was blown. I said nothing.

"It blows my mind. Another 'fun'-raising rep gone. This one fired, according to the woman I talked to this morning from Cheer World Fun-Raising." Twyla was fixing her lipstick as she looked in a tiny mirror that she quickly put back in her front drawer. "Evidently, the wife called the company to let them know that her husband was having an affair with one of the teachers out in a town near Hastings."

In our Monday-morning meeting, Twyla had just thrown a curve pompon at me. "His wife?"

"Yah. Do you remember that Trevor Kula?" Twyla pulled out a chair for me and handed me the brochures for a cheer camp in Iowa.

"Trent?"

"Yah, Trent. 'Y'all want to be a part of Kissermania? You look like you haven't been kissed in a long time.' So inappropriate…but, I will admit, effective as hell. And drop-dead gorgeous to boot."

"Fired?" I pretended to look through the brochure for the summer cheerleading camps.

"According to Winnie, the woman he had an affair with was also married. And the wife was going to surprise Mr. Kissermania with a romantic weekend in his hotel near Hastings. When the poor lil thing got to his room, she got the surprise of her life…"

"The wife?"

I knew exactly how the poor lil thing felt. "I don't want to know." I pointed to the picture of several girls cheering out on a campus lawn. "This camp should work well for our girls."

"Ya think? Oh, and one more thing." Twyla was relentless. "This story is just wack-a-doodle. Turns out, at least according to lady I talked to, the company had already received several complaints from schools that Mr. Kula was even hitting on the cheerleaders…"

"I only have about ten minutes. Did you decide if you want me to call this camp for more details?"

And I thought that Mr. Kula really liked me.

"Oh, yes, yes, yes. The girls said that this was a great camp last year. Most of them said that the second session would work. Can you make a few more copies of the registration forms, and we can get them to the girls at our meeting this week…with permission forms, of course."

He made me feel lovable for a moment, when I needed to feel lovable.

"Of course."

"And I can't be at the meeting. So, are you OK with going over all this with the girls?"

He made me feel kissable.

"Sure, no problem."

He used me.

"You OK, Annie Day?"

I used him.

"Never been better. Why?"

"You look like you just saw a ghost."

Just the Ghost of Kissers Past.

"Never better!"

Twyla yelled as I left, "And thanks again for running the meeting."

A swift trot carried me down the long hallway with bright fluorescent stars shining above. A large body leaned against the wall near the door to room 213. Kinkaid was standing in front of my room, slouched and disheveled. I walked as fast as I could to avoid that bell attack.

"Are you all right, Kinkaid?"

"No." *A single word with a single syllable: so not Kinkaid.*

"Can I help?"

"My dad hates me." *More words, not so much on syllables.*

"No, he doesn't." From what I remember of the rotten dough of a father at conferences, I couldn't believe I was defending Kinkaid's father.

"He does. And I'm OK with that…the arrogant, sanctimonious, controlling son of a bitch." *More words with more than one syllable. Spoken like a true cowboy.*

The bell screamed around us, and a thousand teen soldiers poured into the hall and began marching, only to interrupt our intimate discussion. Kinkaid mumbled, as if to himself, "The son of a bitch can live without a doctor or a lawyer son to showcase to his filthy-rich friends at work. He can rot in hell." *A plethora (power word) of words and hell of lot (cowboy for plethora) of syllables.*

"Hey, Ms. Day! Hey, Kinkaid!" Arty rushed past us.

"I know the truth," Kinkaid whispered loudly. He started to hum and then caught himself and stopped. Most of the students were in the classroom looking out at the two of us. I'm sure our little exchange in the hall looked like an altercation. The last few bodies scurried in.

"I'd like you to all get out your notes from yesterday and look them over," I shut the door.

"Are you going to be all right, Kinkaid?" My thought at that moment was to write a note for Kinkaid to go see his counselor. I wasn't sure what volcano of emotions might erupt all over our notes and discussion on writing a thesis statement.

"I know the truth. I've transcended the muck that is Vincent William Kinkaid, a.k.a. pompous, holier-than-thou jackass."

The word *ass* echoed on the now-empty halls.

Of the abrupt and curt words sputtered from Kinkaid over the past five months, I had never seen this side of him. Most interactions with Kinkaid were over assignments and his academically burdened schedule. What force had changed Kinkaid's mind-set and the comfort in venting his intimate frustrations to his English teacher?

"I've seen the star. I finally realized that I have a star, my own ideas, my own dreams." The whispers erupted louder than before, and Kinkaid's epiphany reverberated against the now-empty halls. "I'm going to be a teacher." Kinkaid spoke more to the world than to me specifically.

Wow.

"You'll make a great teacher, Kinkaid."

So maybe I might receive a call from Kinkaid's father, complaining that I had created problems or supported the wrong team in the Kinkaid Dilemma. I had done nothing but teach his son and given him a B on an early assignment. How would the administration punish such awful behavior? Demote me to a teacher? Wait, too late. Yes, I would be fine with any O'Neill backlash since I could easily defend myself. It wasn't as if I hadn't been called a boring bitch before. The urgency in Kinkaid's voice and his explosive revelation meant more to me than a grumbling, controlling son of a bitch of a father.

I saw a body in my peripheral view while I looked straight at Kinkaid. Maybe another teacher had heard his echoing cuss words and was coming to take us away, *oh no.*

As if snapped out of a trance, Kinkaid looked at me. "I just thought I should let you know." Kinkaid cleared his throat. There wasn't a thank-you attached to this statement, like *thank you for showing me how to break through the muck (my dad)* or *thank you for inspiring me to be a teacher.* There were no such thank-you notations because Kinkaid's epiphany was not about me at all. This was a journey on which he had been traveling a long time. Kinkaid had never wanted to be a doctor.

I just happened to be on the grid when he got to a tipping point, and boy, had Kinkaid tipped.

"Maybe we should get into the room and work on our research papers," I said. Kinkaid sharing his revelation with me made me realize that he considered me safe.

"I think that's a good idea." Kinkaid pushed his glasses up his nose and cleared his throat again. The red from his face was gone. He took a deep breath.

I opened the door. As Kinkaid and I entered room 213, I looked back and saw Nick Stander in the hall. Had he been a witness to my conversation with Kinkaid? Nick looked at me and then looked down. I hesitated. Nick then looked up at me. I waved. He nodded. He walked away. I shut the door.

Awkward.

Nadine had told me that once the football season was over, Nick continued to work with Coach Edwards and his winter conditioning program for athletes who were off-season but maintaining a regimented workout program. Nick was only part time, but Coach Edwards was hoping to bring him on as full time once Nick finished his teaching degree, according to Nadine.

Period Two was a strange kind of quiet as I cleared my throat and smiled. "Are you all ready?"

"For our pop quiz?" Mike Sheridan answered, as though he had a halo above his head and had led the rosary with the class while Kinkaid and I spoke.

"Nah. Let's just talk research papers." I looked down at the empty seat in front of me. Donovan had missed six days in the past two weeks. Gwendolyn's seat was also empty.

"Whew," Arty said, mostly to himself. "I hate pop quizzes."

The word "quiz" used to send Kinkaid into a humming frenzy. He sat with no books open as he took in the discussion.

K-Mart raised her hand.

"Katrina?"

"What would you have quizzed us over? I mean, if you had given us a pop quiz. Our notes are about the process of writing our research papers."

"I wasn't planning on giving a quiz. Mike, where did you get the idea that I was going to give a pop quiz?"

Mike Sheridan's blue eyes smiled back at me. "You know me, Ms. Day. I pay attention to the details. Pay attention to the little deets, and it makes a big dif. You just said to look over our notes. I thought, hey, maybe she's going to pop us a quiz."

"Your what hurts?" I answered quickly without tone.

The class burst out in laughter.

"That was gold, Ms. Day. Hey, have you been out in the sun?"

"Stalling again, Mr. Sheridan? Everyone, please pull out your thesis statement and list of sources for your paper."

"He does have a point," James said as he pulled out his papers. "You do kind of have a sunburn. I mean, more of a tan, but kind of a burn."

Mumbles from the class came in agreement with James.

"Well, I did mow the lawn this week. I guess I got some color. I think what we're going to do today is have each of you present your thesis statement to the class. It'll be good for you to hear feedback from peers and not just me."

"Why doesn't your husband mow your lawn?"

Heads of the bodies in room 213 snapped back to glare at the head behind the voice asking me about my nonexistent husband.

Cami Halloway looked up at the faces scowling at her. "What? Husbands mow lawns. Why is that a stupid question?" Cami's shock was sincere. So, while most teenage bodies in the building were privy to my broken marital status, one body had not yet received the memo: Cami Halloway. And the other bodies in the room came to my defense, if only with a scolding look.

"What?" Cami asked again.

"I'm really very good at mowing the lawn, Cami. It's good exercise after correcting all of your thesis statements and vocab quizzes. We're short on time. I'm going to start with one of my favorite thesis statements. LaTrey, could you please read your thesis to the class."

LaTrey looked around at the class as he heard his name, sat up, and smiled. "For sure, Ms. D.!"

Room 213 was a safe place. As the queen or the mother hen or the dictator, I controlled the climate of the room. Students could not make fun of one another or demean one another in room 213. Phil Timmerman spent a day in ISS, my name at the bottom of the incident report, for calling a student who had picked up attendance a fag. And even though it was under his breath, I heard it and the class heard it. And Phil Timmerman spent a day in the dungeon and was mad at me for about five minutes upon his return. I think—maybe just wishful thinking—that Phil got it. I would do the same if someone had called him a name or bullied him. I may have overlooked an occasional inappropriate remark and a soft cuss word, but I would not allow someone to feel "unsafe" in my room.

After Cami's innocent though untimely question, I, too, felt safe.

My kids would protect me.

I left Belmont right after most students had left the parking lot for the day, feeling safe. I picked up Oliver, and he and I were going to pack a basket of fun food and go up to our tree house in the attic—carpet had been installed the weekend before—and have a little after-school picnic in our finally finished attic. The attic project was done. I had moved most of our books and Oliver's toys up the night before. Oliver did somersault after somersault on the new carpet before the bigger furniture would be moved up.

"Can we bring up chips?" Oliver asked from his car seat behind me.

"Yep."

"Can we bring up cookies?"

"Yep?"

"Kool Aid? Hey, who's that?"

Oliver pointed to a woman sitting on our front porch steps. Her face was down in her hands. As I pulled into the driveway, I saw the box. And

I knew exactly who it was: Annette Graham. Annette had called me the week before to say that she would be coming into town, and I had written a note in my daily planner reminding myself to put the box out on the front porch, behind the porch swing.

I pulled into the driveway, and Oliver and I walked toward the front porch. Oliver ran up to the woman.

"Are you OK, Miss Lady?"

The woman brought her head up and looked at us. We stood, holding backpacks and purses and a bag of groceries.

"I'm fine. Are you Annie Day?"

"I am."

"And I'm Oliver Truett Day," Oliver said.

"Nice to meet you both. I'm Annette Graham."

"I see you found the box. Looks like a lot of family memorabilia that you might want to go through," I said as Oliver dropped his backpack and did a somersault on the grass.

"I found the box!" Oliver said.

"Oliver, if I give you this key, will you go in the house and let Atticus out in the backyard."

"The key?" I wasn't sure if Oliver knew how to use the key, but I knew I could buy a few minutes with Annette. "You bet!" Oliver ran to the front door with the power of the key.

"I want to thank you for taking the time to contact me after finding the...and then knowing it would be important." Annette held a crumpled up paper in her hand.

"No worries."

"Those last days, my dad kept talking about the letter, the letter. I had no idea." Annette was talking so fast that she was barely breathing. "The only two things he remembered in those last days were the letter and his aftershave. He must have felt so bad that he lost the letter. When I look back, I can now see that his mind had started to go. To be honest, he had really been starting to show signs for years. He was always losing things, forgetting things, stopping in the middle of a sentence and then acting like he didn't care about what he was talking about. But I knew he just couldn't recall…It was painful…"

"I'm glad you have the box."

"And, now that I think of it, he was constantly looking for 'it' or something. Where is it? Where is it? And, I…was…condescending…I placated him. I told him we had found it. I told him it was OK. I had no idea. He was looking for this letter."

"How could you know?" I said.

"Well, I know now…what the letter was about…and, uh, why my father was so upset. My mom had given him the letter to give to me, and then he…then he kind of forgot everything."

I heard Atticus bark in the backyard.

"You read the letter?" Annette asked.

Oliver laughed from the backyard.

"Please, tell me you read the letter."

"I did."

"Thank you. Now I'm not alone in knowing…and I want to move on. I don't want to talk to my husband or anyone else. It's over, but I'm not alone. She was a pretty neat mom."

"Sounded like it."

"You know what was in the letter. Oh, my gosh, for years, I obsessed about the woman who didn't want me. I fantasized that maybe she really did want me and wanted to meet me. I was so mad…so, so mad at my mom for not telling me I was adopted. I thought she was so selfish and that she wanted me all to herself…and that she didn't want to compete with the birth mother…You wouldn't even believe some of the names I called her…to her face. I was awful. Now I know she was protecting me."

"She was."

"She didn't want me to feel abandoned all over again. She was protecting me…"

I could hear Oliver and Atticus running on the hardwood floors to the front door.

"Do you think my father read the letter?" Annette was not crying. She pulled her hair back from her face.

"The letter was hanging by a thread, but it hadn't been opened."

"He just knew she wanted him to give it to me...and...I bet he misplaced it. I bet he had been looking for that letter for a long time."

"You have her name."

"Who? Oh, I don't want to meet her." Annette handed me several pieces of the letter, torn up and scrunched together. "Here, please take this and throw it away. I know what my mother said, and I have no desire to go meet a woman who never wanted to even carry me and deliver me. She wasn't my mother."

"Maybe she wasn't in a place in life to be a good mother. She wasn't bad."

"She wasn't bad." Annette repeated the words, tasting them for the first time. Her birth mother wasn't bad.

"Your mom saved your life, Annette."

"She did."

"Atticus licked my face." Oliver was laughing as he shut the door on Atticus, who was not allowed in the front yard.

"You unlocked the door, buddy!"

"I did."

"Oliver, did you know that Annette grew up in this house? Just like you."

"Wow!" Oliver jumped off the low step to the sidewalk.

"Annette, Oliver and I are glad that you stopped by."

"And Choochoo too!" Oliver shouted.

"Choochoo?" Annette asked.

"Choochoo is happy...that you stopped by," Oliver said as he took the keys and opened the door again. He went in the house again (oh, the power of the key) with Atticus, and the running began again.

"Choochoo's his imaginary friend," I said, attempting to sound endearing rather than annoyed. "You have kids?"

Annette stood up. "I do. I have two girls who will enjoy seeing pictures of the grandmother they never had the chance to meet."

"And you as a baby and little girl."

"Thank you, Annie." Annette, a woman I had never met and have never seen again, hugged me. I picked up the box that I had had on my to-do list for many, many months and walked her to her car.

Annette took one last glance at the house and looked up at the attic window. And somehow, I knew who was looking back at her from my attic window.

39

Annie

"So what can I get you two young ladies to drink?"

Our waiter looked way too young to be serving drinks, and his little slant on the word "young" almost made me laugh out loud. Nadine and I had finally found a night to go out. Oliver was at my parents', Hank was working, and Nadine and I were sitting on the patio of a restaurant in midtown Omaha by an outside fireplace. Spring had sprung, but the nights were still cool.

"My name's Garrett. I'll be taking care of you two tonight."

Nadine raised one eyebrow and shook her head without looking at me, and I almost choked on my water.

"I think we may need a few minutes," I said.

"So, Garrett," Nadine said, "where do you go to school?"

"I'm premed at Creighton. I'm also considering law."

"Wow, aren't you the gunner!" Nadine said. She twirled her necklace as she teased.

"Well, I'm just a freshman, so I have time to figure it out."

Garrett lived on the other side of the line.

"Good for you," I said. It wasn't Garrett's fault that he hadn't crossed over the line and seen the real world.

"I have another order to get to a table. I'll check back in a while and give you young ladies time." Garrett set down our menus and left.

"If he says 'young ladies' one more time..." Nadine picked up the menu. "You picked a crazy time to leave town, Annie."

"Why? Did my sub tell you something she didn't tell me?"

"No, just the whole news about the bodies they found. You wouldn't believe the buzzing of the rumor mill."

"Any different from the news in the paper?" I asked.

"You mean that they confirmed that the bones are related to the bones found at our school? My question to that: Are they the actual bones, or are they relatives to the bones? Clarify, people!"

"I mean, any other stories going around?"

"Well, some teachers were talking at lunch about some love triangle of the dead bodies, and I'm like, one man and four women. I'm pretty sure that would be a love polygon."

"Heard that one."

"And someone else mentioned mass murder. But again, what's the connection to Belmont?"

"What were the kids saying in your classes? They get pretty chatty in journalism. And you like to spy."

"One kid, Henry Mason, is convinced that Belmont was built on a Native American cemetery and that the city knew this and built the school anyway."

"Hello? *Poltergeist?* At least be original...what do you think, Nadine?"

"Well, if we're being serious now...sometimes I wonder if the bodies all went to the school at some time. I don't know, like a serial killer who got his jollies throwing it all in our faces and getting away with it. Sounds like one of your murder shows with your boyfriend."

"Keith?"

"First name only now?"

"Yep, but sometimes I like to call him my *Dateline* boyfriend Keith Morrison—you know, like my cowboy ghost. My Keith looks phenomenal in jeans and has a voice I want to drown in. Oh, and I spend every Friday night with him, thank you very much."

"And old enough to be your dad. Do you have any idea how pathetic you sound? You really shouldn't say things like that out loud and sound so perky."

"So what'll it be?" Garrett leaned in on the table as he spoke.

"I'm going with the chicken Cobb salad," Nadine said.

"Same. Let's make this easy."

Garrett smiled, forgot to call us young ladies, and left to put in our order.

"What's wrong with me?" I asked Nadine. "I'm pathetic. I have a crush on Keith Morrison, who doesn't even know I exist, and I'm in love with a man who died over a hundred years ago."

"Did you ever find that cowboy ghost of yours back in Colorado?" Nadine winked.

"Nope, but I did find some closure on the chapter of *my* cowboy ghost."

"Closure?"

"Kind of. Standing at the locked gate of the campgrounds with Oliver and my dad, I decided to move on. No more obsessing or researching. I'm at peace. I'm not the damsel waiting for her ex to come back, waiting for a ghost to come to life, waiting for a knight in shining armor to fix everything. I'm good."

"OK."

"I just still have one tiny little struggle with the whole thing."

"And that would be?"

"I don't know…I just wonder if my cowboy ghost even knows he's dead."

"I can tell you this. Some ghosts just get stuck. Remember how Kenny had a buddy who was a Boy Scout in that tornado up in Iowa?"

Nadine was talking about a tornado that had killed four boys the summer before at a Boy Scout campground in Little Sioux, Iowa. Probably more would have died, except the young scouts set up their own triage unit and cared for one another while waiting for emergency responders.

"I remember."

"One of the mothers of Kenny's friends said that in the chaos of naming the dead, the boys later reported that they kept naming only three boys dead, but they had four bodies. Most were so injured...that they were unidentifiable."

"Wow."

"Anyway, the boys' parents were getting pretty upset that they weren't allowed to get to the campground, but authorities didn't want them there until they confirmed the dead."

"Why?"

"The boys kept reporting that a certain boy had been up and helping. Several kids said they saw him in the aftermath...but he was one of the dead. Had been from the beginning."

"I'm confused."

"The boy's ghost was helping out."

"Wow."

"Point is: your cowboy ghost is stuck, but he doesn't know it. He just keeps busy in the moment he knows. Helping. I'm glad you're moving on, Annie. A heck of a lot of living cowboys out there are waiting for you. Don't get stuck on a ghost that's stuck...and, also, dead."

Nadine's cell phone blasted out a jingle that I had never heard. I was starting to feel really hungry.

"Hey, Hank." Nadine pulled her sweater from the chair next to her.

Silence.

"Oh, God, no. You know that for sure?"

Nadine put her phone down.

"You look like you've seen a ghost, Nadine." I laughed as I took another sip of wine. "Everything OK?"

"A terrible accident, Annie. Some kids from Belmont."

40

Annie

State Street.

Notorious (power word).

State Street is notorious for inviting youthful energy to a death dance.

State Street.

Way out in northwest Omaha is a street where too many teens have died.

Because I could not stop for death,

The challenge: the State Street Jump.

The risk: more than any teen who drives there can comprehend.

He kindly stopped for me.

"You feel like you're actually flying. Well, like your car is flying. It's amazing." One student had shared with me my first year of teaching at Belmont High School. The State Street Jump sounded like the most insane mission a person could go on.

On a long stretch of State Street, in northwest Omaha from about 152nd to 173rd, are actually several jumps: steep, hilly roads that drop off suddenly. Teenagers have been heading out that way to get the "flying sensation" for decades. For thrills. To feel alive. To say that they had done the State Street Jump. Most have walked away or driven home; ten teenagers have died on that stretch since 1994.

"It sounds dangerous to me," I said to that student. I was honest—even then—and attempting to sound adult-like, though I was closer in age to students my first year of teaching than I was to most of the staff.

"Nah, you just drive fast, drop, and drive off. No big deal. You should try it sometime."

I imagined the cars and trucks through the years driving at high speeds in the dark on State Street. I see them getting to the hilltop, and then, airborne, soaring like paper planes, innocent, juvenile, clumsy paper planes thrown aimlessly across the room, diving down without notice, ignoring death.

The immortal teen.

They ignore death, thinking they will live forever. They think they're above death. I know this, since I was once a teenager. Death is something only for the hard of hearing and the elderly with walkers. Teenagers don't die. They have so much ahead of them. Their dreams are realities in their hormonal brains. They're everything. The concept of death is as far from their minds as homecoming is from prom; as pimples should be from a date; as stupid, stubborn parents are from teenagers with the world in their hands.

Teenagers don't die.

Merlin Abernathy of Bennington, Nebraska, a town just on the northwest edge of Omaha, was the first to find the bodies. He was driving late Saturday night to check on his property a mile east of his farm. He lived in town, but as he got older, he was prone to structure and routine. He checked the grounds driving by, but occasionally he stopped and walked around, about every other day, just because he was old and deliberate, because he was cautious and proactive, because he did not ignore death. Every time he drove by the land, no problems appeared. Nothing ever happened. And at age eighty-one, Merlin was just fine with that.

Until May 8, 2008.

That night, Merlin drove by and saw it: just west of the property, the back of the red truck jutting up from a ravine.

"I've heard of the accidents on my road, but none were ever by my property. My gut told me right away. I knew it was kids. It's always kids. Just babies." Merlin told the officers who got to the site at 171st and State right before the ambulance arrived that as he drove closer to the truck, he saw what looked like two rag dolls thrown off the side of the road. "The bodies were right next to each other. One arm of one kid was over the leg of the other. Just thrown out of the car like rag dolls. When I got closer, I could see the babies with the bodies of men. Pretty big men. Still babies."

Nadine's husband, Hank, got the call at 8:54 p.m. that crisp Saturday night in May. He was on duty when fellow officer Mike Becker called for help out on State Street. By the time he got to the road, the lights off the tops of fire trucks and ambulances lit up the area like a carnival, a sick, twisted carnival where the rides came with great cost.

"We realized that there was still another person in the car that needed to be treated after Officer Becker flashed a light in the backseat of the extended cab of the truck. A boy was crumpled over, his seat belt still holding him in. Couldn't say for sure if the two who flew out the front had their belts on or not, or if worn properly. These days, it's just habit to put them on, so, at this point, we surmised the impact was so great that the boys flew out in spite of the restraints. We'll never know.

"The two boys who woke up after they were in the hospital—well, neither could remember even being on State Street. The third boy was never able to talk to officials. He died on impact."

Maybe it was good that Hank didn't initially know the names of all of the boys, or maybe he knew and didn't want us to lose sleep that night. He called Nadine off and on throughout the night. She told me to go to bed and wait for the full story in the morning, but I begged her to let me know. Hank's call to Nadine came with a shock: the young man in the backseat was James Wu.

I left the restaurant and prayed the entire drive home.

The spotty reporting on the ten o'clock news that night kept claiming that three men had been in a serious accident on State Street. That was it. I took a breath at the word "men." The three so-called men had only gotten their first driver's licenses a year earlier. Three years earlier they had started high school. Seven years earlier, they had ridden their bikes to the nearby park. Nine years earlier, they had been collecting Pokémon cards. These men were not men; they were boys. Babies, really. They were just starting off life and too quickly jumped over the line from the side of the dreamers (the view from this side of the line sees all dreams achievable) to the side of the dults. They were much too young to realize that really, really bad things happen, and not all dreams will come true. And, in some cases, your life will end.

The annoying anchor (no longer in aqua) offered this much: "While officials have confirmed that James Wu was one of the men, they're not able to make a statement with the names of the two other men in the accident, one of whom died at the scene. Doctors are still waiting to notify family."

I knew who the two other men were.

I just didn't know who had died.

Teenagers do die.

Especially when they accept the invitation to dance with death.

That night I had strange dreams all night. The only dream I remembered was one where my junior high crush, Sam Piccolo, was driving a truck and waving good-bye to me in a cowboy hat and a grin, sexy and boyish all at once. "My family's moving, Annie."

I started to cry. I knew where he was going.

State Street.

41

May 12, 2009

Annie

We ride and never worry about the fall
I guess that's just the cowboy in us all

—*Tim McGraw "The Cowboy in Me"*

Shock.

A beautiful gift from God that blocks the memories of tragedy.

Neither Arty nor James remembered ever driving in the State Street area the night of the deadly accident. They were in shock.

Neither remembers who was driving. And while the red truck belonged to Arty, the three took turns driving, and on any given day, the driver could be any one of the three. James and Arty remember the plans were to go to the house of a girl later that night. Arty's cousin Libby Toliver lived six miles south, on the other side of town entirely. The good news came back from toxicology report on all three boys: no one had been drinking. Still, the community wondered. Whatever had compelled the boys to drive north and west would never be known.

The coroner's report, also mentioned in an article in the *Omaha World-Herald*, stated that Mike Sheridan died on impact of injuries sustained to the head and internally. The investigation of the accident continued with recurring reports of "still no absolute conclusion as to the driver of the truck."

Arty remained in critical condition at Children's Hospital. I knew that James was conscious and healing at home, as his sister called me to let me know that he would be out for another week, and she offered to pick up his schoolwork daily.

Belmont High School had been quiet, even in passing periods, in the days following Mike Sheridan's death. Students and staff had momentarily forgotten the Belmont Bones as the accident distracted everyone with heavy hearts. Sadness replaced fear, and the sorrow felt heavier than the mysterious bones on the campus had the past year as the people in the building trudged on, attempting to get their heads around the loss of such a vibrant life. I so wished that we could go back to the days when the Belmont bones had disturbed us so much.

Phone trees to notify staff and parents, counselors in place with a list of questions and comments for grieving students, the staff all felt we were doing the "right" thing with this heavy death weight upon the campus, yet none of the little crisis procedures would change the one fact: Mike Sheridan was really dead.

High schools are about youth and life, promise and hormones, today and tomorrow. When a teenager dies, the equilibrium of the youthful, lively environment is thrown off like a really bad simile or a mixed metaphor. And the process of dealing with an untimely death? Well, that process is kind of like throwing a bunch of faulty similes or mixed metaphors out to the world and expecting them to make sense:

If the shoe fits, pay attention to it!

Using a phone tree to let staff know about the tragedy is like getting all your ducks on the same page.

Sending an e-mail about the student death is like leading a horse to water and then forgetting to shut the barn door.

The best-laid plans.

Talking to a teen about the death of his or her friend is like giving a porcupine as a gift and expecting the receiver to hug it and thank you.

Teaching a class of students with three loud, empty seats that stick out like a sore throat is about as funny as an irregular mole, about as fun as an episode of a spastic colon.

The death of a teenager is hell. Only metaphor for it.

"Before we work on the Works Cited page of your research paper," I said as I looked out at Period Two, "do you all need some time to talk?"

The room was silent as three very empty seats blared around us. And I knew right then, Mike Sheridan was the only student who would have known what to do in this exact moment. Room 213 would surely miss his blue eyes and comical wisdom.

The team of experts who had talked to the staff had told teachers at Belmont High School to ask the students class if they needed to talk. Period Two knew all three of the students in a way that no one else in the world could ever understand. Our little island in room 213 with Mike, Arty, and James leading the energy was like a star at the top of a piece of paper. And while most people were below the muck, we all felt a little piece of heaven each school day that year at 8:47 a.m. Ignoring the fact that the energy was gone would be like ignoring the enormous elephant in the room. I walked a delicate line with Period Two, monitoring the balance between ignoring the elephant and shoving grief down the throats of my groundlings. But then again, I was pretty sure that no one wanted to talk about internal documentation on a research paper that we had all started with the three amigos.

LaTrey cleared his throat but said nothing.

Kinkaid's head was down, so I couldn't see if his cheeks were red.

Tears rolled down Gina's face as she struggled to hide her sobs.

Katrina sat up straight and looked at me with no expression at all.

Peaches raised her hand.

"Peaches?"

"Could we do something for his family? I mean, maybe they need help?"

"That's a great thought." A teacher's encouraging words came out sounding like the awkward cheerleader who had forgotten the routine. "I could talk to the adminis—"

Cami stood up. "I want to talk about how we're supposed to get over this!" she shouted and then cried. Cami's beauty was often overridden by her dubious epiphanies and inappropriate questions. Cami was generous in allowing us to see and hear the stupid stuff and honest words we all thought but chose to guard. What I loved most about the girl was her beautiful transparency.

Cami was honest.

"I don't know how to take this with me in my life. I really don't." Cami was sobbing as she walked up and down the row. "I mean, Mike Sheridan… is number forty-five on the roster and number one in our hearts."

I could see LaTrey cover his face as he cried.

Gwendolyn, who finally had shown up, had put her head down on her desk.

Donovan was also with us. His face turned down, hair pouring down to touch the desk.

Cami's beautiful meltdown continued. "Mike Sheridan was the only reason I looked forward to coming to school some days…" She sniffed. "I knew he would smile." She sobbed aloud and caught her breath and yelled to everyone in the class. "I knew he would make me laugh. And I didn't really even know him. Is that crazy? How do I deal with the fact that he's gone? That he's dead? How?"

Most of us knew Mike only in the context of our classroom, but we felt as if he was a good friend or a relative. We felt a great loss.

Cami looked up at me. "Ms. Day. Please, tell us how are we supposed to get our heads around this." Most of the kids were sniffing and wiping tears. "Just how are we supposed to move on?" Cami's hands were on her hips. She wanted an answer. The class looked at me.

Teachers are supposed to have answers. I was, after all, trained by experts. And in actuality, I knew nothing. Most days, I was a liar. I was a poser, a pretender. I tried to be the best teacher ever, and most days, I lied. Cami's question to me was ironic: I had cried myself to sleep the night before, thinking of the boys, the young men, the three amigos.

"I don't know..." My voice quivered. I took a deep breath. I wanted to run into an aisle at Home Depot and have a good cry. And maybe my new friend with the big glasses would come and help me. "I guess... when we start to feel sad about it all and it hurts more than we think we can handle...we just need to remember one good thing, and, well, that's like a step forward."

"One good thing?" LaTrey asked.

Gina no longer tried to hide her sobbing.

"Monty Python." The voice was that of Maggie Whitehead, who hardly ever spoke.

Laughs and sniffles.

"Kneepads on the top of heads," Phil Timmerman whispered.

"One hell of good football player, for damn sure." LaTrey's voice cracked.

"Your what hurts?" Gina was laughing and crying as she spoke the words.

"The American Dream and ice cream." Donovan's voice was loud though he never moved his head up. I saw a tear drop on his desk.

"Your mom goes to college." The words were out of my mouth before I could stop them.

"Marco," Peaches yelled.

"YOLO," LaTrey answered.

"I said Marco!" Peaches shouted.

"YOLO," the class yelled back.

It felt good to shout. It felt good to cry.

YOLO

You Only Live Once.

Mike Sheridan had lived once. That was one really good thing.

That night, I had a hard time falling asleep, playing bits and pieces of the school year over and over in my head like a movie reel, Mike Sheridan as the leading man. The song "Only the Good Die Young" played in the background as my memories of the smiling football player danced around in my head. Atticus struggled to get comfortable on the floor next to my bed, and I realized that the quiet of the house offered no more noises from my attic. Sleep finally overtook me, and dreams came and went, rendering me into a fitful night. I remembered only one dream.

I'm walking toward the main house of the Genoa Place. I see a red truck coming from the main road. The truck slows down, and I see Mike Sheridan sitting in the driver's seat with a cowboy hat tilted just enough to offer the swag. I'm so excited to see him, and I ask him how he's feeling after the accident.

"Living the dream, Ms. Day. Living the dream."

Mike Sheridan drives off toward the tree on the edge of the south pasture.

I know I will never see him again.

42

Annie

ike Sheridan died the death of a salesman.

His funeral was proof. Based on all accounts, the funeral had been standing room only. The Belmont football team wore their jerseys, and Coach Edwards, along with several students, spoke to the grieving community. It was no surprise that the sun was shining, not a cloud in the sky, in sync with the positive energy Mike Sheridan brought to any room, any situation, any day. I can tell you about the touching moments of the funeral, but not in great detail, since I wasn't there. Peaches, Gina, and I drove up to the church after the funeral ended as mourners poured out, leaning on one another for support.

Ah, the best-laid plans.

We did have a plan to get to the church early, so that Gina would be able to sit. She was very pregnant on May 14 but insisted that she be at Mike Sheridan's funeral. Both Peaches and Gina had asked if I could drive there, Peaches with no transportation aside from a bus and Gina on a mission to avoid the popular crowd, most members attending the funeral. The plan was for the Afternoon Club to meet and leave for the funeral, the three of us safe with the people we trusted.

Both Peaches and Gina were standing in the main lobby of Belmont High School at 8:30 a.m. Monday morning. Eyes red and tired, Gina leaned against the wall. Peaches looked like her bodyguard, ready to pounce on the next person to make her cry.

"Let's do this," I said as we pushed open the door and Gina waddled outside. The glare of the sun made it difficult for me to see at first, and then I saw my car and directed Gina and Peaches. "Front row."

Peaches pulled my arm as I walked down toward the east parking lot. She motioned with her head toward a figure on the step. Hunched over and almost hidden from view was a very broken China Doll. Gwendolyn Sparks's head was in her hands as she huddled, rocking back and forth.

Be the bigger person, Annie Day. You have plenty of room in your car for one more.

"Gwendolyn. Need a ride to the funeral?"

Gwendolyn's body shook, and I heard what sounded like a no.

"We're heading that way anyway. It's—"

"No!" Her head stayed down.

"You all right, girl?" Peaches asked as she moved toward the China Doll.

Gwendolyn looked up, black eye swollen shut, fat lip bleeding. She was holding her arm. "Just leave me alone. I deserved it."

"Who did this?" Peaches demanded as she put her arm around her. "Your dad?"

"No, not my dad, and don't bother calling him..." I moved to the other side of Gwendolyn, and Peaches and I guided her up.

"Was it a boyfriend?" Gina asked.

Gwendolyn laughed. "No, no boyfriend."

"We need to get you to the school nurse..."

"No! Not in the school." Gwendolyn said, and then she passed out.

Peaches and I held her before she fell to the ground. Peaches then put both arms around the rag doll, picked her up, and carried her up the stairs. I ran to open doors. Gina waddled behind us.

Peaches laid Gwendolyn on the cot in a small room off of the nurse's office.

"What happened?"

"We don't know anything. We just found her outside, Grace."

School nurse Grace Channing signaled to her aide. "Please go get Mr. Janocek." Mr. Janocek was the assistant principal and probably one of the only administrators in the school, since most had gone to the funeral. "Annie, do you know this young lady's name? Was anyone with her?"

"Gwendolyn Sparks. She's a student of mine. No, she was outside on the front steps." Gina sat on a bench near the nurse's desk. Peaches leaned against the wall. "Is she going to be all right?"

"Her being unconscious right now is not good. Also, it looks like her arm is broken." Grace held a light up to Gwendolyn's eye that wasn't swollen shut. She opened her eye and looked at her pupil.

When Wayne Janocek got to the nurse's office, he had two other men with him I had never seen. "Annie, could you stick around for a few questions?"

"Of course."

Two hours later, the Afternoon Club drove to the church where Mike Sheridan's funeral was held. We sat at an intersection as cars in the funeral procession drove past us, slowly carrying Mike Sheridan to the cemetery. James Wu's sister and parents walked down the stairs. Behind them were two very sad corgies, Arty's mom and dad, anchoring a woman who looked overcome with grief. Neither James nor Arty were able to attend the funeral.

Car after car passed us as Gina cried in the backseat.

"Because I could not stop for death…" Peaches said.

"He kindly stopped for me." I finished the line.

"A girl in my physics class is Arty Elston's sister," Hannah Bixby told me as she filed some essays into student folders at the end of eighth hour. "Erica said that Arty's doctors think he'll be a long time in physical therapy but that they feel pretty good about his recovery. I thought you'd want to hear that."

"Wow." I was exhausted but so happy to hear what my student aide was sharing with me.

"Erica saw her brother…uh, she was pretty upset. He doesn't even look like Arty, she said. I guess he's in pretty serious condition."

"Wow."

"Hey, Ms. Day. I'm all set for college. I had my last final today, since seniors are done…why don't I take your vocab quizzes from last week and correct them. I know it sounds weird, but I like correcting papers."

I looked at Hannah and smiled. I was really behind, as the stacks of papers around me grew higher and higher.

"I'm taking them." Hannah picked up the big pile on the corner of my desk. "I have to come back in the morning since I'm running track, so I'll just drop the quizzes off before school. You've had a rough week. Just hand over the red pen."

"You're the best."

"The best corrector!" Hannah corrected me as she grabbed my red pen and left.

"I have a bone to pick with you, Miss Day."

Nadine's janitor, Lyle, was moving a big box from the floor to a work-table in the teacher's mailroom as I looked in my mail slot. He flashed a disgusting grin at me, and I flashed him a fake smile and nodded. I hadn't seen Lyle in a while, and I hadn't missed him.

"A bone?"

"Well, you see, I was helping clean your hallway yesterday, and, well, you're room is too dang clean. I might have to report you."

I pulled my mail out of the slot marked A. Day. The pile included a district bulletin, an updated graduation schedule for staff, and the schedule for the State Track Meet that would be held at Belmont the next week.

"So next time I clean your room, I want to see a little more dirt, right?" Lyle smirked as he flipped his greasy hair back from his eyes. He was opening a box with a knife. "Ya hear, young lady?" Lyle put his closed knife in his back pocket next to a large marker. My heart skipped a beat when I saw a green marker there.

My note writer.

My breath was short, and I wanted to run out of the teacher mail-room and scream. Was Lyle also the person scaring this campus by placing bones of lost women in random places, taunting us, and watching us squirm?

"I'm just razzing ya. No big deal." Lyle paused. "Ms. Day?"

"Yes."

"Just a joke." Lyle smirked.

A strange laugh came out of my mouth as I put my mail in my purse and walked out of the workroom.

I had a plan.

No one could stop me.

Because no one knew.

I would confront Lyle, the creepy, slimy creature that had been sending stupid notes to rattle me. I would confront him and tell him that he didn't scare me. I would find out if he had any connection to the bones. I would put him in his slimy little place. And I would feel better.

I called my parents right after I got to room 213 and asked them if they could pick up Oliver. An overload of essays (not really a lie) and a meeting with the cheerleaders (a white lie) were the reasons for my request. My parents loved having him spend "special time" with them when I needed a sitter, and, though I felt guilty about the last-minute factor, they never asked any questions and even offered to have him spend the night. "Not necessary, but thanks. I should be back by seven thirty to pick up Oliver."

I was angry.

Angry that this sketchy man was messing with me. Angry that Mike Sheridan was dead. Angry that I felt so out of control. And the built-up anger felt energizing, and I felt the need to regain control. I parked in the lot near the baseball field.

Why are you messing with me, Lyle?

Doc had informed me the week before that Lyle's hours had changed. I had noticed that he no longer worked alone and that he was no longer the late janitor. Doc had watered the reality down. "See, he's serving some time on janitor probation. I'm not so sure that guy is going to be back next year. Not the best cleaner, and, well, that's kind of what we do."

I sat in my car and watched the door by the loading dock. At five o'clock the door opened, and Lyle sauntered out with a bag over his shoulder and a brown baseball cap over his slimy locks. He lit a cigarette as soon as the door to the building slammed shut.

What do you want from me, Lyle? Why are you harassing me?

He walked to his car at a snail's pace. I almost got out of my car, but I froze.

Once in his car, Lyle sat for a while, finishing his cigarette and making a phone call. Fifteen minutes later, he started the car and drove out of the dock area. I pulled out of my hiding spot and drove a good distance behind him. I'm not sure I would have had the nerve to follow this creepy man had I not been in such an overwhelming state of grief over Mike's death, fueled by the news of Trent Kula and the wife and an annoying ex-husband. Great energy. I felt empowered to defend myself. I felt that life was too short to tolerate this man terrorizing me. I felt the need to confront the creep who had been leaving me notes and challenge him to a confession and apology.

That was my plan.

Lyle drove about five minutes to the interstate and then started south on I-680. I followed his green junker car for about twenty minutes. The license read THG 929. I laughed out loud in the car.

"You're just a thug, Mr. Lyle. Thug 929. Mr. Thug 929."

THG is to Thug as Lyle is to thug.

And 929 is the day that my husband told me he was leaving our marriage. The death of a marriage is as bad as Lyle the thug.

Perfect plate for you, Lyle.

THG 929.

I thought I had lost the thug and was almost relieved. THG 929. Green car reappeared. His blinker went on, signaling to turn off at the Forty-Second Street exit. I turned on my blinker.

My head filled with a strange memory of my dad watching my sisters and me attempt to catch frogs at my aunt's farm. We spent the evening chasing the jumping mysteries. "What are you silly girls going to do if you catch one? You won't know what to do with it." My sister Peggy finally caught one and then threw it down and ran screaming to my mom.

What was I going to do once I saw where Lyle was from? Was I going to hide and then leave? Would I report him? Was I really going to confront the green Magic Marker owner? It's not a crime to own a green Magic Marker. Would I ask him questions? *Are you the one writing me notes? Why are you planting bones at our school? Do you ever wash your hair?*

What was I going to do with him once I caught him?

Lyle's THG 929 car turned left onto Hampton Avenue and turned in to the driveway of a run-down beige tract house. I parked down the block and watched the green car and beige house. A board replaced one of the two windows in the front. Peeled paint speckled the house like a bad case of the chicken pox. Ten minutes later, Lyle got out, lit another cigarette, and walked to the side of the house. I sat in my car. Not so brave now, Annie. I watched Lyle open a door that faced the driveway. A surge of angry energy fueled me. I opened my car door and got out.

What are you going to do if you catch one?

I walked down the sidewalk, my cell phone in my hand. I could always call for help if Lyle threatened me. I was one house away from the speckled shack when a woman looked out the window. Before I could turn to run back to my car, I felt a sharp smack to my head, a pain I had never felt before, and then darkness.

Voices. Darkness still.

"The bitch followed you. Do you not get that? She's the nosy one, right?" a screechy woman's voice with a strange accent yelled.

I was on a cold, dirty linoleum floor. I could see a little piece of the floor through a tiny opening in what felt and smelled like an old dish-cloth wrapped around my head, covering my eyes. My feet and ankles were tied up. The room smelled like an ashtray that hadn't been emptied in a long time. My head hurt.

"Yah…"

"What? I can't hear ya? This is the one who's been sneaking around by the dock? Is this the one?" Screechy woman voice, maybe a Spanish accent.

"Yes."

"Kill her." Another man's voice, guttural and slurry, spoke. I couldn't see him, but the image of a giant ogre came to mind.

The woman shrilled again. "We can't kill her, dumb shit. We already have the whole city paying way too much attention to something that Eddie was supposed to keep hidden. You two are no good to me. All you're good for is whining and to throw out stupid suggestions. You're just a bunch of weak whiners."

(Lack of parallel structure. Correction: All you're good for is *whining* and *throwing* out stupid suggestions.)

"I still say kill her." Ogre was persistent.

"Did you not know you were being followed, Eddie? Are you so stupid and in your own little stupid world that you didn't know you was being followed?"

"No. I didn't see her. I—"

"You're going to pay for this, Eddie. I swear, I'm gonna make you pay for this," the woman screamed, and then she slapped Lyle or Eddie, or whoever this man was. Lyle, the janitor, was not Lyle and was not good at cleaning because he was just a bad guy, not a janitor named Lyle.

"What are we going to do with her? Kill her and get rid of her? Eddie can go with me. Him and I can take her to the tree."

(Incorrect pronoun case.)

"Shut up, Ramiro. We're not going to kill her." The woman was beside herself. I was cold and scared but relieved that the irritating woman in charge was voting not to kill me.

"But she's gonna out us. Now she knows where we live." Eddie/Lyle, the unjanitor, didn't sound so greasy anymore. He sounded scared.

"If we kill her," the woman whispered in short, sharp syllables, "the headline is all about the school again. Are you really that stupid? The cops will start nosing around, and the weak links will cave. We need to move this operation. Just shoot her, now."

Wait—I thought you weren't going to kill me. I really just came to yell at Lyle. That's all.

I heard a closet open, and then I felt a needle in my arm.

"Hurry; we've got work to do."

Once the needle was pulled out of my arm, I felt warm and sad. The ogre, the shrill, and the questionable janitor no longer bothered me.

The bossy woman was still scolding, but she was fading away from me. "Ramiro, start packing the car. Eddie, you call all your guys and tell them to stop all recruiting...for the time being. Repeat, for those who don't seem to understand directions: stop all recruiting."

"Me and Eddie got it covered," whispered Ogre.

(I'm silently correcting your grammar.)

I can't save myself.

All I can do is silently correct your grammar, your inconsistent and annoying use of the language. And how's that working out for me? Looks as if my one skill (she can't cook, she can't save her own life) of teaching English didn't really come in handy after all. *The Grammar Queen is a joke, and the whole town is laughing.*

The shrilling commands continued. "Wait, Ramiro. Before you pack, move the girls to the station on I-80. Most are already working. I think three are downstairs. What are you staring at? Go!"

I felt tired, very tired. All those years of telling students that a good command of the English language will open doors and wow people interviewing you for jobs was just a waste of advice. I should have told them that a strong voice and a clear thesis statement will not stop a bunch of thugs from offing you. Better suggestion: go to a shooting range instead.

"But," Lyle/Eddie whined, "I'm not gonna be able to stop them right now." Didn't Eddie hear the screeching woman say that she hated whining?

What if I didn't survive this ordeal, which was starting to feel more like a scene straight out of the movie *Goonies*? What if I never saw Oliver or my family again? My own stubborn nature meant that I might not see my beautiful Oliver again. I heard myself sobbing.

"Shit, she's a crier. Hurry up, Eddie. Move her to the truck. Get her out of here."

"Where are we going to take her?" Eddie whined.

"Figure it out."

I felt someone pick me up, but I couldn't feel my feet and hands. The rest of my body felt fuzzy.

I couldn't save myself.

Join us next week for another episode.

"Hurry, Eddie. We need to do this now."

One woman thought that she could save the world by protecting and promoting the sanctity of the English language, but she couldn't save herself.

Eddie threw me into the back of the car. My head hit the side door.

Neighbors who remember her never saw her death coming. "She always seemed like she was trying to be a good mom. Never went out much, but we never thought she'd follow the bad guys. What was she thinking? How did she get wrapped up in something like this?"

Right before I passed out, I thought of Keith Morrison calmly warning his viewers: "Nothing is ever as it seems."

And Keith Morrison is always right.

Darkness.

43

Annie

"Ms. Day!"

I heard pounding on a door and a voice yelling. My head was pounding like a bass drum in beat with a bad song. I heard a door open.

"Ms. Day. Are you all right?"

Hannah Bixby.

I could make out the shape of her head and body, but her face was blurry and dark. My eyes were mostly shut from swelling, but I knew Hannah was with me as I lay on the floor of what smelled like room 213.

Hannah was talking on her cell phone.

"Uh, yes, my emergency? My teacher...well, she used to be my teacher...and I stopped by before track, and she looks like she's been beat up. She's in her classroom on the floor. I didn't want to run to the office for help because I didn't want to leave her...Her face is bruised and bloody, and she's out of it...oh, in her classroom...Room 213...yes, the door was unlocked...yes, sorry, at Belmont High School. It's pretty early, and no one is around...Please, are you sending help?"

I lifted my hand to her.

"OK, she's moving. Thank God. She's not dead."

I tried to talk.

"Yes, that's her moaning. She must be conscious…No, I don't know what happened to her. I just came to give her some papers. What? I'm not sure if she's the woman the police have been looking for. I'll stay with her. I think she might have been here overnight. Does that sound weird? OK, a man is coming."

Run away, Hannah. Bad people are after me.

"Ms. Day is…she looks like someone hurt her…"

No, don't tell him that. He may be one of them. Just go away from me, Hannah. Somehow I've made someone really, really mad.

The voice of a man spoke to Hannah, but I could not understand. He didn't sound like an ogre.

"Should I give him the phone?"

"Yes, I'm Nick Stander. I'm with the student and Ms. Day…her first name is Annie. She's probably going to need an ambulance. I'll be riding with her to the hospital."

More people entered the room. I felt myself leaving the world again. Blackness.

I was in an ambulance, and I heard Nadine screaming. "Annie girl! Don't you dare leave me, girlfriend! Who would I swap dream stories with, Annie?"

I tried to say I was fine. It was then that I realized my mouth was all swollen. No words came out. Only moans.

Really, I'm not that bad, Nadine Marie. And yes, I do know that Marie is your middle name.

"Annie! Please be OK, be OK…"

Darkness again.

I opened my eyes and looked into the biggest, brownest eyes I've ever seen.

"You're at Methodist Hospital, little missy. You have some bumps and bruises, but you'll be up and at'em in no time."

I could hear Al Roker talking about the weather in every area of the nation on the TV.

"What's the difference between a hurricane and a typhoon? Well, it depends on where your location is. Now let's see what's going on in your neck of the woods."

(It depends on your location.)

No need to correct any grammar today.

"Sweetie, another nurse will be on duty here in about ten minutes. Shelly. She'll take care of you."

I heard a beeping, beeping sound. I was no longer in room 213.

Dorothy, you ain't in Kansas anymore.

A tall man in a suit sat in a chair in the corner of the room. He didn't look like a doctor.

Big Brown Eyes asked the man, "Can I get you a coffee?"

"Coffee would be great," the man whispered.

The nurse held my hand. "You have some people who are coming by to see you this afternoon, Annie. Bye, angel."

The nurse left, and the man in the chair got up and walked toward me.

Who are you?

"I'm here to protect you." The man's voice was calm and comforting. I felt myself falling back to sleep.

I'm walking behind him.

At first, I think the man is Mike Sheridan. Then I remember that I'm in Colorado, and Mike doesn't live in Colorado. Then I remember that Mike is dead, and I start crying.

I keep crying as I follow the man in the cowboy hat. I'm in the cabin in Bailey, Colorado. It's daytime, and the sun is pouring in through every window. I'm the only person in the cabin besides the man I'm following. He's tall and has a nice frame to his body. I can only see the back of the man as I follow him. I want him to turn around.

The sound of wind chimes fills the air.

The man walks faster. I try to keep up.

The hat on his head is cocked to the side. His boots are the only noise in the house as he walks and walks.

The chimes grow louder.

Who are you? I call out to the man.

He either doesn't hear me or ignores me. The man walks through a doorway that leads to the kitchen.

Why are you here?

I walk into the kitchen, but the man is no longer there. I can still hear his boots, walking and walking. The wind chimes stop.

I want to help you.

Walking, walking.

Where are you?

I shout.

Where are you?

Nurse Shelly walked to the window and opened the blinds. "Are you up for some company, Ms. Day?" The nurse walked to the door and opened it. "I think now would be a good time." My parents stood in the doorway with Oliver.

"Mommy?" My mom and dad came in behind him. My dad picked Oliver up and placed him on the bed next to me.

"Gentle now, Ollie," my dad said. "Remember, like we talked about."

"Just a few minutes," the nurse said.

Oliver moved his face close to mine and whispered, "Hi, Mom. I drew you a picture. It's of you and me, only you're feeling better in the picture. Ow, you've got owies all over your face." He smelled like a cherry sucker, and I wanted to just grab him and hug him with everything in me, but my head and body hurt so much.

I sat up. A strong pain shot up my leg to my back. "I see it, buddy." My voice was raw and scratchy. I needed a Diet Pepsi in the worst way.

"Boots?" I managed to ask.

"Yep, I wore my cowboy boots today." Oliver brought one leg up to show me his red boots.

"Where are your tennis shoes?" I whispered. Always in mom mode.

Oliver raised one eyebrow and tilted his head. "Not my day to worry about it."

I laughed and then stopped. My ribs were sore. I found out later that I had three broken ribs and a broken leg.

"Annie." My dad stood with my mom at the edge of my bed near Oliver. "You gave us quite a scare. Just what's going on in your world?"

I could make out the frame of the man in the suit, who was now standing outside the door to my room as Oliver and my parents sat with me for the next half hour.

"Knock, knock!" Avery's voice carried through the room. Avery and Doc stood in the doorway. "The nurse said we could come in for a second."

"Annie, you must really need attention to go through all this." Doc's blue eyes twinkled. The tall man in the suit was no longer in the doorway.

I looked at Doc and Avery standing near my bed, and I felt like Dorothy in *The Wizard of Oz* after she went through her tornado dream. Doc was my Lion and Avery my Tin Man, following the bizarre dream that was the past school year. *Where was my scarecrow?*

"Hey, who was the man in the suit?" I asked everyone in the room. Oliver was pushing the buttons to move the bed.

"We need to be going. Glad to finally meet you two." My dad grabbed his coat, and he and my mom moved toward the door. "Come on, Ollie, by golly."

"Bye, Dad," I whispered.

Oliver blew me a kiss. "Bye, Mom. Get better."

I waved and smiled.

Avery set a vase with flowers on the table next to my bed. "Doc and I thought we'd bring you something pretty to look at while…"

"You heal," Doc said, finishing the sentence. "The flowers are from my garden. Avery supplied the vase."

I smiled and grunted a thank-you. My head was pounding.

The nurse was back in the room. She spoke to Avery and Doc. "I think she's getting tired."

"On our way out," Doc said as he leaned in toward me. "You take care, Annie Day. We'll see you soon."

I waved.

"Bye now," Avery said. "Be safe."

The nurse fixed my IV. "Wanda, the night nurse, set this aside for you. She said you had it in your hand when they brought you in." I looked at the object in my hand and knew that I was holding Oliver's wooden nickel.

"Don't know if you've ever heard the saying about those wooden nickels...you aren't supposed to take any of 'em." She winked.

The wooden nickel was my lucky charm.

It was a miracle.

44

The Interrogation of Mateo Ortiz

"I need to talk to you. I have information about the bones."

Officer Kelly recognized the voice from the other two messages, which he had listened to over and over again. This time the voice was live.

"Anytime; you name it," Officer Kelly said. "Can I get a name, time, and place."

"Only a time and place. I will be at the police station at ten o'clock this morning."

The man hung up.

Mateo Ortiz knew what had led authorities to the bones: Mateo Ortiz.

Mateo Ortiz met with several men down at the police department on the rainiest day yet in the spring of 2009. He was the man leaving the messages. Mateo was the man planting the bones. He had so much more to tell the officers. Officer Kelly offered Mateo coffee and a chair. After the phone call to meet with them, the officers had said they would meet anytime, anywhere, as soon as possible. Two hours after the phone call, the questions started flying.

"So, Mateo, we'll be recording this interview. The recorder is now on. Please state your name."

—Mateo Ortiz.
—Mr. Ortiz, you're admitting to planting bones on the campus of Belmont High School in Omaha, Nebraska.
—Yes.
—Are you also admitting to previously burying the bodies of the recently unearthed bones in Indian Cave Cemetery in Richardson County?
—Yes.
—Did you kill the people who you buried, Mateo?
—No, never killed.
—Why did you bury the bodies where you did?
—My job was to make things go away. But first I was just a groomer. I was a student in the classroom, with no goal of graduating. My goal each day was to find the girls.
—The girls?
—The girls who were easy to groom. The girls who looked neglected. The girls who wanted attention. The girls who wanted someone to make them feel loved. I was their Romeo. Boss called me the Romeo Pimp. I went to high school. I would find the girls. First, I'd make eye contact. Then I'd flirt. Then I'd take them out and buy them things. It was so sad how easy it was to make them trust me. I'd buy them jewelry, the cheap stuff. I'd take them to dinner. Flatter them. Make them trust me. I'd groom them, then take them to the stable, then have them work for Boss. There were a few of us who groomed in the schools. We were young, and the older ones managed the stable.

—The stable?

—The house where they stayed. We called it a stable. Only the grooming was really lying, and the stable...well, it was just a trap. Once the girls were there, Boss got them hooked on drugs. He threatened their lives if they left the stable. Just when you thought those poor girls couldn't be any more broken.

—I'm going to repeat my question: Did you kill these women?

—No, never. That's why I'm here. I want the people killing the girls to pay.

—We can't do that until we have more information.

—We became shorthanded, and then Boss needed me to do more than groom the girls. That's what my orders were. My new job was to hide the bodies. The ones who died. They were our mistakes. The one girl who got too addicted to the drugs that we gave her—she overdosed. Another girl—her john beat her to death after she demanded the money for the trick. She was so beat up that she didn't make it through the night. The man— well, he couldn't keep his mouth shut, so they shut him up for good. I did not kill anyone. I was on cleanup duty. I was to take the broken girls and bury them. Never ask questions. Just get rid of bodies. Far, far from Omaha. To the ghost town. Indian Cave...

—Why did you take the bodies to Indian Cave Cemetery?

—The first night I did what I did, I drove and drove and didn't know where I was going to stop. I was on I-29 going south, and I knew that I needed to go away; that's all. I saw the name Indian Cave on the sign and somehow felt that I should go there. I don't know why. I liked the name. My directions were that I was to drive as far as I could and find a place where no one would connect the bodies to us. I drove west off of I-29 to find the park. Jennifer was the first one. I had to bury the young woman without a proper funeral or coffin or family or...noth- ing was good about it at all. Nothing. I found the tree at the far end of the cemetery. At least she could be in a cemetery. I buried her and prayed over her. I drove back to Omaha as the sun came up.

—Why did you plant the bones at the high school this past year?

—Because I needed to get your attention. I got your attention, didn't I? I couldn't live with knowing where those people were and their families not knowing. That's why I planted the bones—so you would investigate and stop it all. I wanted it to stop.

—Why didn't you just go to the police back then?

—Never. I was a scared, stupid young man...hell, I was a boy, barely seventeen. I hadn't lived at home since I was thirteen. I had nothing or no one but the Boss and the others. They were my family.

—But ten years later, you're here.

—Yes.

—Why?

—Because I fell in love.

—What?

—With one of the girls...one of the girls I groomed. It was considered a crime. It was against the rules. We were supposed to look at the girls as money, as objects, not people. It was against the rules to fall in love. Seriously? How can someone make that a rule? Boss was onto us...he threatened both of us with our lives. We left in the night and went as far as we could. Farther than the Indian Cave. Texas.

—Why are you here now?

—I couldn't live with knowing where those bodies were buried and that I had buried them.

—But not killed them?

—Correct.

—And you wanted them found?

—Found and given a proper burial and...

—And?

—I wanted them found and the ring to be stopped.

—The ring?

—The operation. The stealing of women and making them weak and making them slaves. I wanted it all stopped.

—Why didn't you just tell us? Now, ten years later. Why didn't you just come to the authorities and tell them what you knew?

—Because I was part of the crime that put them there, even though I didn't kill them. I knew that I would face prison time if I came forward. I have a family now. I was torn. I felt such guilt for what I had done. I worked the area—not just the high school, but also restaurants, malls, anywhere I could find, you know... the type. They were easy to find. Eventually, the drugs were a part of the whole plan. I hated the drugs, but the girls were easier to work with when they were high. And then he took them.

—He?

—Boss took the girls. When my job was done, I had roped one in, he would take the girl to the stable. In time, we had the younger ones work truck stops on I-80. He called them lot lizards. Some of us would work the airports following finals; nothing more groom-able than a college girl who's been up all week studying for finals, fragile...And all of them had to work the College World Series. That was, by far, the biggest money and the time when Boss was happiest.

—Who is Boss?

—Was. He was evil. He's dead now.

—Name. We need a name.

—He went by Boss, but someone said that his real name was Alvaro Simon.

—How and when did he die?

—I don't know. I had left by then. Remember...I fell in love. I hated what she had to do for the boss. I wanted to save her. I didn't want to bury her.

—Her?

—No. I won't give her name.

—We can't help you if you don't help us.

—I can't go to prison.

—The phone calls, Mateo. What about the phone calls?

—I tried. I really did. I thought you'd all connect the dots. At first, I thought the soil would help you. I thought you'd find out that the soil in Indian Cave State Park is very unique. So I waited and waited. Then I made phone calls. I got you to the park down where the tree is with the first call, and you connected the bones and even identified them, but you didn't make the bigger connection.

—Bigger connection?

—To the grooming that was going on at school...I hoped you'd find them.

—Them?

—The groomers. Sitting in the classrooms of the city. Roaming hallways after school. Looking for the perfect girls. So I sent the second message, about the ring.

—We were getting close. Before your first phone call, the forensic lab had made the soil connection; at least they knew that the soil came from the Missouri River Valley down in southeast Nebraska.

—Meanwhile, more girls were falling through the cracks. I grew impatient. So I called in with the second message.

—We need names. You know that. We can't do this without names. We appreciate the direction and the help with finding the skeletal remains of the victims.

—That's got to be worth something.

—Something?

—Freedom. I regret it all.

—We're waiting on word from the people who can authorize that sort of thing. One more question, Mateo. How did you get the bones to Belmont without anyone seeing you or suspecting you?

—Because I worked there.

—Worked there?

—Yes, I work at the school.

—So if we ask Belmont High School if you're an employee of OPS at their school, they would say yes.

—No.

—No?

—They know me by a different name.

—Who?

—Nick Stander.

45

May 20, 2009

Annie

The bones belonged to four women and one man.

Nine months after the first skull was found on the football practice field, one month after the unearthing of the bones in Indian Cave Park, the forensic team would name all five Mystery Does: Jennifer Caldwell; Tiffany Manning, the runaway from Belmont in 1998 who had never been found; Carol Wayne, a waitress from Perkins who had disappeared in 2000; Stephanie Hardy, a college student at UNO from Logan, Iowa, whose remains were connected to the skull found in the locker in February; and Carlos Gonzales, a new American citizen who had disappeared around 1999.

Some of their bones and some skulls were missing, but that was because they had been helpful props in the unveiling of a mystery.

The key to the unveiling of the identities of the bones by the tree in a ghost town in southeast Nebraska was Mateo Ortiz.

His role in sex trafficking in the late nineties and his crime of falsifying his identity to start a new life made him a wanted man. But he told the legal team that questioned him in Omaha that he would tell all if they would grant him the freedom to be a husband to his wife and father to his daughter. The practice of swapping information for guilt is protocol in such grave matters. And because Mateo made sure that his freedom was in writing, the investigators heard one long story with puzzle pieces beyond belief.

The room that Mateo had sat in for his interrogation on May 16 was the same room that I was questioned in on Wednesday morning, the twentieth of May.

"Sure you don't want me to go in with you?" My dad looked worried as we sat in the hallway of the downtown police station.

"I'm sure. Just don't leave. You're my ride home."

"I'd go in with you if..."

"I'm good. They said that they just have a few questions. Shouldn't take long."

"For someone who got knocked around a bit, you look nice."

"I am nice."

"Annie, you remind me so much of my Uncle Tru."

"I'll take that as a compliment."

"You're both so damn stubborn."

"Thanks."

"Just like that old cowboy, you think you can take on the world. That it's your job to figure it all out."

I moved my head toward my dad.

"Why'd you follow that man, Annie?"

"Right now, I'm not sure. I thought I was just going to tell him off. Like to quit harassing me."

"And how'd that work out for you?"

"I'm going to change the subject. Thank you so much for helping me with my attic."

"You paid for it..." My dad smirked.

"I'm gonna miss having your Old Spice smell up there."

"Old Spice?"

"Your cologne or aftershave or whatever." My throat was raw. I needed water.

"Hell, I haven't worn Old Spice since the eighties. Your mother said that the smell of it made her sick. And all those years, I thought—"

"Ms. Day?" A man in a short-sleeved shirt that was too small to cover his stomach and a tie that was too wide to be worn in 2008 invited me to his office.

"You don't wear Old Spice anymore?" I looked at my dad as I stood up.

He shook his head no.

I knew then that Choochoo had strange taste in his aftershave.

"I'm Officer Brian Noonan." The man extended his hand to shake mine. "You sure look a heck of a lot better than when I saw you last week, Ms. Day. How're you feeling today?"

I recognized the voice of Officer Noonan as the one who had called the day before to ask me a few questions. I didn't remember seeing him before.

"Much better." I fiddled with my purse. How many high school English teachers can say that they've been questioned by police two times in one school year? The year of living dangerously: running over China Dolls and chasing Thugs.

"Come on in, Ms. Day. Have a seat. As hard as it might be, we need to hear some details about your abduction." Two other men joined the main officer at the table—an older, shorter man in a white shirt and khakis and a tall man in a suit. He looked a lot like the man who had been sitting with me in the hospital. "Officers Templeton and Weidner will be joining us for the questioning." The taller officer smiled as we all sat down.

"We can't thank you enough, Ms. Day," Officer Weidner, his longer hair combed back like a *GQ* model, said as he smiled again and then shook my hand. "Your administration has been instrumental in helping our undercover operation at Belmont. What you may not know is that you have also helped with the investigation, which has been ongoing since August."

"I'm just not sure I have much to offer you other than the street name I gave you on the phone."

Officer Noonan looked down at the report in front of him and tapped his pen. "First, we need to clarify your, uh, relationship with Eddie Tarrington."

"Who?"

"Um, Lyle, the man you followed on the day you were attacked. How were you involved? Or—"

"Wait. I had no involvement with Lyle."

"Well then, let me rephrase the question. You followed a man to a place where you were attacked. We just have to ask. Why did you follow him? Had this man been grooming you—"

"Grooming?"

The short man in the khakis jumped in. "Had he been flirting with you, buying you things?"

I knew what "grooming" meant.

"I followed Lyle to confront him, to tell him to stop leaving me notes. I'm not sure what Lyle's crime is besides leaving me menacing notes and being a really bad janitor."

"As it turns out, we've had our eye on Lyle for months, and he had a few other crimes worse than poor janitorial skills. What kind of notes did Lyle write to you?"

"There were three...the first wasn't a threat. It just proved that he was watching me. It was right after I hit the Chi...a girl in the parking lot."

"Hit?"

"Gwendolyn Sparks moved into my parking spot and I hit her. She was fine, and no one pressed charges. The note said, "Be careful." I think Lyle saw the incident...even though I didn't know it was him at the time. He left a note in my teacher mailbox. And the second read, "Not your business." That note was on my windshield right after I had looked for my purse near the loading dock. I heard a lot of noise in a room down there. I didn't see anything, but..."

"And the last note?"

"That one was left in my car. That came after I saw a man walking a person out to the loading area. I was bringing down work for students in ISS. I saw Lyle down there too. That's when I started to feel, you know, threatened. The note said, "Back off, bitch. We're watching you." Is Lyle—Eddie—the man who was planting the bones?"

"No, but he's related to the bones."

"I'm not sure if I follow."

"Ms. Day." This time the younger Officer Weidner spoke. "Eddie Tarrington is the link into Belmont High School, bringing groomers for a sex-trafficking group into the schools. He brought younger men here to your school to find vulnerable girls to groom for their stable. You found the stable when you followed Eddie Tarrington."

"What?"

"The hallway down by the loading dock, Ms. Day," Officer Weidner continued, "was a transition station, of sorts. That's where the group took the girls to give them gifts and drugs and start the process of controlling them. Grooming. We believe that Lyle and his people thought you were onto them. And when you followed him? Well, let's just say that you're lucky you're alive." Officer Weidner's voice was calming and familiar.

Officer Noonan added, "When you brought Gwendolyn Sparks to the nurse's office, you may have saved her life."

Officer Weidner cleared his throat. "Ms. Sparks was being groomed into a sex-trafficking scheme. She'd been beaten up by one of the team members the day you saw her. She was very helpful in filling in pieces of the puzzle and confirming what we suspected."

"Sex trafficking? Are you kidding me?" My head was spinning.

"You probably don't remember...when we got to the hospital right after your attack." Officer Noonan had a hint of a grin on his face. I shook my head no. "Your doctor allowed us a few minutes with you. We knew we had a small window. We asked who, and...well, to put it lightly, you cussed up a blue streak about the man."

The three officers grinned.

"I did?"

"You did, indeed," Officer Weidner said.

"You told us—and I quote…" Officer Noonan looked down at a report in front of him. "'That greasy-haired son of a bitch janitor was the man who attacked me. He and a damn ogre and his haggy old bossy troop leader attacked me.' You said you followed him, so we asked about the car. You repeated over and over again, 'Thug 929, Thug 929 in an ugly green car…' That was all we had."

Officer Templeton in his khakis took it from there. "We searched the Nebraska license database for Thug 929, TUG 929, THG 929, and jackpot. A green Chevrolet Cavalier belonging to a woman…we found her, and then we found the car down in Kansas City. And Edward H. Tarrington was hiding out…turns out to be Eddie, the greasy son of a bitch. We would never have been able to make the arrests without your help."

Officer Noonan was serious again. "During Mike Sheridan's funeral, the team was cleaning house in the school. They were trying to scoop up all the girls who might leak information. You happened to be at the right place at the right time when you found Ms. Sparks. After your attack, Mateo Ortiz came forward to offer information. His confession came right after the results from the soil forensic specialists. The results connected the soil from Indian Creek Park to soil on the bones planted on your high school campus. We knew that the soil on the bones came from the silty soil down along the Missouri River Valley. The problem was, we were stuck. We only knew what the connection was. We could not get to the why."

"And Mateo Ortiz filled in the holes," Officer Templeton said, "for leniency on his involvement. With Ms. Sparks and Mr. Ortiz and your help, we made the arrest of the three individuals who were working the Belmont campus. The bones had been planted to get our attention, only we couldn't get all the dots connected until Mateo helped us with that."

"If this man named Mateo told you why the bones were buried, and Lyle wasn't planting them, who was?"

"Mateo was."

"Then what does Mateo have to do with the stable? I'm sorry. I'm really trying to keep up."

"Ortiz knew about the stable because he had worked the stable ten years ago. He and a woman whom he had groomed fell in love, and then they ran away. The guilt of his involvement and his knowledge of those bodies he was directed to get rid of and bury far away from Omaha was tearing him apart. Nick wanted us to find the connection and fix it."

"Nick?"

"Nick Stander, a coach at your school, is Mateo Ortiz. He and his wife, Becky, and their daughter had come back to make right, so to speak."

"Becky?"

Officer Noonan looked at his notes. "Becky Ortiz. She had been a student back when Mateo worked the campus. Becky Kershner."

"Wow." Did I have scoop for Nadine.

"The good news is we caught the bad guys."

"Nobody is who they say they are," I mumbled. "The whole thing feels like a Shakespearean tragedy."

"People just need to be honest." The other officers and I looked at Officer Weidner, who spoke the strange words. "I had a teacher once who told me that the purity of the American Dream needs the dream to be worthy and the dreamer to be honest...Ms. Day, you're about the most honest person I know."

Officer Noonan made the reintroduction. "Annie Day, meet Officer Brandon Weidner...or Donovan Hedder." I looked at the man who had spent nine months under my nose in row three of Period Two in room 213.

46

May 21, 2009

Annie

"Some people will do anything to get out of finals," Peaches said loud enough for Gina to hear as we knocked on her door. I set my crutches against the wall and sat in a chair next to Gina.

"And some teachers will do anything to get out of working the state track meet." Gina's radiant smile told Peaches and me two things: (1) She wasn't crying for the first time in a long time, and (2) she was happy with her open-adoption decision.

"You look amazing, girl, for just having a baby and all." Peaches set down a jar of candy that we had just bought in the gift shop.

"I feel good, and Baby Boy came into the world healthy and screaming at eight pounds, eight ounces. All the nurses call him Cowboy, since he's ornery and up all night."

"Wow," I said. "How did that big baby ever fit in you?"

Tears glistened in Gina's eyes.

"Oh, no you don't," Peaches said. "Please just shut off those tears."

Gina laughed. "Baby Boy's parents—they named him this morning… Michael."

I took a deep breath.

"Isn't that beautiful?"

"Damn," Peaches whispered.

"I need to thank you two…for getting me through a tough year. I owe you both so much."

"Are you kidding? You're my hero," Peaches said. "I thought, if this chick can carry this baby for another family, well, then I can go to college."

"Any news on how Arty and James are doing?" Gina asked.

"I talked to Sunny Wu, and she said that the boys are getting letters from strangers all over Nebraska and beyond. From survivors of horrific accidents, begging the boys not to carry guilt with them in their lives. Sunny read one to me that was from a man who said he had allowed the guilt to damage so many things in his life. They have a tough road…"

"I hope we never find out who was driving that night…Ms. Day, I need to apologize for the beginning of the year. I didn't feel well, and…I don't know if you knew that I didn't always like you."

"Really?"

Some secrets are meant to be carried to the grave.

"Yah, you were always so perky and happy about English when I was nauseated and mad at the world. But now…"

"Glad to know you got over it."

A woman and a man stood at the door. "Come on in," Gina said.

"We don't want to intrude," the man said. "We just wanted to check in before we leave. We'll be back tomorrow."

"No, really, I want you two to meet my friends." Peaches looked around the room and then at me. She raised an eyebrow and grinned. I guess we were Gina's friends.

"Ms. Day and Peaches, I want you to meet Tavish and David Kolterman." The formerly self-absorbed cheerleader continued. "Koltermans, this is Ms. Day and Peaches."

"Nice to meet you," Peaches said as she shook the hands of the smiling new parents.

I picked up my crutches and said, "Congratulations." I said no more. I didn't want to cry.

"We need to head out." Peaches caught my cue.

We never did meet Baby Boy. We were there to see our friend Gina.

47

"Mother's Advice"
Brush, Colorado—Morgan County
Nursing Care—July 2006

Rollie

I sat at my mom's bedside, the months before she died in 2006. We talked about how you girls were growing and what year you were in school. We talked about how bad the food was at the nursing home but how wonderful the people who took care of her were. We talked about a lot of things, but mostly we talked about that summer of 1938.

My mother remembered that it was one of the hottest on record. She talked about her brothers and would laugh until she cried when we shared our stories of my uncles throwing me in the trough or cutting off my ears. When she laughed, I swear I could almost see my mother the way she looked back in 1938.

"I wonder how many years Maribel Winters had been running from that monster before she came to Brush."

My kindhearted mother, who hardly ever said a mean word about any person or animal, called Cal Winters a monster. That was saying something. After all those years not talking about what happened to Cal that summer, my mother finally opened up, kind of like she needed to let it all out before she died.

I poured Mom some water and sat down next to her.

My mother loved her brother Truett like you wouldn't believe. Hell, she loved all her brothers, but I could tell her heart broke when she talked about what happened that summer.

"He didn't sign up for it," my mom said. Her defensive statements made me wonder just what she was defending.

"You think Truett killed that monster?"

I asked it, as blunt as that. I felt safe fifty years later with the monster dead and the old sheriff several years dead.

My mother's eyes teared up. She shook her head. "I have no idea." I was secretly hoping that my mother knew something more than the rest of us.

"Something I never told you before."

My mother moved her head toward me.

"I never told you because…well, I don't know if I forgot or blocked it out of my head. Maribel Winters had a gun."

"A gun?" My mother's voice was scratchy. I got up and helped her sip from the cup.

"I saw it when Jeb and I went into town to help Truett fix Maribel's sister's roof. Hell, I was just a kid. I think at the time I was more impressed that a woman knew how to use a gun."

"You…"

"I think I blocked it out, or maybe a six-year-old can't connect dots, but…do you think maybe she might have killed Cal? I mean, the sheriff never said what kind of a gun. Most of the guns Truett had were rifles, and, well, the uncles said he didn't have a gun with him that night. He never took guns into town."

"Well, I never even considered..." My mother started coughing. I helped her sit up.

"I hadn't thought about it either...until now."

"We'll never know...We do know that Truett—and Maribel—carried the truth with them to their graves. I guess, Rollie, some skeletons are meant to be left in the closet."

48

Annie

The bumblebee should not be able to fly.

But you just tell it not to.

As Peaches walked across the stage down on the football field in June of 2009, she held her diploma up to the sky. I knew she was showing her grandmother what she had done for her. Louisa Trumble had passed on in her sleep the day after my attack. Peaches, who wore the bumblebee pin on her graduation gown, told me that her grandma wanted to be there for the graduation, and she was.

I went to Belmont's graduation with my new friend Brandon Weidner. He told me that he wanted to see Peaches graduate. He was, after all, a classmate of hers. Several students and teachers glanced my way during the ceremony, wondering who the man was sitting next to the junior English teacher. Following the graduation, Brandon and I went to dinner. We did, after all, have to eat.

I looked across the table at a man whom I had just met but had spent an entire school year with, and the paradox kept me looking at the deep-green eyes that had been hidden by hair and an investigation. Donovan/Brandon was handsome, in a Keith Morrison way, and then some.

"You look nice." I said to my new friend.

"I am nice." Brandon grinned, and I could now see the physicality that was the line between Donovan and Brandon flicker back and forth, the calm, low voice as the common thread.

In several late-night phone calls, Brandon had shared with me how he had watched over me throughout the year. He was assigned my classroom, as Phil Timmerman and LaTrey Williams, along with several other students, had been flagged as possible groomers, though the real groomers had never been in any of my classes. Brandon had witnessed Lyle putting the second note on my car and had concerns of Lyle bothering me outside of the school day, dissolving the question of the mysterious man watching me on my street and at the holiday party.

"I'm still struggling with the fact that you were Donovan. I have about a million questions. It's just so strange."

"When I was first assigned to go undercover, I was concerned. I'm so much older than a teenager and didn't want to stand out. And then I thought if Dustin Hoffman could pull it off in *Tootsie*, I'd do my best... for the case."

"The fact that you remember the movie *Tootsie* means you're really not in high school."

"After the first week of trying to get lost in the crowd, to not have people notice me, to try to be invisible, I found out something really sad: it's really easy to get lost or overlooked. The poor girls who were taken advantage of, the men taking advantage of them—all under our noses. But we couldn't see them."

"My scarecrow!" I said a little too loud. "You're my scarecrow, Brandon."

"Your what?"

"I'm Dorothy, and a terrible tornado just about ruined my life. Doc and Avery and you were there for me through it all. You were a

Nirvana-loving scarecrow lost in the nineties, and when I woke up, you were the farm hand who was with me all the time."

"Do I have to be the scarecrow?"

"In the real story, Dorothy tells the scarecrow that she'll miss him the most as she heads back to Kansas."

"Well, I'm not going anywhere."

"Sure you want to stick around? I can be kind of a challenge. I might even correct your grammar."

"Not my first rodeo," Brandon said as he grinned a crooked grin and winked.

49

Annie

What if you slept
And what if in your sleep you dreamed
And what if in your dream you went to heaven
And there plucked a strange and beautiful flower
And what if when you awoke you had that flower in your
hand
Ah, what then?

—SAMUEL TAYLOR COLERIDGE

I held a little heaven in my heart after the battles and struggles of one school year, a year with a heck of a lot of muck.

When sorrows come, they come not single spies but in battalions.

I teach American lit, but I took quite a few Shakespeare classes while getting my English degree. I never liked Claudius in *Hamlet*, but his words rang in my head in the spring of 2009. Claudius spoke those words to Gertrude after a plethora of really bad things happened in their world. Trust me, it was a really bad day in Denmark when Claudius spoke those words.

When sorrows come, they come not single spies but in battalions.

Sorrows came in and attacked my world in one school year all at once, like an army or a gigantic bucket of big frogs. And I just didn't know which one to swallow first.

Mike Sheridan's death.

It shattered dreams. The goodness of the young man who could whistle past any graveyard, smile through any thunderstorm, and joke through any rough time. His own cowboy spirit, with a wink of an eye, made the day better. And he was gone. When I think of my last dream of Mike Sheridan—and maybe it was really his spirit connecting with me in that dream as he drove off to the south pasture—I hope that he reached his star, that he found his Camelot. I will never forget Mike Sheridan.

The underworld of sex trafficking in Omaha.

Well, it made us realize that Omaha "what a great place to raise your children," Nebraska, was not devoid of the sinister tyrants who groomed and used easy victims for their own gain. And while we were all glad to find the bones of the missing girls and give them proper burials, we all knew that the sinister tyrants would continue in time, as they have through history, to take advantage of people, to use people.

My attack.

I discovered that with all the might and power I thought I had, I was not invincible. And that was OK.

The city of Omaha moved on as well. Over six hundred scouts headed up to the Little Sioux Scout Ranch to help build a memorial chapel dedicated to the spirit of the boys who lost their lives in the tornado of 2008.

A three-judge panel sent the man convicted of raping and killing twelve-year-old Amber Harris to death row.

They finally did find the killer of the little boy and the housekeeper who lived a few blocks from me after he killed another two people five years later. In 2016, Anthony Garcia, a disgruntled former resident at

Creighton University and a dangerous man, was charged with killing Thomas Hunter and his housekeeper Shirlee Sherman, and later Dr. Roger and Mary Brumback.

On a smaller scale, lighter sorrows sprinkled the days that were tucked into those quarters and semesters and lessons. An unplanned pregnancy, controlling parents, and broken marriages—well, those sorrows soon appeared to be the everyday kind of sorrows. You know, the type that don't show up on any episodes of *Dateline* mysteries.

Peaches went on to law school and works in a firm defending women in domestic abuse cases. She married a fellow law student, and the two had a baby boy last year. I'm the godmother of Peaches's baby; Gina came to the baptism after finals in college.

Sadly, I read in the paper in the summer of 2014 that LaTrey Williams was killed in an incident in North Omaha. The man who shot him didn't even know him and had been aiming for a different person entirely. LaTrey's fears of being killed by a gun—which he had written about in an essay—had been valid. I only hope that through death—the ultimate transcendental experience—LaTrey has found his great big sun or star of peace, as he has risen above the muck.

Choochoo is no longer—Oliver doesn't even remember the Choochoo era.

Brandon and I married in 2010. He's good to Oliver.

So, I have moved on from the Catty Monster and my obsession with *The Jake and Jaymie Show.* Jake shattered one more American Dream as he moved on to another affair and marriage. I never think of Trent Kula, and, if I do, I find that I'm only more repulsed by lip gloss.

Not to sound too Charles Dickens-ish, but looking back at the school year from September of 2008 to May of 2009, I can say only this: it was a wonderful year, it was an awful year. But the world moved on from that year. Nine months. Four quarters, two semesters—however you want to break up a school year, ask any teacher, and he or she will tell you that a school year has its own identity. The personality of a class could be memorable or unmemorable. Famous or infamous.

I will never forget the students from that year.

The thumbprint of the students who met in room 213 during Period Two of that school year was like that of no other class I had taught. I know that while I made lesson plans and hoped to dispense knowledge or at least an appreciation of the nuances of our very messy, complicated language, I learned more from Period Two about myself than I had ever learned. I learned so much more than I attempted to teach to the groundlings sitting before me.

For me, the sorrows of that one school year felt like one great big rubber band being pulled back, and I wanted so badly to know just where that school year would send me. The rubber band finally shot us all out in a trajectory (power word) that we each needed to follow.

We're all flying out on different trajectories from the setbacks and sorrows of that year. We're all going to be OK, but we will never be the same.

Everything is different today than it was that year, although I'm pretty sure that in a cabin in the Colorado mountains, while the hummingbird wind chimes sing, a cowboy ghost, whose psychic souvenir kiss kept me hopeful during a rough time, still wanders room to room, protecting someone, something.

And that works for him.

50

To Oliver: The Code

Annie

When Oliver becomes a man, my greatest wish for him is that he remember the code.

The code that is a beautiful blend of the chivalry that laced the lives of the fictional Knights of the Round Table—he should always remember to open doors for ladies and be kind to animals—and the cowboy code.

The code will come in handy on bad days when a dream crashes to the ground into a million tiny, sharp pieces that will cut him if he sits in the broken dream or walks over it again in regret, years after the dream accident.

Because Oliver will face many broken dreams.

I know this for a fact. And it's not broken dreams that will be a problem for my son. I've learned this fact the hard way. Oliver's choices in reacting to the brokenness will damage or carry him through life.

When a dream breaks, I hope Oliver turns to a spirit that may be racing through his veins from the blood of his cowboy ancestors or tucked in his character from watching my father and listening to his stories. I want Oliver to face each heartache with his head held high and his hat cocked, if he's wearing one. I want him to get back up from the crash and shake the dust off and say something really funny out loud so that people around him will laugh.

I want Oliver to smile through the storms and the muck, to work harder than anyone else in the room. I want him to avoid those who complain and tear down. When he stubs his toe in the late night when no one is around, I want him to grumble a few cuss words under his breath and then laugh at himself. When his friends are going through hard times, I want him to make them laugh. Hell, cut off their ears if he needs to. Just help them to gain perspective. That's what friends are for. I hope that he primps before going out and takes great strides when he meets the world. I want him to give people a hard time and then wink.

I hope that Oliver finds out what he was born to do and loves doing whatever that might be. I hope Oliver is always good with God and at peace with his star. I don't want Oliver to ever forget that he was named after a cowboy who survived a lightning bolt and a broken heart.

And even through the broken dreams, I want Oliver to keep dreaming. Never stop dreaming. And finally, at the end of the day, in the quiet of that good night, my wish for Oliver, my little cowboy, is that he always listen to the messengers in his dreams.

A Note from the Author on Grooming Horses and Humans

ON GROOMING HORSES

Sprinkled within the fictional love story of Truett and Maribel in *Cowboys to Camelot* are the true cowboy stories that I heard from my dad as I was growing up along with actual pictures of him and his uncles in Brush, Colorado during the Great Depression. Many times in my childhood, we went to family reunions in Brush, a small town on the edge of Colorado, the town where my father was born.

The Colorado uncles do exist, and there is no denying the impact their lives and energy had on my father and, in time, on my sisters and me.

As he speaks of that era, a drawl softly envelopes his words in a voice that seems to come straight from a day over seventy summers ago. I think his voice is that of one of his six uncles from the ranch, twenty miles outside of Brush. From his fifth year of life to his teen years, my father had spent his summers helping those men ranch and groom their horses. "They were good to their horses." My dad said that a horse would do anything for you if he trusted you.

He explains to me, a ridiculously solid city girl, that a cowboy may have worn clothes soaked in dirt and sweat during the week as he drove cattle and worked the land, but when Saturday night came, the same cowboy primped like a school girl. My father's similes and metaphors are primitive and raw and likely the residue of memories that only escape when he recalls those cowboy giants and those cherished summers.

At the end of each day, his uncles would place their hats on the mantle with heavy tin cans on each side to hold the hat in a particular shape. The way a cowboy wore a hat meant something. A strong tilt of his hat would boast, but if the cowboy could live up to the tilt, no one bothered him.

I used to wonder how that little boy, who looked up to those horse-man heroes, ended up placing all of his energy in his adult life into raising four daughters in Omaha, Nebraska, with a wife and no horse or no hat. He moved into a career and a nine-to-five life with dinner at six and homework duty after his daughters did the dishes. He drove his daughters to high school dances and financed several mouths with glittering paraphernalia. He promoted post-secondary education and cheered his four babies into adulthood, but I know that those six cowboys never left his head or heart for a moment. Even so, I don't think my father harbors any regrets toward his decision to leave that world. He knew that those summers spent on the ranch as a young boy becoming a man had their place in the great scheme of things. He also knew that he needed to provide a different place for his wife and four daughters. He made that life in Omaha, Nebraska.

He may have moved away from the arid sand hills of eastern Colorado to the humid summers and cold winters of the Heartland, but my dad never really moved away from the spirit of those cowboys and the men who shaped his character. He's kept them alive by retelling his stories to my sisters and me. I have heard each story several times, and I know them by heart. With each retelling of the story, the plot expands just a bit with great detail and thicker dialogue. I would be disappointed otherwise. The countless tales recant the long hours and days those men spent working, the pranks they pulled on each other and my dad to make time pass more quickly, and the Saturday nights with town boots and tilted hats.

Most of the stories he tells are of good times. Occasionally, my dad would share the stories of loneliness. He spoke of their loves and loss of loves; he told of lightning bolts and accidents too far from help, but he never says too much of the uncles' funerals, two of which he missed on account of timing and distance.

Good or bad, the stories have become almost a play in his mind, as his eyes twinkle and his voice dances. My dad never looks at me when he tells a story. I truly believe he is looking at the men before him, acting out a scene in his own living room. I envision the 'uncles' from my dad's stories. The men were handsome, at least in my imagination and from what I could tell in the old black-and-whites of them. They loved their horses, they loved their pranks, they loved their women, and they loved each other.

It wasn't long before I fell in love with their world.

ON GROOMING HUMANS

The storyline of human trafficking at Belmont High School in this novel is fictional. Human trafficking, specifically sex trafficking, in the Heartland is very real.

The plot of human trafficking in *Cowboys to Camelot* came to me several years ago when my daughter came home one day and wanted to talk. After listening to a speaker at her school, Marian High School, address sex trafficking in Omaha—a place where horrible things such as sex trafficking are not supposed to happen—she shared with me the shocking truth of the city in which I was raised, the city in which I raised my children. My daughter told me that human trafficking was actually a pretty serious problem in our own community.

As she spoke, I could see the empowerment that the speaker had given to Morgan and probably all of the other young ladies at the all-girls school. The speaker's message was clear: be aware and be strong. Deplorable individuals are seeking young men, women, and children to join their undertaking, and people should be wary of the "grooming" that might be taking place in the most common of places, including schools. Her words gave me a big pit in my stomach for two reasons. First, I was shocked that Omaha, with its College World Series, Olympic Swim Trials, concerts and other amazing attractions, at the same time, attracted predators who saw opportunity in such events. Second, I was sad that my daughter was aware of a very real travesty.

The irony was not lost on me as the story behind the bones in *Cowboys to Camelot* developed: grooming. Just as the cowboys calm their horses as they brush and attend to their needs, the sex trafficking groomers wine and dine the vulnerable girls they find. The difference between the two: the cowboy loves his horse; the predator uses his victims.

Sadly, sex trafficking in the Heartland has been a quiet problem for decades. Recently, I came across a documentary on the boy from Des Moines, Iowa, who disappeared on a Sunday morning in the fall of 1982 while delivering newspapers. The tragedy of Johnny Gosch was a story I remember when I was in college, but I may have been too self-absorbed to think beyond a paper boy being kidnapped. In 2014, a documentary called *Who Took Johnny* highlighted the journey of the parents in looking for help, unsuccessfully, from authorities.

The documentary spanned thirty years and showed a credible theory involving a pedophile ring, sex trafficking, and reports of well-known community members partaking. Paul Bonacci, a man who claims to have been involved in the abduction of Johnny Gosh, gave testimoney that unveiled a scandal surrounding the Franklin Credit Union in Omaha, Nebraska. The case spawned national interest and eventually helped establish a bill, the Johnny Gosch Bill, which mandates an immediate response from police to reports of missing children.

Wow. Just wow.

Omaha, Nebraska has had a long history of a human trafficking problem.

Make no mistake about it.

Throughout the time that I was writing *Cowboys to Camelot*, I researched the problem in the Midwest. A copy of *Omaha Magazine*, sat on my desk for the last few months of editing, and the picture on the cover haunted me as I worked. A young woman with a barcode over her mouth and her hands seemingly tied in front of her begged for my attention. The feature article by magazine executive director Doug Meigs, in the March 2016 edition of the magazine, well-written, direct, and frightening, was entitled "Gone Girls: Human Trafficking in the Heartland."

The title of the cover story alludes to the hit movie *Gone Girls* in which the main characters are manipulative, narcissistic and often evil. In cases of human trafficking, the characters, the *gone girls*, are subjects of criminal actions of others. The gone girls are victims to the core.

Doug Meigs wrote:

Worldwide, some 20.9 million human trafficking victims are trapped in modern-day slavery, according to the International

Labour Organization. Their horrific experiences generate billions of dollars in profit for abductors and criminal syndicates.

But the scourge is not just a foreign phenomenon. In the United States, the anti-trafficking Polaris Project estimates "the total number of victims nationally reaches into the hundreds of thousands" when estimates of sex trafficking and labor trafficking for adults and minors are aggregated. A 2015 study by University of Nebraska-Lincoln professors Ron Hampton and Dwayne Ball reported that an average of nearly 50 young Nebraska women are known to fall victim to sex trafficking every year, while the actual number is "certainly much higher."

Doug Meigs included in his article one woman's journey:

For Melissa, the path to redemption—to becoming a survivor—has been an arduous journey.

From Wyoming, Melissa and her abductor traveled onward to California. He was "grooming" her, using drugs and violence to instill obedience. He threatened to harm her family if she fled. "I wasn't allowed to be looking in any direction at another man; that was a violation," she says. "I was not allowed to speak. He spoke for me. There were the beatings, the threats, the brainwashing."

While some sex trafficking victims come from troubled families, others come from ostensibly stable households (as with Melissa). The process of coercion to sell sex, however, is often more subtle than what Melissa endured.

"It usually starts by a guy who comes off as her boyfriend, who starts doting on her, buying her things, telling her she's beautiful," Shrader says. The girl hears, "You have beautiful hair, beautiful eyes, whatever," and then she's sucked under the control of the "Romeo pimp," a term Shrader uses for a pimp who methodically targets victims through emotional manipulation.

"We have a girl who took a year [to prostitute herself]; a man was her friend for a year, and his whole intention was to get her out of the state to sell her for sex," Shrader says, noting that the victims often believe they are in relationships without realizing the pimp has a "stable" of four other girls working for him, too.

Doug Meig's article did present good news:

Victims like Melissa are increasingly speaking out. The Polaris Project reported that more than 1,600 survivors of human trafficking had reached out for help in 2015—a 24 percent increase from the previous year—based on statistics from the National Human Trafficking Resource Center hotline and Polaris BeFree Textline.

Rejuvenating Women is part of a growing anti-trafficking network in Omaha. Shrader (Julie Shrader, founder of Rejuvenating Women) says Omaha has become a lynchpin in human trafficking networks stretching from east to west coast on I-80. Mexican gangs have established a foothold in the city, too, funneling sex and labor trafficking victims back and forth on I-29 from Texas and across the border. Meanwhile, Omaha's major events—such as the College World Series, Olympic Swim Trials, and Berkshire Hathaway's shareholder meeting—draw an influx of tourists with a corresponding spike in demand for prostitutes both local and imported.

Local and federal momentum against human trafficking has been building since the turn of the millennium, when Congress passed the Trafficking Victims Protection Act (TVPA) in 2000.

Following the TVPA, lawmakers nationwide have begun to shift punitive focus away from prostitutes—the victims—to increase consequences for the traffickers, the pimps, and those soliciting sex.

The good news is always reassuring.

We are no longer a naïve community turning our heads away from the horrid yet real stories of human trafficking so close to home. We, a sadder and a wiser people, are educating the young be to be wary and be strong. Anti-trafficking groups in Omaha and across the nation are actively participating in a task force to help victims and inform people.

As is often the fact, truth is stranger than fiction. *Cowboys to Camelot* is a work of fiction, but the truth of this tragedy, which has been ignored for decades, is suddenly demanding that we take note.

To read the full article by Doug Meigs, go to *Omaha Magazine* 2016
"Gone Girls Human Trafficking in the Heartland"
March 7, 2016 by Doug Meigs
http://omahamagazine.com/2016/03/gone-girls/

About the Author

Mary Kay Leatherman lives in Omaha, Nebraska with her husband and three children. She manages and teaches for 3MT ACT Test Prep.

Acknowledgements

I have so very many people to thank for help along this journey.

I especially want to thank my sister Robin Boeck, who, just as she has on so many past projects, was an amazing editor, marketing rep, and cheerleader.

I want to thank my dad Richard Mangus and the cowboys who were his heroes as he grew up. So many of the stories in the Rollie chapters are straight from my father's childhood: the cutting off of ears and the incident at Wind Hill. My dad may have raised four daughters in Omaha, Nebraska, but a part of his soul still rides around in Brush, Colorado, the town in which he was born.

I want to thank Doug Meig, executive editor at *Omaha Magazine* and author of the feature article "Gone Girls." His research and well-written article captured the best explanation of sex trafficking in Omaha that I could find.

Special thanks to Marcia Jussel, a woman who loves books and dedicates her life to helping people find the perfect read. Her encouragement and support have been pivotal on this journey.

Special thanks to the team of experts at CreateSpace, especially Heather from the Design Team. Her guidance and wisdom through this process was priceless.

I want to thank Jessa Diebel for her expertise and creativity in promoting and marketing this book through my website.

Special thanks to the 'readers' through the course of *Cowboys to Camelot* and its evolution: my husband Mike Leatherman, my daughter Morgan Leatherman, my father Richard Mangus, my mother Mary Mangus, my sisters Robin Boeck, Patti Grimes, and Julie Hahler, my aunt Sister Barbara Markey, my friends Gary and Sue Boeck, Diane O'Malley, Deb Ward, and Michele and John Trout.

I thank my husband and children for their incredible patience on the days that I, once again, was lost in the story. Mike, Connor, Morgan, and Sean were so patient throughout this process. A special thanks to my husband for his relentless encouragement for a project that was so important to me.